HITHER & NIGH

HITHER & NIGH

WITHDRAWN

ELLEN POTTER

MARGARET K. McELDERRY BOOKS

NEW YORK   LONDON   TORONTO   SYDNEY   NEW DELHI

MARGARET K. McELDERRY BOOKS
An imprint of Simon & Schuster Children's Publishing Division
1230 Avenue of the Americas, New York, New York 10020

MARGARET K. McELDERRY BOOKS is a trademark of Simon & Schuster, Inc.
For information about special discounts for bulk purchases, please contact Simon & Schuster Special Sales at 1-866-506-1949 or business@simonandschuster.com.
The Simon & Schuster Speakers Bureau can bring authors to your live event. For more information or to book an event, contact the Simon & Schuster Speakers Bureau at 1-866-248-3049 or visit our website at www.simonspeakers.com.
Interior design by Irene Metaxatos
The text for this book was set in Joanna Nova.
Manufactured in China   0522 SCP
First Edition   10 9 8 7 6 5 4 3 2 1
Library of Congress Cataloging-in-Publication Data
Names: Potter, Ellen, 1963– author.
Title: Hither & Nigh / Ellen Potter.
Other titles: Hither and Nigh
Description: First edition. | New York : Margaret K. McElderry Books, 2022. | Audience: Ages 8–12. | Audience: Grades 4–6. | Summary: As they uncover their magical powers, Nell and her new friends discover a parallel New York City called the Nigh, where monsters roam Central Park, Finfolk haunt the Hudson River, and a terrifying Minister, who controls it all, holds the key to Nell's missing brother.
Identifiers: LCCN 2022005716 (print) | LCCN 2022005717 (ebook) | ISBN 9781665910385 (hardcover) | ISBN 9781665910408 (ebook)
Subjects: CYAC: Magic—Fiction. | Schools—Fiction. | Friendship—Fiction. | Missing persons—Fiction. | New York (N. Y.)—Fiction. | Fantasy. | LCGFT: Fantasy fiction.
Classification: LCC PZ7.P8518 Hi 2022 (print) | LCC PZ7.P8518 (ebook) | DDC [Fic]—dc23
LC record available at https://lccn.loc.gov/2022005716
LC ebook record available at https://lccn.loc.gov/2022005717

FOR DAD

1

ROOM 101

The whole thing was totally humiliating, starting with the room. Room 101. The kindergarten classroom at Bright Future Academy.

There were three of us, each awkwardly squeezed into the tiny, nubbly plastic chairs. Up in the front, there was Annika, the girl who looked like she had been blessed by a dozen fairies at birth. You know the type. She had tipped her chair backward at an alarming angle so that the ends of her long hair, the color of polished mahogany, hovered inches above the floor. Crossing her long legs on the edge of the desk, she aggressively cracked pumpkin seeds between her teeth.

Behind her, hulking in the corner, dressed in a paint-splattered black shirt and black jeans, was Crud. He was a huge kid with wild dark hair and a jaw like two fists on either side of his face. There were all sorts of rumors about him. People said that he had been kicked out of his last school for trying to strangle his science teacher. And that he ate kittens. Each time he shifted his weight, his chair squealed in pain.

Then of course there was me. Nell.

I stole a glance at Annika, who noticed and returned the stare with her cat-green eyes. She slipped another pumpkin seed between her perfect teeth and cracked it in half.

Sighing, I looked away.

Of all people, why did *Annika* have to be in this club?

I checked the clock on the wall. Its hands were blue oars held by tiny sailors in a red boat that was painted at the clock's center.

3:40.

This thing was supposed to have started ten minutes ago.

"This is the worst," I whispered to the white ferret in a cage on a little table.

Someone had put purple doll-sized pants on the ferret. Probably one of the kids in the class. On the back of the pants was red-glitter script saying *Sassy Pants*.

"Your pants are also the worst," I told the ferret. It stared at me with a peevish look on its face. Then it turned its back, giving me a full view of its sassy pants, before disappearing into a paper-towel roll.

The classroom door swung open, and we all turned to watch The Viking burst in. He was new at the school, newer even than me. An eighth grader, like Annika and Crud—a year older than I was. He had a name, of course, but I didn't know it. In my head I'd always called him The Viking. Not because he was a big muscly kid or anything. I mean, he was tall, but on the thin side. I called him The

Viking because he always wore a Viking hat to school. Not the kind with the horns. Real Vikings didn't wear those, anyway. His was a green cap with brown fur around its rim. He had egg yolk–colored hair that hung down to his shoulders, and his eyes were a pale blue with pinched pupils that looked as though he had been staring out to sea too long.

A red Twizzler was sticking out of his mouth. He removed it and asked, "Is this detention?"

Annika had been watching him with undisguised interest. Now she replied in her raspy voice, "It's called the Last Chance Club." She rolled her eyes at the name. "You know . . . they make you do community service work instead of being expelled. So you'll become a better human being. Supposably."

"Supposedly," I muttered.

The Viking popped the Twizzler back into his mouth and sat down at the chair nearest him. He looked around the classroom, his eyes lingering on Annika.

Shocker, I thought.

His gaze moved to Crud, his eyebrows lifting at the sight of such a monster, then to me. I glanced away, but the next moment I heard his chair scraping against the floor as he dragged it next to mine.

He sat there for a moment in silence while I pretended he didn't exist.

"So what's your story?" he asked.

I glanced at him. He was watching me—I mean, really

studying me, which hardly anyone ever does, except my father. It was very annoying.

"I don't have a story."

"Yes, you do," he said. "And you know what else?"

I hesitated, then said, "What else?" I tried to make my voice sound bored. But to be honest, I was very curious. Because the thing is, I do have a story. Annika knew my story—or part of it, anyway. Up until now, I had thought that she hadn't told anyone at school, but maybe I was wrong.

"I bet your story is a doozy, that's what," The Viking said. "So let's hear it."

I felt a strange mix of relief that he didn't actually know my story, but also irritation that he wasn't wrong. It *was* a doozy.

He leaned in close to me, waiting. In my peripheral vision, I could see Annika watching us. I heard the hard crack of another pumpkin seed.

I forced myself to look at him directly, to focus on the tiny white spot of light reflected in his pupils. It's what Kingsley taught me to do when an opponent accuses me of cheating.

"Go away," I told him.

He started to say something else, but to my relief the door opened again, and a tall, square-faced man stormed in.

2

MR. BOOT

The man wore a black pinstripe suit and a lemon-yellow tie. In one hand he carried a worn leather briefcase with brass fittings, and in the other hand he held a paper bag. His legs were so long and gangly that in no time at all he had crossed the room, flipped open his briefcase, and feverishly sorted through it until he pulled out a pair of chopsticks.

"Excuse me, but how long is this thing going to last?" Annika asked the man. Her legs jiggled against each other, as though she were readying herself to bolt the first chance she got.

The man looked up and gazed around the room. He appeared to be startled to find us there.

"Who said that, please?" he asked.

Annika's hand shot straight up in the air.

The man squinted at her. "Did you receive a yellow slip of paper in your locker?"

Annika nodded.

"And did it have your name on it?"

Annika nodded.

"Then you will remember that on the slip of yellow paper, it clearly stated the Last Chance Club will begin promptly at 3:30 p.m.—"

"You're late," I mouthed silently.

"And will end when we are done, and not a minute sooner," the man continued. "Now . . . is everyone here?"

None of us knew how to answer that.

"Good," he said. "My name is Mr. Boot. That's *Boot* as in *boot*."

He sat down and took a take-out container out of his bag. The smell of garlicky sauce filled the air. Mr. Boot slid the pair of chopsticks out of their paper pouch. He rubbed the chopsticks against each other, then used them to poke thoughtfully at the food. He glanced up suddenly, staring at each of us in turn.

"Why all the sad faces? You look as though you're being punished."

"We *are* being punished," said Annika. "It was either this or get expelled from school."

"Right," Mr. Boot said. "Well, I'm sure you all deserve to be expelled. You look like a bloody pack of hooligans. You especially." He pointed one chopstick at Crud. Crud swiped at his nose with the back of his hand.

Mr. Boot scooped up a lump of saucy chicken in his chopsticks and popped it into his mouth.

Annika's hand went up again, and Mr. Boot, chewing, pointed to her with his chopstick.

"I don't want to do any volunteer work with old

people," Annika said. "I'll work with kids, animals, whatever. Just no old people."

"I'll decide what sort of volunteer work you do," replied Mr. Boot between chews, "based on what I know about you."

"Which is nothing," I silently mouthed to the ferret.

I hadn't spoken a word of that out loud. Not a word. Yet Mr. Boot looked over at me sharply as though he had heard. He parked his chopsticks into his food and began to sift through his briefcase until he pulled out three thick manila files crammed with papers. From the inside of his suit jacket pocket, he took out a pair of wire-rimmed glasses and put them on.

"Nell Batista." He read my name, which was scrawled in purple marker on the front of the top file.

Opening the file, Mr. Boot continued to read out loud.

"'Has a small scar on her right palm from a failed attempt at a cartwheel in Central Park at age six. Has another scar on her elbow where she fell while . . . while simply walking down the street.' A bit of a klutz, aren't you, dear?"

I was too shocked to speak. It seemed impossible that he could know all this stuff about me.

Mr. Boot flipped through some more papers, finally stopping at one. "'Highly intelligent but,' hmm . . . kicked out of four schools? Will this school make number five? I wonder. Only time will tell." He flipped a few more pages and read, "'Is afraid of escalators.'" He looked down at me. "Escalators? Really?"

Annika snorted out a laugh.

Mr. Boot turned to her. "And you must be Annika Rapp."

Annika stopped laughing. Her green eyes nervously blinked double-time.

Mr. Boot put down my file and picked up another one with Annika Rapp written on it in the same purple handwriting.

Annika looked alarmed. I could guess why. If she knew things about my history, I also knew things about hers.

"'Won the state championship two-hundred-meter dash three years in a row.' Well done!" Mr. Boot nodded at Annika, who still looked tense. He rummaged through some more pages, murmuring things like, "Nut allergy. Potty training was an issue, wasn't it? Favorite color orange. Still ties her shoes bunny style. Interesting." He flipped through more pages until he stopped at a green paper with our school's letterhead. "What's this?" He made a frowny face at Annika. She blanched. "Seems you are a rather vicious little bully, Ms. Rapp." He adjusted his glasses and read from the file. "It appears that your bedroom window directly faces the window of one of your classmates. A Ms. Julia Weeks. This report says that you took an embarrassing video of Ms. Weeks, then texted it to all your little chums." Mr. Boot examined the page more carefully, shaking his head. "Tut-tut, Ms. Rapp."

I heard about that video. The video showed Julia dancing around her room, stuffing socks in her bra, and just doing the stupid things you might do when no one is watching. Except someone *was* watching.

Annika flushed, and her eyes flitted over toward The Viking, then back to Mr. Boot.

"How do you know all this stuff?" Annika demanded. "Who exactly are you? You don't teach here. I've never seen you around the school. This is really creepy."

I thought so too. And apparently Crud agreed.

"I'm out of here," Crud announced. His chair squealed as he shifted his weight to grab his backpack on the floor beside him.

There was a rumble, like a storm had suddenly rolled in, and then a mighty clatter as dozens of large alphabet blocks flew out of various bins and tumbled across the floor. They converged under Crud's chair and immediately formed themselves into a tower, lifting the chair until it was seven feet in the air—with the horrified Crud still in it.

3

ALPHABET BLOCKS

The chair wobbled at the tippy-top of the tower, the blocks swaying precariously, while Crud clutched the edge of his chair and tried to find his balance.

We all stared up at him, too astounded to say a word.

It was The Viking who noticed it first: "The alphabet blocks . . . They spell something."

I looked at the blocks. It was true. Reading from top to bottom, they spelled out:

THIS AINT AS EASY AS IT LOOKS.

There was a sudden clattering noise, during which the horrified Crud was bounced up and down like a giant baby on someone's lap. The alphabet blocks had rearranged themselves beneath him, and now they spelled something new:

DONT NO ONE MOVE A MUSCLE.

The clattering started up again, and when they were finished, the blocks spelled:

ESPECIALLY THE BIG KID UP THERE.

"What does it say? What does it say?" Crud cried in a panicked voice.

"It says not to move," Annika told him.

To Crud's credit, he managed to freeze into position. His hands grasped the edges of the chair, and his huge body hunched down as he grimaced.

The blocks rearranged themselves again, and Crud braced himself against the bouncing.

I AM WAITING MR BOOT.

The Viking read this out loud. All of us turned to look at Mr. Boot. His chopsticks were poised inches from his mouth, a lump of chicken pinched between them. He looked at us, and then his eyes slid over to the alphabet block tower and then up at Crud, who was engaged in a mighty effort to not move a muscle.

"Ah." Mr. Boot gave his lump of chicken a regretful look before he put it back in the container. "Yes. Now that I have your attention . . ."

There was a hissing sound, like water being poured onto a campfire, then the clattering again, and the very next second Crud was back on the ground with the blocks scattered on the floor all around him. He was still clutching the edges of his chair, preparing for another quick trip toward the ceiling.

For a moment, there was dead silence in the room. I think we were all too shocked to speak, or to even know what to say.

It was Annika who finally spoke up. "How did you do that?" she asked Mr. Boot.

Mr. Boot held up his chopsticks.

"You did that with chopsticks?" she said incredulously.

"Don't be ridiculous. If that were the case, anyone could do it, couldn't they? I used chopsticks, yes, but I did it with precision, almighty skill, and a particularly good Oomphalos."

"An oomfa-what?" Annika asked.

"You're crazy, you know that?" said Crud. "You could have killed me!"

"Oh, not at all, Mr. Butterbank, not at all," Mr. Boot replied. "We rarely have any deaths in this program."

"Rarely? What do you mean?" I said. "Did someone die?"

"I wouldn't go so far as to say 'died.' Not died, per se. Anyway, you all seem pretty sturdy." He looked more hopeful than confident as he said this. He stood and clapped his hands. "So onward and upward, isn't it? Let's begin our first lesson. Right."

He motioned to a plastic green basket on his desk.

"Everyone, grab a glue stick."

Without hesitation, Annika leapt to her feet, went up to his desk, and grabbed a glue stick out of the basket. She was like that as a little kid, too—always the first to take a dare or to try some crazy new move on her skateboard.

The rest of us just warily eyeballed that green basket on his desk.

"So this isn't really a community service club, is it?" I asked. "We're here to learn magic tricks?"

"Oh, you will be doing community service. A lot of it." He gazed around the room with a look of significance.

"You will also be learning magic. In the next few weeks we will learn about dazzle-shooters, big brass whammies, metamorpha-horses—"

"You're making that up," Crud said.

"And if you learn quickly enough," continued Mr. Boot, "we may even have time to dabble in advanced mummery. Now"—he picked up the basket and gave it an impatient shake—"step up and take a glue stick."

I was next to get up and grab a glue stick, mostly out of curiosity. I knew this guy was hustling us in some way, and I was determined to find out how he was doing it. I'd spent years hanging out with some of the smartest swindlers in the city. I knew all their tricks. I was going to find out what this guy's scam was, because I was a hundred-percent sure he had one.

The glue stick was normal looking, but still I pulled off the little orange cap and cautiously sniffed it. It had the usual plasticky smell. Nothing unusual.

"So what do the glue sticks do?" Annika asked Mr. Boot. She was sitting in her seat and twisting the glue stick way up out of its tube.

"They make things sticky, Ms. Rapp," replied Mr. Boot dryly.

"She means, are they going to do something weird?" Crud asked. He had placed his glue stick upright on his desk, capped closed, at a careful distance.

"That will be entirely up to you."

From the paper bag that had held his food, Mr. Boot

pulled out a handful of chopsticks, still in their white paper wrappers. He walked around the room, handing a set of chopsticks to each of us. When he was done, he stood by his desk with his hands clasped in front of him, his thumbs tapping against each other.

"Right. Who knows how to use chopsticks properly?" he asked.

Annika was the only one who raised her hand.

"Show us, please," he said.

Annika slid her chopsticks out of their wrapper, adjusted them in her right hand, and deftly maneuvered them to take little clicking bites out of the air.

"Your thumb position is excellent." Mr. Boot nodded approvingly at Annika. "Nice mobility, angle of ring finger acceptable. All quite good, quite good . . . except for THE MOST IMPORTANT THING." Here, Mr. Boot's eyes grew wide with contemptuous amazement. "You've completely neglected to wake them up."

"Wake who up?" Annika asked.

"The chopsticks, Ms. Rapp! They'll be useless if they're dozing. And they are always dozing. Pay attention, please."

He took her chopsticks and rubbed them together briskly, as if he were trying to start a fire.

"But that's just to get the splinters off," Annika protested.

"Nonsense. Who told you that? We do it to annoy the chopsticks. Now look. Do you see? They're starting to become more alert."

They didn't look any different to me.

"I want everyone to wake up their chopsticks now," Mr. Boot said. "Go on. Start rubbing them together."

Honestly, if I hadn't seen what had happened to the alphabet blocks, I would have flat-out refused. It was all too ridiculous. But Mr. Boot had done something with those blocks—I just hadn't worked out what it was yet—and if I had to rub chopsticks together to figure out how he was doing his silly party tricks, I would.

I pulled my chopsticks out of their wrapper and started to rub them together.

"Vigorously!" Mr. Boot cried. "You are not trying to tickle them, people. You are trying to irritate them!"

We all rubbed the chopsticks together faster. I glanced at the others. Crud looked like he was trying hard, unlike The Viking, who was sort of tapping his chopsticks together. He smiled when he caught me watching him, and I quickly looked away. Annika was working intently, hunched over her sticks, frowning. Suddenly Mr. Boot hurried to her desk. He grabbed the chopsticks from her and rested them on the palm of his hand. Then he tilted his head up and closed his eyes. After a moment, he nodded once.

"These are ready," he said. "Chopsticks down, everyone, and pay attention. Since this is your first lesson, I'll do it slowly. Ms. Rapp, please dab some glue on the insides of your wrists."

Annika uncapped her glue stick and rubbed the glue on her wrists.

"Now think of something that you've lost and would like to retrieve," Mr. Boot said.

Annika bounced the knuckle of her thumb against her lower lip, considering.

"Don't overthink it, Ms. Rapp," warned Mr. Boot.

After another moment Annika nodded. "Okay."

With the chopsticks, Mr. Boot began to snip and snap at the air in front of Annika, as though he were trying to catch an invisible fly with them.

"For beginners like yourselves," said Mr. Boot as he moved the chopsticks with alarming speed, "chopsticks are particularly handy. These are made of white spruce, a very snoozy type of wood. Even when you annoy it, it's only half awake, so that the magic it produces is reliable. Very little chance of accidents, like the appearance of Moss Necks or, in the worst possible cases, a Stench Mumbler."

I rolled my eyes at this nonsense and caught a glimpse out the window. The sun was already going down. Kingsley calls this time "the dimmery," an in-between time, when the shadows lengthen and you suddenly feel like the world is more mysterious than it lets on. He says it's his favorite time of the day. Personally, it always makes me feel squirrelly inside. I don't like mysteries. I don't like in-betweens.

I looked back at Mr. Boot's chopsticks, which were moving so fast now that they became a whirling beige smudge. A fine vapor of sparks trailed out of each stick. It made me dizzy. I squeezed my eyes shut for a moment, and when I opened them again, the chopsticks had stopped moving.

The very next second there was a coarse scratching sound, like a metal bolt being slid back. Then I heard one quick SPLASH!

"Go on." Mr. Boot gestured to the wooden play kitchen in the corner. "Take a look inside the oven, Ms. Rapp."

4

THE STICKING SPELL

Annika strode over to the play kitchen, grabbed the plastic red handle of the little play oven, and yanked the door open. Water poured out and splashed to the floor. Even from my seat, I could smell the brackish odor.

At first Annika just stood there, the water pooling round her shoes, as she stared into the oven, frowning. Then she reached inside and pulled out an object, still dripping with water. She turned it over in her hands, examining it.

"It's my phone, but . . ." She looked at Mr. Boot. "I lost this thing a month ago."

"Exactly. And with the help of a basic Sticking Spell, it has been returned to you."

Annika pressed her thumb against the button on the side of the phone.

"It's busted," she said.

"Which is generally the outcome of chucking a cell phone into the Hudson River, Ms. Rapp. Really, you must learn to control that temper of yours."

Mr. Boot moved on to Crud and held his chopsticks appraisingly.

"Well done, Mr. Butterbank. These are wide awake."

He told Crud to dab some glue onto his wrists and to think of something he had lost. It took Crud no time at all before he nodded that he was ready.

Mr. Boot began the same quicksilver movements with Crud's chopsticks. When he was finished, I listened for the sound of the sliding bolt again. I guessed that he'd rigged up the room with his tricks. This time, though, the only sound was a dry rustling, as if a breeze were blowing through the classroom, even though the windows were all shut. It took a moment to figure out where the rustling was coming from. The Viking spotted it first and pointed.

"There!"

On the wall nearest to Crud was a poster with the words HELPING HANDS written in green Magic Marker at the top. Thumbtacked to the poster were yellow paper hands, each with a name and a job printed on it—MADDY, PENCIL SHARPENER; AIDEN, SWEEPER; LEE, CRAYON COLLECTOR; CHERI, FERRET FEEDER—and all the paper hands were waving energetically.

"I believe Maddy has what you're looking for, Mr. Butterbank," Mr. Boot told Crud.

I looked over at the hand marked MADDY. A red Bic pen was wedged between Maddy's ring finger and pinkie finger. Crud seemed caught between fear of those weirdly waving hands and wanting that pen. His huge, mounded shoulders hunched forward, as though readying his body to rise, but his hands clamped down hard on the edges of his chair.

"It's all right, Mr. Butterbank. Go and fetch it," Mr. Boot prodded with surprising gentleness. "You'll be fine."

Crud's mouth tightened for a moment. Then he eased himself out of his chair and walked up to the poster of waving hands. He took a breath before quickly snatching the pen from between the fingers, whereupon the paper hands instantly stopped waving.

"A pen?" Annika cried. "That's what you asked for?"

"I lost it yesterday," Crud said.

"But a *pen*?!" Annika laughed.

Crud scribbled on his arm.

"It still works," he said. "Unlike your phone."

Annika stopped laughing. Her eyes cut over to The Viking, probably to see if he was laughing. He wasn't. He was looking up at Mr. Boot, who was heading toward him.

"Chopsticks, please," Mr. Boot said to The Viking, holding out his hand.

The Viking gave Mr. Boot his chopsticks and watched while Mr. Boot rolled them between his palms, gazing up at the ceiling contemplatively. Mr. Boot frowned as though he were confused. He held the chopsticks up to his ear and listened. Then he stared down at The Viking disdainfully.

The Viking stared back and smiled brightly.

"Hello," The Viking said.

Mr. Boot ignored him. He tightened his grip around the chopsticks and snapped them in half. A collective gasp erupted in the room. Snapping them like that seemed like breaking the neck of a bird.

"What did you do that for?" The Viking asked heatedly. Tatty splotches of red appeared on his cheeks.

"It was an act of mercy, Mr. Gunnerson. Your chopsticks had gone quite mad. They were jabbering on about buttered Pilliwiggins. And anyway"—Mr. Boot glared down at The Viking—"anything you would have retrieved would have no doubt been *stolen*."

"I—" The Viking started, but Mr. Boot cut him off.

"There are many types of bad eggs, Mr. Gunnerson, but thieves are among the worst."

5

THE BOY IN THE PLAYGROUND

Mr. Boot turned to me now. I stared back at him squarely. I wanted him to know that I had his number. That he might be fooling the others, but I was no chump.

"Have you thought of your lost object, Ms. Batista?" he asked.

"Yup."

I hadn't, actually. Kingsley always told me that if you're dealing with a scam artist, don't give them anything to work with. *Let them hang themselves by their own rope*, he'd said.

Mr. Boot picked up my chopsticks. He joggled them lightly in his hand, then frowned.

"What have you been doing, Ms. Batista? Singing them lullabies? They're fast asleep!" Shaking his head with disgust, he rubbed the chopsticks together briskly for several seconds then told me to dab my wrists with my glue stick. After I did that, he instructed, "Think about what you have lost, Ms. Batista. Hold that image in your mind."

An image did materialize in my mind. I struggled to push it away, but it kept returning, insistent. Mr. Boot snapped at the air with my chopsticks, making them twist and turn at a terrific speed. It almost seemed as though they were spelling things out in the air—wispy letters, like smoke trails that vanished an instant after they appeared.

Finally Mr. Boot stopped and placed the chopsticks back on my desk. He clasped his hands behind his back and lifted his chin, waiting. The room was perfectly silent. No splashing water, no rustling paper.

"I guess it didn't work," I said after a moment.

"Patience," Mr. Boot replied.

The others were getting restless. Annika's leg had started jiggling again, and The Viking slumped down in his seat and pulled his hat low, as though he were trying to nap.

Then I heard it. A steady, rhythmic squeaking, so soft it hovered on the outskirts of perception. No one else seemed to hear it, not even Mr. Boot, whose brows were knit in concentration.

My gaze skittered across the walls, scanning the reading corner with its rough-hewn wood loft, the shelves with their plastic bins, then over at the row of windows on the other side of the room. They faced the school's small playground—a wooden castle with slides and climbing ropes and four pink elephants set on thick springs. And on one of those elephants was a boy, thirteen, maybe fourteen years old. He rocked the elephant back and forth. He was too tall for it, though, and his legs had to stretch out wide to rock it. He wore a watch-man's cap, pulled down low over his dark hair. There was a tricky bluish half-light that turned him ghostly and shadowed his features, but still he looked so much like River that I stifled a cry. I ran to the window and tried to open it, but the window resisted.

"Leave it shut, Ms. Batista," Mr. Boot ordered harshly. He was now making his way toward the window too.

I ignored him and yanked on the window more force-fully until it finally gave way. A burst of chilly autumn wind rushed into the classroom. I stuck my head out of the window, and my hair instantly blew across my eyes. By the time I pushed it aside to see, the playground was empty and perfectly still, except for one of the elephants, now rider-less, which rocked two or three more times before it came to a stop.

"Ms. Batista!" Mr. Boot was right behind me. "What do you think you're doing?"

His voice short-circuited my thoughts. I now realized just how stupid I'd been.

"I . . . I thought I saw something," I said.

"Was it the object you were trying to retrieve?"

I hesitated. "No."

"Then you have failed a very simple Sticking Spell."

Mr. Boot leaned out of the window for a moment before he did a hasty series of swishes with his chopsticks. Then he slammed the window shut and turned back to the class.

"We're done for today. We'll meet at the same time tomorrow. And a word to the wise—" He stopped short and looked at us all for a moment. "Oh, never mind. You'll just have to learn the hard way. Pity. Off you go."

6

CHESS HUSTLERS

I walked home through the darkening streets, brooding over everything that had just happened. How had Mr. Boot done the trick with the alphabet blocks? How had he retrieved Annika's phone from the Hudson River? My mind toyed with all sorts of possibilities, but none of them made much sense.

And then there was the boy in the playground.

That could have simply been a weird coincidence, I reasoned. It was probably just some kid who happened to resemble River—or what I imagined River would look like now. But all the rest of what had happened? I couldn't figure it out.

I tucked my head down and crossed my arms tightly against the cold. Every so often I had the weird sensation that there was someone right behind me, tailing me. But each time I turned around, no one was ever there—except once when I saw a slim woman in a belted green wool coat walking so close to me that when I stopped to turn, we nearly collided. She blinked in surprise, then quickened her pace to pass me, yanking the belt of her coat tighter.

It was too cold for early October. My own winter coat was still hanging in the back of my closet, hat and gloves shoved into the pocket, ready for me. But I hadn't been ready for it, not yet; so now I shivered in my too-thin hoodie.

When I got to Washington Square Park, I couldn't help myself. I walked around the park's perimeter to the southwest corner to see who was playing. A few of the chess hustlers were at the tables. Kingsley was there, wearing his khaki cargo jacket and a black knit hat pulled low over his dreads, his calm eyes resting on his opponent. I wanted to tell Kingsley about everything that had happened with Mr. Boot. I wanted to tell him about Crud being lifted in his chair and Annika's cell phone, and yeah, I wanted Kingsley to explain it all away. Kingsley, who had seen every hustle in New York, who had taught me how to spot all the tricks.

"Hey, you, Nell!" Serge, one of the other chess hustlers, had noticed me and grinned broadly, flashing a gold tooth. "Vhere vas you been dis morning?" He was short and burly, with hands that looked like they could squeeze the life out of a polar bear.

"School!" I called back.

"School?" He moved his knight as though it were a bishop—an illegal move that he'd done so swiftly, his opponent didn't even notice—then he slapped the timer. He wasn't a great chess player, not like Kingsley. Serge had no strategy. He was just a "wood pusher," shoving his pieces around and waiting for his opponent to make some stupid tactical mistake. Or else he just out-and-out cheated. "Vhat for you going to school, eh? Vhat they can teach you dhere you don't learn vit us?"

He had a point.

"Shut up, Serge," Kingsley told him. "She's a kid. She needs to go to school."

"Pah! Vhat you know?" Serge flapped a dismissive hand at Kingsley.

Serge's opponent was a young guy wearing round, blue-tinted glasses. His mouth was slightly open, head tipped to the left. Right ring finger scraping at his thumb. He lifted his hand and it hovered over his bishop, ready to make his move.

"He'll have you in checkmate if you do that," I warned the guy. He quickly pulled his hand back, as though the bishop had swatted it, and he moved his rook instead.

Serge didn't care. He'd wait for the guy to make some other dumb mistake, and then he'd swoop in for the win.

"Nell." Kingsley gave me a hard stare. "Go home."

He was right. I hated it, but I knew he was right. My father had banned me from the chess tables. In fact, he'd banned me from the park altogether.

"Come on, myshka," Serge said to me. "I finish off this clown right now, den ve play."

My fingers itched to feel the smooth chess pieces, to get so lost in the game that the world around me melted away. . . .

"Can't!" I called, and hurried past before I lost my will-power.

As usual, there seemed to be construction going on everywhere. Dodging the sidewalk sheds beneath the scaffolding, I walked in the street—faster that way—until I reached the bodega on Bleecker Street.

"Hola, chiquita!" Marisol was busy ringing up a customer, but she beamed when she saw me and called to the back of the store, "Hey! Alcapurrias para los Batistas!"

In a minute, Marisol's son Hector came out from the back holding a grease-stained paper bag with *Batista* scrawled on it—alcapurrias made by Marisol. They were delicious, deep-fried stuffed pockets that Marisol only made once a week. They sold out fast, but she always tucked a half dozen into a bag and saved them for us. I think it was because she liked Dad. Most people do.

Outside the bodega, I almost stumbled on Chicken Bone Charlie. He was curled in a nest of plastic bags, sleeping. I'd never actually seen Chicken Bone Charlie sleeping before. Usually he was trudging up and down the street, laughing to himself, or growling, and chasing kids with a chicken bone. All the kids in the neighborhood were scared of that chicken bone, which was dumb, really. It was just a chicken bone. But Chicken Bone Charlie held it like a knife when he chased the kids, and that was enough to terrify them—me included, if I'm being honest.

I stopped to sneak a look at him. He was wearing his usual filthy blue suit jacket, stained white dress shirt, and pants that were shredded at the hem. He looked like he had been on his way to work one day and had fallen asleep for a hundred years. Rip van Winkle—that's who he reminded me of. He stirred, and I hurried past him.

7

4B

Our apartment building was down the block from the bodega, a sooty, mustard-colored brick walk-up with mint-green paint around the window frames. Above the entrance, squatting on a cement ledge, were two gargoyles—both of them ugly monks with bat wings sprouting from their hooded cloaks. River and I had named them Mike and Boomer.

On the door was a badly faded poster with a blown-up photo of River at ten years old. He is staring into the camera expectantly, as if he had just asked a very important question and was waiting for someone to answer it. Above the photo were the words STILL MISSING in red, with information below. After River disappeared on a sunshiny day three years ago while he was in Washington Square Park, that poster was plastered all over the neighborhood. It was taped to every store window and lamppost. But after a few weeks, it was replaced with posters of yoga classes and local bands. People, in general, have appallingly short attention spans. At least Dad and I always made sure that this poster stayed put.

I opened the door and walked into the entryway, where the mailboxes were set into the wall. On the opposite wall was a large painting of giant Q-tips. It was painted by Mrs. Farfle, the lady who lived in the apartment above us. A few years back someone sprayed graffiti all over the Q-tip painting. No one in the building was sad about that. But then Mrs. Farfle replaced it the next day. Apparently, she always painted duplicates, one to sell and one to keep, so we were stuck with that stupid painting.

I dug around in my backpack, pulled out my keys, and opened up the entryway's smudgy glass door. As I passed the red elevator button on the wall, I slapped it, like I always did. Just a dumb habit. There was no elevator anymore, and even when there had been, it had never worked. Five years ago the elevator had been removed altogether and covered with Sheetrock. You wouldn't have known an elevator was ever there in the first place, except for the red elevator button. Who knew why they left it there. Maybe someone thought it would be funny for people to press the elevator button and wait for an elevator that would never arrive.

I started up the stairs, but a scuffling sound stopped me. Leaning over the railing, I peered down into the shadowy niche next to the staircase. A scrawny little girl with rust-colored hair was crouched there, bent over something on the ground. Nyxie McFadden.

"Hi, Nyxie," I called down to her.

She ignored me. She did that sometimes when she

wanted me to leave her alone. Other times, she would follow me up the stairs when I got home from school, chattering a mile a minute.

I squinted into the darkness. There was something on the ground beside her. Something alive and squirming.

"Hey. What have you got there?" I asked.

"Nothing." She hunkered down, hovering protectively over the squirming animal.

"Is that another cat from the bodega, Nyxie? Those cats are half wild. They *bite*!"

Nyxie ignored me, and I hesitated a moment longer, debating whether I should just take the cat away from her. But it would be a fight, and I didn't feel like fighting right now.

"Just be careful, okay?" I said before climbing the stairs to the fourth floor.

There were two apartments on my floor. Apartment 4A used to be the apartment that Annika and her mom lived in. Now it was occupied by Mr. Ramirez and his husband, Saul, who owned the newspaper stand across the street.

I unlocked the door to apartment 4B, tossed my backpack on the couch, and went down the hall, past the tiny bathroom—so small that you could literally wash your hands in the sink while sitting on the toilet. I scratched on the closed door of my father's studio. He taught me never to knock. It might startle him, and in his line of work, that could be a disaster.

"Come on in, Nell!" I heard him say.

He was sitting on a high stool at his worktable wearing his headlamp. In front of him, set on a square of thickly padded cloth, was a porcelain vase. The vase was as big as a small child, even with its top part smashed off. Shards, some large and others minuscule, lay beside it.

"Yikes," I said approvingly. Dad was always happiest when he was restoring. The worse the damage, the better.

"The client said the maid broke it when she was dusting."

"But you don't think she did?"

Dad rubbed his forefinger lightly over the raw edge of the vase. "Doubt it. More likely someone hit it hard with something. Deliberately."

I stepped up to get a better look at it. It was a beauty. Its background was cream-white, and it was painted with brightly colored enamels. Under a baby-blue sky, a group of naked women was crouching by a weedy pond. I looked a little more closely at them.

"They have tails," I said.

"Yes, they do," Dad said, as if he'd spent some time pondering that strange fact.

"Are they supposed to be demons or something?"

Dad adjusted his headlamp so that it shone a small spotlight directly on the women.

"I don't know. I've never seen anything like them before."

He swiveled on his stool, turning his back to the vase, and removed the headlamp. A strip of hair was plastered to his scalp where the lamp strap had been. In the past few years, his face had begun to look shattered, like one of the ceramic pieces he was hired to restore. Fine lines spidered across his forehead. Deep divots had formed between his eyes, twin creases that were almost purple against his dusky skin. Worry lines. It gave me a little ache, because I was pretty sure they were deepening by the day because of me.

"So? How did detention go? What were the other kids like?" he asked. I knew he was nervous that I was going to be in a room with a bunch of scary delinquents.

"It's not detention, Dad. It's a club," I reminded him. "And one of the kids was Annika." I was happy to relieve him of the "scary delinquent" worry, at least, even though one of the kids in the club *was* a scary delinquent.

"Annika? Your friend from next door?" he said, surprised.

"She was River's friend, not mine," I corrected him.

"Poor kid." He shook his head, remembering. "She had it rough."

"I think things have gotten better for her since she moved away," I said. "She dresses like a rich girl now."

"Oh yeah?" He sounded less surprised than suspicious. I knew what he was thinking. That Annika's mother had finally landed a rich guy. "So how was the club?"

"It was . . . It was weird. The guy running it, Mr. Boot—" I searched for the right words but found it hard to know where to start. "Okay, so there's this kid Crud, right? And he was just sitting in his—"

Out of the corner of my eye, I caught a sudden movement behind my father, on his worktable. The vase. It had shuddered as I was talking; I was almost sure of it.

I looked back at Dad and continued. "So this kid Crud was sitting in a chair, and he said he was going to leave—" The vase shuddered again, the thick cloth beneath it muffling the sound. I forced my eyes back to Dad. "And Mr. Boot picked up his chopsticks. . . ." The vase was all-out trembling. I stopped talking, just to see what would happen. The moment I stopped talking, the vase went still again.

Mr. Boot is behind this somehow! I thought. *It's like he's trying to keep me from telling. But how? How is he doing this?* I felt my face heat up with anger.

"And then," I continued pointedly, with angry determination, my eyes flitting to the vase, "this Mr. Boot guy did something with his chopsticks—"

The vase began to shake so violently now that it was inching toward the edge of the table. In another few seconds, it would fall right off the edge.

Go ahead, break the vase, Mr. Boot! I thought furiously. *It's already broken, you moron!*

"And you won't believe what happened next, but it's true," I continued, my voice loud and tight with anger. "Crud was lifted up—"

The vase stopped shuddering.

Just like that.

I had won.

I bit the inside of my mouth to keep from smiling.

Right then, there was a loud rapping sound against the window, startling both Dad and me. Through the window, the last bit of dimmery light had drained from the sky. Still, I thought I could make out a shape moving around on the fire escape.

"It's Mrs. Farfle's cat again," I said.

Gladys, the male ginger cat with one mangled ear and a girl's name, was always prowling around on our fire escape. One time I felt bad for him and took him inside our apartment, but he jumped on my bed and peed on my quilt. When I tried to get him off the bed, he peed on my arm. I put him right back on the fire escape after that.

The window rattled again. This time, however, I was sure that I saw a fist knocking against the window.

Dad must have seen it too, because he rushed over to the window and threw it open. An old brown hiking boot appeared through the open window, and the next second a woman stepped into the room.

8

ᏩHE ᏩXPERT ON ᏩVERYTHING

The woman was young, maybe in her twenties, with dark hair in two braids, the ends of which were dyed electric blue. She wore a brown cargo jacket over a long, flowery dress that reached the top of her hiking boots. Slung over one shoulder was a khaki green backpack that looked like it had been through a few tours of duty. Once inside our apartment, the woman brushed the dirt from the bottom of her dress.

"Well, this is unexpected," she said, as if Dad and I had walked into her apartment.

"Are you all right?" Dad asked her.

"Oh sure. I'm very agile."

"Why were you out there in the first place?" I asked her. Frankly, I didn't like the looks of her.

"I was making my escape from a very boring dinner party upstairs."

"At Mrs. Farfle's?" Dad asked.

"There you go!" The woman pointed to Dad gleefully, like he'd guessed the answer to a riddle.

"Couldn't you have just left through the door?" I said.

The woman looked appalled. "Yeah, if I wanted to be rude!"

"Well, you're welcome to make your getaway through our apartment," Dad said.

"Oh wow!" The woman had caught sight of the vase, and now she clutched her chest dramatically. "*That* is bonkers stunning! Meissen porcelain . . . mid-1700s, I'm guessing."

"You know your porcelain!" Dad said, delighted.

"The front door's just down the hall," I told her. She was definitely a weirdo.

"My daughter and I were just discussing the painting on the vase," Dad said.

The woman strolled up to the worktable, bent over, put her hands on her hips, and squinted at the vase. While she looked, her hips bopped from side to side, like she was dancing to a song in her nutjob head.

"Huldras," she announced with disdain, jabbing a finger at the women with tails.

"You know what they are?" Dad said, impressed.

"Yeah, I'm a bit of an expert. *Yecch.* Disgusting things." She held out her hand toward my father, who took it. "Vanessa Habscomb."

Dad made a little bow of his head. "Luis," he said. "Luis Batista. This is my daughter, Nell."

"Expert at what?" I asked her.

"Excuse me," she replied.

"You said you were an expert. Expert at what?"

"No, no. I said 'Excuse me' because this little fella

here was growling like a tiger." She patted her stomach. "I climbed out of the window before they sat down to eat. All I managed to grab was some salmon on a cracker." She let out a dramatic sigh. Then in a high, girlish voice she said, "I suppose you two already had your din-din?"

"Yes," I said firmly.

"Not yet," Dad said at the same time.

"In that case, I'd be happy to dine with you!" she said.

It turned out she *was* an expert. An expert on everything. She talked and talked—about porcelain and meatloaf and icebergs. She pointed to the dandelion puffball–shaped chandelier above the table—an ugly old thing that came with the apartment—and she told us that dandelions were also called "swine snort," which made her launch into the meaning of different pig snorts, which she imitated very realistically, and she went on and on without letting anyone else get a word in.

I was waiting for her to go home so that I could talk to Dad about the Last Chance Club. However, by ten o'clock, when she showed no sign of leaving, Dad insisted it was time for me to go to bed. Vanessa Habscomb had monopolized the entire evening.

That was when I began to wonder about her sudden appearance. And her refusal to leave.

And if maybe Mr. Boot had won after all.

I got into my pajamas and crawled into bed—the bottom bunk. The top bunk was River's. It still had his quilt covering it. On his bed, near his pillow, was his stuffed owl, George, a battered old toy with one tufted ear missing.

It was like someone had stuck a pin in the day that River had disappeared, and time had stopped. River's ten-year-old-boy clothes still hung in our closet, though he would be thirteen now. His toys were still in his toy chest. There was a third toothbrush in our toothbrush holder, its bristles bone dry. We just couldn't throw it out. Sometimes it felt like we were all holding our breath—not just me and Dad, but the whole apartment—waiting for River to walk through the front door again.

Dad used to say that River and I were twins born eleven months apart. And really, that was how it felt. It wasn't that we were alike—we weren't, not at all. It was just that we were happiest when we were together, which I guess is unusual for siblings. During school, when we were apart, I felt like a mess. Awkward, weird. Never knowing what to say. When we found each other at the end of school, it was always such a relief, like stepping into a warm building when you're freezing cold.

After he disappeared, I was left to live my own messy life alone, a life which just seemed to get messier every year.

I closed my eyes, and as usual I struggled to sleep. I've always had trouble sleeping. That was why River first started telling me stories at night—to keep me from restlessly flipping and squirming in my bed. My favorites were the Elevator World stories.

I remember the exact moment when Elevator World first started. River and I were playing in the lobby by the stairs, in the same spot that Nyxie always played in now. The elevator hadn't yet been removed from the building, but it was always out of order. We'd never ever seen it actually working. I had slapped the red elevator button just for fun. And this time something happened. There was a loud clunking sound, and from somewhere above we heard a motorized whirring. River and I had locked eyes in shock and delight. Had I brought the busted elevator back to life? The elevator never came, but that night River told me the first story of Elevator World.

It was one of those continuing stories in which a magic elevator would take us from one land to another, like a ship. The elevator had only one button, and when you pressed it, it took you to the exact place you were supposed to go. River had a ferocious imagination. He would unravel the most astounding tales like they were coils of rope he kept in his pocket. He told stories about magical white weasels and headless brothers, and forests that turned lost travelers into hemlock trees. His stories sometimes merged, and characters from one story would turn up in another. I loved that.

The Elevator World stories always started the same way:

There once was a rickety old elevator, which everyone thought was broken. But Nell and River and the Girl with the Magic Shoes knew better, and the three of them traveled to Elevator World, where they saw places unknown and met people unheard of.

I always wondered if the Girl with the Magic Shoes was Annika. I asked River once, and he said no, but I think it was just because he knew we didn't like each other very much.

Now, above me, I heard a creaking sound, like someone shifting in River's upper bunk. My eyes flew open, and I froze. On this strangest-of-strange days, I half expected Vanessa Habscomb to hop down off River's bed.

"Hello?" I whispered, clutching the edge of my blanket.

I listened. Hearing nothing, I slipped out of bed and looked up at River's top bunk. There was no one there. His quilt was smooth, his pillow undented. George the stuffed owl sat by the pillow, its watchful eyes facing the window, waiting for River to come home. Waiting now for three years.

9

ULTIMATE
TIC-TAC-TOE

At lunch the next day I sat at the Leftovers Table, as usual. I called it the Leftovers Table because it's where all the kids who didn't fit in at the other tables sat. The weirdos. The pathologically shy. We didn't really fit in with each other, either, but at least we could eat our lunch in peace.

Julia Weeks, the girl whom Annika and her chums had bullied, sat at the far end of our table. Her thin hair was yanked back into a tight ponytail. Her skin was so pale, it was almost translucent, and her eyes were large and dark and doleful, like a camel's. I watched as she reached into her mouth, pulled out a pair of Invisalign braces, and put them in the purple plastic container on the table. She glanced around to see if anyone had seen her do it and caught me staring. I smiled a little, and her eyes startled, then flicked away. It made me feel bad. Like she thought I was one of her bullies. But maybe she didn't know exactly who had seen that video of her, so we were all potential tormentors.

She hunched her shoulders and ducked her head down,

pretending to focus on mixing her yogurt. I knew what she was doing. She was trying not to be noticed. Except she was doing it all wrong. The trick to not being noticed is to notice everyone else. People love to be noticed. It makes them feel important. They think if they're interesting enough for you to notice them, then you aren't as interesting as they are. Boom. Instant invisibility. Who needs a magic cloak?

I pulled out my lunch from my bag—mozzarella-and-tomato sandwich—and looked around the room. At the far corner in the back, I spotted Crud sitting at his table full of goons. The Meathead Table. He had a nasty-looking lump on his forehead—probably a gift from one of his idiot pals.

And there was The Viking, sitting at the Elsewhere Table. Most of the kids at the table were foreign students—you know, from elsewhere. I knew one of them, Omar, who had just moved here from Ethiopia and was in my study hall. Nice kid. He had helped me with my math homework once, and now I cross my sevens because I liked the way he did that.

The Viking wasn't a foreign student, but since he was new at school, I guessed he felt most at home with kids who didn't feel at home. Two tables down from the Elsewhere Table was the Goddess Table. That's where Annika sat. All the girls who sat there were long legged and beautiful. They reminded me of the women on the smashed Meissen vase, except without the tails.

Sitting next to Annika was a girl named Leilani. She was in my gym class and had been my assigned partner at Hantis—a combination of handball and tennis. Of course she was really good at it, and of course I stunk at it. She had been especially nasty to me after we lost the tournament in the first round.

Literally, you are literally terrible at this, she said to me at the end of the game. Then she spit on my sneaker.

Literally.

There were always a few boys who also sat at the Goddess Table. Presumably the goddesses had found these boys to be worthy and had summoned them to their divine realm from other, lesser tables.

Annika caught me looking in her direction, and to my surprise she held my gaze for a moment. It was as if she wanted to talk to me. Maybe she was curious to see what I thought about the Last Chance Club. Maybe, like me, she had tried to tell someone about it, and something strange had happened to stop her. In any case, she must have been pretty bent out of shape if she wanted to talk to *me*. One of the other goddesses leaned in to whisper to her. Annika broke her gaze with me and laughed at whatever the girl said, though she still looked strained.

"Hey, kid." Ruth Rocco plopped herself down at the table, across from me. She was a tall girl with a severe pageboy haircut. She always wore a vest, black or white, and a button-down shirt, and she spoke like a Hollywood agent from a 1940s movie.

It was common knowledge that she had transitioned over the summer. Before that, she had been a point guard on the boys' basketball team and had gone by a totally different name, but I'd only known her as Ruth. Since I'd arrived at Bright Future Academy, Ruth had taken me under her wing. For some odd reason, she also treated me as if I were a foreign student and she were my self-appointed translator.

"So what do you think of this?" Ruth slapped down what looked to be a baby's foot on the lunch table.

"Jeez, what is that thing?" I asked, recoiling.

"A customer left it on the table last night." Ruth's father owned Rocco's restaurant on Mercer Street, and Ruth collected items that people left behind. "It's a squeezy thing. For stress. See." She picked up the foot and squeezed it. "This guy and this chick were sitting at their table, fighting about something, and the whole time she was squeezing this rubber foot. Then finally the chick takes the foot and just chucks it at the guy's head. Plonk! And then she gets up and leaves. But she forgets her foot."

As she spoke, my attention was diverted by a boy at our table who was filling up a piece of paper with tiny tic-tac-toe grids while another boy looked on.

"Hey! Kid?" Ruth snapped her fingers in my face. "My face is over here."

"Sorry," I mumbled, though my eyes were still on the boy. He had a blocky head and bulgy eyes, and I was pretty sure his name was Luke. I saw now that the tiny tic-tac-toe grids were within larger grids. Whatever he was making looked complicated. And interesting.

"What are they doing?" I asked Ruth, nodding toward Luke and the other boy.

Ruth watched them for a moment, then leaned over toward them and rapped her knuckles on the table. "Hey. What are you two clowns doing?"

"Ultimate tic-tac-toe," Luke said.

"Ultimate tic-tac-toe," Ruth translated for me.

"How do you play?" I asked Luke.

"How do you play?" Ruth translated.

"It's complicated," Luke said dismissively.

That made Ruth get all puffed up. "Oh is it? Is it *complicated*?" She mimicked him in a sarcastic voice. "Well, Nell happens to be a genius." She jabbed a thumb in my direction.

"A genius?" He looked at me doubtfully.

"She shames the freaking stars, she's so bright!" Ruth declared.

"Are you a genius?" Luke asked me.

"No. I just like games."

"Yeah," Ruth asserted combatively. "The girl likes games."

Luke shrugged. "Okay." He turned the paper around to show me. "See, there are eighty-one squares. The first player can play anywhere on the board. . . ." He explained the rules to me while Ruth waited impatiently, squeezing the baby's foot and sighing loudly.

"Got it," I said when he was done. "Let's play."

"Ooo-kay!" Luke was happy to have a taker. "I'll go first."

He scribbled an X on the center square in the upper left-hand corner. I put my O in the grid on the upper right-hand corner. As we played, I began to calculate moves, test out variables, find possible traps.

"Ring Ding?"

The voice came from behind me. I turned around to see The Viking, grinning and holding out a package of Ring Dings, with one missing.

"Want one?" he asked, pushing the pack toward me.

"No," I said.

"I'll take it." Ruth grabbed the package out of his hands. "Yummy," she mouthed to me, waggling her eyebrows. I wasn't sure if she was talking about the Ring Ding or The Viking. Both, probably.

I looked back at the grids. I could feel The Viking behind me, watching. It made me really uncomfortable. I mean, I knew he wasn't paying attention to me because he liked me. Guys like him lived in Annika's world. No doubt he'd be summoned to the Goddess Table any day now. So why was he hanging around me? Boredom, maybe. Or else, seeing that I didn't want to be bothered, he was making a point to bother me, just to be annoying.

"What are you doing?" The Viking asked.

"She's playing ultimate tic-tac-toe," Ruth answered for me, with a mouthful of Ring Ding.

The Viking grabbed a chair from the adjacent table and

pulled it up so that he was sitting close by me. Just like yesterday. This was beginning to feel like harassment. I turned to him and gave him a stony glare.

He smiled back. His teeth were pearly white and perfect, like the teeth of a small child.

"Hats aren't allowed in school, you know," I told him.

He shrugged, still smiling, and didn't remove it.

I rolled my eyes, then turned back to the grid and studied it. My mind traveled down several different possible paths until finally I looked up at Luke.

"You've lost," I told him.

"What?" Luke looked down at the grids, frowning. "No, I haven't."

"Really, you can't win this," I assured him.

"You don't know that," Luke objected.

I hesitated, weighing the risks of suggesting a wager. A small one. Just to make things more fun. I felt that familiar flutter of excitement I always got at the chess tables in Washington Square Park.

I glanced around quickly. Mrs. Mahoney, the lunchroom attendant, was busy shushing a table full of noisy sixth graders.

"Well, I don't exactly know it," I lied. "I mean, I've never played this game before, so I'm just guessing."

"You're guessing wrong."

"Maybe. Okay, hey, I'll tell you what . . ."

I stuck my hand in my jeans pocket and pulled out a folded up five-dollar bill. I unfolded it slowly while

Luke watched. I looked at the bill worriedly, as though I were reluctant to possibly part with it. I tightened my lips with pretend resolve, sucked in a breath through my nose, then put the bill down on the table. "Five bucks to whoever wins."

Luke considered for a second. He looked at the grids, then back at me. I shrugged, as if to say, *What the heck, right?* Like I was willing to take the risk. Even though I knew I wasn't taking a risk at all. I would win this.

"Okay." Luke began to dig in his pocket, but before he could place his bet, The Viking reached out and grabbed my five-dollar bill off the table.

"What do you think you're doing?" I demanded furiously. The bell rang then, followed by the sound of chairs scraping against the lunchroom floor, and the thump of food dumped in garbage cans.

I stood up and made a lunge at The Viking's hand, which was clenched around my money, but Mrs. Mahoney stepped up to me at that moment and pointed at my tray.

"Clean up your mess, please," she said, and watched as I picked up my tray, my face hot with anger, and dumped its contents in the garbage. By the time I turned back to deal with The Viking, he was gone.

Yeah, Mr. Boot had called it.

The kid was a thief.

10

GAGGEN-SHTOPPIN

Mr. Boot was late again.

Crud was the only one in Room 101 when I arrived, slouched in his chair in the corner, arms folded against his massive chest. He nodded at me, then looked away.

Today the ferret was dressed in a blue-and-white cheerleader's outfit with pom-pom booties.

"Oh, that's criminal," I muttered to it, shaking my head.

It moved to a corner of its cage, its pom-pom booties shaking as it walked, and then it curled up in a ball and stared at me mournfully.

The door opened, and The Viking ambled in. I gave him a dirty look, but he came up to me anyway. Reaching into his pocket, he pulled out my five-dollar bill and handed it to me.

"What's the matter?" I said as I pocketed my money. "Guilty conscience?"

"Guilt about what?"

"About stealing my money."

"Stealing?" He seemed genuinely baffled. "I was trying to help you."

"Oooh, good one!" I said. "Is that why they almost expelled you? Because you were trying to help someone by stealing from them?"

"I took the money because that kid at the next table was watching you," he said. His usual happy-go-lucky manner had been replaced by something more guarded. I felt a twinge of regret to see the change.

"What kid?" I asked.

"The boy with the hair—" He cupped his hands a foot above his head. I knew who he was talking about. Jay Nardi. He had bushy hair, clipped in an odd way so that his head looked like a mushroom. "He's a blabbermouth. If he saw you placing bets, he would have told."

Just then Annika arrived. She marched up to The Viking and looped her arm through his.

"Sit by me," she said, and herded him to the opposite side of the room. At that moment Annika reminded me so much of her mother—a tall redheaded woman from Russia who seemed to collect men. When she saw that my mother was not in the picture, she had tried to collect my dad, too, without much luck. He had seen the way she treated Annika. He wasn't interested.

From across the room Annika glanced over at me defiantly. She was claiming The Viking, the same way she had tried to claim River so many years ago.

"Back again?" Mr. Boot addressed us all as he walked through the door, briefcase in hand. His eyes landed on The Viking and lingered there for a moment. "There's a no-hat policy in this school, Mr. Gunnerson. You are not so special that you're exempt from our rules."

The Viking removed his hat.

"So," Mr. Boot said, "I trust you have all had a good night's sleep and are feeling as fresh as farm eggs."

I looked around. Except for The Viking, nobody looked like they'd had a good night's sleep. Annika's usually flawless skin sported tired bluish shadows beneath her eyes, and Crud had that swollen purple knob on his forehead.

"I see you have a new growth on your face, Mr. Butterbank," Mr. Boot said.

Crud touched the bump on his forehead and muttered, "My mother's hanging plant accidentally hit me. Hard."

Mr. Boot shook his head. "Hanging plants are such unpredictable things. But tell me . . . when the unfortunate accident happened, were you in the process of discussing what we did here yesterday?"

Crud was silent for a moment, surprised. Then suspicion started to creep into his face. "Maybe."

Mr. Boot nodded solemnly. "Perhaps several of you have noticed that trying to tell people about the Last Chance Club ends in disappointment. Or injury."

Annika crossed her arms against her chest, and her lips pressed together angrily.

Oh yeah. Something had definitely happened to her, too.

"The club has a strict 'no telling' policy. And since we

can't rely on you to keep your big traps shut, we have shut them for you."

"What do you mean? What did you do to us?" asked Annika.

"Nothing harmful. Just a simple Gaggen-Shtoppin Spell."

"I don't like it," Crud said.

"I don't care," Mr. Boot replied. "Each time you talk about the magic we perform here, you will be stopped. And if you persist in trying to talk about the magic, you will be tossed out of the group, your memory will be wiped, and you will be expelled from school. Period." He paced across the front of the room, hands clasped behind his back, his head jutting forward. "Each of you has been given an opportunity. You will learn how to do things that only a handful of humans in the whole history of humankind know how to do." He stopped pacing and looked at us. "Don't bungle it."

"So what exactly are we learning to do?" Annika asked. "I mean, magic, okay, I get that. But for what?"

I snorted, louder than I had meant to, and Annika whipped her head around.

"Do you have a problem?" she snapped.

"Yes, I have a problem," I answered. "Are you seriously buying into all this nonsense, Annika? Magic? Really? He's a scam artist—can't you see that?"

I had gone too far, and I knew it. I get like that sometimes. When I'm on a roll, I sometimes keep rolling till I roll right off the edge of a cliff.

Every eye in the room turned to Mr. Boot, waiting to see what he would do. Even Crud looked nervous.

"Please continue, by all means," Mr. Boot said, flourishing his long hand between Annika and me. "I'm fascinated to see how this exchange will go."

After a quick glance at The Viking, Annika turned back to me and said, "Well, if it's not magic, what is it, then? You're supposed to be so smart, right? Okay, explain it to the rest of us, Einstein."

"I can't explain it," I admitted.

"That's right, you can't," Annika said. "So shut it."

There was a moment of silence, after which Mr. Boot asked, "Are we done?" His eyes shifted between Annika and me. We both nodded.

"Very good. Now, I believe Ms. Rapp wanted to know why you are being taught magic. The answer is simple. You are learning to be angels."

"Never going to happen," Crud said.

"Not to *behave* like angels, Mr. Butterbank. You are learning how to *be* angels. Quite literally."

"There's only one problem with that," I said. Well, there were a few problems with that, but I was being generous. "Angels aren't living people."

"Most aren't, true," Mr. Boot said. "However, there are always a handful of human angels on the planet, and it seems that you sorry lot have been chosen to be among them. You'll be taught how to perform miracles, help avert disasters, et cetera, et cetera, all with the use of magic."

"Why us?" Crud asked.

"Why indeed?" Mr. Boot drawled, appearing to agree with me that the choice was bizarre. "I certainly didn't choose you. I'm simply here to instruct."

"But what if we can't do it?" Crud asked. "I mean, what if we're crap at magic?"

So it appeared that Crud was fooled by Mr. Boot too. I glanced over at The Viking. He looked amused. He wasn't taking this seriously either, which made me like him a little more.

Mr. Boot didn't answer Crud right away. He walked over to his desk and sat on its edge, crossing his long legs at the ankles. He crossed his arms, too, and gazed down at the floor.

"This is called the Last Chance Club for a good reason." He looked up then and regarded us with less disgust than usual. In fact, I thought I detected something new in his expression.

Sympathy.

And frankly, it scared me.

"I would advise you all to try. Try very, very hard."

11

FLATZEN SPURTZ SPELL

Mr. Boot ran us through a series of finger-stretching exercises, without the chopsticks. We all looked totally ridiculous as we wiggled and fluttered our fingers in the air.

"Do we really need to do this?" Annika groused to Mr. Boot.

"Oh no, no, not at all, Ms. Rapp," Mr. Boot said. "It's just that there's nothing I enjoy more than to waste my precious time with you bloody plonkers. Mr. Butterbank, you are flicking those giant paws of yours. You should be fluttering."

And on it went. It was no better when we worked with chopsticks, either. We repeated a series of quick flourishes and swishes, each with dozens of ridiculously tiny variations, over and over.

Years ago Dad made me take jazz dance lessons. My mother was a really good dancer, he said, and he thought I might be a natural. But I hated it. I couldn't follow the series of steps—they made no sense at all—and even when I learned them, I couldn't do them quickly enough.

I dropped out after the third lesson. Mr. Boot's hand maneuvers felt like jazz dance—too fast, too complicated. I struggled to remember which flourish came after the crisscrossing—and was that the left over right or right over left? And then did you make the little sea-waves motion next, or was it the vertical swipes with the sharp uptick at the end? But at least I wasn't the only one struggling. As Mr. Boot walked slowly around the classroom, he muttered to himself disgustedly:

"Clumsy!

"Poorly executed!

"Remember, people, the magic you do is a reflection of who you are. If you are an angry person, your magic will be angry. If you are a sloppy person, your magic will be sloppy."

Finally he marched over to a shelf piled high with board games, plucked one out of the stack, and placed the game on his desk.

"You are each terrible in your own unique way," he told us. "However, you do have one thing in common: you all lack finesse. Come up here, please, all of you. Bring your chopsticks."

The chairs scraped against the floor, and we all, reluctantly, went up to his desk, chopsticks in hand.

"I'm going to be performing the Flatzen Spurtz Spell. Watch closely."

He whipped his chopsticks in the air above the board game, which happened to be the game Operation. I had played it once or twice at birthday parties. Mr. Boot made a series of complex maneuvers with his chopsticks, and then . . .

SQUILCH!

The noise came from inside the box. It sounded like a shoe being sucked out of thick mud. The lid of the board game lifted slightly.

Mr. Boot placed his chopsticks down on his desk and removed Operation's lid. From inside the box, a very small, very naked man sat up.

The little man stared at us with horror, his hands covering his privates. His body was full of gaping holes, revealing bones and ribs and internal organs. It was so shocking, not to mention disgusting, that I looked away.

"It's the Operation guy!" Annika cried with such delight that I forced myself to look at the little man again. That was when I noticed the bright-red, round nose and the thick, bluntly chopped hair, parted straight down the center of his head. Annika was right. This was the cartoon man from the board game, come to life.

"Are you kidding me?" Crud said under his breath.

The Viking clapped his hands and laughed.

Annika turned to me now. She gestured toward the little man. "Okay, so what do you call that? Still think we're being scammed?"

I shook my head. As much as I hated to admit it, this looked an awful lot like magic. There was no other explanation.

Mr. Boot wiggled a finger at the little man. "Lie down, please, Sam," he said.

The little man stayed where he was, looking up at all of us with alarmed eyes.

"Sam? He has a name?" Crud asked.

"Cavity Sam, yes." Mr. Boot wiggled his finger down toward the box again. Sam obeyed this time and lay down in the box, his hands still covering his privates.

"You'll have to put your arms to the side," Mr. Boot told him.

This was too much for Sam. He shook his head, refusing.

"It's okay, buddy," The Viking told him. "You don't have anything down there anyway." He picked up the game's cardboard lid and showed Sam the picture of himself. "See?"

"Oh, for goodness' sake." Mr. Boot peeled off a yellow Post-it note from a pad on the desk and stuck it over the little man's private bits. Satisfied, Sam stuck his arms out to the side, but the horrified expression on his face stayed put.

"Right," Mr. Boot said, addressing us. "We are going to have a lesson on how to use chopsticks with precision, and mmm, yes, perhaps even a touch of elegance. Mr. Gunner-son will start us off."

The Viking hesitated for a moment, then stepped up to the board game and stood there, fiddling with the chop-sticks in his hand. He looked uncertainly at Mr. Boot.

"Go on," Mr. Boot said, crossing his arms over his chest.

"What do I do?" The Viking asked.

"Play the game, Mr. Gunnerson. Play Operation. Have you never played Operation before?"

The Viking seemed uncomfortable. He shifted his shoulders.

"No," he said finally, in a flat voice.

Mr. Boot stared back at The Viking icily. He really seemed to hate the kid.

"Will someone please explain to Mr. Gunnerson how to play Operation?" Mr. Boot said with a sneer on his face.

Annika rushed to The Viking's assistance, outlining the rules of the game, and when she was done, Mr. Boot added one more thing. "But you will not be using the tweezers to extract his bones and organs. You will be using your chopsticks."

Down in the box, the little man whimpered.

The Viking adjusted the chopsticks in his hands. He made a few practice pinches at the air, and after scrutinizing the little man for a second, he aimed his chopsticks at the exposed funny bone in Sam's elbow. Sam lay perfectly still, but his terror-filled eyes followed the chopsticks as they came closer and closer to his body.

"Careful," Annika warned.

The Viking nodded. With the utmost concentration, he inserted the chopsticks into the opening in the elbow. He angled the chopsticks slightly, aiming the tips at the funny bone. Suddenly the little man let out a bloodcurdling scream that made all of us jump. His red nose was blinking wildly as the agonized scream stretched on and on.

"But I didn't do anything," The Viking cried, holding the chopsticks up, warding off blame.

"You touched the edge of his . . . wound," Crud said.

The little man's shrieks had subsided into short bursts of anguished sobs.

"You have failed, Mr. Gunnerson. Mr. Butterbank, you may go next."

"This is messed up, man," Crud said to Mr. Boot.

"We're waiting, Mr. Butterbank," Mr. Boot said.

Crud stepped up warily, his eyes locked onto the terrified face of Sam. He adjusted his chopsticks in his thick hands.

"I'm going for the spare ribs," he announced.

I could see his hand shaking a little as he aimed his chopsticks at Sam's chest. I held my breath as I watched, bracing for Sam's awful screams. Crud's chopsticks pinched the spare ribs. They gripped at the tip, just enough to lift them out of the side of his chest. But before the spare ribs were all the way out, one of Crud's chopsticks grazed the edge of the opening.

"AAAAAAAYIYIIIIII!!!" the little man shrieked, his nose pulsating red.

Crud startled so badly that he dropped his chopsticks on the floor.

"I want to go next." Annika stepped up eagerly.

"What are you, some kind of psychopath?" Crud blurted.

"No, I'm just sure I can do it," Annika replied.

"By all means, Ms. Rapp." Mr. Boot gestured grandly

toward the man in the box, whose gaze was shifting around the room wildly.

"Don't worry," Annika told him, pointing down at him with her chopsticks. "You won't feel a thing this time."

The little man did not look reassured.

Annika tipped her head to the side as she stared down at him, assessing things. Then she positioned her chopsticks in her hand and made some quick, elegant movements with them. She snipped the tips of the sticks together several times, then plunged them into the chest cavity. A moment later she pulled out a heart with a split down the middle. A broken heart. The thing was wet and beating, a fast, fluttery beat of fear. Annika put the heart down on the desk, where its beats began to slow, then settle into a more regular rhythm.

"Nice going, Annika," The Viking said.

Though it annoyed me to admit it, it really was impressive. Even the little man looked amazed.

"It's not the worst I've seen," Mr. Boot said. "Speaking of which . . . your turn, Ms. Batista."

12

THE MAGIC OF POTENTIAL

The thought of making the little man scream made me feel totally nauseous. I switched my chopsticks to my left hand, swiped my sweaty right hand against my jeans, switched the sticks back to my right hand, and then approached the box. The little man stared up at me in terror, and I considered that eye contact might be just one of the reasons doctors anesthetized patients before surgery. I settled the chopsticks into what I hoped was the correct position, giving them a few test snips. I knew that my movements were awkward. Nothing like Annika's. I looked at the little man's bones and organs, trying to figure out which would be the easiest to grab.

The butterfly in the stomach. I vaguely remembered that it was the only thing I was able to pick up when I had played the game before.

I raised my chopsticks.

"Steady," I heard The Viking murmur behind me. For some reason the sound of his voice helped calm my nerves. I took a deep breath and then lowered my chopsticks into the man's stomach. My focus was fixed on the butterfly, glistening repulsively in the stomach cavity.

Steady, steady.

My left stick touched something, and I paused, fully expecting to hear the little man's agonized scream. But it seemed that the stick had simply touched the butterfly's head. I went back to work, nestling the sticks into the groove between the wings. The next moment I was holding the slimy butterfly aloft, free of the man's stomach. The butterfly fluttered its wings, splattering slimy who-knew-what all over my arm. I released it and it flew away, landing on the windowsill.

There had been no screams from Cavity Sam. I had done it!

I glanced over at Annika, expecting to see her look disappointed at my success. But no. She was smiling. She jabbed a finger at Crud and The Viking.

"Girls, dominating!" she cried.

I guess her competitive spirit won out over her dislike of me. For the next half hour, Annika and I became teammates, girls versus boys. We went round for round, sometimes making Sam scream—which always made us all flinch with horror. But after a while, with practice, we became better and better at extracting his innards without touching the sides.

It seemed like the members of the Last Chance Club were beginning to bond, despite the fact that we were four people with virtually nothing in common. Crud wrapped a beefy arm around The Viking's neck when The Viking successfully picked out the wrench in Sam's ankle; and though I still didn't like Annika, I couldn't help but feel a rush of pleasure when she fist-bumped me after I successfully extracted the Charlie Horse, a small horse near Sam's hip socket.

I didn't want to feel flattered that Annika approved of me. She had obviously grown up to be a bully of the worst kind. But the thing with beautiful people is that even though you may not like them, you always sort of want them to like you. I guess beauty comes with its own brand of magic.

We were all laughing and trading insults, until The Viking removed the Adam's apple, and the little man was completely cleaned out of all his bones and organs.

"Congratulations," Mr. Boot said. "You have all managed to make some progress."

He quickly flicked his chopsticks over the little man, who instantly flattened out with a SPLURTZ! and fused with the yellow game board, his face frozen in its look of panic. It was the most shocking thing that had happened during the whole session. We all stared down at Sam's flat, lifeless eyes in silence. It was like seeing someone die right in front of you.

"What happened to him?" I asked in a quiet voice. "Where did he go? I mean, is he just . . . nothing now?"

"Not nothing," Mr. Boot replied as he placed the lid on the box. "The magic only made him more of what he already is. Magic is all about potential. When I look at each of you"—he gazed at us one by one—"I see a wretched pack of thieves, bullies, gamblers, and thugs. Yet there is a tiny possibility—no bigger than a dust mote, mind you—that you will turn into something more. And that goes for anything—a piece of wood or an alphabet block or a board game. Magic is just a way to restructure energy, to give something a fighting chance to be more of what it is."

"Hey, Mr. Boot." The Viking was standing by the stack of board games and had taken the lid off the Monopoly game. "Can you make this more real?" He grabbed some of the paper money and waved it around, grinning.

I groaned. What was it with that kid? He seemed determined to make Mr. Boot hate him.

"You overestimate your charm, Mr. Gunnerson," Mr. Boot said, and added in a voice full of quiet menace, "You are playing a dangerous game. It will end badly for you."

The Viking's expression changed, just a wink of fear that he quickly covered with a sideways grin.

Mr. Boot checked his watch. "Alas, our time is up." He reached into his briefcase and pulled out some dark-blue bound books with gold lettering. "These are the club handbooks. Should your friends or family happen to look at them, all they'll see is a list of club rules and regulations. You, however, will see guides to various spells. Each book is tailored to the individual and what they are capable of. Some of your books will be noticeably slimmer than others." He gave a handbook to The Viking that was about as thin as a comic book. Crud's was hefty, as was Annika's. Mine, though thicker than The Viking's, was not very impressive. On the cover it said *Last Chance Club Handbook, 112th Edition*. "You will study the handbooks and practice your spells before bedtime and then again when you awake."

"What if we make something happen with magic but then can't undo it?" Crud asked.

"Impossible. Your chopsticks are calibrated to work within a highly charged Oomphalos, and only when you will not be seen by anyone else. If any of you actually manages to do a spell correctly at home, which I sincerely doubt, you will produce a very weak sort of magic."

"What is that?" I asked. "An Oomphalos?" I remembered he had mentioned it before, the first time we had met.

"It is a place where energy converges and makes magic not only possible, but probable. In any case, you may safely practice your spells at home without turning your parents into toads."

13

NYXIE

I was so consumed with thoughts about magic and what Mr. Boot had meant about training us to be angels that I almost tripped on Nyxie. She was sitting on the apartment building's lobby stairs, rolling a grubby toy bus back and forth on the wall.

"Hey, Nyxie. What are you doing?"

"My bus can climb walls. It has to make a stop now to pick up more people. *Pshttt!* That's the bus doors opening. Step up, peoples! Off we go! *Whooosh!* See, it flies, too."

She was in a chatty mood today. She swooped the bus in the air. That was when I noticed the nasty raw scrapes along both of her arms and a raw patch on her chin.

"What happened to your arm?" I asked as she made her bus do a loop-the-loop in the air.

"I hate Chicken Bone Charlie." She turned to look at me, her little face suddenly pinched with anger.

"Why?" Chicken Bone Charlie was known to scare kids, but he'd never actually hurt one, as far as I knew.

"He chased me," Nyxie said. "I was going to the bodega this morning, and he screamed at me and did this"—she made stabbing motions—"with his chicken bone. I ran, and that's when I fell and got all scraped up." She held up her arms as though she were surrendering, to show me her wounds more clearly. The scrapes were pretty bad, with bloody pinpricks and dirt lodged in them.

"Come on," I said, starting up the stairs. "Let's get you cleaned up and put some Band-Aids on your arm."

Nyxie swooped her bus in the air pensively, her brows pulled down. She looked ready to refuse. But something made her change her mind. She stood up, reached out, and grabbed my hand. I tried not to think about that filthy paw of hers, which felt dry and grimy.

Upstairs, I took her into our bathroom and washed all her scrapes, put some Neosporin on them, and then stuck some Band-Aids on. I even found a few Curious George Band-Aids that Dad had bought for me ages ago, and I gave her a few extras in case some of them fell off.

"All right, soldier, you're all patched up." I led her out into the hallway, but she stopped at the closed door of Dad's workshop.

"What's in there?"

"It's where my father works."

"Is he in there now?" she asked.

"Yes."

She thought about that, then asked, "Can I see your bedroom?"

I hesitated for a moment.

"I guess so." I led her to the end of the hall and into

my bedroom. She stood in the middle of the room for a minute, staring down at the floor. Years ago my mother had painted the bedroom floor with orange-and-white speckled koi fish swimming in pale blue water. It made you feel like you were walking across an iced-over pond. Dad said she'd wanted her art to make people feel a little off-balance. She managed to do that in real life too, since she left us when I was five and we hadn't seen her since.

"Do you have any toys?" Nyxie asked.

I'd gotten rid of all my toys a few years ago. River's toys were still there, though, in the old toy chest. For a while after River went missing, I would sometimes open up the chest and look at all his stuff. Legos and Matchbox cars. A set of tiny farm equipment, including an oblong piece of farmland with little bumps of plastic corn sprouting out of it. I had loved that farm set. River and I would plow the tiny field and put rice into the spreader to sow the seeds.

It had been years since I had opened the toy chest. Now, impulsively, I walked up to it and lifted the lid. It felt taboo somehow. The sharp smell of plastic toys rose out of the chest, along with the musty scent of cedar.

I heard Nyxie emit a soft "ohhh" of delight and surprise at the sight of all the toys jumbled inside the chest. Yet she didn't move. She didn't fall on the chest and start rummaging around like a normal kid. She just stood there and feasted on the sight of it, as if that was all she would be allowed to do.

"Go on," I told her. "Pick out something you like, and you can have it."

Those are not your toys to give away, I heard a voice in my head say. *Those are River's.*

But River would be thirteen now. Too old for toys.

And anyway, I thought, *he might never come home again.*

I had never before uttered those words, not even in my own head. But something inside me had yawned open, like the old toy chest. Something ugly and hidden.

Slowly Nyxie walked over to the chest and knelt beside it. Rocking from knee to knee, she looked in the chest without touching anything or digging around to see what was beneath the top layer of toys. Finally she reached in and pulled something out. It was the toy griffin—a winged lion with a movable head and wings that flapped when you pulled a lever on its back.

"I'll show you how to move the wings," I said, but when I reached out for the toy, Nyxie swiftly tucked it under her shirt as though she were stealing it and dashed down the hallway and out the front door.

That's when I heard my phone ring from inside my backpack. No one ever called me on it except for Dad, so it was probably a wrong number. But I fished it out of my backpack anyway.

"Hello?"

"Nell?" a male voice said.

"Yes?"

"Don't freak out, Nell. This is River."

"Wait, this is . . . what? Did you say this is *River?*" My voice sounded shrill with nerves, the pitch rising on the tail end of his name as though I were calling out to someone in a dark room.

"Meet me at the Museum of Natural History, Hall of Human Origins. The Neanderthal diorama. Be there at 5:10 p.m. Just you, no one else."

"Hold on. *What?*"

I tried to keep my mind steady as he repeated what he'd said. The voice was deeper than River's had been. But he would be thirteen now, so his voice probably would be lower. He sounded a little breathless and hoarse. He had cleared his throat after he said "Museum."

"How do I know this is really River?" I asked, trying to make my voice more adult. Cool and authoritative, the way Detective Chatterjee would sound.

There was no answer, and the phone went dead.

I checked the time. 4:44.

I did a quick mental risk assessment. I obviously didn't like the idea of going alone. I'm a city kid, which means I'm basically hardwired to expect trouble. But the museum was a very public place, with loads of people milling around. And security guards.

Then I wondered something else—what if the boy I'd seen on the elephant in the playground *had* been River after all? That thought wiped away any misgivings about going to the museum. Hurriedly, I put my hoodie back on and fished through my backpack for some cash and a MetroCard.

Dad opened his door and peered down the hallway at me. "I thought I heard you," he said, smiling. His headlamp was still on, which made it look like a beam of light was shooting straight out of his brain. The light blinded me so that I couldn't see his face, making it easier to lie to him.

"I have to go, Dad. I'm meeting a friend from school at the library."

I didn't like lying to my dad, but I knew if I told him the truth, he would never let me go to the museum. He would call in Detective Chatterjee, and maybe she would call in some officers, and by the time anyone got there, it would be too late.

"Oh? Really? Okay, great!"

I knew he'd be happy to think that I had a normal sort of friend, instead of the chess hustlers in the park.

I checked my phone.

4:45.

"Got to go," I said as I shoved the crumpled bills and the MetroCard in my back pocket and headed outside for the uptown train.

I had been to the American Museum of Natural History dozens of times, mostly on school field trips. I'd never really liked the place. It has this hushed, churchy feeling. Plus, gawking at those poor stuffed animals behind glass always made me feel like a dirtbag.

Inside, I hurried up to the ticket counter. There were only a few people ahead of me since the museum was going to close soon. I checked my phone.

5:06. It was going to be tight.

I had to keep squishing down the anticipation of seeing River, but I couldn't help it. My mind was continuously looping through the moment that we'd see each other—the tears and the hugs and the overwhelming sense of relief.

Was River somewhere in the lobby now? I wondered. I looked around at the crowd, jittery with excitement. I didn't see anyone who looked like the boy on the elephant. Would he be tall now? Probably. He was so gangly as a kid. His hair was dark with loose curls. But hair can be dyed. In any case, I would recognize his face; I was sure of that.

By the time I paid for admission, it was 5:08. They handed me a map, and after a second of perusing it, I headed straight for the Hall of Human Origins, walking as fast as possible without breaking into a run. I knew exactly where it was. First floor. I passed by a troop of rowdy Cub Scouts who were shoving one another, and headed toward the darkened hall where the dioramas were.

I looked at my phone.

5:09.

I hurried past the skeletons and the cases full of spearheads until one of the dioramas in the hallway caught my attention. There was just something about it that sort of flagged me, and sure enough, when I reached it, I saw that it was the Neanderthal diorama. Behind a glass pane, life-sized Neanderthals were going about their business inside a cave. Standing in front of the diorama was a young couple and their two small kids.

No one else.

I glanced around the room. There was a group of tourists speaking German, two elderly women, and a bored-looking guard who appeared as lifeless as the exhibits.

No River.

I paced back and forth as more people ambled past, a few stopping to glance at the Neanderthals before strolling on. After a solid fifteen minutes, it became clear that I had gone there for nothing. The caller had been a crackpot after all. This had all been a sick, cruel joke.

From down the hall, I heard the sound of raised voices. The voices grew louder until there was a full-on eruption of shouting. The bored guard by the Neanderthal diorama perked up and hurried toward the commotion. I did too, feeling a small ping of hope that this might have something to do with River. But by the time I reached it, whatever it was that had happened had already ended. The bored guard was heading back to the Hall of Human Origins with a disappointed look on his face. Behind him was the troop of Cub Scouts, laughing and chattering.

"Hey." I poked one of the Scouts on the shoulder. "What was all that shouting about?" I poked him a little harder than I meant to, and he stumbled. But he didn't even look that surprised. Maybe he was the kind of kid who got poked a lot.

"A cat got into the museum," he said.

"It was a rat," his friend said.

"Nah, it was probably just a squirrel," another kid said. "Some guy caught it and took it out."

So that was that.

I felt exhausted, drained. And most of all stupid. Stupid for coming here. Stupid for hoping. I shot one last rueful glance at the Neanderthal diorama.

And that's when I saw her.

A slender woman in a floral dress and battered hiking boots, carrying a large khaki green backpack. She was hurrying out of a door beside the diorama, which was marked EMPLOYEES ONLY.

It was Vanessa Habscomb, the woman who had appeared on our fire escape the other day. I was sure of it.

The coincidence of seeing her there disoriented me for a moment. But then I began to put it all together. It must have been Vanessa who had something to do with that phone call. I'd thought she was shady that day when she walked into our apartment! There was just something about her that rang all kinds of alarm bells for me, and now it looked like my instincts were right.

I started after her at a fast clip, but the bored guard stepped in front of me, palms up.

"No running."

So I race-walked in the direction I'd seen her go, jogging when there were no guards in sight. I hurried through hall after hall of exhibits—sparkling minerals and giant tree trunks and more skeletons and sharks suspended from the ceiling. It was like rushing through a nightmare. I searched the crowds for that floral dress and those hiking boots, but Vanessa Habscomb, the expert on everything, was nowhere to be found.

14

D-I-Y Magic

The first thing I did when I got back home was go up to Mrs. Farfle's apartment. Vanessa Habscomb had said she'd been at Mrs. Farfle's party the night she stepped through our window, so Mrs. Farfle might know where to find her. But after knocking for a full five minutes with no one answering, the apartment door across the hallway opened up, and a pimply teenage boy with spooky eyes—Nyxie's brother—told me that Mrs. Farfle was out of town.

"I can probably kick open the door if you want," he said leeringly. Then he did a karate kick in the air.

"Yeah, no," I said, and hurried back down the stairs.

That night as I lay in bed, my mind tumbled over itself with questions. Did Vanessa Habscomb have something to do with River's disappearance? I mean, what were the chances that I would see her at the Neanderthal exhibit right at that minute? Plus, the way she had just appeared on our fire escape the other day had been odd. And that brought up something else. She had appeared right before

I was about to tell Dad about the club, which had made me wonder if Mr. Boot was behind it somehow. And if Mr. Boot and Vanessa knew each other, could Mr. Boot be wrapped up in River's disappearance somehow?

It made me feel feverish—it was all too much to absorb. I squeezed my eyes shut and groaned.

But maybe, maybe, it *was* all due to coincidence, I told myself. Maybe Vanessa was at the museum that day because she worked there. Weird stuff happens, right?

Except lately, weird stuff was happening because of magic. Magic and Mr. Boot.

I pulled the blanket over my head, too exhausted to think any more. The neighborhood was noisy as usual, despite an evening rain—cars whining through the streets, their wet tires sounding like packing tape being pulled off the roll. Voices grew louder as they passed beneath my window, then melted back into the damp night. The city sounds were comforting, squeezing out my own troubled thoughts. Pretty soon I began to drift to sleep and was nearly out, but another sound—this one from inside the apartment—rattled me awake.

Scritch, scritch, scritch.

"Dad?" I called sleepily, pulling the blanket off my head. There was no response.

Scritch, scritch, scratch, SCRITCH!!

The noise became more urgent. A rat, maybe, scurrying between the walls? If it was a rat, it was a huge one, from the sound of it. I remembered that Ruth had told me her father once killed a rat the size of a beagle in the basement of his restaurant. I sat up in bed, feeling cold gooseflesh crawl across my body as I searched the dark room for any sign of movement.

SCRITCH, SCRITCH, SCRITCH!!!!

To my horror I saw the front of my backpack twitch. Something was definitely inside it.

The thought of a rat scrambling around in there, touching all my stuff, was totally repulsive, but I was caught between wanting the thing out of my backpack and also very much not wanting it running around my room. After a moment of deliberation, I got out of bed and turned on the light. From my closet, I fished out an old shoebox and examined its contents—a tangle of beaded necklaces I had made in third grade, a few birthday cards, a green plastic Easter egg that had been hidden in there but had never been found. I knelt down beside the backpack and listened. The thing was being very quiet in there, which was even creepier than when it was moving around. Positioning the box with one hand, I unzipped the backpack just a tiny bit, ready to slam the box down on the critter the second it came out of there. I pulled the zipper a little more, wishing I had thought to put on some gloves to protect my hands. There was a sudden scuffling sound in the backpack, and I just barely held back a scream as something jumped out. But instead of a fleeing rat, a pair of chopsticks flew out of the backpack and across the room as though they'd been chucked, and landed on the rug.

"Are you kidding me?" I said out loud, clutching my chest to reassure my racing heart.

I started toward the chopsticks so that I could scoop them up and stuff them back into my bag, but before I could, both sticks popped up off the floor and landed in my right hand.

This was Mr. Boot's handiwork. Of course. I remembered then what he'd said about practicing with the chopsticks before we went to sleep and when we woke up. I was pretty sure that if I tried to put the chopsticks back in my bag now, they'd find a way to get out again.

"Fine," I huffed, staring down at them in my hands, where they felt jittery, like little kids who had been cooped up too long. They quivered and then began to tap against each other, clattering so loudly that I was afraid Dad would hear.

"Okay, shut up, I'll practice!" I whispered.

I took the club handbook out of my backpack and looked through the spells. There weren't many. I settled on practicing the Animagor Airblunken Spell, which made inanimate things airborne. My fingers were clumsy as usual, and one of the sticks dropped to the ground. Instantly, the other stick whacked my left knuckles, hard.

"Ouch!" I cried.

"Okay in there?" Dad called through the door as I picked up the other stick.

"Yup!" I called back.

I glared down at the sticks in my hand. They were

jiggling again, vibrating with energy. It was like they *needed* me to do the spell correctly.

I took a breath and started again. This time things went better. At least both sticks stayed in my hand. After a few more tries, I realized that the sticks were guiding my hands with gentle nudges this way and that. They were teaching me, the way someone might put their hand over a kid's to guide them as they wrote the alphabet.

I began to feel the flow of the movements, how the sticks seemed to be answering each other, movement replying to movement. The way chess pieces do. The black knight answers the white rook. One piece asks a question that the other piece answers. I actually enjoyed the sensation—the way the sticks seemed to gather more and more energy, then release it at the end of the spell. There was a sock on the floor that I managed to make move the tiniest bit, a small hop. After a few tries, though, the sock rose up a good six inches in the air before it flopped back to the floor.

Next I practiced the Grossen-Zetzer Spell, which made things larger. That required some pretty violent movements with the chopsticks that looked as though I was beating a mosquito to death. I had zero luck making anything happen with that one.

After that I tried the Flatzen Spurtz Spell. It was the spell that animated two-dimensional things, the spell that Mr. Boot had done on the little Operation man. Just for fun, I aimed my sticks at one of the koi fish painted on the floor—a large one with Creamsicle-orange splotches.

I focused on the koi. Adjusting my fingers on the sticks, I took a deep breath, then maneuvered my sticks in what I hoped was a decent version of the Flatzen Spurtz Spell. I felt the sticks cooperating, moving smoothly, picking up speed when they were supposed to. A filament of light trailed from the tips of the sticks, and for a split second the fish on the floor twitched and its eyes moved. It looked up at me.

Here's the funny thing about magic—when you watch it in movies or read about it, it's all really exciting and fun. But in real life, magic is very creepy. Seeing the fish look at me like that made me feel squirrelly. But the very next moment, the fish grew still again. It went back to being just a painting on the floor. Weak magic. I guessed it was because of the Oomphalos thing that Mr. Boot had mentioned.

I practiced a few more spells until, all at once, the sticks stopped vibrating. They grew still and cool in my hands. I tried the opening sequence of the Oifen Shoifen Spell, which animated moderately sleepy things, like cloth and plastic, just to see. Nope. The energy had left the chopsticks. Now they were simply two smooth pieces of white spruce—that's all.

The lesson, it seemed, was over.

15

GOOD DEEDS

The next morning I found a yellow slip of paper inside my locker. It looked exactly like the slip of paper I had received the week before telling me I would have to join the Last Chance Club or be expelled. This time, the swirly handwriting said:

> YOU ARE REQUIRED TO DO A GOOD DEED IN
> SCHOOL TODAY.
>
> USE YOUR CHOPSTICKS.
>
> BE DISCREET.
>
> TRY NOT TO KILL ANYONE.

As soon as I finished reading it, the yellow note grew warm in my palm and then melted into a thick, clear puddle that smelled like hand sanitizer. I didn't have anything to wipe it on, so I rubbed it into my hands and hoped it wasn't toxic.

A good deed, using magic?

I looked around, hoping to see someone else in the club to consult, but none of the others were around. Did they all get a note like this too? I felt in my backpack to make sure the chopsticks were in there. The moment I touched them, they buzzed with energy against my hand. They were obviously ready to do some magic.

As it turned out, finding a good deed to do was more complicated than you would think. During a math quiz, I considered causing the fire alarm to ring with the Klangen Tumult Spell. But it was raining outside, and making everyone stand in the rain for twenty minutes to avoid a math quiz that the teacher would make us take the next day anyway hardly seemed like a deed worth doing.

In gym class it would have been nice to help Becca King, the only girl who was worse than I was at basketball, make a layup shot. But, of course, I didn't have my chopsticks with me.

By lunchtime I was beginning to doubt that I'd be able to come up with any good deed at all. I wondered what would happen if I failed the task. Would Mr. Boot have me expelled? It seemed like something he might do. I'd be one less person in the club for him to deal with.

At the Leftovers Table, I picked distractedly at a chicken-salad sandwich while Ruth was frantically trying to finish the final two chapters of *To Kill a Mockingbird* for a test the next period.

I looked around for Annika, Crud, and The Viking.

Over at the Goddess Table, Annika seemed on edge. One of the other girls was talking to her, and she was nodding, but she wasn't paying attention. It was only when I followed her stare that I saw why—over at the Elsewhere Table, The Viking was chatting with a girl named Surinder, who was in my global history class. He was laughing at something she was telling him while unwrapping a Butterfinger. He certainly didn't look like he was searching for a good deed to perform. Or maybe he'd already done his?

Crud was over at the Meathead Table, scowling and hunched over a bowl of something or other, scarfing it down. Good deeds appeared to be the last thing on his mind. But then I noticed something. He was eating his lunch with chopsticks. I narrowed my eyes and watched. It happened so quickly that if I hadn't been staring, I certainly would have missed it. Crud's chopsticks swished around above his bowl, tiny specks of light dripping off the end. Then he continued eating as if nothing had happened.

He did something!

I looked around the lunchroom for signs of magic, but nothing looked out of the ordinary. Kids eating, talking, dumping their trays.

Then I spotted it. Mrs. Mahoney, the cafeteria lady. She was standing by the trash can, gazing up. It took me a second to notice something slowly fluttering down from the ceiling. A blue butterfly. Mrs. Mahoney was transfixed, her mouth open. She held out her hand, and the butterfly landed gently in her palm. She stared at it, smiling. I couldn't be sure, but I thought I saw Mrs. Mahoney's eyes dampen before she sniffed in a businesslike way. She blew on it, and the butterfly flew away.

I looked over at Crud. He was watching Mrs. Mahoney with a little smile on his face. When he caught me staring, his scowl returned, and he plunged his chopsticks back into his bowl and continued eating as if nothing had happened.

It was such a simple and elegant bit of magic. Frankly, I was shocked that it came from Crud.

Also, I realized that the lunchroom was the perfect place to use chopsticks.

I reached into my backpack and pulled out my chopsticks. With some difficultly I managed to clamp the sticks on either side of my sandwich while scouting the room for people who might be in need of a good deed.

"Hey, um, kid?" Ruth had momentarily looked up from her work to notice that I was nibbling at the half-a-sandwich, held aloft in my chopsticks. "What in the dang-diggity-ding are you doing?"

"Just trying something," I said.

"Weird. I like it." Ruth shook her head and went back to reading.

I kept scanning the lunchroom until my attention was diverted by Leilani, the goddess of Hantis. Leilani was heading toward our table, glancing nervously this way and that. Her chin was raised, and her jaw was jutting aggressively, one way and then the other.

When she reached the Leftovers Table, she stopped at the end farthest from me, right behind Julia Weeks, the girl who had been the victim of Annika's bullying. Julia was hunched over a bowl of chili. With one last stealthy glance around the lunchroom, Leilani bent over Julia's shoulder, so close that her long hair brushed Julia's face. It looked as though she were about to whisper something into Julia's ear. Then, so fast that if I had blinked, I would have missed it, Leilani spit into Julia's food.

Pig! I thought, outraged.

I put down my sandwich, and with the chopsticks buzzing between my fingers, I started the Animagor Airblunken Spell. I kept my thoughts focused on what I wanted to animate. My anger seemed to galvanize the chopsticks. They whipped and snipped at the air, trailing sparks.

In a flash, Julia's Invisalign retainer, which had been sitting in its purple plastic case, flew up and inserted itself into Leilani's mouth. Leilani's eyes opened wide with shock. She gagged at first, then began to claw at her teeth in an attempt to scrape off what had nestled itself so snugly against them.

"What did you do?" she demanded of Julia, although the question came out "Wa-ka-deedu?" because of the braces, and Julia could only stare back at her in complete befuddlement.

With a cry of fury, Leilani ran back to the Goddess Table, her fingers tearing at her teeth the whole way.

"Lei, what are you doing?" one of the goddesses asked.

But Leilani couldn't answer her because now the Invisalign had become unhappy with the situation too. In an attempt to free itself from the unfamiliar mouth, the braces made Leilani's teeth clack together uncontrollably. Leilani tried to grab at her teeth again, but this time they bit her. Leilani winced in pain as her teeth continued to clack away.

"Seriously, Lei, you look like a chimpanzee!" shrieked another goddess, and they all started to laugh.

The entire lunchroom was watching the spectacle now, the laughter gradually mounting.

"Sorry, Boo Radley," Ruth said, closing her book and joining the spectators. "This is too good to miss."

All eyes were on Leilani.

All eyes except for Annika's.

She was looking at me.

She knows, I thought.

But I decided that I didn't care. *Leilani deserves it,* I told myself. I met Annika's gaze.

No remorse.

Abruptly, Annika stood and walked up to Leilani, who was in tears now, her hands hovering near her clattering mouth but not so closely that they would get bitten again.

"Let me see," Annika demanded.

Reluctantly, Leilani dropped her hands and let Annika look at the clacking teeth. Annika studied them for a moment.

"Do you wear Invisaligns?" she asked Leilani.

Leilani shook her head, her teeth clacking like mad the whole time.

"Well, you're wearing *someone's* Invisaligns," Annika said.

Leilani stared at Annika for a moment. Then she looked back over at Julia. When she saw the open purple braces container on the table, Leilani turned back to Annika, her eyes wide with horror. Her head jutted forward several times as her teeth chattered away. The entire Goddess Table was watching.

"What is she doing now?" Ruth asked.

Leilani made a retching sound in her throat, and before Annika could back away, Leilani vomited. It was an athletic sort of vomit too, the vomit of a Hantis goddess. It forcefully splattered across the Goddess Table, making the goddesses shriek and jump to their feet. Annika had received the worst of it, though. Her shirt was soaked, as were the tips of her hair, and her boots were a mess. Holding her arms away from her now-disgusting clothes, she looked back at The Viking, who was staring at her, and then she turned to glare at me with rage.

At that moment, the Invisaligns managed to maneuver themselves out of Leilani's mouth and they landed on the floor with a plink, sodden and repulsive.

"Cleanup in the lunchroom!" Mrs. Mahoney called into the intercom by the door. "Vomit!" Which only added to Leilani's mortification.

The fifth-period bell rang. The show was over. Slowly, the kids began to file out.

"Well, if there's a question on the test about the last chapter, I'm in trouble," said Ruth, who was now shoving her book into her backpack. "It was worth it, though."

I slipped my chopsticks back into my bag, but just as I was about to follow Ruth out, Annika marched up to me, blocking my way.

"Why?" Annika demanded. She smelled so awful that I felt a wave of nausea pass over me.

For a moment I considered playing dumb, but in the end I replied, "She deserved it."

"You were supposed to do a *good* deed!"

"Yeah, well, she spit into Julia's chili," I countered, but I felt my certainty dissolving.

"Then you did magic to get even? That's not the same thing as a good deed, Nell. In fact, the only thing you did for Julia was lose her braces for her." She nodded toward Julia, who was looking under the table, presumably for her missing Invisalign.

There was truth to what Annika was saying. But it was hypocritical, too. "Oh, and you know all about being kind to Julia, do you?" I snapped.

Annika said nothing for a moment.

"You are a mess, Nell," Annika said. "You always were."

"I'm a mess?!" I was furious now. I gestured toward the vomit on Annika and laughed. "Look who's talking!"

"Mr. Boot said our magic reflects who we are," Annika said evenly. "And your magic is . . . out of control."

16

ᴛʜᴇ ʜᴏʟʏ ᴘʟᴀᴄᴇ

Mr. Boot was already in Room 101 when we arrived. He was bent over the ferret's cage. The cage's lid was off, and Mr. Boot was poking at the poor animal, which was trying to relax in its hammock, still wearing its cheerleader outfit.

Mr. Boot tipped the hammock over so that the ferret plopped out. It righted itself and looked at Mr. Boot ruefully. Then it stretched, mounted its wheel, and trudged along in a slow and insolent way, the pom-poms on its booties quivering.

Annika had managed to change out of her vomit-splattered clothes, although the new ones were clearly not her own. Probably stuff from the nurse's office. The jeans were too short, and the T-shirt was too large and featured a cat eating a slice of pizza. She must have rinsed off her hair because it was damp and scraped back into a ponytail. She looked so much like the little kid I remembered—scrawny and boyish. The kid who, screeching and laughing, chased River up and down the building's stairs. She always caught him. She was fast even then.

"What's in the bags?" asked Crud suspiciously, pointing to a line of paper bags on Mr. Boot's desk.

"Hopes and dreams, young man," Mr. Boot replied. He put the lid back on the ferret's cage. Then he walked to his desk, grabbed the bags, and plopped one on each of our desks. We peered inside.

"Kindergarten scissors," I said. "And . . ." I pulled out a pair of plastic toy glasses. They had red swirls on the lenses. "X-ray glasses."

Crud put his glasses on. He looked totally ridiculous. "I had a pair of these when I was a little kid," he said. "I chose it as a prize in an arcade because my brothers told me they would really work. I was a chump." He took them off and dropped them back in his bag.

"This afternoon we'll be going on a little field trip," Mr. Boot said. "Take your jackets and backpacks with you."

"Where are we going?" Annika asked.

"A holy place. That means you will all pretend to be civilized."

"What, like a church?" said Annika.

But Mr. Boot had already marched out the door, so we just grabbed our paper bags and backpacks and followed.

"Don't you want to know about our good deeds?" The Viking asked Mr. Boot as we hurried down the school hallway.

"Good deeds are best done in secret," Mr. Boot said.

Outside, Mr. Boot headed toward Eighth Street, walking fast. Annika was the only one who could keep up with him, her long legs scissoring rapidly. Even dressed the way she was and with her hair pulled back, her beauty caught people's eye, and passersby glanced at her in a quick, sneaky way. Crud lumbered along, bringing up the rear.

The Viking had slowed down to match his pace with mine.

"Where's your jacket?" he asked.

"I'm not cold." That was a lie. I was still holding out, refusing to give in to the weather.

"You look cold. You want to wear mine?" The Viking was wearing a long shearling jacket, and boy, did that thing look warm.

"No thanks," I said.

He stopped walking, reached into his sock, and pulled out a Dum Dum lollipop. He held it out to me.

I shook my head. Food from someone's sock wasn't exactly appealing.

"It's mystery flavor," he persisted.

"I'm good," I assured him.

What was up with him? What did he want from me?

"Look, see." He reached into his other sock and pulled out another Dum Dum. "I have more. Do you like orange better?"

I sighed. "Okay, sure, I'll have the orange."

He handed it to me, and I discreetly shoved it into my hoodie's pocket. I'd toss it later. He unwrapped his and threw the wrapper on the street.

I stopped short and nodded at the ground. "Pick it up."

He shrugged, picked up the wrapper, and shoved it in his back pocket.

Up ahead, Annika turned around. When she saw The Viking walking beside me, her face tightened with irritation. I have to say, that felt pretty good.

The Viking stuck the lollipop in his mouth and took a long slurp. "Watermelon-blueberry."

"What?"

"That's the mystery flavor." He held up the lollipop and waggled it between his fingers. "I love a mystery. Speaking of which, what did you do to get put in the club?"

"Shhh," I said, glancing at Mr. Boot up ahead. "We can't talk about it, remember?"

"He said we can't talk about what goes on in the club," he said, "not how we wound up there."

I looked around and weighed the risks. A car could swerve off the road and mow us down. Or something could fall off a balcony and land on our heads.

"You first," I said. "What did you do to get put in the club?"

"I broke into the school at night." He said it so matter-of-factly that I forgot to look around for oncoming danger.

"But . . . why?"

He shrugged. "To see if I could."

"That's a stupid reason," I said.

The Viking just smiled.

"Why does Mr. Boot hate you so much?" I asked.

"I think he hates all of us," said The Viking.

"Yeah, but he hates you especially."

"Well, then he hates me because I know something about him."

"What?"

The Viking drew his fingers across his lips, zipping them shut.

"You won't tell me?"

"Maybe someday," he said carelessly. "So what did you do? Let me guess. Gambling."

"Wrong."

"Really?" The Viking seemed genuinely surprised.

"Criminal truancy," I said.

He frowned at me in confusion.

"It means I skipped school." I glanced over at him. "To gamble." I paused. "I skipped school a lot."

He smiled so smugly that I was almost sorry I'd told him.

"Cards?" he asked.

"Chess. In Washington Square Park."

"Really?" He looked impressed. "How often did you win?"

"A decent amount."

"Make a lot of money?"

I paused. Then nodded.

"Do you cheat?"

"No!" I hesitated, then for no good reason at all I told him, "I just . . . I can often guess what people are going to do next. I know how they'll move their pieces, so I know how to beat them."

"What, like you read minds?"

"Faces. I read faces."

"Really? What does my face tell you right now?" He turned to me and presented his face. Even with the Dum Dum in his mouth, his expression was dignified, his chin lifted, as though he were posing for a portrait.

I looked at him. He had this glow about him. Some people do. It's like the sun shines on them more brightly than on everyone else. It kind of made me uncomfortable. As though I were looking at something I wasn't supposed to.

"It tells me you eat too much sugar," I said, looking away. "You'll rot all the teeth out of your head by the time you're twenty."

Mr. Boot had turned up Eighth Street. I tried to remember where the churches were in the neighborhood. There was the one on Broadway. Chicken Bone Charlie sometimes slept on its steps.

I wondered if Mr. Boot planned to have us do magic in a church. Not that I was religious or anything, but I was pretty sure doing magic in a church would be breaking several major rules.

No sooner had we reached the middle of the block than Mr. Boot stopped and waited for us to catch up.

"Right," he said when Crud finally closed the gap, "here we are. Remember, I expect you all to behave with the utmost decorum. No bellowing, no flicking, no bad language."

I looked around. There were no churches in sight.

"Where—" Annika started to ask.

But Mr. Boot abruptly turned, and the next moment we were following him into McDonald's.

17

CRUD

The place was packed with people hunched over their red trays of food, and the air was thick with the smell of hot grease. I glanced over at The Viking. He was gazing around, a look of fascination on his face.

"What's the matter? Never been in a McDonald's?" I asked.

He shook his head. Then he did the oddest thing. He removed his hat, the way people do when they are paying their respects to something.

"You said we were going to a church," Annika protested.

"I said we were going to a holy place," replied Mr. Boot.

"And you're telling us that McDonald's is a holy place?"

"On Tuesdays it's a dollar-burger-and-free-drink for senior citizens," Mr. Boot said, as though that should explain things.

"But how does that make it holy?" I asked.

"A holy place is somewhere people gather to think and remember. And hope," said Mr. Boot with surprising warmth. "Look around."

The restaurant was filled with elderly people. Many

sat alone. They wrapped their hands around their cups of coffee, or slowly chewed their burgers, gazing off at nothing. Thinking. Maybe remembering. And I supposed some might be hoping.

"Go find a table. A booth is best," Mr. Boot told them.

"You buying, Mr. Boot?" Crud asked in his booming voice.

The man closest to us raised his head to look at him, but Crud glared back, and the man quickly returned to his burger.

"Nicely done, Mr. Butterbank," Mr. Boot murmured out of the corner of his mouth.

"What did I do?"

"A very respectable version of the Notsen-Glotsen Hex. And to answer your question, I will be buying."

"I'll have a Big Mac," said Crud. "Extra pickles, extra cheese, with large fries and a chocolate shake."

"Chicken sandwich," said Annika.

"Just an apple pie for me," I said. That would be all I could stomach here.

"I'll have apple pie too," The Viking said, and grinned at Mr. Boot, who responded with a death glare before turning and heading toward the counter.

We found a booth in the back. I slid in first, and The Viking scooted in next to me. Annika was stuck with Crud on her side, who took up most of the booth's bench.

"Mind moving over?" she said to him.

To my surprise Crud shifted over to give her room.

Maybe Annika was surprised too, because she looked at him for a moment, then said, "So hey. Did you really eat a kitten?"

Crud sniffed. "What do you think?"

"I don't know," Annika said.

After a long pause he answered, "No, I didn't eat a kitten."

I was more than a little relieved to hear that. I think we all were.

"And I'm guessing you didn't try to strangle your science teacher either, right?" I asked.

"Oh, him? Yeah, I did try to strangle him," Crud said, looking me right in the eye. "It took three teachers to pull me off the guy." He smiled, and I actually shrunk back in my seat.

"Why did you do it?" The Viking asked.

Crud looked surprised to be asked that question. Maybe no one ever had.

"He was going to kill a bunch of frogs so that we could dissect them in class. He was going to suffocate them in a jar. It made me really mad."

"And they kicked you out of school because of that?" I said.

He nodded.

"Even though you told them why you did it?" Annika asked.

Crud's eyes flicked away from us for a split second, and then he shrugged.

"He didn't tell them why he did it," I said. "He likes having a bad reputation."

"What, are you a mind reader?" Crud asked.

"She's a face reader," The Viking replied, grinning. It was like he was proud of me or something.

Annika clocked this and quickly changed the subject. "So why do you think Boot chose us to be in the club?"

It was something we had probably all been wondering about. I know I had.

"Well, for one thing," I said, "he picked people who didn't really have a choice in the matter. I mean, it's either the club or we get kicked out of school."

Crud shook his head. "I know at least three other dudes who got expelled recently, and none of them were given the option to join this club."

The Viking leaned forward, his eyes flitting over to the checkout counter to make sure that Mr. Boot was still safely waiting on line. "Did you ever think," The Viking said, "that maybe he chose us four in particular because we all have some secret connection to each other?"

Annika and I exchanged quick glances. Well, she and I certainly did, not that we were anxious to admit it. But Crud and The Viking? What connection did I have to either of them? None.

"The big question is," I said, in part to change the direction of the conversation, "do we trust Boot? I mean, yes, he's teaching us . . ." I almost said "magic" but stopped myself in time, in case it was a violation of the Gaggen-Shtoppin

Spell. "Teaching us . . . you know. But do we trust him as a person?"

There was a pause during which everyone seemed to be considering this question. Crud was the first to shake his head no. Then Annika. Then me. I turned to The Viking. He had tucked his blond hair behind one ear. His skin was as smooth as the finest porcelain vases I'd seen in my father's workshop. I forced myself not to stare at his profile.

"Sure, I trust him," he said breezily, turning toward Mr. Boot, who was heading back to the table, carrying a tray. "Yeah, why not."

Mr. Boot plunked the tray on the table. The only thing on it was a single order of French fries.

"Where's our food?" asked Crud.

"We are here to work, Mr. Butterbank, not to shovel food in our faces," Mr. Boot replied.

"Then what's with the French fries?" I asked.

"Take out your chopsticks," ordered Mr. Boot, removing his from his briefcase.

"Are you kidding? Don't tell me we have to eat our fries with chopsticks!" wailed Crud.

Mr. Boot shot Crud a look that made him shut up fast.

"Wake up your chopsticks, please." He began to vigorously rub his chopsticks together. We all did the same. This time I felt the warmth and tingle in my hands much more quickly. The sensation traveled through my palms and down into my forearms.

"Good. Now assume the Flungen grip." This was one of

the grips we hadn't practiced that much. Mr. Boot waited while we all awkwardly struggled to hold our chopsticks properly. Well, all of us except Annika, who quickly and confidently positioned her fingers on the chopsticks.

Mr. Boot nodded approvingly at her grip, then again at Crud's. But he grimaced at my grip and had to adjust my fingers. To The Viking he just said, "You'll never get the hang of this, Mr. Gunnerson. Your fingers are too gangly. Rather like an ape's. Perhaps you should just sit and watch the others."

But Annika reached across the table and skillfully positioned The Viking's fingers on his chopsticks without any problem. Seeing their fingers intertwined like that, I felt a pang of . . . what? Jealousy? But that was so stupid that I pushed the feeling aside.

"Right," Mr. Boot said. He reached into his own paper bag and pulled out the pair of X-ray glasses and put them on. He looked one-hundred-percent insane. Then he took out kindergarten scissors with a purple plastic handle. "Watch carefully."

In one hand he held the chopsticks the way he had shown us, and in the other hand he held the scissors. Delicately, he picked up one of the fries with his chopsticks. Although it was hard to tell with his glasses on, he seemed to be scanning the room.

After a moment, he muttered, "She'll do."

He lifted his chopsticks, and with a quick flick the French fry sailed over the heads of the couple sitting beside us and hit an old woman two tables down on the back of her neck. Annika snorted, and I had to bite my knuckle to keep from laughing. I mean, it was awful and rude, but funny.

The old lady turned and glowered at us while Mr. Boot made some fast, twisty motions with his hand in her direction.

"What is he doing?" I whispered.

"The scissors," The Viking replied under his breath.

Then I saw it. He was holding the scissors and quickly snipping at the air. The old woman's expression softened. She turned away from us and stared down at the burger in her hands. Then she went back to her meal as if nothing had happened.

"Okay. That was—" Annika started to say.

Mr. Boot held up one finger to shush her. He sat there, staring off at nothing. Concentrating. As we watched, his face grew increasingly somber. Then finally he nodded. "Ahh. It never turns out the way you would think."

"What doesn't?" I asked.

Mr. Boot removed the X-ray glasses and looked at me as though he forgot anyone else was sitting with him.

"Life, Ms. Batista. Life." Mr. Boot sighed. "What I just did is called the Farborgan Maneuver. Humans are separated by a thin yet highly resilient membrane called a Farborgan. It's what stops us from knowing what other people are thinking. A very handy thing. It keeps other people's noses out of our business, yes? Take Mr. Gunnerson for instance.

He doesn't want Ms. Batista to know what he really thinks about her"—I looked over at The Viking, who had turned red—"any more than Ms. Rapp wants Mr. Butterbank to know that she talks to an imaginary friend before every track meet."

Crud laughed. Annika opened her mouth to say something but stopped and then stared at me, daring me to laugh too. I didn't.

"The Farborgan Maneuver allows you to cut a hole in the membrane for a few precious seconds so that you can spy on another person's thoughts."

"But why do you need to throw a French fry at them?" I asked.

"It needn't be a French fry, of course. Anything small and annoying will do the trick. As long as you are clear about your target, the magic turns the French fry into a guided missile. You and the target must lock eyes in order to make the connection, even if it's simply because you've annoyed them. At that moment of connection, you can cut a hole in the membrane and peer through. You only have a few seconds to spy, however, before the membrane regenerates and seals itself up again."

The idea of seeing into another person's thoughts fascinated me. Reading faces was one thing. Imagine being able to actually see what someone else was thinking.

"I'd like to try," I said, raising my hand.

"Ms. Rapp will go now," Mr. Boot said, ignoring me. Probably because he knew I'd mess it up. "But first—" He pushed aside the French fries and put his briefcase on the table. "We're going to add a little something to the Farborgan Maneuver that I think you'll find interesting." His fingers tapped out a beat on the briefcase. The silver buckles snapped open, and he lifted the lid. Inside were dozens of glass vials, each no bigger than my hand, with cork stoppers stuck into them. They were nestled snugly in a blue velvet cushion molded to their shape. Trapped within the vials were tiny creatures—very minuscule birds and monkeys and other creatures that I had no name for.

And in a few of the vials were creatures that looked like very tiny humans.

18

NIBBINS

Whoa!" said Crud.

The rest of us were stunned into silence.

Mr. Boot traced his index finger over the vials until he came to a vial that contained two tiny people, each the size of a thumbnail. Their wire-thin arms wrapped around each other, and their eyes were shut. Carefully, Mr. Boot picked up the vial, and the two little people opened their eyes. They were girls, both with dark hair and thick dark eyebrows. They looked like twins, in fact, except that one of them had a pair of diaphanous dark blue wings growing out of her shoulder blades.

"What are they?" I asked.

"A pair of Nibbins," said Mr. Boot. "Of course, Nibbins *always* come in pairs. The one with wings is the Fetcher, and the other one is the Noodger."

The two tiny girls were staring at Mr. Boot through the glass with rueful expressions on their faces.

Mr. Boot took the cork stopper off the vial, and the girls pressed their tiny hands and feet against the glass, bracing themselves. Tipping the vial upside down, Mr.

Boot gave it a few shakes while the girls tried their best to keep from falling out. The one without wings was shouting something at Mr. Boot, but the sound was so faint that I couldn't make out the words. Mr. Boot paid no attention. He gave the vial one quick, forceful shake, and the two Nibbins came tumbling out into the palm of his hand. The wingless Nibbin was still shouting, the sound of which was something like the buzz of an electric fence. With the tip of his pinkie Mr. Boot flicked her into the empty ketchup cup. This made her even more furious. She banged her tiny fists against the pleated paper walls all around her and continued her tirade.

"I'll be right back," Mr. Boot told us. He stood up and headed for the restaurant's door, the other Nibbin in his hand. We watched as he opened the door and tossed the Nibbin out into the street.

"No!" Crud and I shrieked at the same time.

"Sheesh, you guys, get a grip," Annika said coolly.

Crud tried to get out of the booth, but Annika was in his way, and I was faster. I rushed over to the door to rescue the poor little thing, but Mr. Boot blocked my way.

"Are you crazy?" I screamed at him, searching the sidewalk for the Nibbin. "She'll be stepped on! Or hit by a car!"

"I don't suppose you noticed her wings, hmm?" said Mr. Boot. "She's flown off, Ms. Batista. She's a Fetcher. That's what Fetchers do. Now go sit down. You are making a scene."

Reluctantly, I sat back down at the table. Crud was

shooting daggers at Mr. Boot, while Annika and The Viking were staring at the other tiny girl, who was jumping up and down in a futile attempt to grab the rim of the ketchup container and pull herself out.

"She looks just like a Bitty Bendy doll," Annika said, leaning in to get a better look at her.

The Nibbin appeared to understand English because she jabbed her finger angrily at Annika and said something in a tone that was unmistakably a threat.

"Grab your scissors and put on your glasses, Ms. Rapp," Mr. Boot said.

Annika reached into her paper bag and pulled out the X-ray glasses and the scissors.

"No laughing," she warned, pointing a finger around the table before putting on the glasses.

Mr. Boot picked up the ketchup container and said to Annika, "Hold out your hand."

Without hesitation, Annika extended her hand, palm up. Once again, I had to marvel at her nerve.

"Does it bite?" Crud asked.

"Not very hard," answered Mr. Boot as he turned over the ketchup container on Annika's hand and gave the bottom a quick flick for good measure. The little Nibbin toppled out into the palm of Annika's hand, still screaming in her faint buzzing voice.

"She's called the Noodger. Now you are to say this to her," instructed Mr. Boot. "Alee-oop-desh-noz."

"What does that mean?" Annika said.

"She'll know. Just hold her up to your face and say it."

Annika shrugged one shoulder. She brought the Noodger close to her face and said, "*Alee-oop-desh-noz.*"

The effect of the words on the Noodger was instantaneous. She stopped screaming and waving her arms around. Standing still now, she looked up expectantly at Annika.

"What do I do now?" Annika asked, staring back down at her.

"You put her up your nose," Mr. Boot replied, as though it were obvious.

Annika burst out laughing, but when Mr. Boot's expression didn't change, she stopped. "You're serious?"

Mr. Boot just looked at her, waiting.

"Okay, so do I just, like, shove her up there?" Annika asked, looking down at the Noodger, who was looking up at her.

"Lift her close to your nostril—your left one, please. She'll take care of the rest."

For the first time, I spotted Annika's "tell"—the little gesture that is a clue to a person's emotion. Everyone has one, but some people are better at hiding it than others. Annika was tough to read, but now I noticed her smooth down her hair on the crown of her head. It was an ordinary primping gesture, especially considering that a girl as pretty as Annika would certainly be concerned with the way her hair looked. Except, I realized now, Annika never primped. Never.

"Go on, Ms. Rapp, bring the Noodger up to your nostril," Mr. Boot instructed more firmly.

I watched Annika closely, noticing the tiny twitch of muscle above her eyebrow, the ticking sound of her throat swallowing.

She's scared. Really scared.

The realization gave me a sharp ache in my gut—leftover sympathy, I guess, from knowing too much about her.

"I'll do it," I told Annika, and put out my hand for the Noodger.

But Annika's chin lifted, and her lips tightened with resolve. She had misread my offer of help as a challenge to her courage.

She brought the Noodger up to her left nostril, her eyes fixed on me defiantly. The Noodger immediately leapt up and scrambled into Annika's nose.

Annika's eyes widened for a moment, but otherwise she kept very still.

"She's climbing," she whispered hoarsely.

"Yes, she's heading for your nasal cavity," said Mr. Boot.

"It tickles."

"Don't sneeze, Ms. Rapp."

We all watched Annika's face, which was now wincing as she fought to suppress a sneeze.

After a moment she said, "Okay, it stopped."

"Excellent. She has reached your third eye. The pineal gland. Now pick up a French fry with your chopstick. Use the Flungen grip."

Annika plucked a fry out of the container and held it up between the chopsticks.

"Good. Now, do you see that man there? In the Mets cap?" Mr. Boot nodded toward an old man sitting three tables away, wearing a Mets baseball cap. He was slapping a package of sugar against his palm.

"You want me to hit some old guy with a French fry. Is that what you're telling me?" Annika said.

"That is correct."

Annika shrugged. "You're the boss." She drew her arm back to fling the French fry at him. "Anyway, I'm a Yankees fan." But Mr. Boot caught her arm and stopped her.

"Where exactly will the French fry hit him, Ms. Rapp?"

"His head, I guess." She was squinting at the man now, eager to let the fry go. The man tore open the sugar packet and began to pour it into his coffee.

"Where on his head? Exactly?" Mr. Boot persisted.

Annika assessed the target again, then answered, "On that stupid Mets cap."

"Where on the cap?" Mr. Boot persisted.

Annika stared at the cap for a moment. The cap was blue with an overlapping N and Y in bright orange stitching.

"The stem of the Y," she said confidently. She seemed to be enjoying this. Up for the challenge. I could see why she was a track state champion.

Mr. Boot watched her as she watched the man. Then finally he said, "Go."

It was like she had heard the shot of the starting pistol.

Immediately, she drew her arm back and with a hard flick sent the French fly sailing across the room. Unfortunately, at the very moment it flew over the head of a woman, the woman stood, tray in hand, ready to leave. But instead of the French fry hitting her, which it should have, the thing rose up smoothly and arced over the woman's head, then continued on its course, hitting the man's Mets cap right in the stem of the Y. The man looked up in surprise. His eyes landed on Annika, who was staring at him through her ridiculous X-ray glasses. She smiled at him and waved her fingers.

"You will see the membrane now, Ms. Rapp," said Mr. Boot. "Use your scissors. Snip, snip. Quickly."

Frowning at something in front of her, Annika snipped at the air with her orange-handled scissors, the way Mr. Boot had. Immediately, the surprised expression on the man's face vanished. He looked back down at his coffee and began stirring it with the skinny red stirrer.

"Hey!" Annika said, looking startled. "I can . . . I can see things. . . ."

"Pay attention, Ms. Rapp," Mr. Boot told her. "What do you see?"

Annika grew silent while we all watched her.

"Trees all over the place. Big leaves. A jungle," she said. She adjusted the glasses a little on her nose. "It's raining really hard. I have . . ." She felt the top of her head. "I've got a rain poncho on, and the bugs are, like, everywhere. Biting me. I'm so tired, but I'm not supposed to sleep. I have a gun. . . . Okay. Yeah. I think I'm a soldier."

"Your gentleman is remembering his time in the war," said Mr. Boot.

I looked at the man in the Mets cap. His face was somber now as he stared into his coffee.

"These bugs are just disgusting," Annika continued. Her face was pale, and her forehead suddenly damp with sweat. "They're on my face, in my ears, and—OH!" Annika jumped in her seat and ducked her head, covering it with both arms.

"What happened?" Crud asked.

"There was an explosion," she said. "Right over there—" She waved at a spot behind her. "There's some guy screaming. He says he was hit in the leg. It's . . . Oh, it's awful!"

"Ms. Rapp, you must find one good thing," Mr. Boot told her firmly.

"What? Oh!" Annika flinched again and ducked. Another explosion.

"Ms. Rapp, pay attention. You must find something good to focus your attention on. Does your soldier have a bag with him? A backpack maybe."

Annika paused, then nodded.

"Good," said Mr. Boot. "Now open it up and look inside. See if you can find something pleasant to focus on in there."

Annika's hands moved as if she were unzipping a bag. They were shaking slightly, I noticed. After a moment she said, "There's just socks, cigarettes, and . . . um, that's a grenade! Wait." Annika squinted down at something. "Here's a photo. It's of some lady. She's, like, a hippie chick, I think. With a long skirt and . . . Wow, does she even own a hairbrush? He likes her, though. A lot. I can feel it. Here." She put her hand on her chest. "Benita. That's her name."

I looked over at the man in the Mets cap. He was cradling his coffee cup between his hands, and there was a small smile on his face.

"Wait. I hear her," Annika said suddenly.

"Who?" asked The Viking.

"That thing that went up my nose. The Noodger. She's saying something. *Benita.* She's saying Benita." Annika put her hands in front of her. "Oh! Everything just went black!"

"The membrane has healed over," said Mr. Boot.

Annika whipped off the glasses. She looked around, frowning.

"I can't see anything, though," she said. I could hear an uncharacteristic hint of panic in her voice.

"Your eyesight will return in a few moments, Ms. Rapp. All in all, that was well done. A most satisfactory execution of the Farborgan Maneuver. Now stay very still. The Noodger should be exiting your nostril in just a moment."

Annika's face crumpled into a wince again, and the Noodger appeared out of the left nostril. In a flash Mr. Boot's hand shot out, and he caught the little creature and deposited her back in the ketchup container. The Noodger's skin was wet from Annika's nose, and her hair was a damp mess, but she seemed much calmer than she had before. She sat down in the cup, knees up. Her arms crossed on top of her knees, and she rested her chin on her arms, appearing exhausted.

"But what about the other Nibbin?" I asked. "The Fetcher?"

"All in good time, Ms. Batista," Mr. Boot answered.

19

ZOOPHENLOFT

Right." Mr. Boot turned to Crud. "You're next."

"No thanks," Crud said.

"I'm not offering you a McNugget, young man. Your target will be that lady in the corner booth. The one with red glasses."

Crud leaned across the table, his face inches away from Mr. Boot's. In a very menacing way, he said, "I'm. Not. Doing. It."

I'm pretty sure most people would have backed down at the sight of this giant kid with his squinting eyes and knotty jaw. But Mr. Boot didn't even flinch.

"And what, pray tell, is your objection?" Mr. Boot asked.

"My objection is that I don't want to do it," Crud replied.

"Ahh. You feel it is unethical to root around in someone else's mind, eh?"

Crud looked away.

"Well, perhaps that's true." Mr. Boot was silent for a moment. He seemed to be considering Crud's view of things. I looked over at The Viking, who appeared just as surprised by this as I was.

"I wouldn't want you to do something that goes against your morals, Mr. Butterbank," said Mr. Boot. "You can gather up your things now and leave." But just as Crud made a move to go, Mr. Boot added, "Of course, that means you will be expelled from school. That makes . . . how many schools you've been tossed out of now? Six? I do believe you are running out of options. For dangerous youths like yourself, the only public school left is the Joy M. Blight School."

Every New York City kid knew about the Joy M. Blight School. It was like the bogeyman of schools, where the most violent kids were sent. It was basically a prep school for prison.

The mention of the Joy M. Blight School knocked the wind out of Crud's argument. He scowled at Mr. Boot, and I suddenly wondered how many people it would take to remove Crud's hands from Mr. Boot's throat. But after a moment Crud relented and picked up the chopsticks.

"I'm not shoving that . . . whatever it is . . . up my nose, though." He nodded toward the ketchup container.

Mr. Boot seemed ready to object but then nodded.

"All right. You don't need to use Nibbins in order to perform the Farborgan Maneuver, though you will want to learn how eventually. Proceed, Mr. Butterbank. Remember to put on the glasses."

Crud put on the X-ray glasses, and after a few tries with

his fingers in the Flungen grip, he plucked up one of the French fries.

"Have your scissors ready," Mr. Boot instructed.

Crud reached into the paper bag and pulled out a pair of scissors with lime-green handles.

"Be specific about where the French fry will hit her. See it clearly in your mind first," prompted Mr. Boot.

Crud stared at the woman. I noticed his head shift to the left, then back again, and in a flash he flung the French fry. It rose high in the air, just barely skimming the ceiling, and sailed across the room, passing over the head of his target—the woman in the red glasses—before taking a hard left and heading for the window. A fraction of a second before it hit the window, though, it made a sharp nosedive and bounced off the head of a very small boy.

The toddler had been trying to work out how his Happy Meal toy—a car shaped like a carrot—could turn into a robot. When the French fry pinged against his head, the little boy turned around with a surprisingly nonchalant expression. He locked eyes with Crud. Quickly Crud began to snip away at the air with his scissors. Mr. Boot sighed, crossed his arms, and shook his head.

"Well, that was foolish," Mr. Boot said with annoyance.

"I did what you said. I hit someone," Crud said as he snipped.

"Oh yes, you certainly showed me," said Mr. Boot dryly.

Suddenly Crud let out a yowl and slapped his meaty hand over his head.

"Ohhh! Stop it! Stop it!" he cried.

"Silly boy," Mr. Boot muttered.

"My head!" Crud shrieked, still clutching at his skull.

"Do something!" I said to Mr. Boot.

"There's nothing I can do," said Mr. Boot perfectly calmly.

Crud whipped off his X-ray glasses, put his head down, and banged it against the table, as though he were trying to knock something loose.

"He's going to hurt himself," Annika observed matter-of-factly.

"Oh, he most certainly will," Mr. Boot said as he watched Crud. "Anyone stupid enough to perform the Farborgan Maneuver on a small child is bound to come out with some damage. If he had performed it on an elderly person, as I instructed, he would have been quite safe. But I suppose he thought it would be more ethical to look into a child's mind, where nothing very private is lurking."

Crud lifted his head and began to pound at his forehead with the heel of his hand, his face so crumpled in agony, I could barely stand to look at it. Mr. Boot, however, seemed unmoved as he continued.

"An older person's thoughts are cushioned, softened. Even the bad thoughts or memories have layers of zoo-phenloft covering them, making them less raw. It's a coping mechanism, so that we can get on with our lives after unpleasant events. Even you lot have naturally developed a few layers of zoophenloft. The younger a person is, the fewer the layers, and a child like that"—he nodded toward the little boy who was rolling his carrot car over his Happy Meal box—"will have virtually no zoophenloft at all. The sensation of peering into a toddler's membrane is, so I'm told, a bit like having your brain cut to shreds by tiny shards of glass. It's all very excruciating for poor Mr. Butterbank."

We all looked back at Crud. He was clearly in anguish. The four of us had been thrown together in this club against our wills, but I was beginning to feel like we were . . . well, maybe not exactly friends yet, but definitely a team. It pained me to see Crud in such agony.

"Come on, Boot. You know you can stop it," The Viking said. There was a grimness in The Viking's voice that I'd never heard before.

"There are some things that, once done, cannot be undone," he told The Viking coldly. "The membrane has to heal over." He checked his watch. "Which, if we're lucky, will happen in seventy-three seconds."

"And what if it doesn't?" I asked.

"Ahh, well." Mr. Boot sighed. "Who can say? I did know a membraneolist—a brilliant fellow—who attempted to spy into the thoughts of a two-year-old. Alas, the Farborgan Maneuver went on for a full three minutes and . . . tsk." Mr. Boot shook his head. "It turned the man stark raving bananas. Last I heard he thought he was a biscotti. He panicked whenever someone drank a cup of coffee near him."

Crud's face was slick with sweat, and he was breathing in short, ragged gasps.

Mr. Boot, his eye on his watch, counted off the seconds. "Sixty-nine, seventy, seventy-one."

Crud's eyes began to lose focus.

"Seventy-two, seventy-three—"

I felt a sickening heaviness in my stomach. What would he be like when he came out of this? If he came out of this.

"Seventy-four, oh my, this must be a record." Mr. Boot's voice was rising in pitch. "Seventy-five, seventy-six, seventy—"

Suddenly Crud stopped panting. Though his skin was still damp from sweat, and frighteningly pale, the pained look on his face had softened. His eyes darted about uncertainly without actually fixing on anything.

"Is he—" I started to ask, but Mr. Boot held up his hand.

"Give him another minute."

We waited, watching as Crud's eyes appeared to regain their focus.

"Welcome back," said Mr. Boot evenly. "Do you know where we are?"

After a moment, Crud answered in a hoarse, tentative voice, "A place?"

Not very promising.

"Good, very good." Mr. Boot spoke to him like you would speak to the little boy with the carrot car. "And what is the name of the place?"

Crud had to think about this. But finally he offered an answer. "McDonald's?"

We all blew out a woof of relief.

"That's right," Mr. Boot said cheerfully. "And do you know your name?"

There was a pause. "Carmen."

"Oh no," I groaned.

"No, no, that really is his name," Annika said.

"No wonder he doesn't mind being called Crud," I said.

"Excellent, Mr. Butterbank! Well, this is certainly one for the books. I'll have your name added to the *Journal of Extraordinary Near Misses*." He reached into his pouch, pulled out a few dollar bills, and handed them to Annika. "Go buy him a Big Mac, please. Extra pickles, extra cheese."

"And a shake. He said he wanted a chocolate shake," I reminded him.

Mr. Boot glanced over at Crud, who was still looking ill.

"Very well," he said. He handed her another bill.

As Annika headed up to the counter, the restaurant door swung open, and Chicken Bone Charlie trudged in. I braced for the smell, which arrived at our table within seconds of his entrance. I was already breathing through my mouth—something I always did when I passed him on the street—but other people in McDonald's clapped their hands over their noses.

Chicken Bone Charlie shuffled up to the counter, trailing the filthy shredded strips on the hem of his pants. One of the cashiers hurriedly grabbed a coffee for him, waving off the coins he offered. He took his coffee over to the condiment counter, where he poured five packets of sugar into it.

"Now that we have seen what happens when you don't follow my instructions," Mr. Boot said to us, "who shall go next?"

"I will," The Viking said immediately.

"Fine. Give it a go, then," Mr. Boot replied indifferently.

"What about the Nibbin?" The Viking said. He made a movement toward the ketchup container but Mr. Boot swiftly snatched the container off the table.

The Viking and Mr. Boot locked eyes. The Viking grinned at him. That kid had a serious death wish.

"Nibbins are valuable commodities," Mr. Boot said to him through gritted teeth. "I wouldn't dream of letting a bloody useless bungler like you handle one."

The Viking's eyebrows squinched at the insult, but honestly, I think it was more for show than anything. He turned away from Mr. Boot, and with his far-seeing blue eyes, he squinted at a man wearing a yellow-and-pink Hawaiian shirt who sat in the far corner, reading a newspaper while sipping his coffee.

The Viking put on the glasses. With a sharp flick of his wrist, he sent the French fry hurtling over people's heads, heading toward the other end of the restaurant. But where it should have dipped down to hit its target, it took a sharp right turn instead and then hovered uncertainly in the air. Then it turned around and flew straight back to The

Viking, striking him sharply on the nose before it flopped back down on the table. If it's possible for a French fry to look zapped of all its energy, this one definitely did. Mr. Boot picked it up and gave it a quick wiggle, whereupon it perked up again.

"Well, Mr. Gunnerson, I can honestly say I've never seen a more abysmal execution of the Farborgan Maneuver."

"You did that." The Viking's voice, usually so breezy, turned tight with outrage now.

"Sabotage, you mean?" Mr. Boot said. "Interesting thought, but no, I'm afraid I can't take credit for that, Mr. Gunnerson. The incompetence was all your own. Perhaps you're simply not cut out for this."

Just as Annika returned with the Big Mac and shake, the outside door opened again, and Mr. Boot swiveled in his chair. A woman with a short cap of silver hair and bright, quick eyes entered the restaurant. Long black feathers spilled from the collar of her snug silver jacket.

"Ahh, here she is at last!" Mr. Boot cried.

20

ᴛʜᴇ ꜰᴇᴛᴄʜᴇʀ

Who's that?" Annika asked.

"That," said Mr. Boot, "is Benita. The 'hippie chick' as you called her. She's the woman in the soldier's photograph. The Fetcher found her. They always do. Bonus points to whoever can spot the Fetcher on Benita."

We all looked. Well, Annika, The Viking, and I looked; Crud still seemed dazed and was staring at his food as though he wasn't sure what he was supposed to do with it.

Annika was the first to spot the Fetcher. "She's in the lady's hair," she said. "Right above her ear."

I noticed the tiny flash of dark iridescence. It looked like a speck of dirt that had landed on Benita's head, but, I realized, it was the Fetcher's wings.

"Correct. She has been whispering directions into Benita's ear. That's how she managed to bring Benita to McDonald's. Benita can't hear the Fetcher, at least not consciously. She believes coming here was her own decision, but it's the Fetcher who is guiding her. Watch closely. The Fetcher will turn Benita's attention to the target in just a minute."

Benita started toward the counter while reaching for her shoulder bag, but suddenly she stopped. Turning around, she scanned the restaurant. Her gaze landed on the man wearing the Mets cap, and her hand swiftly covered her mouth, stifling a cry of surprise. She stood there for a moment, as though deciding what to do, her eyes bright with tears. Slowly, she approached the man. She said something to him, and he looked up.

"Benita!" he cried out so loudly, everyone looked his way, but he didn't seem to care. He jumped out of his seat and took her in his arms.

There was a dark flash in the air, as the Fetcher flew off Benita's head and landed in the ketchup container, beside the Noodger. They wrapped their tiny arms around each other, just like Benita and her old friend. There was a high-pitched buzzing sound emanating from the Nibbins.

"Nibbins hate to be separated. It's torture for them, really," Mr. Boot said. "When you separate them, they will do absolutely anything to be reunited."

"Then why did you separate them?" I asked.

"Well, how else are coincidental meetings going to happen?" Mr. Boot retorted. "When someone thinks about a person whom they haven't seen in years, and then suddenly they meet that person in the street . . . who do you think is behind that? Nibbins! Nibbins and a skillful magician."

"But how did the Fetcher hear the Noodger calling for Benita? You separated them," I said.

"There are more ways to communicate than you might

imagine." Mr. Boot opened his briefcase again and picked up the empty vial. With great care he tipped the ketchup container so that the Nibbins could crawl out of it and back into the vial again, whereupon they crouched at the bottom and clung to each other. Mr. Boot replaced the stopper and put the vial back in his briefcase.

"What's that one?" Annika pointed to a vial with a small golden creature. It looked like a tiny seahorse but with feathery hairs covering its body and a minuscule human-looking face. It blinked up at everyone.

"That is an Inkling," said Mr. Boot.

"You mean, when you get an inkling about something, it's actually an Inkling that gives you an inkling?" I asked.

"Exactly, Ms. Batista," Mr. Boot said as he shut his briefcase.

"Will we get our own Nibbins to use?" Annika asked.

"Your own Nibbins?! I wouldn't trust you people to look after a hamster. Our time is up. We'll meet back in Room 101 tomorrow. Ms. Rapp, you don't live far from Mr. Butterbank. You can help him to get home in one piece. Crossing streets may be a challenge for him at the moment. We'll have to wait until tomorrow to see if there has been any permanent damage."

"Wait! I didn't have a turn," I said.

"This isn't a game of Candy Land. Not everyone gets a turn," said Mr. Boot.

"My chopsticks are awake, see," I persisted. "I want to try. Please."

Mr. Boot sighed. He put his briefcase back on his lap. "Go ahead, then."

I eyed his briefcase, wondering if he would give me one of the Nibbins. The idea of putting the Noodger up my nose didn't thrill me, but it seemed like being given one to use was a mark of Mr. Boot's faith in your abilities. Mr. Boot caught my gaze but made no move to open the briefcase. In fact, he clasped his hands protectively over the top of it, as if to send a clear message: Annika and Crud were the superstars in this club, while The Viking and I were "bloody useless bunglers."

I looked around the restaurant for a target. Benita and the man in the Mets cap were sitting across from each other now, happily chatting. I would have loved to get a peek into Benita's mind—she looked like the kind of person with all sorts of interesting thoughts—but I didn't want to break their mood by hitting Benita with a French fry.

My gaze shifted to the corner of the restaurant and stopped on Chicken Bone Charlie. His dirt-encrusted hands were wrapped around a cup of coffee, and his narrow face was bent so low over the cup, it looked like he was staring at his own reflection. His skin, where it wasn't covered with filth, was very pale, and his shoulder-length hair was snowy white. Every kid in the neighborhood knew Chicken Bone Charlie, but what did any of us *really* know about him?

I put on the X-ray glasses and took the pink scissors out of my bag. With some effort I managed to position my fingers correctly on the chopsticks, and then I plucked up a French fry.

I decided I would hit him on his left ear.

I remembered what Annika had said about my magic—that it was messy and out of control. I was going to be precise now. The French fry would hit its target.

I stared at Chicken Bone Charlie's left ear. It was a surprisingly tidy ear, not old-man saggy. I would hit the outer edge of it. No, I would hit the deepest part in the center, which was shaped like a . . . like a peanut. I saw the French fry hitting it right there . . . exactly there.

I held up the French fry and gave it a fast flick. It flew off with alarming speed, like a tiny missile on a direct course for Chicken Bone Charlie's ear. I cringed as it was about to crash into its target, but the French fry suddenly slowed down and simply tapped the ear gently before falling to the ground.

"Chicken Bone Charlie?" I heard Annika cry. "Why would she want to see what's going on inside that head?"

Chicken Bone Charlie turned his head and gazed at me. I had never really looked at him carefully before. He had a fine-boned face with wide, pale lips. It was hard to tell his age—he could have been anywhere from forty to seventy. And strangely, he didn't appear annoyed; on the contrary, he looked surprised and even pleased to see me.

I felt a wave of guilt. Spying on his thoughts suddenly seemed so wrong.

"Cut the membrane, Ms. Batista," Mr. Boot said. I

hesitated, and he ordered, "Cut it now!" There must have been some sort of magic in his words, because I felt myself automatically snipping with the scissors.

At first, everything was a confusion of gunmetal gray framed by ragged edges of the severed milky-white membrane. Slowly, though, the edges of the membrane curled back, revealing more.

My legs were suddenly aching, or rather Chicken Bone Charlie's legs were aching—I was in his memory after all. And I was breathing hard, as though I'd just finished running.

"What do you see, Ms. Batista?" I heard Mr. Boot's voice.

"I'm in a room. A small room. It's dark, but I can see . . . like . . . squiggles carved into the top of the walls. Squiggles all around. And the walls are metal, like in a ship. Yes, I'm pretty sure it's a ship. I can hear water."

My view changed as Chicken Bone Charlie looked down at something. Sitting on a bed in the corner of the room was a figure. I crouched down—or Chicken Bone Charlie crouched down—and I squinted into the darkness. It was a boy, maybe ten or eleven years old. He had dark, curly hair and a pointed chin. . . .

River.

I gasped and reached out my arms toward him, even though I knew it was a stupid thing to do, that this was just a memory, but still, he was right there, right there in front of me.

"How much more time does she have?" I heard The

Viking's voice, though it sounded like he was far away.

"Any minute now," Mr. Boot replied.

As I stared at River, I felt a leaden sense of guilt fill Chicken Bone Charlie's body.

"I'm sorry," Chicken Bone Charlie said to River.

"I want to go home," River said.

Oh, the sound of his voice! It had been so long since I'd heard that voice. I cried out, and I felt a hand on my arm, then heard Mr. Boot's voice command, "Leave her alone, Gunnerson."

"You can't. You can't go home," Chicken Bone Charlie said to River.

And right then the scene in front of my eyes began to grow filmy. The membrane was forming again, growing thicker by the second, and then everything went black.

"Wait, wait!" I cried. "I need to go back in!"

"Hush, Ms. Batista, people are staring."

I didn't care. I looked around for my scissors, which I must have dropped while I was in Chicken Bone Charlie's mind, but the world was just a blur of gray shapes.

"I can't see anything," I said.

"It takes a moment for your vision to return," Mr. Boot said.

"At least you don't have anything climbing out of your nose," Annika put in.

Bit by bit my vision cleared and sharpened. The first face I saw was The Viking's, watching me carefully.

"Are you okay?" he asked, but I ignored him and looked

for my scissors, eventually finding them on the floor by my foot. I grabbed them, and then with my chopsticks, I picked up another French fry.

"What are you doing, Ms. Batista?"

"I have to go back in," I told him frantically as my chopsticks finally managed to grasp a French fry.

"You can't perform the Farborgan Maneuver twice on the same person in one day," Mr. Boot said. "The membrane is too fragile."

"I don't care," I said.

I raised my arm, ready to aim the French fry again. But when I looked over at Chicken Bone Charlie's table, I saw that his cup of coffee was knocked over. The coffee had pooled up on the table and was spilling over the edge, and Chicken Bone Charlie was gone.

21

ᗪETECTIVE ᑕHATTERJEE

I didn't go straight home after the club disbanded. Instead I headed to the Greenwich Village police precinct, a squat brick building that looked like it might have once been a preschool.

I was ushered into Detective Chatterjee's office by the desk officer. It had been nearly three months since I'd seen her. Detective Chatterjee, with her blunt-cut black hair, looked up from her paperwork, then wiggled her glasses so that they bounced up and down on her nose.

"I must need stronger lenses because it looks like Nell Batista just walked into my office."

"I have a question." I got straight to the point.

"Let's hear it."

"Did you ever ask Chicken Bone Charlie about River?" I asked.

Detective Chatterjee gave me a long look. She is extremely hard to read, by the way. I guess if you are a detective, you learn how to keep your emotions buttoned up. "Excuse me?"

"The homeless guy. He sleeps outside of the bodega on Bleecker Street," I said impatiently.

"Yes, I know who he is, Nell," Detective Chatterjee said in her slow, careful way. "What I'm wondering is why you are asking about him all of a sudden."

This, of course, was difficult to explain. Impossible to explain, really, without the risk of her thinking I was crazy, not to mention the threat of magical bodily harm.

"It's just, I was thinking about it," I said. "And, you know, Chicken Bone Charlie is always on the street, and it just makes sense that he could have seen something. . . ." I knew I wasn't sounding too convincing.

"We have spoken to him, Nell," Detective Chatterjee said. "He was one of the first people we spoke to, as a matter of fact."

"And?"

Detective Chatterjee raised her dark eyebrows and sighed. "He's not exactly a reliable witness."

"He did see something!"

"As I recall, he said he saw River step into a garbage can and disappear. And then he told us that it had been raining raisins for the past few days and asked if we could do something about it." Detective Chatterjee smiled. She didn't smile often, and when she did, it was a tired sort of smile.

"But maybe he was the one who took River," I persisted. "He's always chasing kids with that chicken bone. . . ."

"We've looked into that, I promise. We've looked into every possible lead." She left the rest unsaid: that all the leads led exactly nowhere.

Detective Chatterjee and I had become . . . well, not exactly friends since River's disappearance. But she had interviewed me so many times about the day he'd disappeared and for some reason had taken an interest in me.

"We haven't given up, Nell."

I gave her a skeptical look.

"We haven't," Detective Chatterjee insisted. "But Chicken Bone Charlie?" The detective shook her head. "There's nothing to that."

But I know what I saw in his mind, I thought.

Still, I couldn't tell her that.

"How are things going at school?" Detective Chatterjee removed her glasses and scrutinized me. In fact, she was the one who had helped me get into the Bright Future Academy in the first place. The school's admissions committee had seen my history and hadn't been impressed, but Detective Chatterjee had pled my case.

"Things are good," I answered.

"Do you have friends there?"

"Sure."

"She says, as she lies to a detective." Detective Chatterjee smiled at me. After a pause, she said, "Every day I see criminals walk in and out of this building—petty thieves, burglars, vandals. You know what they all have in common?"

"No morals?" I suggested.

"No imagination," replied Detective Chatterjee. "Most of them have been dealt a lousy hand in life; that's true.

They can't imagine a way out. Or at least a legal way out. That's why they keep doing the same stupid things over and over again."

"So you're saying I'm acting stupid?" I said, feeling my anger rise.

"No, I'm saying you might benefit from using your imagination."

"Oh? Am I supposed to just *imagine* River back home?"

"No, Nell. I mean you might imagine what your life could be if you tried to move on."

I shook my head. "River was the one with the good imagination."

My Last Chance Club handbook had gradually been growing. Every so often I'd hear a *snick* sound coming from the manual, and I'd find a new spell had been added. I had been practicing the Oifen Shoifen Spell that night, which animated moderately sleepy things, like plastic and cloth and paper. I tried it on an old Halloween costume hanging in my closet. It was a werewolf costume, just the hairy bodysuit—the mask had gone missing long ago—and amazingly I got it right the first time I tried it. The werewolf costume writhed on the hanger until it broke free and fell to the ground. Then it galloped around my bedroom like a headless dog, leaping on and off my bed a half dozen times, before it sat back on its haunches in front of the window and looked like it was attempting to howl at the moon. Which, of course, it couldn't without a face. Suddenly it collapsed into a heap of cheap acrylic fur and stopped moving altogether—the magic had fizzled. It was when I gathered it up to put it back in my closet that I noticed something strange on River's bed.

George, the stuffed owl that always sat beside River's pillow, was gone.

I was so shocked that for a moment all I could do was stare at the bed numbly. The owl hadn't moved from its spot in so many years that now there was a faint owl-shaped outline on the wall, where it had blocked the sun from fading the paint. I checked between the mattress and the wall and then under the bed, in case George had some-how fallen.

Nothing.

I went to the living room where Dad was lounging on the couch, watching TV.

"Did you move George?" I asked him.

"The owl? Nope. Why?"

"Because he's not there."

Dad looked at me curiously, and I realized I probably sounded bonkers.

"Maybe you bumped against the bed and it fell," he said gently.

"No, I checked. George is gone. Did you let Nyxie come in the apartment today?"

"Nyxie? No." I noticed that crease between his eyes deepening.

"Whatever." I shrugged and backed away. "All good, Dad. I probably did bump the bed or something."

But that owl was gone. Someone had walked into my room and had taken it.

22

MESSY MAGIC

The air was frosty the next morning, and the wind nipped at my face as I walked to school. I zipped up my hoodie and tied the drawstrings tightly so that the hood cinched over my mouth.

As I approached the bodega, I looked for Chicken Bone Charlie, but he wasn't in his usual spot. I checked the church, too, where he was sometimes sprawled across the steps, but he wasn't there, either. In the past, there were times I didn't see him in the neighborhood for weeks or even months, which gave me a flutter of anxiety. What if he simply disappeared altogether and I'd never be able to ask him about what I'd seen in his mind?

At lunch Ruth plunked her tray down across from me. She was wearing glasses with chunky black frames.

"Since when do you wear glasses?" I asked her.

"Someone left 'em at the restaurant last night. They make everything huge! Your head looks like a basketball, kid."

"Wonderful," I said.

I took a quick glance around the lunchroom for The Viking. He wasn't at the Elsewhere Table. I checked the Goddess Table just in case, but he wasn't there either. I felt my energy droop. Besides Ruth, he was the only person in school who actually seemed happy to see me. You can't fake that sort of thing. Next time you run into someone, pay attention to their face during that first nanosecond. It will tell you everything you need to know about the way they feel about you.

"You looking for that cute blond guy?" Ruth asked.

"No."

"He's not here."

"I can see that."

"But you weren't looking for him, right?" Ruth raised an eyebrow.

My mouth quirked involuntarily.

"Yeah, thought so." Ruth pulled a sandwich wrapped in wax paper from a Rocco's restaurant bag.

"Hey, Ruth," I said, picking up my plastic fork and spearing a potato, "you didn't happen to see Chicken Bone Charlie this morning, did you?"

Ruth frowned at me as she bit into her sandwich and replied with her mouth full, "That's a weird thing to ask someone. I mean, *Chicken Bone Charlie?*"

"Forget it," I said.

But once Ruth had latched onto a subject, it would take a crowbar to pry her loose. "Do you talk to that guy? Because listen, kid, he is flat-out bananas."

"I know that—"

"I hope you aren't hanging out with that weirdo."

"No, I—"

"Because let's face it, kid, you are not too fussy about the company you keep. I mean, those sketchy chess guys in the park—"

I made the mistake of saying that they weren't sketchy, and that launched Ruth into a whole new tirade about the chess hustlers. There was no point arguing with her. While she listed all the reasons why the chess hustlers *were* sketchy, I glanced over at the Goddess Table. Leilani was quietly eating a salad, not talking to anyone. Yesterday's incident with Julia's Invisalign seemed to have taken some of the swagger out of her. I didn't care what Annika said; it was worth it, a hundred percent.

The Viking wasn't at the Last Chance Club, either. I kept glancing back at the door, expecting him to bound into Room 101, grinning. Annika was checking the door too. We caught each other checking at the same time, which seemed to annoy Annika to no end.

"And how is your head feeling today, Mr. Butterbank?" Mr. Boot asked.

"Still hurts," he said.

"Yes, well, that's to be expected." He glanced around the classroom. "Ah, I see we're minus one today. However will we manage?" Mr. Boot looked almost cheerful as he placed his briefcase on his desk. We all stared at it expectantly now that we knew that he kept things like Nibbins inside it.

"So." He slapped his hands on the suitcase, and I could imagine all the little creatures in the vials jumping with fright. "I want you all to wake up your chopsticks. Today we will work on our basic animation spells—the Oifen Shoifen Spell and the Flatzen Spurtz Spell."

We all rubbed our chopsticks together, and in no time at all we had woken them up. Obviously, all our practice had been paying off.

"Right. Now have a look around the room, and choose something to animate."

We got out of our seats and explored the cabinets and shelves and colored bins for our objects. I paused over the bin of plastic animals, but sifting through them, I found they were all jungle animals—tigers and lions and rhinos. Not exactly animals I'd want to bring to life while confined in a little room. That could turn into chaos very quickly. I once again remembered what Annika had said about my out-of-control magic.

There were books, of course, but picture books for kids can be full of strange stuff, and I wasn't sure I wanted to have any big surprises, like talking steamrollers or trees that grew children like apples.

"Have you all chosen?" Mr. Boot asked.

Annika and Crud said they had.

Looking around anxiously, I noticed a jar full of Popsicle sticks painted red.

Safe enough.

"Ready," I said.

"All right, Ms. Batista, you can go first. Animate your items."

I focused on the jar, then produced what I thought was a decent version of the Oifen Shoifen Spell. I even created some sparks.

The magic happened with abrupt violence. First came the sound of angry voices from inside the jar, followed by the convulsive shaking of the red Popsicle sticks. They shook with such force that a crack formed along the side of the jar, which lengthened and forked off until the jar shattered altogether and the Popsicle sticks spilled out on the floor.

"Here we go," I heard Annika murmur.

The sticks had turned rubbery and glistening. They moved across the floor like giant flatworms, buckling and stretching out as they inched along, the whole while emitting a cacophony of angry voices.

"JENNA CUT IN FRONT OF ME!!!"

"CARLOS BONKED A PENCIL ON MY HEAD!!"

"LILY SAID MY BREATH SMELLS LIKE DOG POOP!!"

"ETHAN SAID A BAD WORD, AND IT'S SO BAD, I CAN'T EVEN SAY IT!!"

"What are those things?" Crud asked me.

"I don't know," I replied, staring at the slithering, hollering mess, aghast.

"You animated something and you don't know what it is?" Annika rolled her eyes. "Brilliant."

"They are Tattle Tongues," said Mr. Boot. "The children tell the Popsicle sticks the naughty things that their classmates have done and then they put the sticks in the jar. It allows the children to vent without actually tattling."

Crud picked up a Popsicle stick and it screamed:

"ELANA SAYS I'M A BABY BECAUSE I CAN'T WIPE MYSELF."

"Elana is right," Crud said to the Tattle Tongue. "You should be wiping yourself if you're in kindergarten." The tongue lashed around furiously, splattering droplets of saliva on Crud's hand until he put it back on the floor.

The tongues continued their screeching and whining as they slithered, their voices growing louder and louder, each one trying to be heard above the others. Holy cow, those kids had a lot of complaints about each other!

One of the Tattle Tongues started crawling up my leg. I plucked it off, pinching the tip of it between my fingers. It was disgusting, all wet and slippery, and it screamed shrilly, "LEO IS PICKING HIS EARWAX AND EATING IT!!!" over and over again. I quickly trapped the tongue under an overturned garbage can and started off to collect the others.

Except the tongues were everywhere.

Some of the tongues had climbed up the shelves, flopping into baskets of markers or Legos; others slithered under the rugs.

"Can't you stop them?" Annika shouted at me over the screams, her fingers in her ears.

"I'm trying!" I screamed back. I attempted a few spells, but none of them did a thing.

Finally, Mr. Boot raised his chopsticks and slashed them in the air sharply.

The screams stopped immediately. There was a dry-sounding clatter, and then all the tongues—now wooden Popsicle sticks once again—shot out from their hiding places and flew into the center of the room as though a strong wind had carried them there.

"Well, that was fun," Mr. Boot said. He was uncharacteristically lighthearted. I waited for his reprimand, but it never came.

Annika, however, looked over at me, eyebrows raised, and mouthed, "Out of control."

23

ᴮAD ᴾRINCESS

Crud was next. He chose the small plastic jungle animals. I looked over at Mr. Boot to see if he would stop him, but Mr. Boot seemed unconcerned.

"Interesting choice, Mr. Butterbank," he said congenially. "Let's see what you do with them."

Mr. Boot's good mood seemed strange until I realized that it was probably because The Viking was absent. It was amazing that one person could have such a big impact on his attitude, but the truth was, The Viking's absence had changed my own mood too. While Mr. Boot was in high spirits, I felt oddly squashed. Did Annika feel the same way? I glanced over at her. She appeared restless, glancing up at the clock and fiddling with a silver bangle bracelet on her wrist.

Crud placed a handful of the plastic animals on the floor, then worked his spell. The animals that were lying on their side scrambled to their feet, their tiny hooves scratching at the floor. They were no bigger than they were as toys—a tiny zebra, a tiger, a monkey, and a giraffe. They shook themselves off and began to toddle around—wobbly at first but gaining their footing quickly.

"How did you get them to stay small?" I asked, marveling at them. I put out my finger and carefully touched the giraffe's neck, which was warm and as soft as flannel.

Crud shrugged. "Dunno. Just pictured them that way."

The tiger crouched down and, after crawling forward, pounced on the back of the zebra, which shrieked and bucked. Crud simply poked the tiger with the tip of his finger so that it fell off the zebra's back and rolled on the ground, looking baffled. But it let the zebra alone after that. We all watched with delight as the little animals ran around, investigating the room.

A monkey climbed up on Crud's shoe. He plucked it up and held it in his palm, close to his face. With his forefinger, Crud swiped at the air a few times. The monkey froze. Its fur seemed to fuse together and grow dull. It had turned back to plastic again.

Even Mr. Boot seemed surprised.

"That's a Nullification Spell. How did you know how to do that?" he asked Crud.

Crud shrugged. "It's not that different from the Oifen Shoifen spell, except for the end. I just felt my way through it," he said as he tossed the plastic monkey back into the green bin.

"Perhaps you are not the complete muttonhead I thought you were, Mr. Butterbank," Mr. Boot said. "While part of magic is memorizing spells, a truly skillful magician uses their instincts." He looked at Crud with real admiration, and Crud responded by slumping down in his seat, appearing mortified at the attention.

I felt an unexpected pang of jealousy. My own efforts were lousy compared to Crud's. Annika was right. My magic was a mess. I glanced over at her. She was standing in front of a kid's drawing of a princess that was taped to the wall. The princess was just a bunch of shapes, really— a circle head, a triangle dress, lines for limbs, and on her head a row of small uneven triangles for her crown. She wore what looked like pink cowboy boots and held a little purple handbag shaped like a jelly bean.

Annika worked her chopsticks into a Flatzen Spurtz Spell. But did I imagine it, or was Annika not her usual superconfident self? She seemed hesitant. It took her several tries to get her spell to work, and when it did, the princess animated in a peculiar way. She flopped out of the page—three dimensional but still pretty flattish—and fell several feet to the ground in an alarming nosedive. The princess just lay there facedown, her handless arms spread wide, her yellow crown toppled and lying off to the side.

"I think she's dead," Crud said.

Annika shot Crud a look, then knelt down. She nudged the princess with her finger, flipped her over.

The princess's eyes were open. They were black circles with long lashes like tiny knives. Unblinking.

"Get up," Annika ordered.

The princess didn't move. Beneath the stiff, waxy blue material of her triangle dress, I could see her stomach slowly rising and falling, but she seemed too weak to stand.

"Get up!" Annika demanded again, her voice sounding on edge.

Slowly, the princess sat up. Her arm reached out and hooked itself around the crown, then placed it back on her head. Unbending her legs, she stood in her pink cowboy boots. At full height she reached just above my ankle. She gazed around at all of us. There was something genuinely spooky about her. Her eyes, with their knifelike lashes, stopped when they met mine. Her mouth, a single thin line, expanded into something resembling a smile. With her eyes still fixed on me, her arm curled and reached inside her purple jelly-bean bag. I don't know why, but I felt a sudden rush of fear. What was she reaching for?

In a flash, Mr. Boot's chopsticks made a hasty flourish in the air, and the princess burst into flames. She cried out once before she was reduced to a pile of ashes.

Annika looked startled, but relieved, too.

"Thank you," she whispered to Mr. Boot.

"That, Ms. Rapp, was bad magic," said Mr. Boot. "Bad magic born of bad thoughts. Anger, jealousy . . . You had better put a lid on those feelings when you do magic, or you will find yourself attracting things you do not want to attract."

Annika glanced at me. And then I knew. The feelings had been directed at me. Anger and jealousy. And The Viking was at the heart of it.

Mr. Boot clapped his hands together jauntily. "Well,

you are all coming along with your spells better than I had expected. We'll wrap things up today by practicing—"

"Can we see some more of those things in your brief-case?" Crud interrupted, apparently emboldened by Mr. Boot's good mood.

"Hmm," Mr. Boot considered. "Well, we might have some fun with Whirdles. All right, then." He pulled his chopsticks from his vest pocket and flicked them at us.

We all looked around the room to see if something had changed.

"Nothing happened," Crud said.

It was true. No objects had animated. Nothing was moving around that usually didn't move around.

But then I felt a buzzing against my feet.

I looked down at my boots just as I felt something grab my right foot and yank it forward forcefully. I stumbled into Crud, who caught me, but then he promptly stumbled too. Annika was jogging in place, with a shocked expression on her face.

"You animated our shoes!" Annika accused Mr. Boot.

"Yes, and you will find that your shoes all have minds of their own."

But my boots apparently had lost theirs. They were stomping around the room, with me in them, causing me to slam painfully into desks and walls. Crud's shoes, on the other hand, were tiptoeing carefully, sneaking around like, well, sneakers. Annika's flats were hyperactive, forcing her to hop and jog.

"Make it stop!" she cried as she jumped up and did a jerky version of a karate kick. She looked so ridiculous that I laughed out loud. Then my boots stomped smack into Mr. Boot's desk. My laugh turned into a yelp as my hip struck the edge of the desk, which made Crud laugh before his sneakers forced him to tiptoe round and round in a little circle.

At his desk, Mr. Boot tapped a rhythm out on his brief-case. The lock snapped open, and he lifted the lid.

My boots had decided to carry me over to the play kitchen, but I swiveled my head around as I stomped, to keep an eye on what Mr. Boot was doing. He had plucked out a vial from his briefcase and held it up for inspection. I had the feeling that he was deliberately taking his sweet time about things while our footwear was making us look like idiots.

He brought the first vial over to me. Thankfully, my boots had stomped right into a recycling bin and were hav-ing trouble stomping out again.

"This is a Whirdle," Mr. Boot said, holding up the vial for me to see.

There was a creature inside. Its face was craggy, but its body was elegant, with long, muscled limbs. It stood up in the vial, legs astride, keeping its balance without holding onto the glass. In one hand it gripped what looked like a stick.

Mr. Boot pulled the cork stopper from the vial, and the creature scaled the glass and leapt out of it, landing on the toe of my foot. It sat down, its long legs straddling my boot. I felt my boots react. Their crazed stomping stopped. The Whirdle reached back and tapped at the heel of my boot with its stick. Immediately, the boot he sat on took a slow step backward, out of the recycling bin. The Whirdle leapt on my other boot and tapped it, and it did the same. Bit by bit, the Whirdle coaxed my boots around the room, slowing them down when they started to speed up, turning them smoothly this way and that. We didn't bump into anything.

"He's driving my boots!" I cried. "It's like he's a shoe jockey!"

"He is a shoe jockey," Mr. Boot replied, pulling from his briefcase another vial with a Whirdle inside it. "Shoes are very willful things. The moment you animate them, they want to go somewhere, anywhere. So when you animate a shoe, you must also give them a shoe jockey to drive them where you want them to go." He brought the new vial to Crud and took the cork stopper out of the vial, and the Whirdle inside hopped onto Crud's sneaker. With a few sharp smacks of his stick, he urged Crud's heel to go back down to the floor, and Crud began to walk more normally again. Annika was next. Her Whirdle had a hard time staying on her overactive flats. It was like watching someone trying to ride a mechanical bull. But eventually he got his balance, and with some gentle coaxing, Annika's shoes settled down.

"But why would you want to animate shoes anyway?" Annika asked.

"To make people go where you want them to go," I answered as my Whirdle guided me back to my desk.

"Exactly!" Mr. Boot pointed a finger toward me with a pleased expression on his face.

"But why would you need to do that anyway?" asked Annika.

"It seems like Nell is using her brain today. Can you answer that?" Mr. Boot gestured toward me.

I thought for a moment. "What if someone were about to walk into trouble? Or you wanted them to see something or meet someone? You could just redirect them."

"Correct." Mr. Boot waved his chopsticks across the room. I felt my shoes die. There was no other word for it. They simply stopped being alive. Suddenly it felt odd to have the lifeless things on my feet.

Mr. Boot went to each of us, plucking the Whirdles off our shoes and putting them back in their vials.

"Don't you think it's kind of cruel to keep them in those little bottles?" Crud said.

Mr. Boot's expression tightened. "That's what they were born to do, young man."

"They were born to be trapped in a tiny bottle and carried around in a briefcase by some dude?" Crud said incredulously.

"Our time is up," Mr. Boot announced brusquely, his good mood deflated. He tapped a beat on his briefcase, the locks snapped into place, and he stalked out of the room.

24

CRIMINAL TRUANCY

Outside, the air felt damp and weighty. It would rain tonight. Lousy weather for ceramics. Dad would have to put aside his restoration work, which always made him antsy. When he wasn't working, he was worrying, usually about me.

As I walked home, I kept a sharp lookout for Chicken Bone Charlie.

I knew exactly what I would say to him. I'd ask him if he'd seen River on the day he disappeared. I'd tell him that if he knew something, he wouldn't be in trouble. That we just wanted River to come home.

What I didn't know—what was much more iffy—was how Chicken Bone Charlie would react. When I was in his mind in McDonald's, I could feel his guilt—a tight-fisted ache in the pit of his stomach—so maybe there was a chance he'd tell me something. Maybe it would be something that he wouldn't tell the police. But then again, I might just make him angry. Or probably more likely, he was just too crazy to tell me anything that would make any sense at all.

"Hey!" I heard a voice call from across the street.

I spun around. There, sitting on the steps of an immaculate brick town house with a white portico, was The Viking. He wore his hat, as usual, and his long shearling jacket. He raised a hand, smiling, and I felt a chime of excitement at the sight of him.

As I crossed the street, I caught a glimpse into the town house's window through a parted curtain. White furniture. White piano. Pink and lavender peonies spilling out of vases. It was the sort of place I would have imagined Annika would live in with her wealthy stepfather and her gold-digging mother.

It appeared as if The Viking was stinking rich.

"You weren't at school," I said. There was more than a hint of accusation in my voice.

He smiled and shrugged one shoulder. "I thought I'd give criminal truancy a try."

He reached into his jacket and pulled out a handful of Hershey's Kisses.

"No thanks," I said when he held them out toward me. "So, what did you think?"

"About what?"

"Criminal truancy."

"It was nice at first," he said as he unwrapped a Kiss. "Then somewhat boring." He popped the chocolate into his mouth and tossed the wrapper over his shoulder on the steps.

"There's a trash can right there." I pointed to the curb.

He reached back and grabbed the wrapper, then did a free throw, and the wrapper went directly into the can.

"See? Was that so hard?" I said.

"So . . ." He stood up. "Are you ready?"

"Am I *ready*?" I stared at him. Had he been waiting for me? "I'll need more information."

"I have something to show you," he said.

"Still more information," I said, crossing my arms.

"Trust me," he said, smiling.

"When people say 'trust me,' it makes me a hundred-percent not trust them. I'm going home."

"No, no, you don't want to do that," he said.

"Why not?" I asked.

"Because that's no fun for me," he answered in a small, pained voice. He was perfectly serious, too. No irony at all.

"I have homework to do," I said.

"Please?"

It was such an open plea, a plea that smacked of loneliness. Loneliness is something that I understand.

I sighed. After hesitating a moment, I slipped my backpack off my shoulder and fetched my cell phone from an outer pocket. Dad picked up on the first ring.

"Hi, Dad. Listen, I'm going to be home a little late."

There was a pause.

"You're not at the park, are you?" he asked, his voice brittle.

Oh yeah. I could tell right away how he'd been spending his day. He had been picking at all the scabs in his life—Mom and River and my bad behavior and the strained relationship with his older brother and all the other regrets and anxieties that riddled his life.

"No, Dad. I'm just hanging out with my friend from school."

"The one you met at the library?" he asked.

I winced at having to revisit that lie.

"Yep."

"What's her name?"

He didn't believe me. That made me mad. Until I remembered that I was lying. So I lied some more.

"Lauren," I told him.

"Lauren what?"

I looked over at The Viking. He was watching me. He watched me in the same way I watch other people when I'm trying to read them.

"Gunnerson," I told him.

The Viking smiled.

"Okay," Dad said, his voice relaxing.

"I'll be home by five," I told him.

"Six," The Viking whispered.

I hesitated, then added, "Five thirty, latest."

The Viking led the way, weaving through the busy streets, until I saw we were headed straight for Washington Square Park. The great white marble arch was dead ahead, planted at the entrance like an upside-down magnet.

I stopped short.

"What's wrong?" The Viking asked.

"I can't. I'm not allowed to go into the park," I told him.

"Why not?"

I hesitated. The reason was both simple and complicated. I told him the simple part.

"Because I was skipping school to hang out with the chess hustlers."

"Right." He nodded. "The gambling thing."

"Yeah, that thing."

"But we're not going there to gamble."

"It doesn't matter," I said. "My dad banned me from the park."

The Viking raised one eyebrow. I could see that he thought Dad was being unfair. I thought so too, but I didn't like the idea of The Viking thinking it.

"Anyway, we're not going into the park," he said.

"Where are we going, then?"

"Trust me, Nell," he said.

Again with the "trust me." But here's the funny thing. . . . I hadn't heard him say my name before. He pronounced it "Nall." Sometimes when a person mispronounces your name, it makes you feel like you might be a whole other person.

A girl named Nall.

A girl who trusts people a little more than the girl named Nell does.

"Fine," I said.

We started walking again, coming closer and closer to the park until we were right beside the arch. I stopped again.

"I told you I can't—"

"We're here," he said.

"That's right. In the park. Where I can't be."

"Just wait, okay," The Viking said, backing up into the park.

When I didn't answer, he looked worried.

"Promise you'll wait? Promise you won't run off."

I rolled my eyes, but then nodded.

He jogged ahead a few paces, looked around, then disappeared around the side of the arch. After a moment he reappeared.

"Okay, let's go," he said.

I followed him around to the side of the arch, where he stopped by a little door. Although I had passed it thousands of times, I had never stopped to think why on earth there was a door there, set into the arch.

After glancing around, The Viking gave the door a sharp nudge with his foot. It opened, and the next moment we had both slipped inside.

Let me just say for the record that I knew we weren't supposed to be in there, but there aren't many secret places left in New York City. They've all been sniffed out by tour guides who charge buckets of money to take people to see them. But this little door in the side of the arch? This was a secret. And it was irresistible.

25

CONFESSIONS

The Viking pushed the door closed again, and we found ourselves in total blackness. The first thing that struck me was that there was absolutely no smell of human pee. Every tucked-away place in New York smells of human pee. But here, I only smelled a dank, cavelike smell.

The Viking switched on a flashlight. I pulled out my phone and turned on the flashlight app. The walls were brick—old brick, from the looks of it, that badly needed repair. I swept the light along the ground to check for rats. I didn't see any, but that didn't mean they weren't there.

We both stood still for a moment, listening. That was the most amazing thing. It was completely silent. It felt like we were deep underground instead of just feet away from one of the busiest little parks in the city.

"You'd think they'd lock that door," I said. My voice sounded alarmingly loud as it echoed off the walls.

"You would, wouldn't you?" I could hear the smile in his voice even if it was too dark to see it.

He had broken in. Of course he had. He was a thief, after all.

I'm ashamed to say that this realization didn't make me turn right around and leave. Being in this hidden place, and being there with The Viking, was just too interesting.

The circular stairwell was narrow, hemmed in by a crumbling brick wall on one side. The steps were uneven, and although I was careful, I stumbled and fell painfully on my knee.

The Viking turned around, his flashlight blinding me.

"Whoa!" I said, shielding my eyes.

"Sorry. You okay?" he asked.

"Yup," I said, but my knee throbbed, and after that I kept my left hand on the cold brick wall for support. By the time we reached a landing, I was out of breath, but as it turned out, there was yet another staircase to climb before we came to a skylight. The Viking reached up and pushed it open, and we both stepped outside onto a narrow rooftop.

I don't like heights, and rooftops make me nervous, so I kept away from the edge as I took in the view.

"Amazing, right?" The Viking said, watching my reaction.

I nodded. It really was. You could see the entire neighborhood spilling out from the edges of the park. Below us I could see blocks and blocks of the clay-colored brick buildings on tree-lined Fifth Avenue, stretching farther and farther north, their awnings poking out into the street like tongues.

"You can see the park better if you come closer to the edge," The Viking said, sitting on the low parapet and patting it.

"The murderer said, right before he pushed her off the roof," I said.

For a moment something shifted in his expression and flattened his breeziness, as though I'd actually offended him.

"Kidding," I said quickly. "I just don't like heights."

He hopped down off the parapet and walked over to me with his hand outstretched. "Come on. I won't let you fall."

I hesitated, then took his hand. I'd never held a boy's hand before. I knew my cheeks were going bright red, so I turned my face away from him as we walked over to the roof's edge. I looked down at the park below. From this height, it resembled a giant spider, with the fountain, now dry for the season, as its body and the footpaths stretching away from it like skinny legs.

"Nice, right?" he said, watching my face, and I nodded, smiling.

On the southwest corner of the park, I spotted Kingsley, the dark green scarf I had given him last winter wrapped around his neck. He was playing against a kid whose father stood behind him, filming them. The boy made a move, but Kingsley shook his head, then showed him what would happen next. That was how he taught me, all those years ago. That made me sad somehow. A time in my life that I couldn't get back.

I glanced over at The Viking. His eyes met mine. They were the same color as the sky now—dimmery gray—and watching me intently. He seemed to vacillate between looking old and young. It was the way the light fell on his features. Framed by the sky, with the setting sun casting bluish shadows beneath his eyes and along his cheekbones, he now looked like a storm-hardened sailor, much older than his years. His brows pinched together suddenly as if he were weighing something in his mind, struggling with a decision. His hand tightened around mine, and it struck me suddenly that he might kiss me, and, I don't know, maybe it was nervousness, or the feel of his hand in mine, but I blurted out, "You asked me what my story was. Back when we first met. Do you still want to know?"

His expression changed, like he was abruptly snapped out of his thoughts.

"Okay."

"Three years ago," I said, "my brother went missing. We were in this park when it happened."

"I know," The Viking said.

For a moment I was speechless.

"How did you know?" I asked.

"Annika told me."

Of *course*. Annika.

I dropped his hand and took a step back. "Did she tell you how it happened?"

He nodded.

I was gripped by anger so raw that it pulsed through my

veins and rushed into my head, turning my vision blurry.

"I've got to go." I turned to leave, but The Viking leapt in front of me, arms spread out, like a kid playing tollbooth.

"Don't!" he said. "Come on. Please? I'll tell you some things about me that no one knows."

I hesitated. Though I hated to admit it, I was interested, despite my rage.

"Okay. Hmm, let's see," he said, "confessions, confessions . . . I am afraid of marionette puppets." His eyebrows rose when I reacted to this. "It's true. Those arms and legs clattering around, and the painted eyes! Don't laugh. What else? I hate caraway seeds. I've been known to bite my toenails. Just the big one." He smiled, but when I didn't return the smile, he grew serious again. "I hate being alone. It kind of frightens me." He paused. "Sometimes I steal things."

He checked my face for a response, for me to be shocked or something. I wasn't. I'd spent a lot of time sitting on a park bench with people who had done things they weren't exactly proud of.

"Is that enough information?" he asked.

I thought for a moment. "What's your name?"

"You don't know my name?"

I shook my head. "Not your first name. I've been calling you The Viking. In my head. Because of your hat." I didn't mention the part about his eyes or his hair.

"Okay." He smiled lightly and nodded. "My name's Tom."

"Tom?"

"What's wrong with that?" he asked.

"Nothing. You just don't seem like a Tom, that's all."

We stayed up on that rooftop for another hour, sitting on the parapet, talking and eating Lemonheads from a box that he had in his jacket pocket, and watching as the park below slowly became glazed with the shadowy blue of evening. It was so easy and comfortable to be with Tom. It was the first time I'd felt like that with someone since River had vanished.

"What do you think happened to him?" Tom asked suddenly. "Your brother, I mean."

"I think someone took him. He'd never have run away." I paused, then added, "A lot of people think he's dead by now. Even my dad. He'd never admit it, but he does, I can tell. Sometimes I do too. But mostly . . . Mostly I have this feeling that he's still out there somewhere. Waiting."

Tom stared at me with those seafaring eyes that suddenly flashed bright, as though they had spotted land in the distance. "We're going to find him."

It was such a crazy thing to say. Probably he was just trying to make me feel better. But I believed him. I don't know why, but I did.

26

ANNIKA

The following morning I took the long way to school, past Washington Square Park, in the hopes that Kingsley might be there.

I walked along the fence line, not actually going in the park, which was quiet now—just a few dog walkers and three elderly women doing tai chi. It was a little early for the chess hustlers, especially now that the mornings were cold, but Kingsley was often there before the others. It had occurred to me that he might know where Chicken Bone Charlie was. He knew the neighborhood backward and forward, knew all the shopkeepers and the local characters. He knew Chicken Bone Charlie, too—I had seen Kingsley give him money now and then, or hand him a sandwich. If there was a secret place where Chicken Bone Charlie liked to tuck himself away, there was a good chance that Kingsley would know where it was.

That morning, though, the benches were empty. I could just wait for him, I thought. He'd probably be along soon. So would the other guys. Maybe I could even play a few games. The idea took hold of my mind, and before I knew it, I was walking back toward the park entrance, in the opposite direction of my school.

"Skipping school again?" a gravelly voice called out.

I swung around to see Annika in a black peacoat with a military cut. She was standing across the street, watching me. I felt my anger rise at the sight of her, the feeling just as raw as yesterday.

"That's my business," I called back.

Annika crossed the street and walked over to me.

"Boot won't like it," she said evenly. "He might throw you out of the club. Which means you'll also get expelled."

She was right. I hated that she was right, but she was. I couldn't risk it. Getting expelled would crush Dad, for one thing. But also, I realized that I very much *wanted* to stay in the club. I wanted to stay because of the magic and because of Tom and because I suddenly felt like my messy life had some sort of purpose.

I turned my back to Annika and started walking in the direction of school again. Behind me I could hear Annika's heels clicking against the pavement, and in a second, to my annoyance, she was right beside me. We walked in silence for a few moments until Annika said, "That video of Julia Weeks . . . It wasn't my fault."

"Oh, no, of course not. The video was only filmed from your bedroom window on your phone and then sent to everyone you know."

"Yeah, well, you don't know everything about me, Nell. Hard as that is for you to believe."

"I'll tell you what I *do* know." I stopped walking and turned on her, no longer able to wrestle down my anger. "I know you told Tom about River, about how he disappeared."

Annika pressed her lips together, and for a moment she said nothing. Then "Tom was asking about you."

"Asking what?"

"Just . . . I don't know . . . what you were like, how I knew you . . ." Her voice sounded brittle. I could imagine how much that must have infuriated her.

"And *that's* what you decided to tell him? About what happened when River disappeared? *That*, of all things?!"

I stopped short. Annika did too. The wind whipped her hair across her face, and she shoved it away. As angry as I was with her, I couldn't help but be aware of her beauty. Her wide cheekbones that sloped smoothly toward her nose. Her upper lip that curved like an archer's bow. But there was something more. She had a patina about her, a polish. Like a memory of someone special whom you haven't seen in a long time.

"What are you staring at?" Annika asked.

"I'm just staring because I can't believe what a jerk you've become," I said, hating to be caught out. "If River were still around, he would never have stayed friends with you."

It was a low blow, and I knew it, even as the words were coming out of my mouth.

Annika winced as if I had smacked her. But there was a

steely core to that girl. I watched as she regrouped on the spot, pulling herself together. Even if I didn't like her, I had to admire her toughness.

Right then River's voice rose up in my mind, like a ghost, reprimanding me: *Take it back, Nell. You know what things used to be like for her. We were all she had. Take it back.*

But River was good. He was a much better person than either Annika or I was.

I hopped off the curb and crossed the street. For the rest of the way to school, we walked parallel to each other. She could have walked much faster than me, but for some reason—probably to annoy me—she kept to my pace, a tall, black-coated figure in my peripheral vision that I just couldn't shake.

27

CLASS PETS

I had expected Tom to come bounding over to my lunch table that day, a big grin on his face as usual. My eyes kept skittering over to the lunchroom's double doors, watching for him. But when he did arrive, he wasn't smiling. And he didn't come over to my table. He sat down at the Elsewhere Table with his back to me.

"Go on," Ruth said, watching me watch him. "Invite him over."

I hesitated. But just as I got up and started toward him, Annika suddenly rose from her seat and made a beeline for him. She snaked her arm through his and brought him over to the Goddess Table, with a quick defiant glance in my direction.

"Didn't see that coming, did we, kid?" Ruth said, smirking. "I bet if we checked the inside of his collar, it would have a label that says, 'Property of Annika Rapp. Hands off.'"

Mr. Boot was decidedly unhappy to see Tom that afternoon.

"Back for more, Mr. Gunnerson?"

I waited for Tom to say something that would annoy

Mr. Boot. Maybe even just flash him a smile. But Tom didn't respond. He had come in late and sat by himself near the windows, somber. He'd removed his hat without being asked. It sat on the tiny desk in front of him, and he fiddled with the brim distractedly. He never looked my way. In fact, it seemed like he was deliberately avoiding me. Had I said something yesterday that offended him?

Or maybe, I thought with a sickening lump in my gut, after hanging out with me, he decided he didn't like me that much after all.

"Hey, the ferret's gone," Crud said.

I looked over at the cage. It was empty.

"What happened to him?" Annika asked.

I braced for bad news. I'd grown fond of that dumb ferret.

"Escaped," Mr. Boot said indifferently. "I'm sure he'll be found. Now, down to business." He swept his arm toward a line of colorful buckets on his desk.

"What's in the buckets?" asked Crud. "A goblin?"

Mr. Boot looked at Crud disapprovingly. "You've been reading too many fantasy novels, Mr. Butterbank."

"Oh yeah? Well, what about them fairies in your brief-case?" Crud said.

"They aren't fairies; they're Nibbins. Totally different things. Fairies are quite stupid in general. It's from all the inbreeding. They have a terrible sense of direction, too, which is a liability when you have wings and an addiction to nectar. In any case, I had planned a lesson on manipulating weather systems." He gestured to the water table, which was filled to the brim with water. "However, since we have Mr. Gunnerson in attendance today, the water table might get a bit crowded. Our buckets won't go to waste, though. You can use them when you clean out the cages of the classroom pets."

"That has nothing to do with magic!" Annika protested.

"But it has everything to do with *community service*," Mr. Boot replied. "Doing the repulsive chores that no one else wants to do is an excellent volunteer activity. You may all step up and take a bucket."

After we grabbed our buckets, Mr. Boot gave us each a classroom number, with instructions for cleaning.

"Ms. Rapp, you'll go to Room 304. You will be mucking out the guinea pig cage, lucky girl."

"Gross," Annika said.

"Animals go in the bucket while you clean. You'll find fresh cedar chips below the cage, along with a shovel. Off you go."

Annika reached for her chopsticks, but Mr. Boot said, "No need for those. You'll be getting your hands dirty. And stay in your own assigned rooms, please. Absolutely no socializing."

After she left, Mr. Boot sent Tom off to Room 308 to clean the turtle tank. Crud was assigned the goldfish in the first-grade classroom at the end of the hall, and I was assigned to the room next door to his.

"You'll be tending to the bearded dragon in Room

112, Ms. Batista. Not as scary as it sounds."

Crud and I headed down the hall together. I'd never actually been alone with him before. I'm not a big talker, and I was pretty sure he wasn't either. For a minute we walked in awkward silence. Then I remembered that there *was* something I wanted to ask him.

"Hey," I said, "yesterday? When you turned the monkey back to plastic without using chopsticks. How did you do that?"

I noticed his massive shoulders relax a bit. I guess he felt awkward with me too and was glad to have something to talk about.

"I don't know. It might have been a fluke or something . . . ," he began uncertainly. "And maybe it's just me . . . but whenever we're doing spells with the chopsticks, I can feel the magic in the air. I mean *after* I've done the spell. The magic sort of, like, hangs out. The air looks a little bluish too."

The moment he said it, I knew exactly what he meant. I'd noticed that too, but between trying to get the spells right and the surprise of seeing the magic happen, I didn't pay much attention to it.

I nodded. "Yeah. Sort of an electrical feeling, like the air is ionized."

"Exactly!" He seemed relieved that I had felt it too. "I've been thinking about it, and I'm starting to wonder if you could do magic without the chopsticks. I mean, if there's enough of that Oomphalos stuff around. So I've been trying it out here and there. I guess it worked with the monkey. You should try it too."

I thought about what I'd seen of Crud's magic. It was elegant and skillful. He was better at it than I was.

"Maybe," I said doubtfully.

The bearded dragon wasn't too awful. In fact, it was sort of adorable. It was a baby bearded dragon, and when I picked it up, it sat quite happily in the palm of my hand, looking around the room. I pet its tiny head with my index finger. It seemed so content to be held that I hated to put the little thing in the bucket. I carefully placed him in there, and then I took him over by the window to be in the sunshine. Out on the street below, people were hurrying here and there. Always moving, moving, moving. Not moving in NYC signaled that you were a tourist. Or a maniac.

Which made me think about Chicken Bone Charlie . . .

"Hey."

I turned, and there was Tom, standing at the doorway. His sleeves were soaked, and there was a big wet splotch on the front of his shirt.

"They're psycho," he said, his eyes wide.

"Who is?"

"Those turtles. Every time I grab one, the other tries to bite my fingers off. Can you help me?"

"Annika is in the classroom next door to you. Why don't you ask her?" I tried, unsuccessfully, to keep the bitterness out of my voice.

"Please, Nell." He smiled. It was the first time I had seen him smile that day. It lit me up too. I guess that's what people mean by charisma—when a person makes you feel like you want to help them, even when you're sort of mad at them.

Even when there are biting turtles involved.

They must have been studying ancient Egypt in Room 308 because there were models of Popsicle-stick pyramids on the windowsill and posters of hieroglyphics on the walls. The turtle tank was in the back of the room, and boy, that thing was filthy. The water had a greenish cast, and there were tiny specks of who-knows-what floating in it. I could barely make out the two shadowy shapes moving through the murky water.

"When do you think the last time someone cleaned that tank is?" I said.

"Probably never, because no one can get near those two fiends to clean it," Tom said.

"*Fiends?* That's a little dramatic, don't you think?"

"You'll see."

The trick, I knew, was to grab the turtle by the back of the shell so it couldn't bite. But of course, there was the other turtle to consider. I looked around the room until I spotted a clipboard on the teacher's desk.

"Here." I handed it to Tom. "Hold this in the water between the two turtles, so the one won't bite me as I grab the other one."

He stuck his arm in the tank and positioned the

clipboard between the two turtles, while I rolled up my sleeve. I could smell the putrid water. No wonder the turtles were mean, living in that mess. I eyeballed the shadowy shape of the turtle lurking way down at the bottom of the tank. It was as though it knew I was trying to catch it and wanted to make things as difficult as possible. I'd have to reach in up to my armpit to grab it.

Cringing, I plunged my arm into the warm, greenish water. I aimed for the turtle's back end, keeping a sharp eye on it in case it decided to pivot around and bite. I had to stand on my tiptoes now in order to reach it.

"I'm sorry," Tom murmured.

"Blechh, me too," I said.

Suddenly Tom grabbed my wrist. Tightly. I felt a ferocious downward pull, and then I found myself completely submerged in water. It happened so fast and was so extraordinary that I cried out and swallowed a mouthful of fishy water. My mind tried to piece things together logically, to make sense of what was happening, but there was only one conclusion: Tom had pulled me into the turtle tank.

The tank's glass sides had vanished, and all around me was a vast swampy ocean. Tom's hand was still wrapped around my wrist, and he was dragging me down deeper and deeper in the water, which swirled with silty clouds and stringy pieces of nastiness. I tried to twist my hand away from him, but his grip was as ruthless and unyielding as an iron cuff. The water made his skin appear greenish, and his pale hair writhed like some weedy plant. Our eyes met.

He had a look on his face I'd never seen before—piercing, determined. But the next moment his expression changed to confusion, then panic. He began to flail like a fish caught on a line. Something had gotten hold of him, though I couldn't see what it was. As he struggled to hang on to me, I was being yanked downward with short, sharp tugs, until his hand was wrenched off my wrist. I watched him drift backward until he was swallowed up into the watery gloom, and then he was gone.

I began to kick frantically, trying to propel myself upward. But the water's surface must have been very far above me because as hard as I kicked, I couldn't seem to reach it. My chest was burning from the lack of oxygen, and I knew it wouldn't be much longer until my mouth would open involuntarily to take a breath. I wanted to breathe more than anything in the world. Just one breath.

Don't breathe.

Just one breath.

Don't breathe.

The water around me began to darken and grow colder. I felt consciousness slip out of my body. The pain in my chest eased. I was dying. I knew it. I wasn't afraid. *What a strange thing, to die in a turtle tank,* I thought. I felt like laughing, but nothing worked in my body anymore.

That's when I heard the voice, so clear it felt like someone was right beside me, saying, "*Hold on, hold on.*"

28

THE ANGEL
OF THE WATERS

My head broke through the surface of the water, and I gulped at the air, my arms thrashing in an effort to keep myself afloat. I tried to tread, but my legs wouldn't move, and I realized that I wasn't floating at all. The ocean was gone, and I was kneeling on solid ground in shallow water. I tried to stand, but I was so wobbly with exhaustion that my knees buckled and I almost went down again before I steadied myself.

Now I could see that I was standing in a fountain, at the center of which were two stone tiers, both with bronze statues on them. All around, outside the fountain, was an expanse of redbrick pavement and, yards away, a set of grand staircases on either side of walkways beneath vaulted tunnels, the color of yellowing paper. It looked at once ancient and strangely familiar.

Something small and hard struck the back of my head, and I whipped around. Sprawled across the lower tier in the fountain, behind a curtain of water that fell from the basin above, was an oversized toddler. He was fat, with slick skin like a seal, his bronze-colored body nearly naked except for a swath of cloth around his middle. He stared at me with an eager, idiotic smile on his face. Then he reached down, scooped something up from the fountain, and threw it at me.

I tried to sidestep it, but it hit my head anyway and plunked down in the water. A coin.

"Stop that!" I told him.

His smile grew wider, and his body shook as though he were laughing, only he made no sound at all. On either side of him were two other toddlers, both as unnaturally large as he was. Having noticed what he was doing, they joined in, flopping down on their bellies and tossing handfuls of coins at me.

"Cut it out!" I yelled at them, shielding my face with my arm. That made them laugh even more—silently—their dumpling heads bobbing up and down.

At that moment, a hand the size of a spade descended from the upper tier. It swatted the head of one of the toddlers, then slapped another one on its behind.

"That's enough, Holy Terrors!" said a voice, which I assumed belonged to the person with the huge hand. In order to see who it was, I had to back up to get a view of the fountain's upper tier. Standing at the top of the fountain was a lady. Or more precisely, an angel. She was tremendously tall—maybe eight feet or more—and was the same sleek bronzy color as the toddlers. Sprouting from her back was a pair of muscular wings, thickly feathered and poised as though she were about to take flight. She gazed down at me for a moment, then shook her head. Her wings collapsed against her back, their feathers settling. She sat down on the edge of the stone tier she stood upon. Her massive legs dangled near the toddlers below, who took the opportunity to jump up and hang on her feet.

"Oh, honey," the angel said to me, "you are crashing the wrong party." Her voice was deep and buttery smooth.

"Party?"

"Metaphorically speaking, honey." With a quick jerk of her leg, she dislodged the toddlers from her foot, and they all tumbled away, laughing their silent laughs.

"Did you see a boy?" I asked her, gazing around the plaza. "A blond boy?"

"No, you came solo. Looks like you were ditched, baby. But that's men for you," the angel said breezily.

"He didn't ditch me. He was the one who pulled me into the turtle tank."

"Did he now?" The angel nodded knowingly. "Ahh. You got snagged by an Imp; that's what happened to you."

"An Imp? What? No, he's a boy," I said.

"Imps are boys. Or a type of boy. Was he charming, your Imp?"

Considering that he had just practically drowned me, I hated to admit that he was. I nodded.

"Mmm, they always are," said the angel. "Dangerous creatures. They make mischief wherever they go, but they have a particularly bad habit of stealing Humans."

Mr. Boot's words came back to me then. That Tom was a thief.

"But why would they steal people?" I asked.

"Sometimes for the fun of it. To entertain themselves. To prove that they can. Imps get bored very quickly, though, so nothing good ever happens to the Humans they steal. And of course, there are always the Imps who take Humans for profit. Anyway"—the angel's voice brightened—"looks like you are one of the lucky ones who got away."

I tried to wrap my mind around the idea of Tom betraying me like that. Of Tom being an Imp. It seemed impossible . . . yet he *had* pulled me into the turtle tank. Deliberately. Maliciously.

And now here I was.

But where was I?

I looked all around me. The two staircases. The vaulted tunnels, their stones turning a deep mustard color in the setting sun. The fountain. I looked up at the angel.

And then I knew.

"I'm in Central Park, aren't I?" I said. "This is Bethesda Terrace. And you're the statue. The one in the fountain!"

"I *am* Bethesda!" the angel said. "*The* Bethesda. Angel of the Waters."

So I was still in New York! I could grab the B train at the Seventy-Second Street station, which wasn't far from Bethesda Terrace. I'd be home in about fifteen minutes.

But the statue could talk.

And the park was eerily empty.

"Where is everyone?" I said, half to myself.

"It's too early in the morning for Folk," said the angel.

"No, it's not," I said. The autumn sky was descending into the deep blue half-light of dimmery. "The sun's going down."

"It's coming up, baby. Up."

I looked at the sky and saw that it was true. The sun was rising behind the buildings flanking the east side of the park. But those buildings also looked odd. There were skyscrapers, yes, but there were also houses nestled among them, some of them little more than shacks, and what appeared to be farmland.

The air felt different too. For one thing, it was warmer. Much too warm for an autumn in New York. My soaked clothes were already beginning to dry. And there was also a charged feel to the air, as if a steady current of energy was coursing through it, like an unbroken breeze.

I caught sight of movement in one of the underpasses. Horses, three of them. All of them were white, slim and leggy with riders on them.

"Magicians," Bethesda said darkly before scooping me up in her massive hand and depositing me on the fountain's first tier with the toddlers. "Don't move," she ordered as her wings folded over me. The feathers on her wings were huge, the longest nearly as tall as I was, and about two inches thick. Within that downy shelter, the air quickly grew very warm, and it smelled, quite honestly, like a dirty birdcage. The toddlers were there too, also enveloped in the angel's wings. They were staring at me and smiling, and I half expected them to pinch me or poke at me. But they stayed perfectly still, as if they had done this many times before.

I peered out at the plaza through a narrow space between Bethesda's wings. The approaching animals weren't horses after all, though they were easily as big. They were dogs. Or anyway, they looked like dogs that had been supersized.

"What are those things?" I asked.

"Dogges." Bethesda pronounced the word *doe-eggs*. "Now hush!"

The three huge, rangy, white dogges had long, elegant legs and narrow, triangular snouts. They were saddled, and ridden by two men and a woman, all of them with stony expressions—the Magicians, I guessed. They were dressed very drably in tweedy grays and browns, with suit jackets.

As they neared, Bethesda's wings shifted slightly, and my peephole was closed. In near darkness, I listened to the click of the dogges' toenails against the pavement, growing louder, then finally stopping.

"Bethesda." It was a man's voice.

She didn't answer.

"Bethesda!"

The angel's wings stirred.

"Come back in an hour," the angel murmured, her voice convincingly husky with sleep, her wings tightening around us.

"Wake up!" the man barked at her.

"Hush! What is wrong with you?" the angel snapped at

him. "You're going to wake the Holy Terrors if you keep going on like that."

The toddlers all giggled silently at this.

"Has anyone come through the fountain's Wicket this morning?" the man asked.

"Oh yes, someone came through," Bethesda said.

I sucked in my breath. It occurred to me then that Bethesda's wings might not be protecting me; they might be trapping me. I felt a sickening rush of terror at the thought of those three people seeing me. I didn't know why. There was just something about them that made me feel cold inside. I thrust my hand into the depths of the feathers, trying to push them up so I could at least make a run for it, but the wings held firm, locked by powerful muscles.

"She was about yea high," the angel continued. "Says her name is Mary Carpenter. Ever hear of her?"

"All right, all right." The man seemed to back down.

"Well?" Bethesda persisted. "Isn't that what you're all fired up about? Now, come on, Mr. Barnabas, if Mary Carpenter came through here, don't you think I'd alert the authorities?"

There was a pause, during which I could hear my own breathing. One of the Holy Terrors wiped its nose with the back of its hand.

"Fine morning, isn't it, Bethesda?" said another voice. The second man. His voice was as slippery as baby oil. "The air is so deliciously sweet this time of day."

"I love what you've done with your hair, Nester,"

Bethesda said. "How did you get it to come out of your nostrils like that?"

"Ha, yes. So, tell me," the man continued, "how many Holy Terrors are there now?"

Bethesda didn't answer. The muscles in her wings twitched, making her feathers ripple. Beside me, the Holy Terrors had stopped their silent laughter.

"How many, Bethesda?" This came from the woman in the group. She had a sharp, high voice that sounded coiled, as though she were just barely keeping her rage under control.

"Three," Bethesda answered.

"I remember when there were four of them," the oily-voiced man said in a mock tone of wistful reminiscence. "There was the smallest fellow with the lovely curls. Pity about him. I'm sure the other Holy Terrors miss him. I'm sure you do too, Bethesda. Don't force the Minister to take another one away, please."

Bethesda's wings shifted, tightening around us.

"Please remove yourselves from my plaza," Bethesda said coldly. "You're stinking up all my sweet morning air."

I heard the click of dogges' toenails again, retreating, growing fainter, and then silence. The great wings opened. I looked up at Bethesda, her face grim, a mask of barely controlled outrage.

"You've got to go, sugar," she said. "You've got to go now. No one knows you're here yet . . . no one except your Imp, of course, and he'll be looking for you. You've got to get yourself to another Wicket, the sooner the better. This one is closed now."

She made a hissing sound in the direction of a stand of trees. There was a stirring in the treetop, and the next moment a small creature bounded across the plaza.

It wasn't any sort of animal that I could identify. It was squirrel-like, but not a squirrel. And although it was long-bodied, like a weasel, its face was flat and short, like a pug, with a pair of large ears that stood up. And most of all, it was blue. A beautiful dusty blue, the exact color of the sky right before a storm.

The creature perched on the edge of the fountain, its brushy tail twitching alertly.

"What kind of animal is that?" I asked Bethesda.

"He's a skrill, of course." Then to the skrill she said, "Tiller, this child needs an escort to a Wicket." Bethesda spoke to the creature as if it were a person. "Take her to Wiffle's, and have her get on the 7:05."

The skrill's eyes moved from Bethesda to me.

"Does he understand?" I asked.

"Of course."

Bethesda lifted her wings and pressed them together behind her back, making them snap like a crisp bedsheet. Slowly and gracefully, she bent down and scooped up water from the fountain.

"Take a sip," she told me, holding her palm out toward me.

"No thanks," I replied.

The Holy Terrors took angry stances at this, their

chubby arms folded against their chests as they glowered at me.

"It's nothing personal," I said defensively. "It's just that people do disgusting things in New York City fountains."

One of the Holy Terrors made a move to kick me, but Bethesda stopped him.

"This is not your New York City," Bethesda said to me. "Haven't you realized that by now? You're in the Nigh. You can drink this water. In fact, you'll need to, for when you have to spit."

"What? Why will I need to spit?"

"Drink."

Bethesda's hand moved beneath my chin. I examined the water cupped in her bronze palm. It looked clear. I took a sniff. It smelled okay.

Bending my head down, I took a noisy slurp of water, then swiped the drips from my chin. It tasted pretty clean, actually, with a slight metallic taste, probably from Bethesda's hand.

"All right, now get going," Bethesda said. "Follow Tiller. Do what he does. If he runs, you run. If he hides, you hide. When you reach the Ramble, you'll have the Boggedy Cats to deal with, and they mean business, honey, so stay alert."

29

THE RAMBLE

The moment I stepped out of the fountain, Tiller leapt to the ground and started off toward a wooded grove. His blue fur had a shadowy quality, and I imagined that if he wanted to, he could melt into the undergrowth. He was fast, too. I had to jog to catch up with him, my feet sloshing in my waterlogged boots.

We followed a dirt path, narrow and scrubby. I had that same unnerving feeling of things being both familiar and strange. Central Park—this Central Park—looked wilder than the other one. The trees grew more thickly together, and the land occasionally plunged into a sharp drop alongside the path, ending in a gorge. Plus, there weren't any lampposts or benches.

And there was something else, too. The only way I can describe it is that everything seemed much more alive here. Everything had this twitchy electric quality, even the grass and the sky, which seemed to shimmer with an extra dose of light and color. It was mesmerizingly beautiful but also unsettling.

As we hurried along, my thoughts turned back to Tom's

betrayal. It was so raw, so shocking, that I felt it like a physical pain. I replayed all our past conversations. He must have been laughing to himself the whole time. He must have thought I was a first-class moron. I made a sound—a snort of self-disgust—and I murmured, "I'm such an idiot."

The skrill looked up at me, and I asked, half kidding, "Can you understand what I say?"

Then the weirdest thing happened: I could hear his answer. Not with words but with a *knowing*. When I had asked if he understood me, I had, of course, assumed that he didn't. And now I knew that he did. It was that simple. I looked at him in surprise, and he stared back at me with steady, gentle eyes. Honestly, he didn't look any more or less intelligent than a dog.

"So can you hear what I *think*, too?" I asked him.

I'm not a mind reader! Again, I felt the words of his answer rather than hearing them. Then there was a burst of jiggling lightness, which I knew was the skrill laughing.

I liked talking this way. I'm not a fan of blabbermouths. The skrill's silent conversation was strange but pleasant.

"What is this place anyway?" I asked.

Central Park, the skrill answered, as if shocked I didn't know that.

"But it's all wrong for Central Park," I said. "There are too many trees, and statues shouldn't be talking, and we don't have things like skrills."

Yes, imagine that! Well, this is the Nigh, after all, so there are bound to be differences.

"What's the Nigh?"

This. All of this. It's a vast place. New York City is only a tiny part of it. And you live in the Hither . . . the . . . What is it you Humans call it again? The Earth. Of course, we once lived all together. In the beginning, as the story goes, we were all Eve's children.

"What, like Adam and Eve? The first people? That Eve?" I asked.

Yes, that Eve. She had twelve children. And one day the Great Spirit came down from the sky to see the children. But only half of the children were bathed and groomed, while the other half had been playing in the mud and were filthy. So Eve hid the dirty children. But the Great Spirit sees everything and was insulted by Eve's trick. To punish her, the Great Spirit said, "Since you're so eager to hide your dirty children, I'll hide them forever. Half of your children will be banished from the world. They'll be Hidden People."

"So the people in the Nigh are the Hidden People?"

I felt Tiller laugh. Then he said, No, no. The Humans on Earth are the Hidden People. They were the ones who were banished.

I must have slowed down as I absorbed this.

You'll need to walk faster if we're going to make it to the Wicket before it closes.

I quickened my pace and asked, "What is that anyway? A Wicket?"

A Wicket is a way in to the Nigh. And a way out of it. There are timetables for the Wickets, but they are shifty and unpredictable. *If we don't make it to this one, it might be a while before another one opens.*

"Hours?"

Hours. Days. Weeks.

You'd better believe that made me walk faster.

The woods grew thicker now, and the path disappeared. The skrill moved along more carefully now, taking frequent, cautious sniffs at the air.

"So who's Mary Carpenter?" I asked.

Tiller looked back at me, as if this took him by surprise. *How do you know about her?*

"Bethesda mentioned her name."

Tiller was silent for a moment. Then he said, *Mary Carpenter is a legend.*

"In what way?"

It depends who you ask. Some Folk think she's a criminal.

"Do you?" I asked.

I think she's a hero. The most important hero we've ever known in the Nigh. We've just entered the Ramble incidentally. Stay alert.

I had been in the Ramble many times before, back home. It was a section of Central Park with quiet winding paths twisting through shady woods and over rustic bridges. But this? This was much wilder than the Ramble I knew. This was straight-up forest.

We have to keep to the Ramble as long as we can, Tiller said. *Less Folk here. Of course, Folk won't see you very well in general, but we don't want to take any chances.*

"What do you mean? Am I invisible here?" I whispered.

Not invisible, no, but difficult to see. In the Nigh, Humans appear as something like a ghost. At least for a little while.

"But you and Bethesda can see me."

I'm not Folk. Neither is Bethesda.

There was a riffle in the treetops. Tiller stopped, and we both looked up.

"What is it?" I could feel my heart begin to thump more quickly.

Just a Willaweeper, the skrill said. See it? It's flying between the low branches.

I stared into the treetops until I could make out a pearly figure darting through the air. It had paper-thin wings like a giant moth, yet its body was shaped like a human.

"It's a fairy!" I whispered.

Oh no, not at all! There are no fairies anymore. But the Willaweepers are dwindling too. As are Nibbins and Inklings.

"Nibbins? They live in the Nigh?"

Of course! It used to be that you'd find a pair of Nibbins in every Iffiny shrub. But nowadays you're lucky if you see any at all. The Smugglers steal them from the Nigh and bring them to the Hither.

Which meant that Mr. Boot's briefcase was full of smuggled creatures.

Hmm.

I watched the Willaweeper land on the tip of a branch. Its tiny legs lifted quickly, one then the other in a speedy jig.

"It's dancing," I said, entranced, and I moved closer to

the tree to get a better look. Right then a fine stream of liquid spilled down from the Willaweeper and would have splashed on my head if I hadn't jumped aside.

"Is it . . . Did it just pee?" I asked the skrill.

Yes, it did, said Tiller wearily, as though he'd been the target of a Willaweeper a few times. *Willaweepers are nuisances, but they're good for the flowers, and they sound the alarm when there's danger approaching.*

That reminded me of Bethesda's parting warning.

"What are Boggedy Cats?" I whispered.

Don't! If you think about them, they'll come. Now hurry, we're losing time. Tiller trotted onward, his delicate paws flicking out at each step.

"Well, great, now I'm thinking about them," I whispered back as I jogged after him.

But the next second I began to see images in my mind, like an internal movie. It was a silly story about a flying mouse and a bakery. The skrill turned to look at me with his gentle eyes, and I thought I detected something playful in them. He had sent me the story to crowd out thoughts of the Boggedy Cats.

I noticed a flash of color off to my right—a huge tree, as wide around as a trampoline, and draped with scraps of cloth and little toys and fishing nets and beaded necklaces and all sorts of other things. It looked like a Christmas tree decorated by a lunatic.

I paused to look at it.

Devotion Tree, the skrill remarked. *An old Folk practice.*

When a person dies, you take something that belonged to them—
a bit of clothing or an object that they liked—and tie it to the tree.
The object represents their soul. Tying it to the tree is supposed to
help them travel to the Isle of the Dead.

The skrill stopped suddenly. His tail coiled tensely as he tipped his head to the side, listening.

Hshhht! he said. *Lie down! Over there, behind the brickle brush! Folk are coming.*

I had no idea what a brickle brush was, but there was a copse of low bushes with tangled branches and golden leaves. Brickle brush or not, it was thick enough to hide a person. I dropped to the ground by the bushes while Tiller scrambled up a nearby tree, perching on a low branch.

Then I heard it. Voices. They grew louder, and from the depths of the Ramble a man and a woman appeared. Their clothes were strange, mismatched, as though they had tossed on things they'd found in an old trunk. The woman wore a long, silky lavender gown with a faded denim jacket. The man wore a green T-shirt coupled with old-fashioned gray pantaloons and boots. He held a child in his arms, limp with sleep, her face buried against the man's neck.

The man and the woman were startling looking. Of course, I had seen beautiful people in New York City before. Greenwich Village was crawling with models, loping around the streets as they talked on their phones, a Starbucks or a cigarette in their other hand. I always thought the models looked sort of monster-ish, with their too-small heads on giantess bodies and lamppost legs. But these two? Their beauty shimmered, as if they were made of something more than muscle and bone. There was a phosphorescence that radiated off their skin. It reminded me of the light that Mr. Boot's chopsticks created as he whipped them through the air.

The man and the woman were on the small side, not much taller than me, but long-limbed and slender. The woman's hair was short and dark. Her thick, dark brows sheltered wide-set, tip-tilted eyes. Her nose was blunt and short, and two long dimples played beneath her cheekbones. The man, who moved with a skittish energy, was dark-haired too, with a delicate face that was even more beautiful than the woman's.

"They're so . . . so . . . ," I murmured.

Yes, Folk are like that, Tiller said simply. *Shhh.*

The woman passed so close to me that I heard the sluff-sluff of her lavender dress. A pair of basketball sneakers peeked from beneath the dress. I had a powerful urge to reach out and touch her. Even as I felt this way, I knew it was rooted in some sort of magic, something about the way they were made, and I forced myself to keep still.

"Does it matter where?" she said.

"Anywhere is fine," the man replied, looking around nervously. He shifted the child in his arms so that the girl's head lolled against his shoulder and her hair spilled down his back—lackluster brown and tangled. When the woman scrutinized the area another minute, the man lost his temper. "Hurry up," he snapped.

The woman glanced at him, frowning, and I thought her eyes looked damp. But then she pointed at a spot of ground that was covered with bright green moss.

"Here, I suppose," she said.

The man bent down and laid the child on the mossy ground. When she was flat on her back, I could see the girl was probably about eight or nine. And she was human. Her eyes were open and blinking up at the trees. There was something strange about her. She was too still. Her mouth was open slightly, as though she were about to say something, but she didn't make a sound.

The woman knelt down beside her and brushed the girl's hair away from her face.

"Let her be. She'll be fine," the man said.

The woman resisted. "Are you sure they'll fetch her—"

"Yes," the man said gruffly, grabbing the woman by her elbow and tugging her to her feet. "The Minister says so, but we have to leave right away or they won't."

From above us, in the treetops, came a thin warble. *Wickle-wickle-feee!*

With one last look at the girl, who was eerily still, as immobile as a doll, the woman joined the man, and they hurried away. I started to rise to go to the girl when I heard it again: *Wickle-wickle-feee! Wickle-wickle-feee!*

Looking up, I saw the Willaweeper darting from branch to branch, its tiny pink tongue warbling out its call, like a bird.

Get down! I heard Tiller's order. His command sent

me crouching down behind the bush once more. Then I remembered what Tiller had said about Willaweepers—that they sound an alarm when danger is approaching.

There was a dry rattling in the undergrowth, and a massive creature rose up beside the girl. Its body was a wide slab of muscle covered with mottled oblong scales, like oyster shells, that quivered as it moved, making the dry rattling sound. The scales started at its enormous tail and went all the way up to its bullish neck, which tapered toward a head that resembled an alligator, except for a brutal-looking horn that rose up from the top of its snout. I could smell the creature, a putrid wormy stench, as if it had just tunneled through the earth, had fought past roots and sludge and buried things, and had clawed its way up to the surface.

Sewer Mahamba, the skrill said. *Don't. Move.*

30

SEWER MAHAMBA

I watched as the creature's tail swept at the earth, fling-
ing dirt and stones in the air. Its squat legs with their
thick black claws scraped at the ground while it swung
its head around so wildly that I wondered if it were
blind. But no, that brute could definitely see, because its
eyes suddenly locked onto the girl. The beast grew still.
Slowly, almost pneumatically, it lowered itself close to the
ground. I caught a flicker of fear in the little girl's placid
eyes.

She knows that monster is there, I thought, *but she can't
seem to move.*

My mind scrambled for some way to stop what was
about to happen. My body must have shifted, instinctively
readying itself to do something.

Stay where you are, I heard the skrill command again.
I felt an impulse to keep still envelop my muscles—the
skrill's handiwork—but I fought it off and looked around
for something to throw at the beast. All I could see were
sticks and small rocks, which wouldn't do much more than
annoy him. I wished so badly that I had my chopsticks

with me. I could have tried a spell, and even if I didn't do it perfectly, it might have been good enough to buy some time, to grab the girl and run.

Right then I thought about Crud, and what he had said about the monkey that he'd turned back to plastic. He hadn't used chopsticks to do that. My panicked mind tried to recall the conversation we'd had in the hallway. He had said something about the magic being in the air, about that buzzing feeling. It occurred to me then that the air in the Nigh felt like that—charged and buzzing, as if the magic were just loitering in the atmosphere. I had no chopsticks. But maybe I could use my hands, the way Crud had with the monkey.

I looked around the woods for something to animate. There were plenty of trees and rocks, of course, but Mr. Boot said that animating things like trees and rocks was very difficult since they were essentially in a coma. My eyes landed on the Devotion Tree with all its crazy decorations—ribbons and cloth scraps and toys. I spied a cloth doll hanging from the tree. It was creepily faceless, as though it were more an effigy than a toy, but someone had made it a simple white shirt and pants, and fastened a red ribbon around its wrist, which was tied to a low branch on the tree. Swiftly, I performed the Oifen Shoifen Spell, a half-twist with my right hand, and then the three circles, two clockwise, one counterclockwise.

I felt the air around me thicken and crackle. Its filmy blue cast deepened. The leaves greened up and shimmered with such brilliance that they looked like they'd been glazed.

Despite all this, the doll still hung limply from the tree. To my horror, I saw the Sewer Mahamba's front shoulders tense abruptly, its muscles readying itself to pounce on the girl, as if my feeble attempt at magic had somehow stirred it to action.

I tried not to panic and held my focus while I repeated the spell. This time I caught a glimpse of fine sparks around my fingers, like fireflies. The doll shivered, and then its legs kicked out once, twice. Its free arm began to flap up and down, and it let out a thin, pitiful cry.

It was enough to divert the beast's attention. The Sewer Mahamba swung its head around toward the tree.

In a flash, I darted out from behind the bush and started toward the girl to snatch her up and run, even as I heard the skrill in my mind crying, No, no, no! But before I could reach her, the Sewer Mahamba turned its head again, and this time its eyes found me.

I froze. The beast heaved its massive body around to face me, its shell-like scales rattling softly. Under hooded lids, its eyes were a milky blue, its pupils diamond shaped.

I could feel the skrill in my mind now. I could sense him preparing to leap down on the creature, waiting for the right time . . . but what could he possibly do to help, as small as he was? Nothing.

This is how I will die, I realized. In this strange place that is New York City but also not New York City. My father would never know what had happened to me. I cursed Tom, and I cursed Mr. Boot, too, because if it weren't for his club, I'd never have met Tom in the first place and wouldn't be in this situation.

The girl moved. A small movement—the fingers on her left hand fluttered. Her eyes were on me, wide with fear. A sound came out of her mouth—no words, just a sound. The Sewer Mahamba heard her. It pivoted on its squat legs with alarming speed and rushed forward, and in a flash it grabbed the girl in its mouth.

I cried out as the Sewer Mahamba whipped its head back and forth violently. There was a dry snap, and then the girl disappeared within its jaws. The creature's head lowered to the ground. Satisfied, it crawled off, the underbrush hissing beneath its belly, until it was gone.

In my life, I have seen all sorts of things that kids shouldn't have to see. That happens when you grow up in the city. But never, never had I seen someone killed. And killed in such an awful way. I fought back nausea. I felt cold all over and damp with sweat, and I couldn't control the shaking that racked my body.

A sudden scratching sound made me jump. But it was only Tiller, climbing down the tree. He tipped his head up, and the flexible flaps on the sides of his nose pressed in and out, pulling in a scent.

Something's coming.

I knew what he said, but I couldn't hold the words in my mind.

"How could they have left her there?" I asked. "She was just a little kid."

Something's coming.

This time it registered.

"Boggedy Cat." I said this rather than asked, because, having just seen the worst thing I could think of, it seemed only natural that the next thing would be another horror show. My wild thoughts anchored to the image of massive lionlike creatures, silent and unseen until they were right on top of you, gouging your skin with their razor claws, their teeth tearing you apart.

No. Not Boggedy Cats, Tiller said. *Something else. We have to go.*

I heard him, but I couldn't move. Wouldn't move. It was as though there were still something I could do about what had just happened. Something I simply hadn't thought of yet. It made no sense, but my mind hadn't caught up with what I had seen.

We have to go, the skrill repeated more vehemently. He filled my mind with a sense of urgency, and I felt my body respond to it like a puppet, and we both hurried off again into the woods.

Numbly, I followed Tiller through the woods, feeling like a walking target. My ears strained for the warning cry of the Willaweeper as the image of that poor little girl being devoured was crashing around in my brain. When the sobs rose up in my throat, Tiller attempted to settle me down—I could hear him chirping softly into my mind—but I was too distressed to be soothed.

Tiller was small and agile and could dart between the brambles, but it wasn't long before my arms and face were scratched and bleeding. It was when we had reached a portion of the woods that was nearly impenetrable with scrub that I noticed something behind us—a glimpse of movement, quick and stealthy. A shadow slipping behind a fallen tree. A flash of red. But when I looked back again, and several times after that, I didn't see anything.

I couldn't be sure, but I didn't think it was an animal. And then I thought of something—what if it was Tom? The idea of seeing him again made my blood heat up with anger. I would let him know that I hated him for the way he'd betrayed me, that he was despicable for pretending to be my friend. But then I remembered how he'd grabbed my wrist and pulled me into that water. He was strong, too strong for a boy his age. No—I decided that, after all, I did not want to face him again. Definitely not.

The land began to slope upward, and just ahead I could see that the woods were growing thinner. Fine-spun columns of morning light penetrated the canopy. I suspected we were coming to the end of the Ramble, thankfully. Bad things could happen anywhere, but the Ramble was a place that felt primed for trouble. As we climbed the slope, which grew steeper with each step, the woods seemed less woodsy and more parklike. Above our heads flew a brilliant iridescent green bird, the sort of bird you would see in a rain forest, not in Central Park. I watched it hover in the air for a moment, then circle back, diving into the depths of the Ramble. That's when I caught another glimpse of whatever was following us. Just a flash of movement, a shape that certainly looked human. Or Folk.

Or Imp.

"There's something—" I started to say to Tiller.

Yes. It's following us.

"What is it?"

I'm not sure.

Behind us, I could hear the snap of slender woody stems, the rustled brush, and then the slow, heavy thrum of unbalanced footsteps.

Don't run.

"Why not?"

Because it's been following us for a while, so if it was going to do something, it would probably have done it already. If we don't alarm it, it may just keep its distance.

I can't even tell you how hard it is not to run when you have something creepy tailing you. Every cell in my body wanted to bolt. But I kept to a fast walk, my heart thudding in my chest, my legs shaky with adrenaline. Every moment, I expected to feel the thing leap on my back.

Tiller kept closer to me now, trotting right beside my feet. I couldn't help myself and started to turn to check where the thing was, but Tiller stopped me. *Don't look at it.*

Off in the distance, I could see an expanse of green, a large meadow divided by meandering paths on which some Folk were walking. They were dressed in the same strange way as the man and woman in the woods—a mash-up of clothes. Men in waistcoats and bell-bottoms. Women in Jane Austen–style gowns and bomber jackets. One chubby little girl in a Halloween fairy costume, holding a wand with a glittery star on the end. Seriously, it looked like a thrift store had exploded on them.

There was a line of carriages, just like the one I'd seen in Bethesda Terrace, hitched to those huge dogs. *Dogges.* Some were white, like the other dogges I'd seen, but there were a few sleek tricolored ones and black ones with thick fur—all of them enormous. The carriage drivers, wearing white top hats, were sitting in their carriages, looking bored.

Behind us, I heard the soft rustle of something brushing against a shrub. Whatever was following us was closer now.

Don't turn, I told myself. Don't turn.

But I did. I couldn't help myself. I caught a quick glimpse of a boy, or anyway something boy shaped. Its face was horribly twisted, as though someone had tried to wring it out like a washcloth. Its arms and legs seemed boneless, buckling, walking with a weightless limp. I caught a flash of red—blood?

When I tell you to, Tiller said, *head for Mrs. Wiffle and tell her you're traveling.*

"What?"

The yellow food cart, past the carriages.

At the far end of the meadow, close to the tree line, I could see the food cart. Bright yellow with pink stripes.

Attached to its front was a giant fake waffle griddle, the size of a truck's wheel, with the words MRS. WIFFLE'S WAFFLES painted on it. There was something about the cart that held my attention. It flagged me, the way there are certain faces that make you look at them twice.

There was a sharp crack of a branch behind us, the unbalanced footsteps close now, very close, and Tiller cried out, Run!

31

MRS. WIFFLE'S WAFFLES

Now that my muscles were given permission to do what they had been aching to do, I took off as fast as I could. I ran toward the food cart with the same cold panic I used to feel when Chicken Bone Charlie used to chase me, the whole while wishing like mad that I had Annika's speed.

Up ahead, one of the carriage drivers—a large man with a mustache and a cloud of black hair beneath his white top hat—stood up in his carriage and squinted in my direction. He didn't look right at me, just in my general vicinity. It seemed as though he couldn't see me very well, like Tiller had said. But he could see *something*.

A few seconds later I reached Mrs. Wiffle's Waffles, but the food cart's serving window was sealed with a metal shutter. I rapped on it frantically, making the shutter rattle.

"We're closed!" I heard a voice say from inside the cart. "Come back in a half hour."

I knocked on the shutter again, harder this time, creating a thunderous clanking.

The shutter lifted a few inches, and a pair of annoyed green eyes peered out at me.

"I said we're closed. No waffles. Stop knocking."

The first thing that struck me was that the person could obviously see me.

"Are you Mrs. Wiffle?" I asked.

"That's me."

"I'm traveling." I repeated Tiller's words.

The shutter opened a few inches more. Now I could see that Mrs. Wiffle wore a yellow-and-pink-striped cap and coveralls to match the cart. Her face was wide and short, like a balloon that's been sat on.

"Anything to declare?" Her tone was all business now.

"What?"

"Are you bringing anything back with you?" Mrs. Wiffle asked impatiently.

"No."

"Turn your pockets inside out," Mrs. Wiffle demanded.

"Listen, I need to—"

"If you have nothing to hide, then turn your pockets inside out."

I jammed my hands in my pockets and turned them inside out. A few coins dropped out, but that was all.

"Come closer," she said, crooking two fingers. "Closer."

I leaned across the truck's narrow food counter, and Mrs. Wiffle's fingers instantly began to rummage through my hair. I pulled away, but she grabbed a hank of my hair in her fist and held it.

"If you're not a Smuggler, you won't mind me having a look."

It was clear she wasn't going to back down, so I let her paw through my head, then stick a finger in each one of my ears until she seemed satisfied.

"Bethesda said there was a Wicket—" I started to say.

"Bethesda? Well, why didn't you mention her before, you goose? You could have bypassed security." She leaned across the counter and started to point toward something on her cart. But the very next moment, a hand grabbed my throat from behind. I tried to twist around, but the grip tightened, squeezing my windpipe.

"Keep still," whispered a voice in my ear.

I stopped struggling and the grip loosened a bit, just enough for me to take quick wheezing breaths.

"Well, heyo!" the voice said cheerfully. "I've caught myself a Peeper!"

The hand shifted roughly on my neck, and for a moment I thought my attacker was letting go. But no, he simply turned me around to face him. It was the carriage driver with the black mustache. He examined my face, squinting again, trying to see me clearly, I guessed. Like the man and woman in the woods, his skin had a luminescence, but beneath his white top hat, his features were sharper, his nose and mouth thin. And there was something weird about his eyes.

"Let her alone!" Mrs. Wiffle shouted across the counter. She chucked something at the man—a ball of butter, it looked like—but it missed him.

"How old are you?" the man asked me.

When I didn't answer, he shook me hard.

"Oy!" Mrs. Wiffle warned, and threw a spatula at him, but it simply landed at his feet without touching him. Mrs. Wiffle had lousy aim.

"How old are you?" the man demanded again.

"Twelve," I said.

My voice must have been as wispy to him as my body because he frowned and said, "What? Say it again. Louder."

"Twelve."

"Twelve, you said?" It was difficult to tell what he thought of this. His face gave away nothing. It was then that I realized what was weird about his eyes. He had no eyebrows. None at all. Apart from his hand on my throat, it was the single most terrifying thing about him. That is, until he muttered his next words: "There's my luck, isn't it? Catch a Peeper, and it's next to useless." He looked at me again. "You might have another good year in you. Maybe not even that. Ah well. I'll take you anyway, and we'll see what the Minister can get out of you."

"Heyo, Sheffer!" The call came from across the meadow, where the other carriage drivers loitered.

"What do you want?" the man holding me called back, without taking his eyes off me.

"Your carriage is on the loose, Sheffer!"

The man swung around to see. Behind him, one of the carriages was careening wildly around the meadow. The dogge hitched to it—a squarish, thickly muscled tan beast with a head as big as a mini fridge—was bucking and kicking and lifting the carriage's wheels precariously off the ground, tipping it from left to right, before sprinting off again. Running beside the dogge, nipping at its legs and harassing it into its breakneck frenzy, was Tiller. It would only be a matter of time until the carriage toppled on its side altogether.

You could see the man trying to make his decision—to save his carriage or to hold on to me. Finally he released me and made a beeline for his carriage.

I sucked in a big gulp of air as Mrs. Wiffle hurriedly asked me, "Did you drink from Bethesda's fountain?"

"Yes," I gasped.

"Then spit on the griddle!" Mrs. Wiffle said. "Quick now! The Minister has spotted you." She nodded toward the other end of the meadow where Folk were watching the runaway carriage. A few were staring in our direction, but if there was a Minister among them, I certainly couldn't tell.

"The griddle?" I said, confused.

"Yes, the griddle, the griddle!" she said, and jerked a thick finger toward the giant waffle iron sign by the serving window.

"You want me to spit on *that*?" I asked, baffled.

"Yes! It's your token for the Wicket, girl. Spit!"

I gathered up some spit in my mouth. There wasn't much. I hoped it was enough. I took aim and spit at the

MRS. WIFFLE'S WAFFLES sign as hard as I could. It wasn't a great shot, but it must have been good enough because the giant griddle lid flipped up with a clang, revealing a round opening just big enough for me. I scrambled inside it, and the griddle lid slammed shut behind me.

On my hands and knees, I crawled through the narrow metal passageway and onto a dirt floor, surrounded by craggy, dun-colored stone.

I wasn't alone.

A few yards away were half a dozen people. They were nothing like the Folk. These people were filthy. They had long, matted hair and were mostly naked except for scraps of pelts that they wore around their waists. Most of them were sitting on the ground, but there was a boy standing off to the side, not far from me. He held a long stick, sharpened at the tip. This group wasn't much more inviting than the carriage driver and the Magicians.

I stood up and looked around, considering my options. There were none. I was surrounded by rock wall on all sides. The only way out was to walk right past these people. And that kid with the stick looked like he meant business.

"What do you think you're doing here?" a voice from behind me demanded.

I turned and found myself face-to-face with a large and very irritated-looking woman standing in a doorway I hadn't noticed before. She wore tight black slacks with a radio clipped to her belt and a white button-down shirt with a badge sewn on the arm.

"Out!" she ordered before I could answer, sweeping her arm toward the open door, like I was a stray cat she was shooing away.

I didn't argue. I hurried through the door that led into a large, dimly lit room. There were people milling around—regular people, not Folk—peering down at maps and into glass cases filled with fossils and skeletons.

Now I knew where I was.

The American Museum of Natural History.

The Hall of Human Origins.

I was back in New York, my New York.

I turned around to see the half naked Neanderthals that had scared me a minute ago, frozen in their poses behind a pane of glass. I had been *inside* the Neanderthal diorama. The Wicket from Mrs. Wiffle's Waffles must lead right into the exhibit.

I looked back at the door I'd just walked through. On it was a sign that said EMPLOYEES ONLY.

Just a few days ago, I had seen Vanessa Habscomb walk out of that very same door beside the Neanderthal diorama. So either she was an employee at the museum, which I very much doubted, or else she had just been visiting the Nigh.

A thought occurred to me then, something that filled me with dread. Vanessa Habscomb had been here when I'd gotten the call to meet River in the museum, which even back then had smacked of more than a simple coincidence. So was it possible that River was in the Nigh? What if he'd also been stolen by an Imp—maybe even Tom himself?! I thought of that poor little girl and the Sewer Mahamba, and the notion that River might have met a similar fate wormed its way into my mind and made me sick to my stomach.

Stop it, Nell! I told myself. *Your most powerful weapon is your next move. Kingsley always said that. What's your next move?*

I took a breath.

My next move was obvious. On Monday I would confront Mr. Boot, because there had been too many connections, too many coincidences, and I was pretty sure that Mr. Boot was somehow at the heart of them.

32

ʘUSTED

At home that evening, everything was weirdly normal. I had taken the subway back to our sooty, mustard-colored brick apartment building with its mint-green window frames. I sat across from my dad, under the ugly dandelion puffball chandelier, eating the rice and pigeon peas, which he always made on Friday. The world of Folk and skrills and Imps felt like it had never really happened.

"So what's going on at the club these days?" Dad asked.

"What? Oh. Um. I cleaned out a turtle tank today," I told him.

Avoiding any talk of magic in the club came so naturally now that I didn't even have to try.

"That sounds unpleasant."

"It was. Very."

Two sharp knocks on the door made me startle—I was still feeling pretty jumpy—and to cover for it, I popped out of my chair and said, "Got it."

At the door, I stood on my tiptoes and looked through the peephole. To my surprise I saw Annika's face staring back at me.

"Who is it?" Dad asked.

"Annika," I whispered.

"Annika Sokolovsky?"

"Rapp now. Annika Rapp."

I took a breath, tried to wipe the surprise from my face, and then opened the door.

"Hey," I said, and smiled.

Annika held out my backpack without returning the smile. "You left this at school."

Right. I had forgotten all about my backpack. I had left it in the kindergarten classroom when I went to clean the lizard tank.

"Thanks," I said, taking it from her.

"Is Tom here?" She looked past me into the apartment.

"Tom? No." I lowered my voice to a whisper. "Listen, Tom is not what you think he is. I can't talk about it now, but—"

"Did you two have a good time ditching the club?" Annika interrupted loudly, her voice tight. I widened my eyes at her and shook my head, silently urging her to shut up. But of course she wouldn't. "I hope so," she continued, "because Tom will be expelled over it. You know that, right? You might be expelled too, but he *definitely* will since Boot can't stand him."

My dad's chair scraped backward. He'd heard her.

"Hi, Annika," he said, walking up to us.

Annika's face softened. My dad had always been nice to her when she was a little kid.

"Hi, Mr. Batista."

"Thanks for bringing Nell's backpack." He took the backpack from me and hooked it over his shoulder. It was a small gesture, but he was sending me a message, and I knew it. He'd have better control of me from here on in. I could no longer be trusted.

"I hope your mom is well," he said to Annika. Normal chitchat, but I could hear the strain in his voice.

"She got married. But, you know, she's . . . sort of the same." Annika sounded very young suddenly, as if seeing my dad had flung her back to that time when she lived next door with her tall, redheaded mother whose endless supply of boyfriends—some of them truly dangerous—had landed Annika in our apartment so often.

Dad nodded and smiled at her. "You know you can always visit us whenever you like."

"Sure." She nodded and turned to leave. I knew she'd never take him up on it, for which I was grateful. "Thanks, Mr. Batista."

The second he closed the door, I turned to him.

"Dad, I *was* at the club today! I cleaned out a turtle tank, like I said. Here, you can probably still smell it on me!" I stuck out my arm for him to smell my sleeve, but he gently pushed it away. He shook his head and laughed. It was an awful laugh, full of bitterness, and it scared me. I'd never heard him sound like that before.

"Why are you laughing?" I asked, gazing up into his face. His eyes were faraway, like he was scanning his memories or staring out at his future.

"I spend all day repairing things that are broken," he said softly. "But I can't fix this."

"Me?" I choked out. "You mean you can't fix me?"

"No, not you, Nell. Just . . ." He looked at me. "It's been three years. We have to face it—"

"Dad, no," I begged him, because I knew what he was going to say, and I couldn't bear for him to say it, even though it was the monstrous thought that lurked under our beds and in the back of the closet and in every dark corner of our lives.

"It's been tearing us up, Nell. The waiting. The hoping. Why do you keep going back to the park?"

"For . . . To play chess. You know that."

"It's more than the chess, Nell."

I shook my head, but my mouth crumpled.

He wrapped his arms around me and pressed the side of his face against the top of my head.

"You're waiting for River to turn up there again," he said softly.

"No!" But my voice broke as powerful waves of heartache pulsed through me, as if they'd been straining against a locked door for a very long time and had finally burst free.

Because he was right. He was right.

33

MORONIFICATION OF THE MASSES

Dad grounded me for the weekend—a light punishment considering everything, I guess, but still, it meant I couldn't go out looking for Chicken Bone Charlie. A precious two days of tracking him down were wasted.

In school on Monday, people were acting strangely around me all day. They stared at me in class and whispered to one another when I walked by them in the hallway.

"How you holding up, kid?" Ruth plopped herself across from me at our lunch table.

"I'm fine." I poked at a soggy, deflated ravioli.

"Yeah, that's the way! Don't give them the satisfaction."

"What are you talking about?"

Ruth looked surprised. "You didn't hear?"

"No."

"Hey, it's just moronification of the masses, kid. People acting stupid." She opened up her Rocco's bag and pulled out a foil-wrapped sub.

"Okay, what's going on, Ruth?"

She hesitated, then put down her sub and looked at me squarely.

"There's a rumor going around . . ."

Uh-oh. That was possibly even worse than "I've been thinking . . ."

"People are saying you deliberately got that cute blond guy in trouble because you made him skip detention."

"It's not detention. And I didn't."

"Oh good, yeah. It didn't sound like you." She started to unwrap the foil from her sandwich, but I could tell there was something she wasn't telling me.

"What else are they saying, Ruth?"

Ruth flapped her hand in the air dismissively without meeting my eyes.

"Just stupid stuff," she said.

"Tell me." I tried to keep my voice calm, even though I was feeling tiny tremors in my belly.

Ruth looked at me. You could see that this conversation genuinely pained her. I'd never thought of her as a good friend, exactly; she was just a funny and nice kid I sat with at lunch. But I realized now that I liked her more than I knew.

"That boy who disappeared in Washington Square Park a few years ago—" she started.

I felt my stomach contract and my mouth go dry, but I tried to stay calm.

"Was he your brother?" she asked.

I nodded.

Ruth winced. "Oh, kid. I'm sorry."

"What are they saying about it?" I pursued.

Ruth shook her head, looking away.

"I want to know," I insisted.

Ruth sighed. "Some people—some idiots—are saying that you had something to do with his disappearance."

Annika.

I glanced over at the Goddess Table. Annika was talking to the goddesses and laughing. I felt dizzy and not quite in my own body. The real details of River's disappearance were something that only a few people knew—my dad, Detective Chatterjee, and Annika. Tom, too, thanks to Annika.

Now the story was out there in the school's ether. Ruth must have heard some version of it. I might as well tell her mine.

"It's true," I told her.

"Stop."

"No, it is," I said. "River, Annika, and I all used to walk to school together. The school was just down the block, so Dad thought it was okay for us to go by ourselves. Annika's mom didn't care one way or the other." I glanced over at Annika. She was staring back at me. "On the way to school we would pass right by Washington Square Park. I liked to watch the chess players, you know, so one day as we were walking to school, I said that I was going to go in the park to watch them play chess for a while. River tried to talk me out of it. He said it would make me really late to school and I'd get in trouble, but I told him I didn't care. Annika called me a brat, which made me mad. I ignored them and walked right into the park anyway. I knew River wouldn't leave me there alone. I knew that he wouldn't. So Annika went on to school and River stayed with me while I watched them play. I asked one of the guys if I could play him. It didn't take long for him to beat me, of course. When the game was finished, River said we should go, that we were going to be crazy late to school, and also . . . also he said that there was someone who was giving him the creeps. I heard him say it, but I didn't even bother to look up and see who he was talking about. I wanted to stay. So I played another game, and when it was over, I turned to River, but he wasn't there. I didn't see him leave. I didn't even see him stand up. He was just gone."

A small sound came from Ruth, air hissing between her teeth. She shook her head and was silent for a moment. Then she said, "I remember the posters all over the neighborhood. My dad put one up on the restaurant's window."

I nodded.

"And they never found out what happened to him, right?" Ruth asked.

I shook my head. "Annika always blamed me. If I hadn't insisted on going into the park—"

"Hey, kid, that's just stupid talk. That's just Annika being Annika, right? You know what? Let's just forget this whole thing, and by the way"—Ruth placed the other half of her sub on my tray—"you are eating this because, no joke, your food looks like it was pulled out of a dumpster."

Unfortunately, I couldn't forget the whole thing because Leilani, the Hantis Goddess, was now swanning over to our table. She stood in front of me, arms crossed. I covered my food in case she was planning to spit on it.

"What's your problem, princess?" Ruth said to her.

I'm telling you, I could have hugged Ruth right then and there.

"Shut up, *Robert!*" Leilani snapped at Ruth. Then she turned to me. "Just because you are trash whose own mother didn't want anything to do with her, doesn't mean you have to go around messing up other people's lives."

I knew I had Annika to thank for feeding Leilani that information about my mother.

"Oh, and by the way, we never understood why Tom was hanging out with you," Leilani continued, her eyes narrowing. "I mean, like, why? I guess he felt sorry for you or something. And you repay him by messing up his life. Like you did to your own brother."

I flinched at this. Leilani was pulling out all the ammo, and it was working. I was pretty sure that she'd never played chess in her whole life, yet she had managed to put me in checkmate. I wanted to jump out of my chair and wring her neck. And while I was wringing her neck, I would have liked to tell her exactly why Tom was hanging out with me. But I couldn't do either thing, since the consequence would be certain expulsion.

It was Ruth who stepped in for me, yet again. She had taken a notebook out of her backpack and was making a show of jotting things down as she nodded extravagantly at Leilani.

"What are you doing, Freak Show?" Leilani asked her.

"No, no, keep talking," Ruth answered. "I'm just diagnosing you. So far I've got raging narcissist with a probable eating disorder."

There was a smattering of laughter from other kids at the Leftovers Table.

Leilani shifted her stance, readying herself to respond to Ruth, when Luke, the ultimate tic-tac-toe guy, threw his hands over his head and shouted, "Take cover, she's going to yak again!"

Even Julia Weeks was laughing now. Some of the kids at other tables were looking at Leilani too. She turned bright red, pivoted on her flats, and retreated to the safety of the other goddesses.

It was a victory, I guess, mostly for the Leftovers Table, who suddenly no longer seemed like a random collection of leftover people. For the rest of the lunch period, the kids at our table actually talked to one another. Maybe not Julia, but you could tell she was listening at least.

"Moronification of the masses defeated, kid!" Ruth declared, and put up her fist. I bumped it, but I knew she was wrong. Goddesses aren't that easy to defeat.

34

THE NOTSEN-GLOTSEN HEX

F erret's still missing," Crud said when we had taken our seats at the Last Chance Club.

"Astute observation, Mr. Butterbank," said Mr. Boot. "But while the ferret will be back eventually, Mr. Gunnerson will not. He has been expelled for failure to comply with the rules of our club."

Annika's hand shot up.

"Yes, Ms. Rapp?"

"I don't think it's fair that Tom gets expelled and Nell gets a free pass for doing the exact same thing." She shot me a scathing look.

"I see." Mr. Boot nodded thoughtfully. "Anything else?"

She shook her head.

"Excellent. Now today we will be practicing the Notsen-Glotsen Hex."

"Mr. Boot, I need to tell you what happened on Friday—" I started, but he held up his palm to stop me.

"Not now, Ms. Batista."

"But this is important—"

"I said, not now."

"Then when?" I refused to back down.

He glared at me so fiercely that for a moment I was genuinely afraid he might put some spell on me. But then he answered, "Talk to me after we're done here," and he continued the lesson.

That afternoon we worked nonstop on the Notsen-Glotsen Hex. You used it to deflect people from looking at you. It didn't require much chopstick work, thank goodness. Mostly it required lots of mental focus—my specialty. Annika, Crud, and I took turns at staring contests, trying to force each other to look away. To my surprise, I was able to do this better than the other two, although Crud was good at it also. When he performed the hex on me, I felt a nearly irresistible urge to look away from him and had to fight every impulse in my body to hold his gaze. Annika, however, was terrible at it. Maybe it was because she was so used to being gawked at. Or maybe she wanted me to feel the full effect of her hateful stare as we locked eyes.

"Time's up for today," Mr. Boot said finally. "Tomorrow you will be doing in-school service again."

"I can't tomorrow," Annika protested. "It's the school dance."

"Well, what a coincidence. That's exactly where you will be doing in-school service."

I had successfully avoided school dances up until now, and from the way Crud groaned, I assumed he had too.

"Before the dance, you'll be helping with decorations, moving tables—"

"Using magic?" Crud asked hopefully.

"Using your arms and legs."

"So then we don't have to go to the actual dance itself," I said. The thought of being at one of those dances, even if it was to help out, made me cringe. And now that pretty much the entire seventh and eighth grades despised me, it was going to be pure torture.

"You will all attend the dance as volunteers."

I took some vindictive pleasure in seeing Annika's mouth pop open, aghast. You could just tell she was imagining what the goddesses would say when they saw her working at the dance.

"But why do we even have to be there?" she said. "I mean, we're not chaperones."

"Trust me, you'll find ample opportunity to use your magic."

"So we're supposed to do spells in the middle of the school dance?" she asked. "Don't you think everyone will notice our chopsticks waving around?"

"Hmm, good point, Ms. Rapp," Mr. Boot replied, tapping his chin thoughtfully. "I wonder, though, if there's a spell that will make people look away while you perform magic. Ah yes, the one you have been practicing for the past hour should do nicely."

Crud laughed, but Annika took one more desperate stab at it. "Mr. Boot, I already bought my dress."

"Then I hope it goes well with manual labor," Mr. Boot replied.

When Annika and Crud left, I went up to Mr. Boot's desk, ready to tell him about Tom and the Nigh. But before I could utter a word, he said, "And how is dear Bethesda these days? Still as saucy as ever?"

It took me a second to absorb this.

"You know?" I asked.

"That you were in the Nigh? Oh yes. Word gets around quickly in certain communities."

"Did you know that I was pulled into the turtle tank? The one in Room 308?"

"Yes, you were pulled in by an Imp who saw the perfect opportunity. A Wicket right in the turtle tank he just happened to be cleaning. And the Human he is trying to steal is so close by. Imagine that!"

When I play chess, my mind works like lightning. I can see a dozen moves ahead. But for some reason, I had missed this. I hadn't understood until now. I felt that little pa-ping that I always feel when I figure something out. Usually the pa-ping is deeply satisfying, but this time I was simply outraged.

"You knew there was a Wicket in that turtle tank!" I said.

"I did," replied Mr. Boot.

"And you wanted Tom to pull me in. You wanted him to try to steal me!"

"He was bound to steal you at some point or other; that much was clear. Do you know what an Imp is, Ms. Batista?"

"Not really, no."

"They're creatures who are neither dead nor alive. They live in an in-between place, alone, hungry for the company of other children. Your *Peter Pan* story? That comes remarkably close to the truth, except that Imps are far more cruel than Peter Pan. We wanted the Imp to steal you, Ms. Batista, because we knew that he would, and this way we could keep an eye on things. Do you really think he would have let go of you in that water if there hadn't been some magical intervention?"

"I almost drowned!"

"And yet you didn't."

"What if he comes back?" I asked.

"It's possible, but not likely. Imps have very short attention spans. He's probably moved on to some other mischief by now." He picked up his briefcase. "You escaped from the clutches of an Imp. Not many do. Count yourself lucky, and let's leave it at that."

"But why did you let him stay in the club all this time if you knew he was an Imp?"

"I said, *let's leave it at that*, Ms. Batista." Mr. Boot headed for the door.

I remembered then that Tom said he knew a secret about Mr. Boot. Maybe that was why Mr. Boot hadn't simply tossed him out of the club right from the start. And though it was clear that Imps were not to be trusted, and were certainly big fat liars, maybe sometimes they also told the truth.

"Mr. Boot," I said.

His hand was on the doorknob, but he stopped and turned around.

"Yes?"

"Do you know where my brother is? Tell me the truth. I'm sure you know he's missing, since you seem to know everything about all of us."

I waited, my heart thumping in my chest, as Mr. Boot took his time to answer.

"Not everything, Ms. Batista. I have no idea where your brother is." His eyes met mine, and I saw a flash of genuine compassion in his face. "I'm sorry."

35

COSTUMES

The goddesses were plotting their vengeance. It was obvious from the way they huddled together at their table during lunch the next day, laughing too loudly, their precisely lined eyes—flicked up at the corners so that they all looked like gorgeous Halloween cats—flashing at me every few minutes. Leilani's jaw was shuttling slowly back and forth. Her "tell." Revenge was in the works. They were going to discipline me somehow, and goddesses' punishment is always diabolical, isn't it? They chain people to mountains. Turn them into monsters. I'm sure Annika and her pals had something hideous in store for me.

The one bright spot that day was finding out that Ruth was also going to the school dance that night.

"Really?" I said. "That doesn't seem like you."

"Oh, I love school dances," she said, not at all ironically. "What are you wearing?"

"I don't know. This, I guess," indicating my T-shirt and jeans. I had no intention of getting dressed up for this thing. I could already imagine the snide comments from the goddesses if I showed up in something swanky.

"Wow. Okay, yeah. Rebel move, kid." She nodded in approval.

That's when it occurred to me that not dressing up was going to make me stand out even more.

When I got home that afternoon, I went straight to my closet, which was just a shallow recess in my wall with a bedsheet strung across it. I didn't have any clothes that would be remotely considered dressy. Still, maybe I could cobble something decent together. I swiped the hangers along the rack, one by one. Jackets that no longer fit, jeans, jeans, and more jeans. A few okay-ish shirts. Other than that, I had exactly two other outfits squashed against the wall at the end of the rack: one was the werewolf costume, and the other was a dress. Bright blue, scoop-necked. I'd forgotten I even had it.

My mother had mailed the dress to me when I turned eight. It was the first birthday present that she had sent me since she'd left. I remember seeing the long, flat box wrapped in pink-and-purple striped paper and being so excited. I opened it very slowly and carefully, like opening a long-searched-for hidden treasure. The blue dress was inside, wrapped in white tissue paper. I took it out and held it up. It was way too big. More for an adult than a child. I sobbed. I mean really bawled, in that hysterical, breath-gasping sort of way. Not because the dress was too big, but because I was such a stranger to my mother that she couldn't even fathom what I looked like now.

I remember Dad sat me in his lap and wrapped his arms around me until I calmed down.

"She loves you, Nell. She does," he insisted. "She was just never mother material."

Mother material. What was "mother material"? I had wondered. Was it that soft stuff they make drugstore socks out of? If my mother was made of any material, it was lace—nice to look at but totally useless.

When I tried the dress on now, though, it fit. I looked in the full-length mirror behind the door. The hemline was just above my knees. The armholes were a little big, but they'd work. It looked nice, I guessed, but I felt like I was wearing a costume.

It's either this costume or the werewolf costume, I told myself.

There was a knock on my door, and then my father came in, his face registering shock when he saw me.

"Excuse me, ma'am, but have you seen my daughter?" he asked.

"It's for the school dance." I was at least happy to be able to tell him I was doing something normal-ish, even if I was working at the dance, not dancing. "And if you say something embarrassing, Dad, I'm going to put on my werewolf costume instead."

"Okay then. You look awful."

"I guess I'll just have to wow people with my sparkling personality."

"No, seriously, Nell, you look beautiful."

"That's good, because I don't actually have a lot of sparkle."

There was a pause in which my dad seemed to be considering something.

"What is it?" I asked.

"No, nothing. Nothing. It can wait." He started to leave.

"Come on, Dad, what?"

After a moment of hesitation, he said, "Detective Chatterjee stopped by."

I felt my heart lurch. There were only two reasons she would have come here. To deliver good news or to deliver bad news. And it probably wasn't good news.

"A witness came forward," he said.

"Now? Three years later?"

"A young man from Spain. He had been a tourist and was in the park, playing chess, on the day River disappeared. He flew back to Spain the next day and had no idea anything had happened to River until recently. He said he was reading about a kidnapping in Madrid, when he noticed a related article, clicked on it, and saw River's photo. After he read the article, he called the police. He remembered you. He mentioned your silver backpack. And he remembered River."

The blood in my veins seemed to become tidal, surging through my body, rushing to my head.

"What did he see?"

Dad paused. "He saw River walk off with a man in the park. He said the man looked homeless. He had white hair and he wore a suit jacket."

"Chicken Bone Charlie."

Dad nodded. "The man identified him when Detective Chatterjee sent him some photos."

I felt a rough tangle of emotions—anger at Detective Chatterjee for not listening to me, and the tiniest bit of hope. Stupid hope, maybe, but hope anyway, because as crazy as Chicken Bone Charlie was, at least we knew him. He wasn't a faceless creeper. Would he have hurt River? Would he have killed him? I didn't know. He had never laid a hand on us kids before. But that didn't mean anything. He was nuts. He threatened kids with a chicken bone. But was he capable of a lot worse? I'm sure Dad was thinking the same thing.

"Did they arrest him?" I asked.

Dad shook his head. "They haven't found him yet. But they will." He scrutinized my face and frowned. "Remember, Nell," he warned, "it's nothing until it's something."

Detective Chatterjee's favorite saying.

I nodded.

But still I knew. This time it was something.

36

SCHOOL DANCE

The school cafeteria was filled with magicians. Well, they were chaperones and teachers dressed like magicians—or their version of it anyway—with witch's hats and turbans and fake long white beards. A few of them were hanging silver paper stars and moons from the ceiling. Ms. Dannigan, the gym teacher, was filling a cauldron with punch, while Mr. Oberbeck, my science teacher, was setting up a projection light in the corner.

"Okay. What am I looking at?" I heard a voice say behind me.

I turned to see Crud, his arms folded against his barrel chest as he surveyed the room.

"Magic," I told him, then added, "Well, magic according to the school dance committee."

Crud snorted. He was dressed pretty spiffily, for Crud. Black jeans and a black dress shirt that might have possibly been ironed. He'd even managed to tame his hair, which was glazed with gel.

"You bring your chopsticks?" he asked.

I patted my silver handbag. The bag had been Mom's,

hanging in Dad's closet with some of her other clothes. In fact, it had been the perfect chopstick concealer—long and thin, like an eyeglass case.

"What about you?" I asked Crud.

He was smuggling his in his socks.

Mr. Oberbeck had finished with the projector, and suddenly the cafeteria was bathed in a deep purple light with tiny stars speckling the ceiling and walls, rotating slowly.

The door swung open, and Annika walked in. She was dressed all in gold, with a lacy gold dress, a narrow gold beaded belt, gold sandals, and a gold clutch. It was a look that deserved a full-on entrance—music stops, dancers stare, murmur, murmur, murmur. Instead, she had to make do with just Crud and me staring at her. I don't think she cared, though. She gazed around the cafeteria, looking fairly dazzled as the projected stars glided across her face. That's the thing with school dances—either you buy into the whole dreamy fantasy, or you spend the entire evening rolling your eyeballs. Annika was obviously all in. She didn't even react when Ms. Dannigan came over with a carton of cheap plastic magic wands and instructed us to put them out in the baskets around the room.

"What are people supposed to do with them?" Crud asked her.

"They're for fun. You know . . ." Ms. Dannigan picked one up and swished it around. "Abracadabra."

"The kids are just going to whack each other on the head with it," Crud told her.

He was right, but Ms. Dannigan clearly thought he wasn't giving them enough credit, because she took a wand and waved it over him, saying, "Abracadabra, you will have more faith in your fellow humans."

"I wish it were that simple," I said.

"So true." Ms. Dannigan nodded at me as though I were very wise.

Of course I was talking about magic while she was talking about human nature, but never mind.

Annika, Crud, and I spent the next hour filling bowls marked MAGIC BEANS with jelly beans, setting out baked goods and paper plates and boxes of pizza, and placing dry ice around the cauldron full of "Magic Potion," aka fruit punch. We also set up a table for the fortune-teller—who was Mrs. Blum, the seventh-grade social studies teacher— and a cardboard backdrop for the photo booth. It had a picture of a castle with lavender turrets—more Playmobil than Hogwarts.

By the time we were done, I was embarrassed on magic's behalf.

At go-time, six o'clock, tinkly music was piped through the speakers as the purple light projector swirled stars. Crud, Annika, and I were stationed behind the snack tables, plastic gloves on our hands, looking like overdressed cafeteria ladies. I was handling the punch bowl while Crud and Annika were in charge of pizza and chicken wings and balls of Rice Krispies Treats covered in purple candy stars.

The doors opened to a crowd of kids, all decked out

in their finest. They gazed around the cafeteria, ooing and whoa-ing. They were genuinely astounded. I have to admit, that part was satisfying. Not as satisfying as actual magic, but nice anyway.

The tinkly music stopped abruptly and was replaced by loud dance music. In a flash the dance floor was filled with kids, mostly girls. Annika's goddess friends glided over to us and swept Annika out on the dance floor, where they gyrated around one another like a sequined amoeba.

"And then there were two," I said.

Crud shrugged, picked up a piece of pizza, and shoved half of it into his mouth.

It was going to be a long night.

My knee-jerk thought was I wish Tom were here, but as quickly as I thought it, I knew it was ridiculous. Tom was a weasel and a liar and who knew what else. A murderer probably.

"Isn't that your friend?" Crud asked.

For a nanosecond, I thought he was talking about Tom, and I froze. But then Crud nodded toward the dance floor. Ruth was out there, wearing a satiny maroon 1950s-style dress. That was surprising enough. But also, that girl could dance! Her spine was as supple as spaghetti. She didn't care that no one was dancing with her either. She just tore it up out there.

"She's bonkers," Crud said.

I opened my mouth to defend her, but Crud was look-ing at her with admiration.

"Good dancer," I added, and Crud nodded.

To complete the whole cheesy magic theme, there was a magician in a black cape and top hat who walked around the cafeteria, pulling silk scarves out of people's ears and doing card tricks. It was so hokey that the kids sidestepped him whenever they saw him headed their way.

For the first half hour or so, the snack tables were not very popular. People were too busy dancing, or else they were standing in the corners, making fun of the dancers. It gave me a chance to look around and spy on my schoolmates. There weren't many people from the Leftovers Table—just me and Ruth and Luke, the ultimate tic-tac-toe guy.

My eyes snagged on the goddesses who appeared to be holding some sort of conference on the dance floor. Then, in unison, they all turned to look at me, and when they saw me staring back, they swiveled their heads away. Oh yeah. I was top priority on their hate agenda. The goddesses were working on something special for me.

Ruth, sweaty and pink-faced, had spotted me. She strutted over to the snack tables with a big smile on her face. "Hey, kid! You're missing all the fun. I'll take over if you want to go dance."

"Thanks, but I'm safer over here." I nodded toward the goddesses.

"Grrr." Ruth bared her teeth at them. Right then a new song came on, and Ruth's face lit up. "Love this song!"

"Go dance." I shooed her away.

"Okay, but I'll be back soon. You." She pointed a finger at Crud. "Keep an eye on this one. Don't let anyone mess with her."

"Okay," Crud agreed. I couldn't tell if he was taking her seriously, but she seemed convinced.

"Good man," she said, nodding approvingly at him before heading back to the dance floor.

"She's cool," Crud said, watching her as she left. There was a pause during which he looked at me guardedly, with side-eyes.

"She shames the freaking stars," I replied.

37

THE GODDESSES' REVENGE

The snack tables were getting busier now. I ladled up cup after cup of punch while Crud slapped pizza slices on plates. Hardly anyone really notices the people serving them, which was just fine with me. Only a few people bothered to look up and see who was handing them their food.

"Prison duty?" asked Luke, the ultimate tic-tac-toe guy.

"Basically," I told him.

A few of Crud's friends heckled him, but otherwise we were mercifully ignored.

I looked around for the goddesses, just to keep tabs on them. Annika and her pals were over at the fortune-teller's booth. Annika was sitting across from Madam Destiny, aka Mrs. Blum, who wore a green turban and, weirdly, what looked like an old Halloween pirate costume—a white buccaneer shirt cinched with a red cloth strap over striped breeches. The goddesses were smirking as Madam Destiny shuffled her tarot cards, but Annika was watching attentively.

"If Boot saw her slacking off like this, he'd turn her into a snail," grumbled Crud.

I shrugged. "It's better this way. If she were working with us, all her idiot friends would be hanging around here too."

Crud nodded thoughtfully. "So why do they all hate you so much anyway?"

"Because they think I got Tom expelled," I told him.

Crud shook his head. "Nah, he was headed for trouble without your help."

"Really? Why do say that?" I was cautious. And curious.

"There was just something off about that kid," Crud said. "I felt it from the beginning."

After a pause, I admitted, "Well, you have good instincts."

"Yeah? What do you know about him?"

Then I told him the whole story. I told him about the Nigh and about Tom being an Imp and Mrs. Wiffle's Waffles. All of it. Every so often I was interrupted by someone who wanted drinks or pizza, which Crud thrust at them impatiently before turning back to me to hear more.

When I was done, Crud was silent. Finally, he asked, "Did you tell Boot?"

"I didn't have to. Boot knew all about the Nigh. He knew about Tom, too."

"Then why didn't he kick him out of the club? Send him back to the Nigh?"

"Because Tom knew something about Boot that he wasn't supposed to know."

Crud crossed his massive arms and shook his head.

"I don't trust Boot. And those little creatures he keeps in his briefcase? That's just wrong, man."

"The skrill told me that there used to be lots of Nibbins, but Smugglers steal them and bring them here. Maybe Mr. Boot's creatures were smuggled out of the Nigh."

"*Excuse* me. Is there any pizza with mushroom?" The goddesses had arrived. They were done with having their fortunes told and were now crowded around the snack tables, practically asphyxiating us in a perfumed fog of jasmine and vanilla.

"Just what you see," Crud told the goddess gruffly.

Leilani was eyeing me in a spooky way while Annika sauntered behind the snack tables and stood next to me.

"Do you know what the fortune-teller told me?" Annika said in my ear.

"You mean Mrs. Blum, the social studies teacher?"

"She said," Annika ignored me, "I'm going to have an unforgettable night."

"That's a little vague," I said.

"And do you know why it's going to be unforgettable?" Annika raised one eyebrow.

"Because Crud and I are going to do all your work for you?"

"Because you are going to get what's coming to you."

There was a sharp popping noise, and I turned in time to see a small glass bottle shatter in the air in front of Leilani, the pieces tinkling to the ground and clear liquid pooling out. Leilani looked shocked, and the goddesses behind her were glancing around the room shiftily. Only Crud seemed composed as he bent down to readjust his sock.

Oh. Right.

The chopsticks were in his sock.

I was pretty sure he had just performed some kind of magic that made the bottle break. Probably the Sprakken-Boorst Spell.

"She was about to pour booze into the punch bowl," Crud said, nodding his blunt chin toward Leilani.

"Really?" I glared at Leilani, whose face was set in defiant indifference at having been caught. "Good thing the bottle broke. Because otherwise"—I turned to Annika—"people might have gotten the idea that it was *me* who had spiked the punch."

Annika's sour expression was as good as a confession.

"You're stooping really low, Annika," I said quietly, "and there's stuff you don't know about Tom, which I can tell you if you'd just—"

"No thanks," Annika said, holding up her hand to my face. She turned and stalked away, leading a trail of goddesses over to the photo booth.

"They're like a herd of wildebeests with lip gloss," said Crud.

"Hey." I turned to him. "Thanks for that." I nodded toward the smashed bottle.

Crud shrugged. "I promised your friend I wouldn't let anyone mess with you."

"I'll let her know that you kept your promise," I told him.

"Now?" he asked.

"Oh? You want me to tell her now?" I realized that Crud might have a little crush on Ruth.

"Whenever." He shrugged.

"I have to find a broom anyway to clean up the glass, so I'll just tell her now," I said casually, so as not to embarrass him.

"Don't mention the magic," he warned.

"Don't worry," I said. "I have no desire to have a disco ball fall on my head."

I skirted around the dark edges of the cafeteria, trying to go unnoticed while looking for both a broom and Ruth.

"Excuse me," I asked Mrs. Blum, who was checking her phone between fortune-telling duties. "Where can I find a broom?"

"I don't know," she said as she swiped her screen. "Broom closet, maybe?"

"Where is that?" I asked.

"Somewhere over there, maybe?" She gestured to a corner of the room.

Her directions were as vague as her fortunes, but I followed them anyway. That awkward feeling of wearing a costume returned as I sidled my way past dancers.

"Hey, kid!" It was Ruth, who had seen me and danced over. "You finally decided to dance?"

I shook my head. "Looking for the broom closet," I shouted over the music.

"It's next to the kitchen," she shouted back.

"Thanks. And oh, Crud? He actually did what you asked him to do—not to let anyone mess with me. Leilani was going to pour alcohol into the punch, and he . . . He swatted the bottle out of her hands just in time."

"Did he? Kid's a solid gent." She nodded approvingly.

I'd tell Crud she said that. He'd be pleased.

I had just finished sweeping up the broken glass by the snack table when Julia Weeks walked into the cafeteria. A really popular song was playing, and I wondered if Julia had been lurking outside the cafeteria door, timing her entrance for when most of the kids would be on the dance floor. She slunk in, head down, and hastily found a wall to lean against near a garbage can. She definitely did not look like she wanted to be here. She wore a pale yellow three-tiered dress that looked like it had been salvaged from a bridesmaid's closet, and her hair was curled and poufed.

I glanced over at the goddesses, who were, as usual, in the center of the dance floor. They were all too busy gyrating to notice Julia. All except Annika. She had spotted her and was clocking her now. I put my hand on my bag and felt the reassuring shape of the chopsticks inside. If Annika tried something, I'd be ready.

"Good song," Crud said, his head keeping time to the beat.

"Go ahead." I nodded toward the dance floor. "I've got this under control."

"Nah." He shoved his hands into his pockets.

"By the way, Ruth said you were, quote, a solid gent."

"Yeah?"

"Yeah. Seriously, go."

After a pause, during which he ran a hand through his hair, he headed for the dance floor. I watched as he awkwardly shouldered his way through the dancing crowd until he reached Ruth and began dancing in her vicinity, not too close but near enough for her to notice him. When she saw him, Ruth smiled, leaned back, and pointed two fingers at him. That was that. They looked so happy, dancing together, and my reptilian brain thought wistfully of Tom again. But I put a stop to that quickly, and instead I watched the annoying magician bother people around the lunchroom.

The guy was doing card tricks for kids who didn't care and were trying to ignore him. I watched with some amusement as he pestered the goddesses, who looked mortified that he had joined their dance group. He pulled a ring out of Leilani's ear and pretended to swallow it, and then it wound up on his finger. The goddesses turned their backs to him. It was a little sad, actually. I hoped he was getting paid well at least.

I looked over at Julia. She hadn't moved from her place beside the garbage can. Impulsively, I ladled up a cup of punch and headed over to her. My good deed for the day, and I didn't even have to take out my chopsticks to do it.

"Punch?" I said to Julia, holding out the cup. She looked at it suspiciously. "I would never have come to this stupid dance," I continued, my hand with the cup of punch still outstretched toward her, "but I was forced to."

Julia's face softened a little. "My mother made me go."

"I have to work the snack tables," I said, nodding toward them. Annika was lurking around the baked goods at the far end, probably trying to escape from the magician's attention.

"You sure you don't want some punch?" I said.

She took it now but didn't drink from it. I stood there with her. I don't know, it just seemed like the right thing to do, so that she wasn't so totally alone. Anyway, Annika could make herself useful and watch the snack tables for a little while.

After a moment Julia said, "Your friend who got in trouble? The boy with the blond hair? He got kicked out of school, right?"

I nodded. I guessed she wanted a little gossip about it straight from the person who had gotten him expelled. I hadn't expected that from her, and it disappointed me a little, frankly.

"Then he's probably not supposed to be at the dance, right?" Julia said.

"What?"

"I saw him when I came in," she said. "He was standing outside the cafeteria."

I felt a sickening pinch in my gut and a wave of dizziness.

"Are you sure it was him?"

"Pretty sure."

I forced myself to breathe. *Think, think.* I had my chopsticks with me. I could try the Fetzen-Zetzen Spell if he tried to do anything. I hadn't mastered it, but if I got lucky, I'd be able to disable him for a few minutes.

"Don't worry," Julia said, touching my arm tentatively, misinterpreting my concern. "I think he's being careful not to get caught. When he saw me coming, he took off down the hallway."

"Oh, good, good," I said distractedly. "Okay, well, I should probably get back to work."

Julia nodded. She looked sad to see me go, but I needed to think.

There were so many people on the dance floor now that I couldn't skirt around the edges, but had to wade through the dancers to get back to the snack table.

I was halfway across the room when something flew right over my head. It looked like a sponge except it was too aerodynamic. I followed its progress suspiciously, watching it soar over the dancers, then angle down in a precise arc to hit Julia Weeks right on the head. I saw Julia's hand dart to her hair, where the object had lodged itself. I squinted at the thing. It looked like . . . Yes, it definitely was a Rice Krispies Treat ball—I could see the purple stars all over it. Julia looked around and seemed to spot the person who had thrown it. She stared across the room for a moment. I followed her gaze to see who she was staring at, but there were too many people dancing in front of me.

Now Julia was struggling to remove the sticky thing from her hair, pulling out strands as she did and wincing in pain. It just steamed me! And I had a pretty good idea who had thrown the thing at her.

I pushed my way through the dancers toward the snack table, where I had seen Annika lurking just moments before. I was going to full-on throttle the girl!

Ruth spotted me. She waved, a big smile on her face, and then danced her way over with Crud right behind her.

"Dance with us!" she shouted above the music. Crud was smiling—a rare sight.

"Can't right now!" I shouted back, and kept on weaving between the dancers.

But by the time I reached the table, Annika was gone, lost in the crowd again. The roving magician, however, was there. I groaned. He was definitely not someone I wanted to deal with now. Tall and skinny with a long, bony face, his ridiculous top hat squashed down a mass of curly red hair that spilled out beneath it. His eyebrows were black, and it looked like he was wearing eyeliner.

I tried to walk past him, but he stepped in front of me and pulled out a deck of cards from his jacket pocket. Right away he began to fancy-shuffle them, holding them high, bending them back, and letting them fall through the air into his hand below.

"Excuse me," I said, starting to sidestep him.

But he put up a hand in a *wait* gesture. He fanned the cards and held them out for me, then nodded his chin toward me, which I knew meant *pick one*. I sighed.

"Fine," I said, and I plucked out a card and held it up for him to see. It wasn't what you were supposed to do, and I knew it. You were supposed to look at your card and put it back in the deck, and he'd reshuffle, then magically pull the exact same card out again. *Ta-da!* He would have been laughed right out of Washington Square Park for doing such a cornball magic act.

He shook his head and gestured for me to look at the card instead.

I sighed and flipped the card around.

There was a message printed on it in big block letters:

CORNER OF BLEECKER AND MERCER STREET THURSDAY 7:37 AM

"What is—" I started, but the magician put a finger to his lips. He swept his other hand behind my ear, pulled something out, and placed it in my hand. I looked down at it. It was a large bronze coin with a hexagon cut out of the center. Around the rim, embossed above a crosshatched background, were the words, "Good for One Ride."

The magician closed my fingers around the coin. He smiled, his eyes widening as he did, as though we shared a secret, and then he disappeared into the crowd.

38

RIVER'S ANNIKA

I found Annika slumped on a stool near the castle back-drop, her head in her hands.

"Why?" I demanded when I reached her.

"Stop shouting." Annika lifted her head from her hands, wincing as she did.

"Why are you so mean?"

"What are you talking about?" She seemed genuinely perplexed.

"Julia! Julia Weeks! Do you know how much courage it must have taken for her to even come to this stupid dance? And what do you do? Throw food at her? Humiliate her?"

Annika didn't reply. She dropped her head down to her hands again and pointed at something behind me. I turned and caught a glimpse of Julia Weeks, still standing by the garbage can. But now Omar, the kid from Ethiopia, was standing with her, both of them talking and smiling.

Annika said something, but with her head buried in her hands, it came out muffled.

"What?" I asked.

She looked up, her face cinched in pain, and repeated,

"I hit her with the Rice Krispies ball so I could do the Farborgan Maneuver." She opened her gold clutch, and showed me the chopsticks and a pair of X-ray glasses.

"But why?" I asked.

"To see what she was thinking about. Why else?" she snapped at me.

"What was she thinking about?" I asked.

Annika looked at me as though she could not believe how thick I was.

"She was thinking about Omar."

A new song was playing, one that had been popular last year but now was a bit of a joke. Most of the kids had drifted off the dance floor, but Julia and Omar were dancing to it—awkwardly, but whatever. They looked happy as they stiffly dance-swayed, Omar listening attentively to something Julia was saying.

"I told Omar that she liked him, and he went over to talk to her," Annika said.

"That was . . . nice," I said, surprised at Annika. "Who needs a Nibbin, right?" I smiled at her, but she just winced and groaned in response.

"Are you okay?" I asked her.

"Boot wasn't kidding about those layers of zoophenloft. Julia didn't have much padding in her brain. I don't think it was as bad as what Crud felt with that little kid, but still, my head's killing me."

I had never understood why River liked Annika so much. I used to think that he just felt bad for her. But maybe he had seen this other side of her when I hadn't. The side of her that was kind, even when it cost her something.

"That video of Julia," I said. "Why did you do it?"

"I didn't."

"It was on your phone," I said. "Filmed from your apartment."

"Did you ever see the video?" Annika asked.

"No. I heard plenty about it, though."

Annika reached into her little gold clutch bag and pulled out her phone.

"No thanks," I said quickly. "Not interested."

But Annika ignored me as she scrolled through her phone, still wincing in pain. She stopped at something, then handed the phone to me.

"Just watch."

I sighed and looked down at Annika's phone, where a video was playing. There was Julia in her bedroom. The video was definitely filmed from the building next door—you could see other windows in Julia's building too. Julia was doing all those stupid things people do in private—dancing around her room, checking her reflection in her mirror, then stuffing socks into her bra and rechecking.

But then I noticed something. The video also captured the apartment below Julia's, where a man walked across his living room and opened his apartment door. A tall red-headed woman entered the apartment, and in about two seconds they were kissing.

"That's your mom," I said.

"Yeah."

"And I'm guessing that's not your stepfather."

"No, it's not," Annika said wearily, taking back the phone. "She's going to mess things up like she always does. I took the video to stop her. I was going to threaten to show it to my stepdad if she didn't break things off. But then Leilani saw me looking at the video, and she snatched the phone out of my hands. She's never met my mom—I keep my friends away from my mother because, well, you know what she's like. . . ."

I did.

"Leilani noticed Julia Weeks in the video, and before I could stop her, she'd sent the video to a bunch of my friends. And then they sent it to a bunch of their friends. You know the rest."

"I'm sorry, Annika," I said. "You need better friends."

"Yeah."

I wondered if I should tell her about Tom now, since she seemed more likely to listen, but she buried her head in her hands again and groaned.

"Do you want me to get you some punch?" I offered. "No one's spiked it lately."

Annika responded with a snort that threw her into another paroxysm of pain.

"Okay, hold on," I told her, and I started for the snack tables.

What happened next occurred so quickly that for a few seconds after, I questioned what I had seen.

The lunchroom door had swung open, and Mr. Boot stalked in, carrying his briefcase. His long legs were moving faster than I had ever seen them move, and his face was gripped with angry determination. He walked straight to the back of the lunchroom, where the magician had just pulled a fake dove out from under his handkerchief for a group of snickering boys.

Suddenly I felt a tremendous urge to look away from the magician. It was as irresistible as the need to sleep after exhaustion or to drink when you're parched. When I looked back, the magician wasn't there anymore. I caught a glimpse of a pair of small hind legs and a snowy white tail being swiftly tucked into Mr. Boot's jacket pocket. Then Mr. Boot exited the lunchroom just as briskly as he'd entered it.

"What just happened?" Crud approached me, looking just as confused as I felt.

I took a moment to gather my wits and sort out what I'd just seen. "Mr. Boot just did the Notsen-Glotsen Hex." I looked around. Everybody seemed a little dazed. Mr. Boot had performed it on everyone at the dance; I was sure of it.

"Why?"

"Because I think Mr. Boot found the missing ferret," I explained. "He was wearing a top hat and pulling coins out of people's ears."

The dance lasted only a half hour more. The music stopped abruptly, almost rudely, and the lights went up.

Some of the kids looked a little embarrassed, like they had been caught doing something they shouldn't.

Annika had already left—she'd told Ms. Dannigan that she had a migraine—so Crud and I cleaned up without her. When I told Crud what Julia had said about seeing Tom in the hallway, Crud insisted on walking me home. I didn't refuse. To be honest, I had been worrying about that walk home the whole time. I considered calling my dad to come get me, but having Crud with me was better. At least he knew why I kept obsessively looking behind me.

On the way we traded theories about the ferret/ magician while keeping a sharp eye out for any sign of Tom. I carried a handful of swag that Ms. Dannigan had given me before I left. It was the kind of stuff I knew Nyxie would like—magic wands and felt wizard hats.

"Do you think Julia was wrong about seeing Tom?" Crud asked when we reached my building without any sign of him.

"Maybe. I don't think she knew him all that well. It could have been some other kid who looked like him."

"Give me your phone." Crud held out his hand.

I gave it to him, and he typed something in, then handed it back. I looked down at my screen. It was his phone number. His contact name was Carmen.

"Text me if something happens," he said. "I don't live too far from here."

"Thanks . . . Carmen?"

"Crud's fine."

In my room I opened the toy chest to put the magic swag away for Nyxie. And that's when I saw it. The stuffed owl. George. I hadn't put it there. And when I asked Dad, he said he hadn't either.

That night I went through the apartment and checked the latch on every window, then made sure all three locks on our door were fastened and the chain was on. And even then, I slept with the lights on.

39

ᗷODEGA ᑕAT

After a tough night of bad dreams, I woke up with a racing heart and a raw throat, squinting at the sunlight that was too bright for 6:30 a.m. I thought I must have slept through my alarm until I remembered that there was no school today—it was one of those in-service days for teachers.

The first thing I did was check River's bed to see if anything had changed there since the night before. It was a creepy thought, but if Tom had been sneaking into my room without my dad knowing, he could be doing it while I was asleep, too. But no, it looked the same as it had last night.

Maybe if I lie low, I thought, *and avoid any possibility of seeing Tom, he might lose interest.* Mr. Boot had said that Imps had short attention spans. So I hunkered down and spent the morning in my pajamas, reading. I fully intended to stay in my room the whole day.

Until I heard the screaming.

It wasn't hard to figure out where it was coming from. There were only two apartments above us: Mrs. Farfle's,

who lived by herself, and Nyxie's, whose family was con-
stantly battling with one another. The fights generally
ended with a loud crash of someone or something hitting
the floor. Usually it was Nyxie's teenage siblings I heard
fighting, but now there was a thin, high-pitched shriek in
the mix, which I was sure came from Nyxie.

I am embarrassed to say that I did nothing. I waited, my
book open in my lap, my eyes on the ceiling, hoping the
screaming would stop.

It didn't.

I cursed that whole crappy family, then got dressed and
hurried up the stairs to the fifth floor.

I knocked on Nyxie's apartment door. Loudly. A tall,
skinny girl appeared a moment later. She had an angry pink
face and greasy auburn hair. She looked just like Nyxie,
only stretched out and meaner.

"What do you want?"

"I heard Nyxie scream," I said, meeting her hostile glare
with my own.

The girl leaned against the doorframe and looked me
up and down. "You're the kid who lives downstairs, right?"

One thing I've learned is that when sketchy people ask
you questions, don't answer them. If you do, it just puffs
them up and makes them bolder. It's better to ask them the
questions.

"Why was she screaming like that?" I asked.

"Because she's a brat," the girl said.

There was a sudden yowl from within the apartment.

The girl turned away from me and bellowed back, "GET RID OF THAT THING NOW, NYXIE, OR I WILL TOSS THAT ANIMAL RIGHT OUT THE WINDOW!"

For someone who probably weighed about eighty pounds, she had an impressive pair of lungs. But more than that, I was pretty sure she meant what she said.

I guess Nyxie thought so too, because a second later she appeared at the doorway, her eyes red from crying, clutching something swaddled and squirming in a grubby fleece blanket printed with pink elephants—probably the same bodega cat she'd been playing with by the stairs. I was relieved that she at least had the sense to wrap it up so that it didn't scratch her to shreds.

"Want me to walk you to the bodega, Nyxie?" I said, keeping an eye on her sister in case she decided to make a grab for the cat.

I expected Nyxie to refuse me as she usually did, but she nodded. From inside the blanket, the cat yowled again, and Nyxie hurriedly squeezed past her sister and dashed down the stairs at a furious clip. I followed her lead, also running, since I figured Nyxie knew her sister might just be spiteful enough to chase her down.

Once outside, I gave the street a quick inspection in case Tom was lurking. There was no sign of him, so we headed down the block toward the bodega.

"You okay?"

Nyxie nodded but looked miserable as she clutched her cat to her chest. Poor kid.

"Maybe you can get a hamster or something," I said.

She ignored me, and I guess I didn't blame her. A hamster wasn't much of a pet. And anyway, her sister would probably wind up chucking it out the window sooner or later.

Nyxie stopped short suddenly and stared down the block.

"He's there," she said ominously.

For a heart-fluttering moment, I thought she was talking about Tom. But then I looked down the block to where she was staring. Pacing by the entrance of the bodega, alternately muttering to himself and shouting at passersby, was Chicken Bone Charlie.

He was back.

I reached into my pocket, pulled out my phone, and called Detective Chatterjee's direct line, which she had given to me years ago.

"Nell?" Detective Chatterjee answered right away.

"He's here. I'm looking right at him," I whispered into the phone.

"What?" I heard an unusual burst of excitement in her voice, and I realized she thought I was talking about River.

"Chicken Bone Charlie," I told her. "In front of the bodega by my building."

"Okay, hold on." I heard her call to someone, and then an exchange of muffled voices before she came back on. "Has he seen you, Nell?"

I looked back at him. He was wearing his usual raggedy

suit, but now he was missing his left shoe. Instead he wore what looked to be about a dozen pairs of socks on his foot. He was all worked up, worse than I'd ever seen him. His arms flailed, the chicken bone clutched in his right hand, and his head thrust forward aggressively as he marched back and forth in front of the bodega like a soldier on guard duty.

"I don't think so. He's just freaking out in front of the bodega," I told her.

"Nell, I've already got people on this. Go back home now. Don't approach him."

Nyxie said something to me while Detective Chatterjee was talking.

"I'm dead serious, Nell. Don't say anything to him about River. It will spook him. Just leave now."

"Yeah, got it."

"Do you?"

"Yes."

Nixie pointed at Chicken Bone Charlie.

He was looking right at us.

"He's going to chase us," Nyxie whispered.

"All right," I said to Detective Chatterjee, maneuvering myself in front of Nyxie, "got to go." I hung up even as I heard the detective still talking.

Chicken Bone Charlie lifted his chicken bone in the air, yelled something incomprehensible, and then launched himself down the street, headed right for us. I heard Nyxie squeak in terror.

"Go home, Nyxie!" I told her.

"I can't. My sister will kill her . . . ," Nyxie said, nodding down at her bundle.

"I'll bring her back to the bodega." I scooped the bundle from her arms. "Go on. Go home."

Nyxie just tucked herself behind me, but she wouldn't leave. I don't know if it was me or the cat that she was worried about.

I turned back to Chicken Bone Charlie. He was approaching fast, even with his one shoeless foot. His chicken bone was raised in the air, and his eyes looked wild. His lips were pulled back so that his teeth—the few he had left—were bared. I stood my ground. The plan in my head was to keep my eyes on him as long as I could until Detective Chatterjee's officers arrived. Of course, there was a real possibility that he would just barrel right into me since he was coming closer and closer without slowing down at all.

I widened my stance to steady myself, and when he was practically right in my face, he stopped short. His body tilted to the side, favoring the foot that had a shoe on it. He smelled awful, no joke, and he held that chicken bone like a knife, poised to strike, but I stood my ground. He glanced around me at Nyxie, who was cowering behind me. When I moved to block his view, his eyes darted back up to meet mine. Worn brown eyes, like the edges of Mr. Boot's briefcase. The fury in his face abruptly disappeared. He took a deep, rattly breath and tucked the chicken bone into his jacket's breast pocket, tapping it down with one filthy finger.

"She's too nosy," he said, nodding toward Nyxie. "Tell her to stay away from the bodega."

It took all my self-control not to grab him and shake him until he told me what he knew about River. But there was always the chance that he would run, and I needed to keep him here. I needed him to stay put as long as possible until Detective Chatterjee's officers showed up.

"Why don't you want her near the bodega?" I asked him, my voice shaky with rage.

At that moment the cat began to squirm frantically in my arms. Maybe she could smell the bodega and was anxious to get back home, where she no doubt enjoyed the perks of dropped deli meat and the occasional mouse. I adjusted my arms to contain her, but she found an opening in the blanket and out she leapt, her long blue-gray body arcing in the air. I lunged for her—the last thing I wanted was for her to dart out into traffic in a panic and get hit by a car right in front of Nyxie—but she was too fast for me. She sprinted down the street, limping badly, with her billowy tail held high. She turned to look back at us, and I caught a glimpse of her squashed puglike face with its large ears.

That was no cat.

It was a skrill.

40

NOOKS AND CRANNIES

The shock of seeing a skrill on Bleecker Street had only sidetracked me for a moment, but it was enough. In a flash Chicken Bone Charlie bolted. He charged across the street, slipping between traffic and pedestrians. I ran after him, trying to keep him in my line of sight. On Mercer Street, though, a UPS man with a dolly cart full of boxes crossed my path, making me swerve around him and then nearly collide with a guy whose nose was in his phone. After a moment of doing that awkward side-shuffling dance with the guy to avoid walking into each other, I returned to the chase, but Chicken Bone Charlie had vanished.

I looked up and down the street for any sign of a man with paper-white hair and a suit jacket, but he was well and truly gone.

Nyxie, however, had stuck with me like glue.

"That animal . . . Where did you find it?" I demanded. My voice was harsher than I intended, and Nyxie frowned, hurt.

"In the bodega," Nyxie said. "Hiding behind the money machine. Her leg was hurt."

"She's not a cat," I said.

"I know."

"Didn't anyone in your family notice she wasn't a cat?" I asked incredulously.

"They just thought she was ugly."

For once I was glad that Nyxie's family were such a bunch of dummies. But how did a skrill wind up *here*? The animal didn't look like she was in the best shape. Maybe she wandered through a Wicket by accident and couldn't find her way out again.

I looked at Nyxie. She wasn't crying or anything, but she was watching me with wide, nervous eyes, her small body very still.

"It's okay, Nyxie. You took good care of her. She'll be okay."

After I sent her home, I walked around the block and then several blocks more in every direction. There was no sign of Chicken Bone Charlie. New York City can do that. If you want to hide, it can tuck you in its nooks and crannies, stuff you in its pockets or under its hat, and hide you so well that no one will ever find you. Not even the police.

Still, there was one person who might be able to find him. And right now, he was likely sitting in Washington Square Park.

For the second time in less than a week, I broke my father's rule and entered the park. This time, at least, I had a good reason. At the chess tables, Kingsley was sitting opposite a blond guy in a yellow puffer jacket, both of them moving their pieces at a furious clip, slapping the clock, like it was a mosquito that wouldn't stop annoying them. Even at a distance I could see that his opponent was good. He was making Kingsley work; I could tell by the way Kingsley's left hand was tapping out a nervous beat on his knee.

I approached them, and without looking up from the board, Kingsley said, "Go to school, Nell."

"I have off today," I told him.

Kingsley raked his eyes over me skeptically, which I ignored.

"I need to ask you something," I said.

The blond man took Kingsley's knight with his pawn.

The moves and the slapping grew more furious now. I saw what was coming. It would take just five more moves. *Slap, slap, slap, slap, slap.* Checkmate. The man in the puffer jacket looked disappointed but not surprised. When you play chess hustlers, you sort of expect to be beaten.

"What are you doing here, Nell?" Kingsley asked as he set up pieces for the next player.

"Where does Chicken Bone Charlie hang out?"

"The bodega."

"But when he's not at the bodega? Where does he go?"

Kingsley looked at me hard. "Why are you asking?"

"I . . . I have a problem that I need to take care of."

"A problem, huh? You have a problem?" He reached

into his jacket pocket and pulled out a fistful of change. "Hold out your hands."

I held out my hands, and he poured the change into them.

"What's this for?" I asked.

"Here's what you do. You take that money and you go to the dollar store on Ninth Street. You know the one I'm talking about?"

I nodded.

"And you buy a mirror. A little hand mirror. Understand?"

"Okay."

"And then you hold up that mirror and look at yourself."

"Kingsley—"

"Look good and hard. Because the biggest problem you have right now . . . is you." Kingsley tipped his head to one side, and his eyes bored into mine. "What are you doing in the park, Nell? You know you're not supposed to come in here anymore. And don't think I didn't spot you with that boy, up on top of the arch. That's right." He made a V with his fingers and pointed at his eyes. "I'm always watching."

I put his change on the table. "Just forget it." I turned and started to walk away, seriously annoyed with Kingsley, partly because he was right.

"Try the Herron Theater on Great Jones Street," Kingsley called after me.

I turned. "What?"

"Go around the side of the building to the box office."

I smiled. "Thanks, Kingsley."

"And I mean it about the mirror!" he called as I walked away.

41

CHICKEN BONE CHARLIE

The Herron Theater was on the bottom floor of a stocky townhouse, its crumbling bricks painted lavender. One window was plastered with black-and-white photos of actors and a handwritten sign that said BOX OFFICE AROUND THE CORNER. I walked around the side of the theater and saw a short staircase leading down to a door marked BOX OFFICE. Sitting on the ground at the bottom of the staircase, beside a table full of playbills, was Chicken Bone Charlie. He was cradling the skrill in his arms, his head bent low as he whispered to the creature.

I started to back up slowly as I felt in my pocket for my phone to call Detective Chatterjee, but at that moment Chicken Bone Charlie looked up. Our eyes met. He looked calm now. He watched me guardedly while he stroked the skrill's head.

If he saw me reaching for my phone now, or if I walked off to call Detective Chatterjee in private, there was a good chance that he'd run again. I couldn't risk that. I inched closer to him, and when he didn't move,

I started down the short flight of steps.

The smell in the entryway was outrageously disgusting—a powerful blend of body odor and old urine—but I forced myself to sit down on the bottom step.

Where's River? I wanted to blurt out the question, but I controlled myself, squeezing my hands into fists so tight, my knuckles ached.

Don't scare him, I told myself.

"Where did you find her?" I asked, nodding toward the skrill.

After a pause he answered, "She finds me."

"I think she's hurt. She was limping."

He didn't respond, but I saw his hand move to her hind legs and feel them.

"Are you hungry? I could get you a sandwich or something."

He shook his head, then muttered something to the skrill as he stroked her spine.

"My name's Nell." When there was no response, I added, "I live near the bodega."

"I know," he said.

"You've seen me around?"

He nodded.

"Then you also must remember my brother, River."

Chicken Bone Charlie winced at the mention of River's name, and he stopped petting the skrill.

"River went missing three years ago," I said.

Chicken Bone Charlie leaned his head against the

lavender brick wall and closed his eyes, as though he were suddenly exhausted. The skrill shifted in his lap so that she could clock me. She was wilder-looking than Tiller had been, her fur smashed down in mats, her eyes cagey.

"You know what happened to him, don't you?" I said. Detective Chatterjee would be furious at me right now, but I didn't care. The end to three years of hoping and waiting and wondering was right here, right in front of me.

But Chicken Bone Charlie didn't answer. He didn't even open his eyes.

"You took him," I said, my voice growing shakier. Any control I had over my emotions was quickly melting away. "I know you took him. What happened to him? Tell me!"

I saw his throat click with a hard swallow, and his fingers began to tap at his forehead, hard, as though he were trying to smash his way into his brain.

Okay, Nell, calm down, I told myself. *Calm down, or he won't tell you anything.*

I took a breath and looked at him more carefully. His hair was very fine and so white. Not old-man white, but the sort of platinum hair you see on young children. It suddenly occurred to me that he had a name, an actual name, and none of us ever knew it.

"What's your name?" I asked him.

His fingers stopped tapping, and he opened his eyes. Up close, I could see that his face was deeply creased, and his skin was splotchy, but his features were delicate. The worn-out brown eyes met mine. I'd never seen him smile before, but now he did, a small, sad smile as he said, "My name is Mary Carpenter."

42

MARY CARPENTER

My mind struggled to absorb all of it. Was Chicken Bone Charlie a woman? And could she be the same Mary Carpenter that Bethesda had mentioned to the Magicians? Was this the woman Tiller had said was a legend?

"Have you . . . Have you ever been to the Nigh?" I asked. She was silent for a moment.

"They took me there when I was six," she said. The crazy didn't exactly leave her eyes, but something had changed, as though a high fever had broken.

"Who took you?" I asked.

"A Poacher. It's always a Poacher. The Minister sends them here to take the children."

The Minister. The Magicians had mentioned the Minister to Bethesda—as a threat.

"Did a Poacher take River?" I asked quietly.

Mary returned my gaze, though her eyes seemed to be seeing something far away. Her head moved a little.

"Is that a yes, Mary?" I asked.

The sound of her name made her blink. She nodded.

Okay, okay, I thought, *remember who you're talking to. This person chases kids with a chicken bone.*

And then, as though she knew what I was thinking, she said, "I keep the children away. When the Poachers come looking for new ones to take, I chase the children away so they won't get caught." The skrill hopped off her lap and warily crept up to me, checking me out. "I knew there was a Poacher watching him."

"Watching River?"

Mary nodded. "He'd been watching him for months."

"Was the Poacher in Washington Square Park that day, the day he was taken?" I asked.

"He was watching you play chess."

I thought back to that day. I tried to picture the people in the crowd, standing by the chess tables. I knew they were there, but I'd been so immersed in the game I barely noticed them. And River had said someone was giving him the creeps.

"I tried to protect him. But the Poacher was fast." She shook her head. "I tried, but they wanted him, him especially . . ." Mary's eyes dampened, and the skrill jumped back into her lap and settled her head on Mary's leg.

"Why?" I asked.

"Human thoughts make things grow." Her hand began tapping at her forehead.

"I don't understand."

"They take the children with the powerful minds. The ones with the best imaginations. They take them and they use them up and they throw them away."

"Use them how?"

"The children build their cities."

She kept tapping her forehead, harder and harder.

"Mary." I reached out and stopped her hand. Her eyes met mine. They were twitchy with fear and memories and something else that I couldn't pinpoint. "Is River alive?"

I felt a trembling deep in my gut as I waited to hear the answer to the question that had tormented Dad and me for so long.

Mary lowered her head and put a shushing finger to her lips. Then she nodded.

I felt such a staggering sense of relief that I couldn't speak for a moment. "Is he in the Nigh?" I asked.

She nodded again, smiling. A whole bunch of her teeth were missing on the left side of her mouth. "I hid him."

"Where?" I asked.

She stopped smiling. Her eyes took on a faraway cast, and then her brow furrowed.

"It's not in my head," she said.

"What isn't?"

"Information. It's not safe to keep information in my head." She tapped her forehead again. "They take things from my head."

"Mary, I need to find him."

"I feel very uncomfortable right now," she said to me, squirming with such agitation that the skrill jumped out of her arms.

"River needs to come home," I urged. "Where did you hide him?"

"I'm very uncomfortable," she repeated, her voice edging toward panic. She stood up and began to pat her jacket pockets, as though she were looking for a wallet, and then she pulled out the chicken bone.

"Go away," she said, holding up the bone like a knife.

I looked at the skrill crouched on the ground. The animal returned my stare. It didn't have gentle eyes like Tiller. Her eyes were sharp and feral. I wondered . . .

I knelt down beside it. "Do you know where River is?" I asked the creature.

I waited for the answer to appear in my mind, the way Tiller had communicated with me.

Nothing happened.

I felt a sharp stab in my neck and turned just as Mary was about to jab me with the chicken bone again. The papery skin on her face crumpled, as though an invisible hand had reached out and wadded it up. I knew that expression. Wild rage. I had seen it on her face so many times when I was a child and she chased us with the chicken bone. But she had never touched any of us. Until now. She bared her teeth, the chicken bone raised in her hand, poised to strike again. I jumped to my feet and walked backward up the stairs, my hands held in front of me.

"Mary, please—" I tried once more, but she cut me off with a rough-throated animal howl of fury and lunged at me.

I ran. It was like I was seven again and Chicken Bone Charlie was chasing River, Annika, and me down the street, our legs pumping and our hearts pounding until we reached the safety of our home.

In the morning I shoveled down a chocolate-chip muffin before putting on my jacket and hitching my backpack on one shoulder. I glanced at my dad, still asleep on the couch, wrapped in a quilt. I fought the urge to kiss him goodbye. Nope. No. No drama. I needed a steady mind.

"See you later," I whispered. Just like I always did.

Outside my building I was surprised to find Crud, leaning against a tree, waiting for me.

"What are you doing here?" I asked. I didn't mean to sound rude, but I had plans this morning, and Crud was not part of them.

"I figured I'd walk you to school," he muttered, obviously insulted. "You know, in case Tom . . ."

He left that hanging.

I quickly glanced up and down the street, but Crud added, "No sign of him yet."

I nodded. "Thanks, Crud, but you don't have to escort me. I don't think Tom will try anything with lots of people around in broad daylight."

"Okay. Well. Since we're going in the same direction anyhow, I'll walk with you."

This kid was in serious bodyguard mode.

I sighed, debating how much I should tell him.

"Listen, Crud, I'm not going to school today."

"Yeah? Where you going?"

He knew so much already that I went ahead and told him everything else. I told him about Chicken Bone Charlie who was really Mary Carpenter. I told him what Mary had said about River.

Crud put his meaty hands to his head and then flicked them away. Mind blown. "So you think River is in the Nigh?"

I nodded.

"And that's where you're going now?" he asked.

I hesitated, then admitted, "That's the plan."

Crud considered this. "Okay."

"Okay what?"

"Okay, I'm in," Crud said.

"You're in?"

"I'm going with you."

"Um, no. Crud, you are a hundred-percent not going with me."

I'll be honest with you. I a hundred-percent wanted Crud to come with me. I'm not a brave person, and the Nigh was no joke. But I'm not a total jerk, either. I wouldn't let a friend accompany me to a place that I knew was dangerous. Even if that friend was built like a linebacker.

Crud slipped his hand into an inner pocket of his jacket and pulled something out. He held it in his fist for a moment, looking around cautiously, and then opened his hand to show me what it was.

It was one of Mr. Boot's vials. Inside was what looked like a small golden seahorse with a human face, which was watching us through the glass with sharp, clever eyes.

"Is that an Inkling?" I asked, astonished.

Crud nodded.

"Are you kidding me?! Where did you get that?" I whispered.

"Swiped it from Boot's suitcase when he was putting a Whirdle on your shoes. I didn't know what to do with it until you told me about the Nigh. I'm taking this little guy back there. I wish I could take Boot's whole briefcase with me too, but at least I'll get this one home again."

I held out my hand. "Give it to me. I'll take it. It's stupid for both of us to go."

"Nope." He tucked the vial back in his jacket pocket.

"Don't you trust me?" I asked.

"I do, but I'm going anyway."

"Why?"

"I'm curious."

And here's the part where I did act like a total jerk. I didn't argue with him. I told myself that the chances of getting River back were better if we went together. Power in numbers, right? And maybe that was true, but the bottom line was that having Crud with me made me feel less scared.

"Okay," I said. "Let's go."

43

ᴛʜᴇ ʙᴏᴅᴇɢᴀ

The bodega was packed with people waiting for break-fast sandwiches or lottery cards or both. Marisol, the owner, was behind the boothlike checkout counter, framed by plastic containers of Blow Pops and beef jerky. Ribbons of scratch-off cards were on the wall behind her, and over-head, hanging like stalactites from the top of the booth, were packages of pantyhose and rat poison and a dozen other items that made no sense together.

"Hey, big boy!" Marisol pointed at Crud. "Leave the backpack with me."

I guess there had been some shoplifting recently, and Crud had a tendency to look like a thug, so you couldn't really blame her for being suspicious. I left my backpack with her too, just so Crud wouldn't feel bad.

"Are you sure the Wicket's here?" Crud asked as we squeezed through the aisles of food.

"Not *sure* sure. But pretty sure."

I had worked it out in my mind. Chicken Bone Char-lie, or really Mary Carpenter, had always hung out by the bodega. And it was here that she chased kids away with her chicken bone. If she was protecting kids from Poachers, that meant there was most likely a Wicket nearby.

I examined the refrigerated section, opening doors and peering behind cans of soda and cartons of milk. I wasn't exactly sure what I was looking for. In my limited experience with Wickets, they were well hidden. Other than that, they had nothing much in common—a turtle tank, a waffle cart, a museum diorama. But still, there had been something about the diorama and the waffle cart that had flagged my attention and held it for a few seconds longer than they should have.

I moved on to the boxes of pasta, and after that to the shelves of breakfast cereal. A movement on the lower shelf caught my attention, and I quickly crouched down, only to find that it was a small black bodega cat lurking behind some boxes of Pop-Tarts.

I lingered at the ice cream freezer and the ATM.

Nothing was flagging me.

I considered that I might be missing something. And the other problem was that I had no idea when the Wicket would open. Not exactly, anyway. I was simply operating on a guess—Nyxie had been chased away from the bodega in the morning. I checked my watch. 7:37.

7:37. Why did that sound familiar?

Then I remembered. That magician at the dance. Or really, the ferret/magician. The card that I had picked from his deck had said CORNER OF BLEECKER AND MERCER STREET THURSDAY 7:37 AM.

The bodega was on the corner of Bleecker and Mercer Streets.

And today was Thursday.

"Come on!" I said, and I rushed out of the bodega with Crud behind me.

The moment we stepped outside, a yellow cab careened around the corner and came to an abrupt stop in front of the bodega. On the passenger-side front door were the words ANYWHERE TAXI. There was something about the cab—besides the weird name and the fact that it looked vintage with its big hood and a fat rounded back end—which made it stand out in a street teeming with cars and people.

It flagged me.

I grabbed Crud's jacket sleeve. "Let's go!"

We ran to the taxi, yanked open the door, and flung ourselves onto the black vinyl seats.

The driver turned around and looked at us. He was an older man with thick silvery hair that reached his shoulders. He wore a yellow cap with a shiny black rim and the words ANYWHERE TAXI on the front.

"Token," he said flatly, and held out his hand.

I hesitated, not sure what he meant. "We're going to the Nigh," I told him.

"You're not going anywhere without a token, sister." He shut off the ignition. Without turning around, he reached one hand back toward us and wiggled his blunt fingers.

A token, a token? How had I gone through the Wicket

last time? Well, in the turtle tank I was forced through it, and with Mrs. Wiffle's Waffles . . . I remembered Mrs. Wiffle had said that I had to spit. She'd said that was my token.

I looked at the cabdriver's outstretched hand, winced briefly, then spit.

"You nasty little punk!" The cabdriver whipped his head around and glared at me before wiping his hand on his wool jacket.

"Sheesh, Nell," Crud muttered.

"No, it's just the last time, I had to spit. . . ."

"No token, no ride," the cabdriver said. "I'll give you"—he checked his watch—"fifty-seven seconds."

Crud reached into his back pocket and pulled out his bus pass. "How about this?" He held it up for the cabdriver to see.

The cabdriver eyeballed the pass in his rearview mirror, snorted, and then looked back at his watch. "Forty-two seconds."

I racked my brain for something that might serve as a token.

Suddenly I had an idea. It seemed like a long shot, but it was all I could think of. I fished around in my jacket's pockets, first the large pockets on the side, then the smaller chest pockets.

"What are you doing?" Crud asked.

"Hang on, I'm sure I put it here somewhere. . . ." I found it in the little inside zippered pocket. It was the bronze coin that the ferret/magician had given me. I had kept it, although I had no idea what it was for.

"How about this?" I shoved the coin at the cabdriver. To my astonishment, he took it and plunked it into a slot on top of the meter.

Crud and I looked at each other in disbelief. That was the token. We were on our way to the Nigh.

"Nell!" Crud gripped my wrist suddenly. "We left our backpacks in the bodega. My chopsticks are in mine."

"Mine too!" I couldn't believe I'd forgotten that! The Nigh was full of danger, and not having our chopsticks was going to make it that much more dangerous.

"Can you wait just a second?" I pled with the cabdriver. "We have to get something in the bodega."

"Too late," he said, and he turned on the ignition.

So that was that. We'd just have to make do without our chopsticks. This trip wasn't starting off too well, and I doubted things were going to get any easier.

"You'd better buckle up," I told Crud resignedly, fumbling for my own seat belt. "In my experience, Wickets are not smooth rides."

Crud reached for his buckle, but before he could fasten it, the cabdriver turned off the ignition.

"But we gave you the token," I objected.

"Yeah, so what's your point?" the cabdriver asked as he opened his door.

"My point is, we gave you the token, which means you're supposed to take us to the Nigh."

As a response, the cabdriver got out of the taxi and slammed his door shut.

Crud and I looked at each other. "Well, that was a waste of time," Crud said.

But the next second the door on the passenger side was opened by the cabdriver, and he said, "Out."

"But we haven't gone anywhere," I said.

"Nell, look." Crud nodded toward the open door. I leaned forward to see past Crud. Outside the passenger-side door it was completely black, as though the door had opened straight into the night sky. Yet the windshield in front of us and the window on the driver's side still showed us the same view of Bleecker Street.

The cabdriver leaned down and poked his head in the cab. "Well? You getting out or what?"

Crud shifted over on the vinyl seat, then stepped out, and I followed. Once my eyes had adjusted, I could see it wasn't quite as pitch black as I'd thought. I could make out shadowy, lumpy mounds on the ground all around us. A few yards off was a vast stretch of water on which the moon had laid down a pale stripe of jagged light. In the distance I saw the outline of a ship—a full-rigged sailing ship—anchored offshore and listing slightly in the wind. The night air had a chill to it, and I was grateful that I had finally given in and worn my jacket that morning.

"Where are we?" I asked the cabdriver.

"Hudson Barrows," he replied as he walked back to the driver's side door.

"Wait!" I had just remembered something. "Will the Wicket always open up in this spot again?"

"It will until it won't," he replied offhandedly. Then as he stepped back into the taxi, he and the taxi vanished on the spot, as though the night had swallowed them whole.

44

HUDSON BARROWS

O kay, this is weird," Crud said behind me.

"It is, but you'll get used to it," I said, staring at the spot where the cab had vanished.

"No, not the cabdriver," Crud said. "This."

I turned, and in the darkness I could see him twisting his hand through the chilly air. Filaments of light trailed from his fingertips.

"No chopsticks or anything," Crud said. "The magic is just . . ." He whipped his hands one way and then the other, watching the light show it produced. "It's just there. It's in the air. It's like this whole place is an Oomphalos."

I had noticed the strange electric quality in the air last time I was in the Nigh and had even been able to produce a decent Oifen Shoifen Spell on the Devotion Tree's doll without my chopsticks. So maybe not having our chopsticks with us wouldn't be a total calamity.

Maybe.

Somewhere, punctuating the night, was the far-off sound of music and laughter, rising above the tidal splash of the water. There were buildings across the street—tumbledown tenements. Apart from some winking lights in the distance, the city was dark.

Crud turned to me and stuck his hands in his coat pockets. "Okay, boss, what's the plan?"

"The plan is to find River," I told him.

"Yeah, I got that. But how?"

When Kingsley first taught me to play chess, he didn't show me specific moves. That came later. Instead he taught me how to think.

Go in with a plan. When you don't know what move to make, just keep your blood cold and your mind open. Don't panic. Look for the logic.

I had a plan. I wasn't sure where it would lead me, but it was the next logical move.

"We need to talk to a statue," I said. "Bethesda. She helped me before. She's in Central Park, which should be—" I turned to face what I suspected was the north end of the city.

That's when I saw the boy. He was only a few yards away from us, sitting on a pile of rocks. A wiry kid, maybe six or seven at most, with a head that looked too big for his body topped with an aviator cap. But even with that big head, he still radiated the Folk beauty. It was as though the moonlight clung to his skin and hair. He stood up, and as he walked toward us, he reached inside his coat—a tattered old thing that looked like it was sewn from roadkill—and pulled out a wooden club.

"Okay, here we go . . . ," Crud muttered, straightening

his spine. I braced myself for some kind of fight. But the boy smiled—it was a nice smile—and he held out the club toward us. It was then that I realized that it wasn't a club at all.

"It's bread," I told Crud.

Crud made a move to take it, but I waved it off. "No, we're good," I said to him.

"I knew you would come," the boy said.

"You did?"

"Of course. If you wait by the barrows on Winterfest night, you'll catch a ghost," he replied simply. "Okay, now you have to eat the bread."

I looked over at the loaf. It was coarse-looking. Definitely something that someone had baked themselves. Crud reached for it again, but I grabbed his sleeve and stopped him.

"Not a good idea," I whispered.

"Why? I'm hungry."

"Something I heard one time. A fairy story where if you eat their food, you won't be able to go home again." Had I read that, or was it something River had made up for one of his stories? I couldn't remember. In any case, it was probably a good idea not to eat stuff here.

"He's not a fairy," Crud objected.

"No, but . . ." I turned to the kid. "Why do we have to eat it?" I asked him.

"To bring you back to life," the boy answered, frowning as though this were obvious and he was wondering how we couldn't know it.

Crud and I looked at each other, confused. Then I remembered what Tiller had told me about Folk not being able to see humans very well.

"Because we're ghosts," I said to the boy. "Right?"

The boy nodded.

Crud looked at me questioningly. "Later," I whispered. "It's okay, we like being ghosts. You eat the bread," I told the boy. The kid looked like he needed the bread more than we did. Frankly, he looked like he could use a few trips around a sundae bar, too. "What's your name?"

"Jack."

"Hi, Jack. I'm Nell. That's Crud."

"Which are your barrows?" Jack asked.

I hesitated for a moment, but Crud said, "Over there," and pointed vaguely to the stones farther down along the riverbank.

Our barrows. Right. He meant our graves.

"Jack!"

I turned to see a girl striding up to us. Too skinny, a wild shock of brown hair partly covered by a mangy fur hat.

"I've been looking all over for you, you idiot!" the girl said as she walked, her arms bent like an old-timey gunslinger. "What were you doing?"

"I've caught some ghosts, Tammany! Two of them!"

The girl—Tammany—squinted at us in that half-light, trying to make us out. When she saw us, her eyes widened, and I heard her pull in a sharp breath. She had a tough-looking mug, with a rounded jaw and a flat face, but despite that, she had the Folk glow about her.

"They're not ghosts," Tammany said to Jack quietly, her eyes still on us.

"Of course they are. Look at them," Jack insisted, but Tammany ignored him. She moved in close to us.

"Where's the Poacher?" she whispered to us, glancing all around.

"What?" Crud said.

"The Poacher who took you. Where are they?"

"No one took us," I answered, remembering what Mary Carpenter had said about humans being poached and taken to the Nigh. "We came on our own."

"So you're Peepers." A tone of disgust had entered her voice. "Well, if I were you, I'd go back to the Hither before someone does poach you."

The singing in the street had been growing louder. Now I could see figures approaching, silhouettes of strange hats with horns and feathers. They seemed to be holding lanterns, the lights of which darted all around them like fireflies.

"But they're mine!" Jack countered. He grabbed my hand and then Crud's, and he tugged at us to go with him.

The parade of Folk was just across the street, singing loudly, swinging lanterns around themselves to form liquid hoops. Frankly, I suspected they were drunk.

It didn't take much urging from Jack's small hand. Crud and I ran alongside the little Folk boy, his sister tailing us, lecturing him even as we ran. "You can't take them home!

Mams will smack your bottom for this! You will be crying your eyes out for days!"

But it didn't stop him. He charged ahead, running along the strip of land beside the water, dodging the stone piles. He was surprisingly fast, so that Crud and I really had to burn rubber in order to keep pace.

The streets across the way were lined with what looked like a shantytown—tumbledown shacks tilting on their foundations. Some of them were so busted up that it seemed impossible that anyone actually lived in them, yet there were puffs of smoke trailing out of chimney pipes.

Our mad dash caught the attention of two Folk sitting on chairs outside a shack.

"You'd better run, you filthy Water Creepers!" one of them called out, which I assumed was directed at Tammany and Jack, since Crud and I would have been hard to see from across the street. The man leapt up and made an aggressive lurch toward us, which caused us to run faster. The man didn't follow us, but still we kept on running until Jack and Tammany veered off toward the water and stopped beside a tree, its slender branches bending low and concealing a little boat. Or a rough approximation of a boat anyway. It was patched together with mismatched planks of wood, and it definitely did not look like something that would float. Yet Tammany was now dragging it toward the water, and Jack was ordering us to get in.

"It's too small for all of us," Crud said nervously.

"Don't get in, then," said Tammany flippantly as she continued to drag the boat.

"Get in, get in!" urged Jack.

"It's better than being poached," I said to Crud, and stepped inside the boat.

"Is it? Is it really?" Crud asked. But he got in anyway.

45

PIDDLEBANK

The river was choppy close to shore, and the boat—which was literally one step above a homemade go-kart without wheels—wobbled around so badly that I was sure we were all going to wind up in the water. Beside me I could hear Crud's panicky cursing under his breath.

Tammany rowed with quick, skillful strokes, and within a few minutes the river grew calmer. The water was black, with only fitful rays of moonlight touching it when the clouds moved off. *This must be the Hudson River,* I thought. In my New York, the Hudson was always illuminated by ribbons of lights reflected from the high-rises of the city and, opposite, New Jersey. But there were no lights here. I don't know how Tammany was able to see where she was going, but she worked the oars calmly, making the boat glide through the water with ease, her incandescent skin cut sharply against the sky.

"Where are we going?" I asked her.

"Home. Mams will know what to do about you."

That had an ominous sound to it. I had considered asking her about River, but now my gut told me to keep my mouth shut. I glanced over at Crud to see if it had alerted him, too, but he was preoccupied with his own terror of being in the boat. I could feel his bulky body next to me, cringing every time the boat tipped a little.

"Don't tell Mams about them," Jack complained. "She'll take them away from me."

"You'll be lucky if that's all she does. Probably we'll both be punished for the rest of our lives for sneaking out."

This made Jack cry, until Crud took a break from his own terror to reassure Jack that no one gets punished for the rest of their life, to which Tammany replied, "You haven't met Mams."

With Tammany at the oars, we made steady but slow progress. The city receded behind us, and we were out in open waters. This Hudson River smelled a whole lot better than our Hudson River. I leaned over to dip my hand in the cold water. Immediately, something large and eerily human-shaped broke through the surface and leapt high in the air, twisting, then diving back in the river again. I yelped and nearly tipped the boat over as I lurched backward.

"What was that thing?!" I asked.

"Finfolk," Tammany said offhandedly. "Keep your hands out of the water."

"Are they dangerous?" I asked.

"It depends."

"On what."

"Different things."

This kid was exasperating.

I spotted something up ahead poking up out of the river. It was tall and lumpy, yet the shape of it was familiar. I stared at it for a while, trying to figure out what I was looking at.

Crud had been staring at it too. "What is that thing?" he asked.

"It's the Statue of Liberty, of course," said Jack.

Now that he said it, I could see that it was. But also it wasn't. For one thing, it wasn't tall enough. Plus, it wasn't a lady; it was an old man. Instead of the spiky crown, the man had a head full of disheveled hair. And instead of that heavily draped toga, he wore something that resembled a hospital gown. His hand was raised in the air, like the original statue, but he wasn't holding a torch. I squinted up at it.

"It looks like he's holding—"

"A television remote control." Crud finished my sentence.

I nodded and whispered to Crud, "That's how it is here. The same but different."

"Hard to get used to," Crud said.

After a while I could make out the craggy rise of land up ahead. Large rocks lined the shore, and behind them was a wilderness of trees and undulating hills that stretched back into the night.

"What is that?" I pointed at the land.

"Brooklyn," Tammany answered.

"Brooklyn? Nah," Crud said in disbelief. "Maybe Brooklyn three hundred years ago."

Tammany turned to glare at him. "It's Brooklyn," she said firmly. "I think I'd know."

She sailed the boat into a small cove, which tapered into a narrow canal. Tammany expertly guided the boat through the canal, which snaked between the woods that grew on either side. Apart from the sound of water rippling around the oars, the wild woods were silent. Spanning the canal were roughly cobbled wooden bridges, and bobbing near the banks were other little boats, most looking about as seaworthy as Tammany's, moored to large stones set in the ground. Farther up the canal, flanking the banks, were thatch-roof cottages, their windows adorned with painted shutters and flower boxes. The place seemed like something out of a fairy tale, and for the first time since we arrived in the Nigh, I felt the tension in my muscles begin to unravel.

"This is Piddlebank. We live by the second bridge." Jack had turned around to tell us, then stared at Crud and me with wide eyes. "Oh! You look different now!"

Tammany gave us a cursory glance. "Their bodies are coming in," she said.

"Excuse me, what are our bodies doing?" Crud asked.

Tammany nodded her chin up and down at us as she rowed. "You're getting more solid. That's what happens to Humans who are in the Nigh for a while."

Jack was clearly disappointed. "They aren't ghosts."

"I told you that already," his sister said. "Now listen, you two," she said to us. "When we get back to the house, Jack and I are going to sneak into our bedroom window. Wait a few minutes, and then knock on the door. You can tell my mams that you came through a Wicket and now you're lost. But don't say a word about us being in the city. You never met us, got it?"

"Tammany!" Jack whispered in warning, then pointed to the bridge up ahead where a wide shadowy figure was leaning over the low railing.

Tammany turned to look, then muttered something under her breath. She changed the oars' rotation, stalling the boat's forward motion for a moment, then moving it back in the direction we'd come from. She was attempting a retreat.

"Don't you dare, Tammany Nerriberry!" the woman on the bridge yelled.

"That's Mams," Jack said darkly.

"Yeah, we figured," Crud said.

Tammany sighed loudly. She stopped her retreat and began to row toward the bridge again, glum-faced.

I looked up at Tammany's mother. The clouds had drifted across the moon, so all I could make out was a bulky silhouette with a wild halo of hair, like her daughter's.

"Are you two mad?" Mrs. Nerriberry hollered. "Your father was frantic. Frantic! What were you thinking, running around in the middle of the night like this? And on Winterfest when Folk are blasted out of their minds with

Nectar Tonic? A big girl like you, Tammany—"

"We wanted to see the costumes, Mams," Jack said.

"There were plenty of costumes right here in the village," their mother said. "And sweets. And Mrs. Frecklepelt was giving out honey rizzles—Jack . . . *Jack?* What do you keep looking at?" She had noticed Jack was barely paying attention to her. Instead he kept glancing back at us. I waved a frantic no-no finger at him. We didn't need any more attention from Folk, especially an angry one. But at that moment the clouds decided to move away from the moon. The darkness lifted. Jack's mother leaned over the bridge and squinted at us. I guess we were still a little ghostly because it took her a moment to make us out. When she did, she clapped her hand over her mouth.

"Tammany Nerriberry, what have you done?" she cried.

"It wasn't me. It was Jack," cried Tammany. "He found them by the barrows—"

"I thought they was ghosts," Jack piped in.

"Shht!" their mother told them, glancing around, then turning back to us. I could see her more clearly now. Dressed in a long bulky coat, she had a tumble of unbrushed hair and a flat face with a heavy chin. "You'd better just come home with us for now."

"Should we?" Crud whispered to me.

Mrs. Nerriberry miraculously heard this. "Should you?! Well, you can wander around in the dark if you like, dodging Night Mumblers, but I wouldn't advise it."

"What are Night Mumblers?" Crud asked.

I didn't know, but I didn't like the sound of it. It made me think about the horrible Sewer Mahamba.

"I think we should," I said.

Tammany's home was a quaint stone cottage, hunkering low along the banks of the canal. Inside, it was kind of a mess, to be honest. In one corner of the house, a patch of grass had grown up through the dirt floor, and a creeping vine clung to a corner of the wall and snaked all the way up to the ceiling. Here and there were shallow divots in the floor in which puddles of water had collected, and no one had bothered to clean them out. At least the cottage was warm—a fire was burning in the fireplace. There were sudden mysterious movements in the house, quick darts and flitters, which I caught with my peripheral vision. Yet when I looked around, it was just us. Well, except for a portly man lounging in an armchair with a book splayed out across his knees. Tammany and Jack's dad, I assumed. He didn't look very frantic. In fact, I was pretty sure he was sound asleep.

"Sit." Mrs. Nerriberry nodded toward a thick slab of a wooden table, around which were a half dozen chairs. We all sat, Tammany and Jack too, and waited while Mrs. Nerriberry ferried plates of food back and forth from the kitchen pantry to the table—small iced cakes, and something that looked like a jelly roll, and more of that rustic bread, and a bowl of small yellow fruit the size and shape of an almond. And then finally four steaming cups of something that smelled like hot chocolate.

I looked at Crud eyeballing all that food, and I mouthed "Don't" to him.

Tammany dug in to one of the iced cakes right away. I guess all that rowing had made her ravenous. They had lousy table manners, by the way. Tammany shoved the whole cake into her mouth, leaving half of it on her face, while Jack slurped up his drink, spit it back into his mug because it was too hot, and then slurped it again.

Beside me Crud shifted in his chair as he watched them gobble all that delicious-looking stuff.

"Don't even think about it," I hissed at him.

But when Jack then stuck his finger in a jelly roll and popped it into his mouth, Crud said, "I don't care if it makes me turn into a goat or something." Before I could stop him, he reached over, grabbed one of those cakes, and took a bite.

"Mmmf!" he said appreciatively with his mouth full of cake.

"Fairy cake," Mrs. Nerriberry said. "Glad you like it."

I poked my finger into Crud's rib, hard. "See! *Fairy cake!* I told you!"

Crud ignored me. He had finished off one piece of cake and had reached for seconds when something dark and slimy-looking scrambled across the table, snatched the cake out of his hands, and then leapt to the ground and jumped onto a puddle of water in the dirt floor.

"Mams!" Jack cried. "The Noxious Vexx is stealing food again!"

Mrs. Nerriberry immediately opened a kitchen cabinet and pulled out a pair of gloves and a ladle with a very long handle. She jammed her hands into the gloves as she marched over to the puddle. Kneeling down, she stuck the ladle into the water. The puddle was deeper than I thought, because she reached in until the water was up to her wrist and felt around.

"Got you!" she cried as she yanked the ladle out of the water, then scooped something out of it with her gloved hand. It was hard to see what it was exactly, since the thing was squirming so violently. She managed to pinch its stubby tail between her fingers and held it up. It looked like a fat see-through slug with legs—you could see a tiny black heart beating beneath its skin, as well as some globular items which I assumed must be other internal organs. It had six short legs and a blunt nose between two gleaming dark eyes. Hanging upside down, it twisted itself around and bit Mrs. Nerriberry's glove with sharp white fangs. That glove must have been pretty thick because Mrs. Nerriberry didn't even flinch. She just casually shook the Noxious Vexx until its teeth dislodged and it hung upside down again.

"You ungrateful little thing!" Mrs. Nerriberry said.

"If they bite you, your fingers turn black and fall off," Jack said.

"Sheesh," I muttered, and watched in horror as Mrs. Nerriberry held the Noxious Vexx perilously close to her face and scolded it.

"I feed you three good meals a day, which is better than you've had in your whole life, so there's no need to steal from the table! If I catch you at it again, out you go, and you'll have to fend for yourself in the canal."

"Why does she keep something like that in the house?" I asked.

"She takes in Fates who are hurt or sick," Jack replied. He reached for the saltshaker on the table and held it out for me to see. What I thought was salt was actually a puff of cotton. And nestled on the cotton were two little creatures.

"They're Nibbins!" I cried.

46

ᴛHE ᴛATES

W hat's wrong with them?" Crud asked, leaning across the table to look at the saltshaker. I saw his hand reach for his jacket pocket protectively, and I remembered he had the Inkling in there.

"The Nibbins?" Mrs. Nerriberry smiled down at them fondly. "Sweet little things. The Noodger had a bad cough, so the Fetcher insisted she come to me for a mustard cordial. Fixed her right up. I'll send them on their way in the morning."

"The Pilliwiggin came in yesterday too." Jack pointed to the corner of the house where a climbing vine crept up the wall. At first I couldn't make out what he was pointing to. But after a moment I caught sight of a small, sleek turquoise creature clinging to one of the delicate leaves.

"Someone found him in their garden, sprawled over a pebble," said Mrs. Nerriberry. "Looked in bad shape, but he did eat some diced earthworms this morning."

"Blech." Jack made a face.

"Well, you're not a Pilliwiggin, are you?" Mrs. Nerriberry said to her son. "Anyway, he seems a little stronger today, but he still won't sing, and if a Pilliwiggin won't sing, there is something the matter with him."

Now I began to look around the house more carefully. That's when I saw them. There were dozens of tiny creatures all around—peeking through the grass that had grown up from the floor, climbing up the table legs, popping their heads out of the puddles in the floor. One was even walking upside down on the ceiling. He looked like a hairless pink rat with a ridge of pineapple-like prickles along his spine. Four short legs gripped the ceiling as he waddled above our heads. I stared up at him nervously.

"He's not going to fall on you, you know," Tammany said snidely.

And then the thing fell.

I shrieked and jumped out of my seat. But the creature hadn't landed on me; it had landed on Crud's shoulder.

I'll tell you what—Crud was full of surprises! He didn't even flinch as the creature righted itself, then ambled down Crud's arm and finally curled up in his lap.

"Well, now, that's a first," said Mrs. Nerriberry. "You must have a way with Auguries."

Crud shrugged. "I don't know. Never met one before." Carefully, with one finger, he touched the creature's prickly back. The prickles flattened against its body, like a cat retracting its claws.

"They don't have Fates in the Hither?" Jack asked.

"You mean Nibbins and things like that? We do sometimes," Crud said. Carefully, so as not to disturb the sleeping

Augury, he reached into his jacket pocket and pulled out Mr. Boot's vial with the Inkling in it. Mrs. Nerriberry gasped at the sight of the little creature imprisoned inside.

"What have you done to the poor thing?" she shrieked, lunging toward the vial and snatching it out of his hands.

"He didn't put it in there," I hurriedly told Mrs. Nerriberry, because Crud seemed in danger of being whacked over the head by her. "Someone else did. Crud was just trying to return it to the Nigh."

"Smugglers," Mrs. Nerriberry said scornfully. "They steal our Fates and bring them to the Hither, then use them as though they were playthings. It's criminal. They aren't toys. They are living things with as much right to their dignity as any of us." She removed the vial's cork stopper and tipped the vial into her hand so the creature could crawl out. The little thing sat in Mrs. Nerriberry's palm for a moment, and then all the hair on its tiny body puffed out, and it drifted weightlessly through the air like a dust mote before landing on a blade of grass in the corner of the house.

"Now, you two"—she turned to Tammany and Jack—"off to bed."

"But what are you going to do about them, Mams?" Tammany nodded toward us.

"Never you mind."

"They can stay in our room," Jack offered.

"I'll sort them out," Mrs. Nerriberry assured them. "Now go. Your father and I will discuss punishment for you. He was beside himself with worry."

I glanced over at Mr. Nerriberry, who was snoring away in his chair.

"I don't see why I can't listen," Tammany objected. "I know everything anyway."

"You know too much, that's true," Mrs. Nerriberry said. "But not everything. Off to bed!"

Mrs. Nerriberry sat down heavily at the table.

"I suppose you should tell me your names."

We did, and she leaned her chin on her fists and examined us for a moment. "You two are a little old to be poached. How did you manage to escape?"

"We weren't poached. We came here on purpose," I told her. "We're looking for my brother. He was poached three years ago."

"Oh, dear." Mrs. Nerriberry pursed her lips together and frowned. "It's an awful business, this poaching. Here in Brooklyn, we keep ourselves apart from it. We stick to old Folk ways. I only saw poached children once, many years ago, at the Great Market Parade. I was a girl myself, not much older than Jack. There were five of them, dressed beautifully and riding on top of dogges, like princesses and princes. The Minister led the parade, and Folk clapped and threw flowers at them. Everyone made such a fuss over those children. I couldn't understand why. I thought they were ugly, even with all their fancy clothes. But then Humans are not very beautiful. Oh, I'm sorry! I do tend to talk before I think."

I guess I should have felt insulted by this. But the thing

is, compared to Folk, humans *are* ugly, even the good-looking humans.

"Still," Mrs. Nerriberry continued, "I did feel sorry for the littlest one. A girl. She was riding on a black dogge, a huge beast. They had her all trussed up, with a gold dress and red silk sashes. But if you looked closely, one of those sashes was tied to the dogge's saddle. They had made sure she couldn't get away. Her eyes were all swollen like she had been crying. Tssst. They take them so young."

"Why do they take them?" Crud asked.

Mrs. Nerriberry tapped her head. Like Mary Carpenter had done. "For their thoughts. That's why they take them young, and only certain ones. The Poachers are always watching for the good ones, the ones with powerful minds. The ones with strong imaginations."

"Why do they need their thoughts?" I asked.

"Greed, why else! Those children's thoughts have built the Nigh into what it is, for better or worse. Worse, in my opinion."

"But how?" I asked.

"It's a skill that Human children possess, and it only works in the Nigh. It's called casting. The children think about something, and poof, there it is! Well, no, not quite poof, not quite that simple. The children need to be gifted to begin with, and then they have handlers—Magicians—who train them to cast. Anyway, my brother Reynold once explained it to me. It is something to do with the way Human children are made and the Nigh's . . . Oh, what do you call that darn thing . . . ? The Om . . . the Oom . . ."

"The Oomphalos?" Crud offered.

"Yes, that's the word."

"I feel it," Crud said fervently. He turned to me. "It's like this whole place is wired for electricity, and we're the plugs."

He waved his fingers in the air, and the luminescent tendrils appeared immediately, dancing between his fingers.

"Well, look at that!" Mrs. Nerriberry exclaimed. "I guess Reynold knew what he was talking about! That certainly looks like magic, doesn't it? Although I don't suppose you could conjure up the Statue of Liberty without some training."

"That statue was made by one of the kids?" Crud asked.

"Oh yes, the statue, the buildings, the whole city, all of it casted by Human children. I don't know exactly when they started poaching children. Several hundred years ago, certainly. Before poaching, Folk just kept the Human children who accidentally wandered in through a Wicket. Peepers, we call them. That happens more than you would think. Folk used the children for small things back then—to make the crops grow well, to make the rain fall. They'd only keep them for a short while, and in the end they'd send the children back home, bearing stories about the Nigh that no one believed. It was the Magicians who realized that Human children—certain Human children in particular— could be more valuable than anyone had imagined. That's when the poaching began. And mind you, Magicians are not Folk." She waved her finger under our noses to stress the point. "They may live here in the Nigh, but they are not one of us, no thank you. You couldn't imagine a more wicked bunch, bent on destroying all the old Folk ways, though there are plenty of Folk who go along with the Magicians, out of ignorance or greed or usually both. And they're led by the worst of them all—"

"The Minister?" I said.

Mrs. Nerriberry's upper lip lifted with disdain. "A bad egg, that one, mean as a meat-ax. I've heard such stories that would turn your hearts to ice—" Mrs. Nerriberry stopped abruptly and shivered her shoulders as if to rid herself of some memory. "Anyway, the very gifted children work for the Minister, building the cities. Others are sold to wealthy Folk, who use them to become wealthier still." Mrs. Nerriberry paused here, looked at me. "The children are only useful for a few years, and rarely past the age of twelve. Then they become . . . used up."

"Where do they keep the kids who've been used up?" Crud asked.

It was a good question. It seemed like the fairy cake had not done anything to his common sense at least.

Mrs. Nerriberry shook her head. "I'm not totally sure, dear."

But there was a slight hesitation in her answer, and I saw her blink, off time.

"But you've heard something," I prodded.

She frowned at us, debating if she should go on. "It was something a skrill told me while I was nursing her back to health—she was half starved, all skin and bones. She told me she had become friends with a Human boy. Skrills seem to like Humans, though it often turns out badly for the skrills. The boy had become very ill. He couldn't speak or move, but he was aware of everything. The skrill said that's what usually happens to these children—their bodies finally give out."

I felt a gut-pinching rise of fear. What if this had happened to River? Mary had said she'd hidden him, but what kind of condition was he in?

"The boy couldn't cast any longer, so the Folk who had bought him left him in the Ramble in Central Park, and . . . well, the child was killed by some creature. The skrill said she'd heard rumors that the Minister was disposing of the children this way."

"A Sewer Mahamba," I said.

I felt nauseous at the memory—disgusted by the idea of a child being tossed away like garbage when they were no longer useful, and in such a horrifying way. Once again the thought that River might have come to a similar end ripped at my heart, and I had to force my mind back to what Mrs. Nerriberry was saying.

"Perhaps that, or some other thing. There are a lot of terrible creatures roaming the Ramble, more and more all the time. They're created by the children themselves, you know. If a thing is real to a child when they lived in the

Hither, they can create it here in the Nigh. Monsters under their beds, creatures in their nightmares . . ." She stopped and looked at me gravely. "Are you sure your brother is here in the Nigh, dear?"

I nodded. "Mary Carpenter told me he was. She said she'd hidden him here."

At the mention of Mary's name, Mrs. Nerriberry's eyes lit up. "Mary Carpenter! You've met Mary Carpenter?"

Mrs. Nerriberry seemed positively starstruck. She peppered me with so many questions about Mary that I couldn't bring myself to tell her the truth—that in our world Mary was living on the street, sleeping on garbage bags, and not exactly sane.

"I really only met her once," I said, which was sort of true.

Mrs. Nerriberry put her hands to her chest. "She's a wonder, Mary Carpenter, a hero in our lifetime. She's helped rescue dozens of Human children, if you believe the stories, which I do, absolutely. The Magicians caught her once, you know. The Minister tortured her, and some say that Mary was never quite the same again after that. But she managed to escape and went on to sneak more children through Wickets and bring them back home to their families. Imagine losing your child and then one day they just appear at your door, safe and sound. Imagine the joy!"

I could imagine the joy. I could imagine it very well. "Then why didn't she bring my brother back home?" I asked, the bitterness creeping into my voice. "Why did she hide him instead?"

Mrs. Nerriberry frowned and shook her head. "I don't know. But Mary Carpenter is as sly as a Garden Squiffin. If she's done a thing, you can believe that there's a good reason for it." She leaned back in her chair, folded her arms across her chest, and scrutinized us through narrowed eyes. "Now. Tell me. Do your parents know that you're here?"

Crud and I exchanged glances. It was something that had been weighing heavily on my mind, and from Crud's expression, his, too. Time seemed to work differently in the Nigh than in the Hither—I had seen that when I'd been here last—but I wasn't sure how. There was a solid chance that I would fail to come home this afternoon. And if that happened, Dad would be beside himself with panic. Honestly, I couldn't stand to even think about it.

"Clearly the answer is no." Mrs. Nerriberry sighed. "All right, here's my advice. Stay here tonight. In the morning I'll check with my brother Reynold for the nearest Wicket back to the Hither. He keeps track of all the new ones that hardly anyone else knows about. That's the most sensible plan, my dears. And when I say 'sensible,' I mean it's the only plan in which you two will not come to a bad end." She looked at me. "Your family has already suffered the loss of one child. Don't make them lose another one."

I could feel Crud's eyes on me, waiting. This would be my call. He had delivered his Inkling. He had completed his mission. He could go home. But I knew he wouldn't.

He would stay with me. He would keep going until we either found River or the poachers found us.

"Okay," I said to Mrs. Nerriberry, nodding. "You're right."

I saw the look of surprise register on Crud's face. He was shocked that I would give up so easily. But I had a plan. I kept my mouth shut about it, though, because I was pretty sure both Mrs. Nerriberry and Crud would have hated it.

Suddenly there was a sharp rap on the door that made us all jump. Even Mr. Nerriberry was roused from his sleep and grumbled, "Who's coming round at this hour?"

"It's been a very strange night indeed, my love," Mrs. Nerriberry said to him, but he had already drifted back to sleep.

47

MRS. MUCKWORT

C rud and I hid in Tammany and Jack's bedroom while Mrs. Nerriberry went to the door.

Tammany and Jack were already asleep. I could hear their measured breathing in the darkness. The sound of it calmed my racing heart.

"Mrs. Muckwort!" said Mrs. Nerriberry, loud enough for us to hear. "Is everything okay?"

"I came here to ask you the same thing," said a woman's baritone voice. "Are the children back home yet?"

"Of course. They had just taken the boat down the canal a bit for a romp. You know how they are. They're all tucked up in bed now."

"Good. Because there is an Imp on the prowl."

My heart sped up again at this, and Crud and I looked at each other in alarm. Tom. Could he have tracked us here?

"An Imp? What would an Imp want with us?" Mrs. Nerriberry asked.

"You never know with those creatures," said Mrs. Muckwort. "And this one was bold. He came right to my door. I thought it was a little one wanting some sweets. He asked if I had seen any Humans tonight. Can you imagine? As if I'd help him find a Human, even if I did know where one was! I'm not a monster! Anyway, I know your children can be a bit . . . adventurous." There was an edge of judgment in her tone, and I guessed that Tammany and Jack had a reputation as local troublemakers. "We wouldn't want them out and about with Imps creeping through the neighborhood."

"Thank you, Mrs. Muckwort," Mrs. Nerriberry replied in a tight voice, offense having apparently been taken. "My children are safe and sound, but I appreciate the warning."

We heard the door shut, and the next moment Mrs. Nerriberry opened the bedroom door and gestured for us to come out of the room.

"If the Imp's in the canal," she said, "he's probably been following you. They rarely come here. Nasty things! The Magicians sometimes recruit them to entice Humans to the Nigh, and they are diabolically good at it."

"If we stay here, he's going to find us for sure," I said.

Mrs. Nerriberry didn't argue. She knew I was right, and maybe she also wasn't too keen on having an Imp come to her house, with her kids in the next room.

She made a hissing sound, and a lumpy creature popped its head up from beneath the book on Mr. Nerriberry's knees. The creature was roughly the size and shape of a piglet, with fold upon fold of thick, gray, dimpled skin. It leapt off Mr. Nerriberry's lap with a plop, its skinfolds quivering, then ambled to the door, its backside waddling.

"She'll take you to my brother Reynold's house," Mrs. Nerriberry said. "It's not far, and Reynold can help you get to a Wicket. Keep to the western banks of the canal. The path is narrower there and harder to see from the road. And walk *quietly*." She was too polite to say Humans were unbelievably clumsy compared to Folk, but I knew that's what she meant.

She gave us both a hug. It was just a quick hug, but it made me a little weepy. I hadn't been hugged by a mom-type person in a long time.

We followed the creature out into the night, trailing its waddling hindquarters as it led us back down to the canal. But when it turned up the path along the bank, I caught Crud by his arm.

"Hey. This is where we part ways," I told him.

"What do you mean?"

"You did what you came to do, Crud. You brought the Inkling back to the Nigh. Go home now."

"And what about you?"

"I'll leave when I find River."

"But you have no idea where he is," Crud countered.

"I know he's not back home." The creature turned to look at us and grunted impatiently. "Go on."

I turned my back to him and walked away. To be honest, I kept expecting to hear Crud's footsteps behind me, hurrying to catch up. I knew he should go home. It was the right thing to do. But a part of me was hoping he'd insist on staying anyway. I turned to glance back down the canal and saw Crud's shadowy bulk lumbering after the creature. I felt a rush of resentfulness, then mentally slapped myself on the wrist.

Don't be such a selfish beast! I told myself. *He came this far with you. He didn't have to. You're fine, Nell. You can do this.*

I found Tammany's moored boat, which looked even lousier than all the other lousy-looking boats in the canal. The boat was listing even though the water was calm. Still, I told myself, Tammany had managed to keep it afloat, so it couldn't be totally unseaworthy.

I started untying the mooring, struggling with the complicated knot. That was a bad sign. I mean, untying the mooring should be the easy part. I felt bad about stealing Tammany's boat, but I intended to leave it where she could find it again. That is, if we didn't both wind up in the bottom of the river.

On the upper banks behind me, I thought I heard footsteps, and for a moment my hope rose that it was Crud. But no, Crud's footsteps didn't sound like that, and anyway, these were coming from the other direction. I looked off into the darkness just above the canal, my eyes combing through the shadows for a flash of Tom's pale hair, while my fingers fumbled frantically with the rope until I managed to loosen the knot. I stepped into the boat, making it rock so wildly that I was nearly dumped right out of the thing. But after a few dodgy seconds, I found my balance, sat down, and took up the oars.

Rowing was harder than I thought. The moon had slipped behind clouds so that the canal was pitch dark. Trying to make out the banks was nearly impossible, not to mention the fact that managing the oars was way more awkward than I had imagined. I would accidentally thump the front of the boat against the bank, struggle with the oars to push off again, then smack the back end of the boat against the opposite bank. Tammany's boat was taking a beating that it couldn't afford to take. I hoped it would hold together long enough to get me where I wanted to go.

The other thing that began to worry me was all the noise I was making—the splash of the oars, the shhhh of the boat cutting through the canal, and then the drip of the water off the oars when they were lifted out of the canal again. If Tom were lurking anywhere close to the canal, he would hear me for sure.

As soon as this thought came into my head, I heard a soft hissing somewhere behind me. I stopped rowing and listened. Yes, there it was! A stealthy sound of something stirring in the water.

I stared into the blackness behind me, straining my eyes to see what it was, and caught a glimpse of a shadow on the canal. Someone was in a boat heading toward me, moving at a quick clip. I put my oars back in the water and rowed hard. For the amount of effort I put into the rowing, the boat just didn't seem to move fast enough. I could hear the other boat behind me, coming closer, closing the gap between us.

It was useless. I'd be caught if I stayed in the boat. I did the only thing I could think of. I steered the boat right for the bank. It smashed into it so forcefully that I fell off the plank seat and dropped an oar into the water. I made an awkward scramble from boat to land, stumbling into the cold canal water, soaking myself to my shins. Once again, I was in the Nigh with my boots filled with water.

"Nell!" It was a whispered cry. The sound of it made me freeze where I stood.

I should have run. I should have sprinted off into the woods, and chances were he wouldn't have found me and would have given up and left.

But I'm a selfish beast.

I waited by that bank, my icy sodden jeans plastered to my calves, and watched as Crud rowed his way toward me in a large, sturdy-looking boat.

"Really, Nell, with all the boats in this whole canal," he said when he was close, "you steal the lousiest one."

48

ALEE-OOP-DESH-NOZ

"Where are we going?" Crud asked once I had gotten into the boat he'd taken.

"Back to Manhattan," I told him, then added, "Their Manhattan, not ours. We're going to talk to Bethesda. The angel. She'll help us."

Crud was struggling to keep us in the center of the canal, and his rowing was worse than mine, so I took the oars until we reached open water, then handed them back to him. The river was calm, thankfully. A sheet of black glass. In the distance I could see a few flickering lights. Manhattan. It looked like the city during a blackout.

I kept checking the water around us, looking for boats that might be following us. But we seemed to be the only ones on the river. In the river, it was another story. As we drifted along, we heard splashes all around us. Fish, I hoped. But every so often something large would jump out of the water—too large for a fish. More Finfolk? It was too dark to tell, but you can bet that I kept my hands in the boat.

When I took my turn at the oars, Crud began to twist his hands around each other, crossing and uncrossing his wrists, flicking his fingers, then snapping them open, creating wide ribbons of pale green light that melted together, then dissolved.

"What are you doing?"

"Gedink-Gedank Ward," he said. "Trying to, at least."

"What does it do?"

"It's a protection spell. I saw it in the club handbook. If someone's about to attack you, it's supposed to make them suddenly have second thoughts. Anyway, I'd like to have something locked and loaded in case Tom catches up to us. Or in case of, you know, whatever other terrifying things are lurking in this place." He dropped his hands and let the light fade out. "You realize that if Ruth finds out I didn't stop you from coming here, she'll wring my neck."

"Yeah, so let's not tell her."

We left the boat behind a tumbledown barn on a farm close to the banks of the river, farther north than the Hudson Barrows. I was aiming for the Upper West Side of Manhattan, but it was hard to tell exactly where we were. The geography of New York City in the Nigh was different from what it was back home. Just when you thought you knew exactly where you were, something popped up that wasn't quite right. It was like following a map drawn up from someone's fuzzy memory of a place.

"This is probably how the city looked a few hundred years ago," Crud said, gazing at the vast undulating fields all around us, separating sprawling farmhouses.

"But then there's that." I pointed over to the cluster of skyscrapers in the distance, some of the windows lit up. "I've been thinking about what Mrs. Nerriberry said. About how kids have been poached for ages. So if they poached a kid two hundred years ago, that kid would create things from two hundred years ago. And a kid poached from today would create the stuff from today. That's why you get this mash-up. And that weird Statue of Liberty? It's like some kid's version of it, you know?"

Crud nodded. "Makes sense."

We tramped through the fields as the darkness was beginning to lift. The farmland gradually gave way to dirt roads with a smattering of nicer houses, their windows dark. I guessed it was about two or three in the morning, so everyone must still be in their beds.

The roads grew steeper, and up ahead I could see the tops of trees peering out above a long stone wall barrier—Central Park. Beyond it, in the distance, were those magnificent skyscrapers. They rose up, straight and golden, with their filigree rooftops, side by side, like a fortress wall.

"I've been thinking about something else," I said. "Maybe Mr. Boot is one of those people who smuggle Fates. I mean, he does have a briefcase full of them. So maybe that's the secret Tom knew about Mr. Boot. Maybe that's the reason he didn't kick Tom out of the club."

Crud nodded. "I wouldn't put it past him."

We walked on in silence for a while until I stopped by one of the houses that had an old barn beside it.

"Hey, um, I've got to pee," I said.

"Oh, yeah, sure," Crud muttered, embarrassed. He turned his back to me. I guess he thought I was going to squat down and pee right then and there.

"No, I'll just go behind the barn," I told him. "Be back in a sec."

"Sure, sure." Crud still kept his back to me. I was pretty sure he wasn't going to turn around until I told him to.

Once I got to the other side of the barn where Crud couldn't see me, I reached into my pocket and pulled out Mrs. Nerriberry's saltshaker. The Nibbins were sitting inside, arms around each other, and staring up at me. I felt a sharp pang of guilt. Crud never would have approved of this, which is why I had slipped the saltshaker into my jacket pocket when he wasn't looking. And of course, Mrs. Nerriberry would be furious to know I had stolen her patients. But she had said she was going to release them in the morning anyway. And this was technically the morning.

I unscrewed the saltshaker's lid and tipped the shaker over in the palm of my hand. The Nibbins tumbled out and stared up at me. They didn't look scared, just curious. I felt another wave of guilt, which I pushed aside. *Means to an end*, I told myself.

I looked at the Nibbins carefully. The Fetcher was the one on the right. I could make out the delicate wings, thin as a lemon's membrane, folded against her back.

I wasn't sure if this would work. After all, when Annika

had used the Nibbins in McDonald's, she had been snooping around in someone else's mind, not her own. But still, why couldn't the Noodger latch on to a thought in my own mind—the way the Noodger had latched on to that old man's memory of Benita—and have the Fetcher bring me what I wanted?

I wouldn't need to perform the Farborgan Maneuver, either, since I didn't need to sneak into anyone else's mind.

"I'm sorry," I whispered to the Nibbins. As carefully as possible I started to pull the Fetcher away from her Noodger. They both cried out in a reedy shriek of protest—too quiet for Crud to hear. It was awful, so awful that I almost lost my nerve, but then I felt the Fetcher pull loose from her wingless friend, whose wire-thin arms reached out pathetically for her mate. With a quick flick of my wrist I flung the Fetcher so that she sailed over the fence and into the dark night.

Quickly I plucked up the Noodger, and just as quickly she bit my finger, hard. I stifled a yelp, then held her up to my nose.

"Alee-oop-desh-noz," I said, and she immediately scrambled up my left nostril. The sensation was bizarre, like a sneeze going in the wrong direction. I felt her climbing, her tiny hands pulling the hairs in my nose, stinging pinpricks. It was probably what getting a tattoo felt like, I thought. At a sudden sharp pain in my sinus, I yelped.

"You okay there?" Crud called.

"Shh! Yes," I whispered back. The pain eased, then

stopped. The Nibbin was in place. I could have kicked myself for crying out like that. What an idiot! Why couldn't I be brave like Annika? She had done this in McDonald's without uttering a sound. And she didn't even know what was going to happen; she just shoved that Nibbin up her nose, no questions. I thought of something else, too. . . . If anything bad happened to Crud while we were in the Nigh, it would prove Annika right—that I messed up other people's lives because I was too impulsive.

I forced myself to stop considering this and focused my thoughts on River. I conjured up his face in my mind, blurry at first but then growing more and more clear until I heard a shrill cry, an urgent high-pitched buzzing. The voice was in my head—in my pineal gland to be precise. It was the Noodger calling out to her Fetcher.

It had worked.

It had worked!

The Fetcher would find River and bring him to me.

Just like that.

I didn't know how long she would take. The one in McDonald's had worked quickly, but maybe Benita had been close by. River, on the other hand, might be very far away.

I felt the Noodger climbing back down my nostril, which was just as uncomfortable as it sounds. I had to suppress the urge to sneeze as I held my hand beneath my nose. In a moment, the Noodger fell into my palm. I carefully put her back into the saltshaker, replaced the shaker in my pocket, and hurried over to Crud.

"You all right?" Crud gave me a quizzical look.

"Too much coffee this morning," I muttered.

Once in Central Park, we headed for the paved path, which felt safest and most likely to lead us somewhere. I had a vague idea of how to get to Bethesda, but since New York City in the Nigh and New York City in the Hither didn't always match up, it might be tricky.

"It's weird to be in here at night," Crud said, looking around at the deserted park and its shadowy outcroppings of rocks and shrubbery. "I keep thinking a mugger is going to jump out at us."

"No muggers," I said. "At least I don't think so. Boggedy Cats, maybe."

"Boggedy whatsits?"

I felt like an idiot the second I said it. Tiller had told me not to think about them or they would come, and here I was mentioning them to Crud. Now the both of us would have to not think about them.

"Nothing, forget it. We'll just steer clear of the Ramble," I told him.

But the path had ideas of its own. It kept leading us to the edge of the heavily wooded area that shed the scent of leaf mold and earth. We backtracked each time, taking a different fork in the path, but it always wound back to the Ramble and its darkly dense thickets.

"Okay, this is ridiculous," I said, throwing my arms up in exasperation.

"All roads lead to the Ramble," Crud said.

"Then we're not taking the road."

I headed off the path, and we started across a meadow flanked by boulders. It was hard to tell where we were exactly, but once we climbed on top of one of the boulders for a better view, I saw something familiar: the model boat pond. It had been a favorite spot for River and me. We had loved to lean across the pond's low stone barrier, scratchy against our forearms, and watch people—mostly grown men—race their remote-controlled boats. Afterward we'd climb onto the Alice in Wonderland statue, and I would sit in Alice's lap and hold her huge, cold, bronze hand.

Off in the distance, past the pond, I could see the silhouette of the familiar statue—Alice perched up high on a giant mushroom, the Mad Hatter's huge top hat, a dark cylinder set against the sky.

And then I saw something on the statue move.

It took me a moment to make it out—a pair of legs, long and lanky, were swinging back and forth. Someone was sitting on one of the giant mushrooms in front of the Mad Hatter.

Crud spotted it too.

"Nell!" he whispered.

"I know," I replied. My voice didn't sound alarmed like Crud's. It sounded excited. Because I was pretty sure the person was River.

The Fetcher had done her job.

49

COMPANY

I ran toward the statue, and Crud followed, though I'm sure he thought I'd lost my mind. I didn't have time to explain. And also, I didn't *want* to explain, since he definitely would be angry that I'd stolen the Nibbins.

The figure hopped off the statue. Crud and I both stopped short and stared.

"Is that—" Crud whispered.

I squinted into the darkness.

"I think so . . . but I don't understand how . . . ," I whispered back in astonishment.

"*Pssst, pssst, pssst!*" Annika put her hands on her hips. "Are you two going to just stand there and whisper about me like a couple of second graders?"

"What are you doing here?" I asked her.

"We're looking for you two clowns," she replied.

"We?" I asked.

"Nell." Crud's voice was low and grim. "Behind Alice."

He had been half hidden by the giant mushroom, his pale hair easily mistaken for a spot of ragged moonlight glinting off the bronze statue.

Tom.

He ducked under the mushroom and stepped toward us, smiling.

"Hey, Nell. Hey, Crud," he said lightly.

"Stay where you are, Gunnerson," Crud demanded. He raised his arms and twisted his hands around each other. I saw ribbons of light project from his fingers and undulate in the air toward Tom. Tom reached up and swatted them away like bugs. They fell to the ground, dimming, then extinguishing.

"Decent ward, Crud," Tom said. "No, seriously, Boot would be proud. It's just, wards don't work on me." He reached into his pocket and pulled out a candy bar, unwrapped it, and tossed the wrapper on the ground.

"Annika," I said, "get away from him now."

"Sheesh, Nell," Annika said, not moving an inch. "You've spent too much time with those chess guys. It's made you think everybody is up to something shady."

"Really? So did he tell you that he's an Imp?"

"Yeah, Nell. He told me a lot of things. He told me that he tried to rescue you."

For a second I was so outraged that I couldn't even get my words out. "He . . . ? What? Annika, he nearly *drowned* me!"

"No, that's not true!" Tom said. "I wasn't trying to drown you. It's just that the Wicket in the turtle tank opened up suddenly, and Leland was roaming the school—"

"Leland? Who's *Leland?*" I asked.

"The ferret. You know, the magician at the school

dance. He's an actual Magician from the Nigh."

"What would a Magician from the Nigh be doing in our school?" Crud asked skeptically.

"Looking for Nell," Tom replied.

"Me? Why me?"

"To help the Minister find River," Tom said. "They thought if they had you, they could draw River out of hiding. But Boot caught him and changed him into a ferret. He was keeping him in the cage until they figured out what to do with him. And when Leland didn't come back to the Nigh, the Minister sent me in to grab you. They figured I'd blend in at the school, just another kid."

Tom started toward us, but Crud jabbed a finger at him and said, "Not another step closer, Gunnerson."

Tom stopped. Crud's ward might not work on Tom, but his fists still would.

"I could have stolen you, you know," Tom continued sullenly. It seemed like he was insulted that we didn't trust him. "When we were on the arch in Washington Square Park? There was an open Wicket in a vent."

"Oh, so that's why you took me up there," I said, now as insulted as he was.

"No. I mean . . . yes, at first. But then I . . . I just couldn't do it."

"What a prince," Crud sniped.

Tom ignored this. "But then Leland escaped from the ferret cage, and I knew he'd try to grab you. He'd escaped once before and had almost gotten you then. He was the one who called you to get you to go to the museum. He was going to pull you into the Wicket, the one in the Neanderthal exhibit."

"But I didn't see him there," I said.

"That's because Boot got to him first. He turned him back into a ferret and hustled him out of the museum."

Then I remembered. "There was something about an animal loose in the museum."

"That was Leland. Then he escaped the second time, and when a Wicket opened up in the turtle tank, I knew he'd try to take you through it. The only way I could think to stop him was to take you myself. But Boot must have summoned some Finfolk to pull me away from you."

"And what were you going to do once—" I started, but Crud grabbed my arm and held up a warning finger to his lips.

"Shh! Look." He was tracking something by the boat pond that was stumbling toward us. It was a boy. Well, it was *shaped* like a boy, but even in the darkness I could see there was something wrong with it. Its face was twisted, and its eyes were too large and misplaced—one practically on its cheek while the other was too close to its temple. I recognized the creature immediately. It was the thing that had followed Tiller and me through the Ramble. I had only caught the briefest glimpse of it that time, but now I was looking at it squarely. And, listen, I had seen some pretty weird stuff in the Nigh. But this thing? This thing was different. It looked like something that wasn't supposed to exist. It stared at me with its all-black eyes, its body weaving around like a plastic bag caught in a current of wind. A red ribbon was tied to its wrist, the end of it trailing.

"On three, we run," Annika said.

"No. It's fast," I said. "It chased me once before. I have another idea."

It was risky, and I couldn't be sure what the end result would be, but it wasn't as if we had a whole lot of options.

50

THE MAD HATTER

My hands are my chopsticks, I told myself.

With all the focus I could muster, I took my best shot at the Oifen Shoifen Spell. It was the spell I'd always had the most luck with. I produced the strings of light right away, but as I worked the spell, my eyes flitted toward the twisted boy coming closer and closer to us, and the lights dissolved and blinked out. I tried again, this time keeping my attention squarely on the statue. I felt the air grow heavy around my fingertips. The tendrils of light formed in the air, swelling out in all directions, like a miniature Milky Way hovering above our heads. Honestly, my attempts at magic in my own world had never worked so well. There was a loud CRACK, and the light formed incandescent blue branches that arced over the statue like a net and blasted to the ground, barely missing Annika and Tom.

"Are you trying to kill us?!" Annika shrieked.

But something was definitely happening to the statue. The shine on its bronze patina dulled. The creatures on the statue twitched, then shivered. The Dormouse was the first to move. It leapt off the bigger mushroom onto the smaller one, then bounded to the ground.

I had hoped to create a diversion, and it had worked. The boy-shaped creature stopped in his tracks when he saw the flash of light, his twisted face cocked to the side.

But before we could run, everything went wrong. The White Rabbit bounded straight at Annika, his umbrella held out like a sword. He jabbed at her, driving her backward. At the same time the Mad Hatter sprang to life and charged at me, bowlegged and cackling. His head was huge, easily three times the size of mine, and his face . . . I remember being creeped out by that face as a little kid when we climbed on the statue. But animated? It was ghastly. He would have barreled right into me if I hadn't dodged him, but then he swung around, ran back at me, and scooped me up under his arm, football style.

"Let me down!" I screamed.

"If I let you down, we won't get there. You're too slow," said the Hatter as he ran. He had a nasally voice, as though his giant nose were stuffed up.

"Get where?" I asked. "Look, my friends are back there—"

He sneezed, and I felt a wet spray on my neck.

"Don't worry, just allergies," he said, looping around and running back toward everyone.

"Watch out for that thing—" I warned him about the twisted boy.

"What thing? You're a thing."

"I mean that creature back there," I said, ignoring the insult.

"Oh, you mean the Wraith," the Mad Hatter said. "Scared of him, a big girl like you?"

"Yes."

"That's funny, since he's one of your own kind."

"That thing is not a human," I said.

"Was a Human. *Was*. He's dead. His toy was tied to the Devotion Tree, and *someone*—and I'm not mentioning names, but it was you, dingbat—did a little hocus-pocus on it and turned him into a Wraith."

"A Wraith? What do you mean?"

"*What do you mean, what do you mean?*" He mimicked me. "You don't know much, do you?"

He about-faced and crashed right into the woods, weaving around trees wildly. I shut my eyes as the branches scratched at my face and pulled out my hair while the Hatter ran along.

A *Wraith*.

I realized then what he was talking about. Back when I was with Tiller and the Sewer Mahamba had appeared, I had performed the Oifen Shoifen Spell on the doll hanging on the Devotion Tree. And what had Tiller said about the Devotion Tree? That the things tied to it represented a dead person's soul. Without chopsticks, without finesse, and, let's face it, without much talent, my magic had created a ghost. I didn't know if I should be proud or horrified. I guess I was both.

The woods were growing thicker by the second, and suddenly I realized where we were.

The Hatter complied by spinning in a full circle and smacking my head against a tree trunk, which I was sure he did deliberately. "Watch your head." He then continued on in the exact same direction, heading deeper and deeper into the Ramble. Below me I spotted a huge rat running alongside us and screamed, then realized it was only the Dormouse from the statue.

In the distance I heard an eerie, high-pitched wail that ended with a sharp thiiith, like someone hissing through bared teeth. The wail came again, and it was answered by still more wails, as though animals were calling to one another, the sound growing louder and more excited. And closer.

"Go faster," I told the Hatter.

That's when he dropped me on the ground.

"Don't tell me what to do," he said, cackled, then off he ran.

Stupid jerk.

I scrambled to my feet. The wailing had stopped completely. It was utterly silent except for the sound of labored breathing. Something—many somethings—had run far and fast, and now they were here. All around me. I could smell them. A sour public-bathroom smell.

A thin bar of pale morning light passed between a break in the trees, and for a split second I saw them—several large cats, thickly muscled with a hump above their shoulders. And then they were gone, lost in the darkness again.

Boggedy Cats.

Keep still.

I felt the words, the same way I had felt Tiller's words, but it was different this time. These words were a command. My muscles instantly relaxed. My heart stopped racing. It was like being anesthetized—I knew the terror was there, but I couldn't feel it anymore.

Keep still.

That nasty smell was stronger now, and I felt the air around me grow warm as the cats circled me, but I wasn't afraid. One of them stepped right up to me, its face inches from mine. Its breath was disgusting but fascinating, too, and I looked straight into its eyes, with its pinpoint pupils that were slightly crossed, and I had the funniest thought—of Kaa in Disney's *The Jungle Book*, the snake who hypnotizes Mowgli with those swirly eyes. I saw images in my mind, thoughts that weren't my own. They belonged to the animal in front of me. I saw myself in its eyes as it drew closer to my neck. I could smell my own sweat, mixed with the thick, complicated reek of adrenaline and the coppery smell of my own blood just below the thin surface of my skin, skin that was thin enough to pierce with the slightest pressure.

With a sudden jolt, I was in the air once more, scooped up by a pair of cool, powerful arms. I was facing down, so all I could see were a pair of tremendous Mary Jane shoes stomping through the underbrush with impressive speed.

Alice.

All the terror that the Boggedy Cats had somehow suppressed now burst out of me. I cried out, hyperventilating. A huge pair of hands flipped me over. Now I was cradled in Alice's bronze arms while she was tromping along at a brisk clip.

"Thank you!" I gasped. "Oh, thank you, thank you!"

Alice looked down at me and smiled.

I had only been to church once in my life. I went with my grandmother, and I literally spent the whole time wondering what eyebrows were for. In other words, I'm no expert on saints or religious stuff. But at that moment, when Alice smiled at me, I thought she looked just like a saint—full of patience and kindness.

It all spilled out of me. As she ran along, I told her everything. About how River was poached and how I had to find him and bring him home with me. "There's a statue of an angel in the park," I told her. "Her name is Bethesda, and she stands in a fountain. She's got a bunch of fat toddlers." I was pretty sure that's where Crud would go, since we were separated. "If you can just get me to her, Bethesda will help me."

I gazed up at Alice, and she looked down at me serenely. She raised one of her massive fingers and pressed my nose. "Boop," she said. Then she giggled.

"Okay, so . . . Bethesda—"

She pressed my nose again. "Boop."

What's wrong with her? I thought.

Then I remembered something. In *Alice's Adventures in Wonderland*, Alice was just a little kid.

That's when I began to wonder if I actually did know what saints looked like after all, and if maybe my fate was in the hands of a giant-sized seven-year-old.

51

ᴹYSTERY ᶠLAVOR

Alice ran through the Ramble, the Dormouse appearing at her heels every so often, then darting off. Before long we emerged in a clearing and headed toward a steep, rocky outcropping with steps carved into its side. Alice's huge Mary Janes pounded up those steps effortlessly. I don't think statues have lungs because she wasn't even breathing hard.

"Where are we going?" I asked.

"To the top," she said.

"Yeah, I can see that. But, like, why?"

Alice looked down at me and smiled. "Your head is the size of a crumpet."

"I feel like you were a lot more mature in the book," I said.

There was nothing to do but sit tight in her beefy arms and wait until she put me down. At least we were out of the Ramble. If I twisted my neck around, I could see the dark mass of woods at our back, below us. I wondered where the others were.

After a solid ten minutes of climbing, Alice reached the

summit of the rock, and she put me down on the ground. Standing beside her, my head didn't even reach her armpit. I gazed around. We were probably at the park's highest point. I'm not great at judging feet and yards, but when I looked down the side of the summit's cliff, I guessed that we were about as high off the ground as a two-story building. The sun had risen. Fingers of vermilion and orange stretched across the sky. Just beyond the park's boundaries were the glittery skyscrapers, like bars of gold rising out of the pavement. I could see the rich green meadows of the park, with their looping footpaths, skirting the edges of the woods. I hoped the others had enough sense to stay out of the Ramble.

And just as I thought that, I saw three figures emerge from the woods far below.

They were running fast, now heading up the steps in the huge rock we were standing on. How they had found me, I had no idea. I was so happy to see them all, even Tom, who was the first to reach the summit.

"Are you okay?" he asked.

Alice made little kissy sounds at me.

"Shut up, Alice," I said.

A moment later Annika arrived, followed by Crud, huffing and puffing, both of them clearly in bad moods.

"Nice going with the magic, Nell," Annika said. "I had to climb a tree to get away from that rabbit." She suddenly leapt backward into Crud and pointed. "*Rat!*"

"It's a Dormouse," I corrected her. The thing had

popped out from behind a pile of rocks near Annika's feet.

"Same difference," Annika said, which appeared to offend the Dormouse, who skulked off.

"How did you find me?" I asked them.

"Good instincts," Annika said, tapping her head. "At least one of us has them."

A small creature flew out of the depths of Annika's hair and landed on my shoulder, shrieking indecipherably into my ear. Hurriedly I reached into my jacket pocket and pulled out the saltshaker. As soon as I unscrewed the cap, the Fetcher flew down into the saltshaker and grabbed the Noodger around her tiny waist. With her friend safely in her grasp, the Fetcher flew off, the two of them disappearing into the treetops.

"I had a Nibbin on me?" Annika cried.

"That makes no sense," I objected. "I wasn't thinking of you. I was thinking of River."

There was silence during which I felt Crud's eyes boring into me.

"Where did you get the Nibbins from, Nell?" Crud asked, staring at the empty saltshaker.

I hesitated, then said, "You know from where."

"You stole them?! After everything Mrs. Nerriberry said about the way humans use Fates?"

"I know, I know, but they were right there, and I thought that they might lead River straight to us. . . ." But then I remembered that I had thought of Annika and her bravery when the Noodger went up my nose—who knew

Nibbins were such sticklers to details—and now I had lost a solid chance at bringing River right to us. Stupid!

"What are we doing here anyway?" Annika asked.

"I have no idea," I said glumly. "Ask *her*." I pointed to Alice.

"What are we doing here?" Annika asked Alice.

Alice pouted, her brows furrowed. "She told me to shut up," she complained to Annika, nodding at me.

"Yeah, she can be a real pain sometimes," Annika agreed.

"Do you like sweets?" Tom asked Alice.

Alice nodded sullenly.

Tom kneeled down, reached into his sock, and pulled out a Dum Dum lollipop. He held it up toward Alice.

"Hey, Willy Wonka," I said testily. "You can't solve everything with sock candy."

Tom ignored me and wiggled the lollipop between his fingers.

"It's mystery flavor," he told her.

"What's mystery flavor?" Alice said, her curiosity piqued enough to wipe the frown from her face.

"That's for you to figure out." He unwrapped it—tossing the wrapper on the ground, of course. "You can have it if you tell us why we're here."

Alice thought for a moment. "I came here because this is where the boy went."

"What boy?" Tom asked.

"The one she said about." Alice pointed to me. "River. That boy."

"River was here?" I cried. But then my better senses prevailed. Alice had been a statue up until today. "Wait, how can you know that? You weren't able to even move before."

Alice took the Dum Dum from Tom. The lollipop wasn't even the size of her pinkie fingernail. She stuck it in her mouth. It clattered around against those bronze teeth of hers, and then she chomped it in one bite.

"The skrills sit on my head, and they yakkety yak-yak all day long," Alice said. "I heard all about that boy. One of the skrills told another one that Mary brought him here."

"Mary Carpenter?" I asked.

"Yes, her," Alice said.

Okay, now we were getting somewhere.

"Why did she bring him here?" I asked.

Alice frowned, and she thought for a moment. Then her eyes opened wide, and she lifted a finger in the air. "Wait! I know the answer!"

We all stared at her, waiting.

"Root beer–cherry." She smiled at Tom. "That's the answer to the mystery flavor, right?"

I jumped up and waved my hand in front of her face to get her attention. "Okay, Alice. Look at me. Look at me." She turned to me glumly, not happy that I had spoiled her Dum Dum discovery.

"I'm looking."

"Great. Now focus, Alice. Why did Mary take River here?"

She glowered at me, then blew out her cheeks and sucked them back in.

"To do this—" she said.

And with a sudden lunge, she shoved me right off the cliff.

52

FAIRY-TALE WOODS

It happened so fast that before I could even scream bloody murder, I was already on the ground. I had simply stumbled to my knees. It felt less like falling off a cliff than missing the last step on a footstool.

A second later Tom tumbled to the ground next to me, looking as startled as I had been.

"Are you okay?" he asked breathlessly.

I nodded. "You?"

He nodded too.

A moment later we were joined by Annika and Crud, who were both caught midscream before they also landed on the ground with an anticlimactic thump.

I looked up and saw Alice standing on a low stone ledge just above us. She was so close to us that I could have jumped up and touched her Mary Janes, though, by the way she was looking down in our direction but not at us, it was clear that she couldn't see us.

"That wasn't a real cliff," Crud said, getting to his feet.

"Well, we know that now," Annika said as she brushed

herself off. "And by the way, Alice is a straight-up psycho. She *pushed* me!"

"She pushed me, too," I said. "She probably knew we wouldn't jump, not even if she told us that the cliff wasn't real."

"She didn't push him," Crud said, nodding toward Tom. "When you went off that cliff, he jumped after you." He turned to Tom. "That was hard-core, man."

I looked at Tom, who muttered, "Reflexes," in an uncharacteristically embarrassed way.

"I guess it was camouflage of some kind, made to look like a cliff to keep people out of here," I said.

"Yeah? Well, they shouldn't have bothered." Annika swept her arm around. "No one in their right mind would want to come in here anyway."

Although we had landed in a small glade, we were surrounded by the type of woods that always pop up in the scary bits of fairy tales. A ring of black thorny brush stood sentry in front of gray-barked trees, whose long, spindly branches hung like jellyfish tentacles. The air was thick with damp morning fog that slithered along the ground. Above all, it was silent. No singing birds, no scampering critters. I mean, it was the whole enchilada of creepiness.

"Have you ever noticed," Crud whispered, "that in every story, bad things happen to people when they're in the woods? *The Blair Witch Project. Friday the 13th. Little Red Riding Hood.*"

Something shot out of the trees, snapping branches and

sending leaves raining down. The thing circled above us for a second, then disappeared back in the trees.

"And bats," Annika said. "Bats happen in the woods."

But when the creature emerged again and hovered above us for a moment, it was clear that this was no bat. Yes, it had wings like a bat, but that's where the resemblance ended. Gaunt and gray-skinned and wearing a hooded cloak, it had the face of a homely man. It swooped within inches of me, then barreled into Tom, knocking him to the ground before diving up into the trees and crashing through the canopy, and then it was gone.

"What was that thing?" Crud asked as he helped Tom to his feet.

"It had a face like an old potato," Annika replied.

"That was Boomer," I said, my voice rising with excitement.

"What's a Boomer?" Crud asked.

"Boomer and Mike. They're gargoyles in front of our apartment building." I looked at them all, feeling dizzy with this new realization. "He's here."

"River?" Tom asked, his eyes flitting toward the woods. I nodded.

"You don't know that," Annika said. I could see in her face that she was struggling between hope and disappointment, a painful battle that I knew only too well.

"Not a hundred percent, no," I admitted. "But . . ." I walked up to the edge of the woods and stared into its impenetrable thickness.

"River!" I called out.

The others came up behind me, and together we all waited, listening. The only answer was heavy, bleak silence.

I felt the familiar ache of disappointment rising up into my chest, but I shoved it away and again called out.

"River!"

The next moment there was a dry squeaking noise, as though a huge nail were being pried out of a piece of lumber. The sound grew and grew until it filled the air. All round us the trees leaned in toward one another, their roots creaking with the stretch, and their long, spidery limbs lacing themselves together, forming a wall all around the glade. One nearby branch stretched itself out toward us, its trunk listing, groaning with the effort, and with a quick swipe the branch jabbed at Annika's face, just missing her eye. Another branch shot out and poked me painfully in the ribs.

The trees were herding us backward. There was nothing else to do but retreat, back, back.

"River!" I shouted again.

But the angry fortress of branches kept building furiously, advancing closer and closer, the sound deafening.

"We're going to have to climb back out of here in a minute," Crud shouted.

He was right. We were nearly to that low stone ledge, back to where Alice was still waiting.

I took a breath, and as loud as I could I shouted, "There once was a rickety old elevator, which everyone thought was broken! But Nell and River and the Girl with the Magic Shoes knew better!"

I ducked when a tree took a swipe at my head, and Annika grabbed my arm and tried to pull me back, but I shook her off.

"What are you doing?" she cried. "Let's go!"

"And the three of them traveled to Elevator World," I shouted, "where they saw places unknown and met people unheard of!"

The horrible shrieking of the trees suddenly quieted. The branches stopped weaving their wall, though they twitched restlessly, like horses being reined in. The woods went silent again, but now it felt as if they were alert and listening.

The branches began to move again. This time, though, they coiled up, lifting like a series of curtains, one behind the other, until finally revealing a green clearing hemmed in by a protective stand of hemlocks. In the center of that clearing was a sooty, mustard-colored brick apartment building with mint-green window frames and a line of ancient fire escapes trailing up the side of it.

And standing on the front stoop, wearing a pair of red boxers and that's all, was River.

53

RIVER

I had imagined this very moment so many times—how we'd throw our arms around each other and scream and laugh and cry with sheer joy and relief.

But it turned out that I had imagined it wrong.

I ran over to him, and then we simply stared at each other in shock. He was thin, his face so spare it made him look much older than thirteen. A new scar, like a white thread splicing the right side of his upper lip, gave him a permanent sneer. His dark hair was long and wild-looking, dried mud clinging to a patch of it above his ear.

"River."

My voice could only muster a rough whisper. I felt tears burning at the edges of my eyes, my throat swelling with both elation and sadness, making it impossible to swallow. Sadness, because now I understood something that I hadn't anticipated. Three years had been stolen from us. Three years which we would never get back. We had both changed in those years, and when you change when you're apart from each other, sometimes you fit together again, and sometimes you don't.

"You got so tall," I said in wonder.

He stared at me intently, his face racked with confusion. I saw his Adam's apple—that was new—tick up and down once. Then he reached out and pulled me in and hugged me tightly. And there it was. The reunion I had dreamed about for so long—the hug, the tears. Maybe not the boxer shorts, and he smelled all armpitty like a teenaged boy, but everything else.

I felt his arms loosen as he stared over my shoulder.

"Is that Annika?" he asked me.

I nodded.

"Nice boxers," Annika said, folding her arms across her chest and smiling. She was trying to play it cool, but I could hear the happiness in her voice. River looked awkward suddenly. He wiped his tears away roughly with the heel of his hand. Then he smiled back at her, his scar twisting his lips on the one side, making him look like a comic-book bad guy. He went over and hugged her, quickly. I think they were both embarrassed about the boxer-shorts thing.

"And this is Crud," I said.

"You said Crud?" River frowned at me, checking that he heard right.

"Nickname, man," Crud said, smiling. "Good to finally meet you."

River smiled back. "Hi, Crud."

When River saw Tom, though, his face hardened with suspicion. Like his Adam's apple, this was also new. The River I had once known was so trusting—too trusting for New York City, my father had always worried.

"He's an Imp," River said.

I thought about how Tom had jumped off the cliff when none of us knew it wasn't really a cliff. He had jumped because of me. And what he had said about Leland, the Magician . . . I believed him.

You just want to believe him, a voice in my head said.

But I checked in with my gut, and my gut said, Trust him.

"He's okay," I said decisively. "I'll vouch for him."

"You can't vouch for an Imp," River replied darkly, glaring at Tom.

"It's all right, I'll go," Tom said, backing up.

But Crud put a hand on Tom's shoulder and stopped him. When Crud wanted to, he had an air of authority that could rival Mr. Boot's. "You're staying." He turned to River and said, "I don't know much about Imps and whatnot. Probably they're all a bunch of dirtbags. Except for this one. This one's okay."

When River asked how we'd found him, I told him the story—well, the abbreviated version anyway.

"So she hid you here?" I said. "Mary Carpenter?"

River nodded.

"But why didn't she just bring you home?" I asked.

"I don't know," he replied, but I thought I saw his eyes dart away from mine for a split second.

Just then Boomer, the flying monk, dove out of the trees and glided down to the cement ledge above the door. He squatted next to his fellow gargoyle, another bat-winged man in a monk's robe.

"Mike and Boomer," I said, smiling at the two gargoyles I had seen thousands of times perched above the door of our apartment back home. Boomer placed his sinewy arms on the ledge and leaned over to keep a sharp eye on us.

"Boomer's a good bodyguard," River said. "Better than his friend." He nodded toward Mike, who was dozing, his head resting on his knees.

Annika had walked up to the building and touched it, then rapped her knuckles against the brick.

"It feels real," she said.

"It is real," River said. "I made it. Casted it. Come on, I'll show you."

Inside the building, the dingy entryway was exactly like the real one—the smudgy glass door, the intercoms. Even Mrs. Farfle's Q-tip painting was there.

We walked past the red elevator button set in the wall and up the staircase. I automatically peered over the railing to look for Nyxie. Stupid, I know, but the place was such an exact replica, I half expected to see her there, playing in the dark niche.

When we got to the fourth floor, Annika reached out and wistfully trailed her fingers across her old apartment door.

River opened apartment 4B's door, and we followed him inside. While he changed into clothes, I looked around. It was our apartment, yet it wasn't. I mean, everything was the same, except the couch looked too big and the windows' views were of trees rather than other buildings. It was all so familiar that I kept expecting Dad's workroom door to open, and for him to pop his head out and ask where I had been.

"Is our room the same too?" I asked River when he emerged from down the hallway, dressed in a sweatshirt and jeans.

"Go look."

I went down the narrow hallway to my bedroom, stood at the threshold of our room, and gazed around. It was all there—the bunk bed, Mom's painted koi fish on the floor, the dresser. The toy box was in its place, between the windows, which didn't look out onto Bleecker Street but were shaded by the hemlocks.

He must have been so lonely and homesick to have created all this. The thought raked at my heart.

"Oh, River," I said sadly.

But I was immediately sorry. He suddenly looked embarrassed, and I realized that he was proud of his creation. All alone, with nothing and no one, he had re-created his home.

"It's amazing, River," Annika said. I think she really meant it too—she wasn't just trying to one-up me. She walked into the room and gazed around, genuinely in awe. And of course, it was amazing. He had remembered every detail—the tiny white birdcage on the windowsill filled with a molting toy parakeet, the tin London phone booth on the dresser beside a Quaker oatmeal canister filled with colored pencils, a plastic statue of the Eiffel Tower.

I looked up at River's bed. It was so weird to see it look slept in. The rumpled blanket, bunched up at the bottom of the bed. The pillow with a dent in it where his head had been. And my bed below, untouched, with my old red quilt on it—the quilt that Mrs. Farfle's cat had peed on a few months ago, and which we tossed after we couldn't get the smell out.

Then I noticed something.

"You forgot George." The owl wasn't on his bed.

"Give the guy some slack," Crud said to me. "He made a freaking *apartment* building. If he forgot something, I think you can forgive him."

"I didn't forget him," River said. He walked over to the toy chest, opened it, and pulled out the owl. "I just put him in the toy chest. It felt kind of silly, still sleeping with a stuffed animal."

"Wait!" I said, frowning. "Back home, George went missing a few days ago, and I found him in the toy chest. I didn't put him there. Neither did Dad."

River looked as baffled as I did.

"Can you do something in the Nigh that affects things in the Hither?" Crud asked Tom.

Tom thought about this. "I've heard about things called bleed-throughs," he said. "Like when someone in the Hither thinks they see a ghost, a lot of times they're just catching a glimpse of someone in the Nigh, and vice versa."

I thought about when I had done the Sticking Spell, and saw the boy who looked like River—a ghostly River—out on the playground. Maybe that had been a bleed-through.

"But moving things around?" Tom nodded toward George. "That's a new one."

From outside the window came the crack of what sounded like thunder, sharp and explosive. In a moment we were all at the window, staring down at a pile of debris on the ground below. It looked like pieces of a stone that had been smashed to bits, as though it had been blown up. Fragments of it were scattered in a wide radius, and a few pieces were embedded in the trunk of a hemlock.

A face appeared at the window—Mike, the sleeping gargoyle monk. He hung in the air, his bat wings bending and flexing frantically. Then he let out a sound—not a human sound, but it was undeniably the sound of anguish. He swooped down to the ground and squatted beside a shard of stone next to a hemlock tree. A smashed bat wing. Mike looked up at us and wailed again.

Boomer.

"The Minister's here," Tom said grimly.

54

ᴛʜᴇ ᴍɪɴɪꜱᴛᴇʀ

The window began to rattle violently. With a loud pop the glass was sucked out of its frame, as though hit by a microburst, and fell to the ground outside.

"That's better," a high, young-sounding voice from outside called up. "Now we can chat more easily."

Down below, holding a wand with a glittery star on the end of it, was a chubby little girl with glasses. She wore a full-on fairy dress with green tulle and fabric wings, and I was pretty sure she was wearing tap shoes.

"Are you kidding me?" I said. "That's the Minister? She's a little girl."

River grabbed my elbow and pulled me away from the window. "She's old, Nell," he said gravely. "She's centuries old."

"Turns out, the Dormouse is quite a blabbermouth," said the Minister. "He told us exactly where to find you."

"That's because you called it a rat," Crud hissed at Annika.

"Tut-tut, River!" the Minister continued. "This place

doesn't look too sturdy. Not your best work, is it?" She made a frowny face.

"He didn't build it for you, so get lost, Tinker Bell!" Annika yelled back at her.

"Shh, Annika!" River hissed.

The Minister was silent for a moment. She adjusted her fairy skirt, then said, "Children are so rude these days. Well, we've changed with the times too. When a child is too mouthy . . ." She stuck out her tongue and made a scissor gesture with her fingers.

I heard Annika suck in her breath.

I looked over at River. He stood to the side of the window, his head leaning against the wall. His face had turned so pale that the fine scar on his lip looked red.

"Okay, I'm getting grumpy now, so let's move this along," said the Minister. She turned around and yelled toward the woods, "What's that Imp's name again?"

"His name is Tom." A tall, lanky Magician in a dull brown corduroy jacket emerged from behind one of the hemlocks. There was something so familiar about the guy. I took in his auburn hair and bony face, the way his spine bowed out, like he was leaning down to talk to someone shorter than he was.

Then I knew. It was the ferret. Leland. The magician at the school dance.

Now I saw other Magicians emerge from the depths of the woods, dozens of them, all dressed in their drab clothes.

"Tom, dear," the Minister called up, "be a good fellow and escort River down here."

I looked at Tom, the blood draining from my face. He had betrayed us. Of course he had. He was an Imp. Bethesda had warned me, hadn't she? So had Boot. I'd been warned but just didn't listen because I wanted to believe that he was good.

"What have you done, Tom?" I choked out the words.

Tom glanced at me with his blue seafaring eyes, and right then I thought that "The Viking" had been the right name for him after all—the Vikings, who stole what they wanted and destroyed what they didn't.

"We trusted you, man," Crud said.

"I told you," River said. "No one can vouch for an Imp."

Tom said nothing but walked past us, stepping up to the window. He reached into his jacket and pulled out a packet of Twizzlers. He bit the edge of the packet and tore it open, then pulled out a couple of Twizzlers and stuck them in his mouth.

"So here's the thing," Tom called down to the Minister as the Twizzlers bobbed around out of the corner of his mouth. "River's not coming down."

There was a pause, and then the Minister turned to Leland and said, "Why are Imps the stupidest creatures in the universe?"

Leland shrugged.

"I'll count to twenty," the Minister said, "and if River isn't down here by then, we'll have to come in and fetch him ourselves. And that will not be a fun time, kids. Not for any of you. Including you, Imp. Twenty . . . nineteen . . ."

"I'm going," River said.

He started for the door, but Tom grabbed him by the arm. "Wait!"

"For what?" River struggled against Tom's grasp. I knew from painful experience how strong Tom was, but I was grateful for that strength now.

"I need to think," Tom said.

There was a quick *rat-a-tat-tat* sound from outside. I looked out the window to see the Minister dancing on the front stoop—a clumsy tap dance, her chubby arms stretched out to the side. She glanced up and giggled, pointing her fairy wand at me.

"Oops, you caught me! Couldn't resist the stairs." She lifted her fleshy chin and called up, "Fourteen . . . thirteen . . ."

"Let me go!" River's eyes were now wild with panic. "You know what they'll do to the others if they come up here!" He wrenched his arm so violently that it looked like it would pop out of its socket, but Tom held on easily. In fact, it looked like he was using no effort at all.

"Is there another way out of here?" Tom asked.

"No."

"They're all around the building." Crud had been walking from room to room looking out the windows.

"Ten . . . nine . . ."

Annika ran into the kitchen. She yanked open the

kitchen drawers, one after the other, until she finally pulled out a knife. It wasn't much of a knife. Serrated, cheap. I recognized it from the real kitchen back home, where we used it to saw away at loaves of bread. She grabbed a saucepan off the stove and held it out to Crud.

"We'll fight them," she said.

"They're Magicians, Annika!" he said. "Real Magicians. What are we supposed to do with a bread knife and a saucepan? And, by the way, how come you get the knife and I get a saucepan?"

"Because you won't use the knife and I will." She shoved the saucepan in his hand. "And we know some magic too."

With that, she bolted out of the apartment. Crud and I followed her down the stairs, all of us running smack into the thick of it.

It was strange how familiar it felt. Annika in the lead, tearing down the apartment stairs, while I trailed after her, not knowing what she had in mind, but not wanting to be left out. We had done this very same thing dozens of times when we were little kids, Annika, River, and me. Except of course we were now running headlong toward an army of ruthless Magicians with, in my estimation, zero chance of survival.

By the time I reached the lobby, Annika and Crud were already by the glass door, watching the Minister and her Magicians enter the building's vestibule. When the Minister saw us on the other side of the glass, she stopped short. She glanced at the knife and the saucepan, then back at us.

You would have thought she'd have laughed or rolled her eyes or something. But no, she wasn't taking any chances. She was sizing us up. Which didn't take long. She said something to the Magicians, but the glass muffled her words. They nodded. The Minister reached for the door, and Annika went into what they call in gym class an "athletic stance." Knees bent, arm akimbo. Knife poised. Ready.

The Minister gave the door a tug, rattling the glass. It was locked. Of course. That door was always locked in our apartment building. If you didn't have a key, you had to buzz up on the intercom in the vestibule to be let in. A fact which I was pretty sure was not much of an obstacle for the Minister.

She raised her glittery fairy wand and began to slash at the air in front of her.

"She'll be through that door in seconds, you guys," I said, not even bothering to keep the panic out of my voice.

"Yeah, she will," Annika said in a voice that was practically purring with anticipation.

Whatever spell the Minister was using was so easy for her that she actually looked bored doing it. I saw the left toe of her foot idly tapping out a rhythm and her eyes roving around the vestibule as her wand slashed through the air crisply. I looked around the vestibule too, and my eye caught on Mrs. Farfle's big, ugly painting of the giant Q-tips.

The moment the idea came to me, I wasted no time. My hands began to work the Flatzen Spurtz Spell. Once again I felt the astonishing gathering of energy, as if I were pulling molecules from the air and shaping them with my hands. I felt something else, too, like an undertow beneath my own spell—its power more concentrated, more adept—and when the Minister's eyes met mine, I knew it was her magic I was feeling. She was pushing back. Still, one of the Q-tips in the painting shivered, then pulled away from the canvas, followed by another one and another one. It was enough to divert the Minister's attention, and I felt her magical counterstrike slacken. The Q-tips, about a dozen of them, hovered in the air, each one the length of a large candlestick. Leland began to work a spell on them, his bony hands moving fast, but one of the Q-tips launched itself right into Leland's ear and violently twisted back and forth. Leland screamed loudly enough that I could hear him through the glass. The other Q-tips made their move then, ramming themselves into the Magicians' ears, twisting as though they were trying to tunnel right into their brains. One Q-tip swatted the Minister's fairy wand right out of her hands and then worked its way into her right nostril.

"Nell Batista!" Annika cried out. "That was amazing!"

It was. I mean, I was amazed that it had actually worked. But we didn't even have time to bump fists before the spell was shattered. With a flick of the Minister's hand, the Q-tips went limp and melted into small pools of paint on the ground.

55

THE AOA-SANCTIONED WARD

A nnika turned to me. "What else have you got?"
"That was it," I said. "What have you got?"
"A bread knife."
We looked at Crud.
"I can try the Gedink-Gedank Ward," he said without much confidence.

His hands started to work the spell, but the filaments he was creating kept breaking, their light slowly dying as they fluttered to the floor.

"She's doing something," he said with frustration. "I can feel her messing with my spell."

"I know. I felt it too," I said.

Through the glass door, I could see that the Minister was smiling at him, a thread of blood coming from her nose where the Q-tip had attacked her. She adjusted her glasses, then lifted her fairy wand and waved it at the door. This time she wasn't even going to bother with the lock. First there was a sound like a whip cracking, and then a fine fracture started along the top of the glass door, forking off into two fissures that traveled down the length of it, popping and snapping as they moved.

Some tragedies take you by surprise—car crashes, heart attacks. But other tragedies are things you see coming, and all you can do is watch helplessly as it happens. We stood there, the three of us—Annika with her bread knife, Crud with his saucepan, and me . . . me with nothing at all—waiting for the nightmare that was about to storm the building.

The sound of the cracking glass stopped abruptly. The Minister frowned and repeated the spell with the fairy wand. Nothing happened. She turned and said something to the Magicians, who in unison raised their hands to help, but before they could, there was a loud metallic SNAP! The mailboxes set in the wall of the vestibule had flipped open all at once. Flying out of them came postcards, hundreds and hundreds of them. They hurtled at the Minister and the Magicians like ninja throwing stars, their edges slicing at their clothes and their skin, driving them back, back, back, out of the vestibule, out of the building.

I turned to Crud in astonishment.

"How did you do that?" I asked.

Crud put his hands up and shook his head. "It wasn't me."

I turned to Annika questioningly.

"Don't look at me," she said.

"Then who did that?" I asked. "And why do I smell popcorn?"

"I know," Crud said. "I smell it too."

The postcards were still racing around the vestibule,

slapping against the walls. One of them stuck to the glass door. I stepped closer to read it. It had a picture of two crossed swords above a pigeon. Printed in bold purple letters were the words THIS PROPERTY IS PROTECTED BY AN AOA-SANCTIONED WARD. WE ARE NOT RESPONSIBLE FOR SKIN BOILS, HAIR LOSS, BRAIN LEAKAGE, SWELLING OF THE EYEBALLS, OR DEATH.

I heard the sound of pounding feet behind us and turned to see River hurtling down the stairs with Tom right behind him.

"What happened?" River asked, staring at the chaos in the vestibule.

"We don't know," I said, "but it looks like they're leaving."

"They're not," River said with certainty. "They won't leave without me."

"But why?" I asked him. "Why do they want you so badly?"

"I'm not sure. I don't think it's just the casting. They kept moving me around, like they were hiding me from someone."

I turned to Tom questioningly, but he shook his head. "Magicians may work with Imps sometimes, but they don't tell us anything if they can help it."

A thunderous ripping sound came from outside. Just past the glass doors I saw mustard-colored bricks tumbling to the ground from above.

"What's she doing?" Crud asked.

And then, as if she heard his question, the Minister shouted, "What's that old saying . . . ? Where there's a will, there's a way! We may not be able to get into the building, but we can tear the building down around you!"

"Don't Imps have any, you know . . . superpowers?" Annika asked Tom.

"None that will help us right now," Tom said.

An idea flickered through my brain then. The odds of it actually working weren't great, but since an entire New York City apartment building was about to fall on our heads, it couldn't hurt to try.

I ran to the red elevator button and slapped it. I listened for a metallic clank or a whirring, for the sound of an elevator that could take us out of here and into Elevator World.

Nothing happened.

I slapped the red button again and again until River put his hand over mine to stop me.

"There's no elevator here, Nell. There wasn't one back home, so it's not here, either."

"But Elevator World was real for us, wasn't it?" I said. "Wasn't it? I mean, it felt real when we were little kids."

River nodded.

"So if it was real for you in the Hither, wouldn't it be real in the Nigh? It would be part of this place, right?"

I watched River process this, then slowly shake his head. "But the story always started with us already in the elevator. We never actually entered the elevator from this building."

I thought back and realized he was right. In the Elevator World stories we moved from one floor to another, but we never started from home. Still, something nagged at my thoughts. . . .

Then I remembered.

"*We* never entered the elevator from the building, but someone else did!" I said. "The first time we met the Girl with the Magic Shoes, she came through the hatch on the elevator's ceiling." I remembered that part of the story so vividly because it had bothered me at the time. River and I were in the elevator, and the Girl with the Magic Shoes tumbled through the hatch, bold and loud and ready for anything. I hadn't seen why we needed her in the story, and I told River to take her out of it next time, but he never did. "She'd said that she came through Gladys's secret cat door in Mrs. Farfle's apartment, remember?"

"I remember." River nodded and looked at Annika.

"So the Girl with the Magic Shoes *was* Annika, wasn't it?" I said to him accusingly.

"Wait, who's the Girl with the Magic Shoes?" Annika asked.

There was a loud pop from above, and chunks of ceiling plaster fell down, filling the air with white dust. Outside, the bricks were falling like rain, thudding to the ground.

"Fifth floor! Mrs. Farfle's apartment!" I shouted to everyone above the noise.

We all bolted up the stairs, and when we reached the

fifth floor, I went straight to Mrs. Farfle's apartment and tried the door.

"Locked."

"Wait, I think I remember how to do an unlocking spell," Annika said, but before she could attempt it, Tom grabbed the knife out of her hands.

I tensed up, and Crud took a threatening step toward him. But Tom simply bent down and expertly worked the knife into the crack of the door, picking the lock.

There were ominous sounds throughout the building— the squeal of nails being pulled up, the thud of falling wood and the shattering of glass. The Minister and her Magicians were taking the place down brick by brick, beam by beam. Yet underneath all the crashing and squealing, I heard a voice. And I was pretty sure it was coming from inside Mrs. Farfle's apartment.

Tom picked the lock in no time and was about to open the door when I grabbed his wrist and cried, "Wait! She's in there. The Minister. She's in the apartment."

We all listened. From inside Mrs. Farfle's apartment came a whoop of laughter followed by the thunderous crack of wood splintering, shaking the floor beneath our feet.

"Okay, I'm going to try something." Annika raised her hands and began working up a spell, tossing the filaments between her hands.

"What are you doing?" Crud asked.

"Dazzleshooter. It was in my handbook."

"That wasn't in my handbook," Crud said.

"Mine either," I said.

"I've never tried it," said Annika, "but I think I remember how it goes. Sort of."

She was stretching the strands of light, then coiling them up in her hands, but they kept flickering weakly. She was beginning to break a sweat with the effort, and frankly it wasn't looking too promising.

"Yawn," Tom said to her.

"Oh, sorry if this is boring you," Annika sniped at him as she worked, "but magic is a little more complicated than picking locks."

"No, *yawn*," Tom insisted. "Yawning helps to pull in the Oomphalos."

"Really?" Annika, Crud, and I all said at once.

"That's the funny thing about you Humans," Tom said. "You have all these skills that Folk don't have, but they're totally useless in the Hither. Like yawning. You don't yawn because you're tired. Back when Humans lived in the Nigh, they used yawning for magic."

"Humans used to live in the Nigh?" I asked.

"They don't teach you much in history, do they?" Tom said.

"Well, they don't teach us *that*," I replied.

Already Annika was opening and closing her mouth, working up a yawn. She managed a small one, then a wider one, and yes, the filaments began to pulse with energy. She tossed them from hand to hand, compressing them into a ball. It must have hurt her hands because she winced as she did it, as though she were juggling a piping hot potato.

"Open the door," she urged Tom in a strained voice. "Quickly."

As soon as Tom flung open the door, Annika lobbed the ball of light into Mrs. Farfle's apartment. It whizzed through the air, and then there was a crash and an angry shriek, and the next moment Vanessa Habscomb marched up to us holding a piece of broken ceramic in her hand.

"Well, what did you do that for? That was a nineteenth-century Pearlwood teapot!"

56

Amscray Ward

"What are you doing here?!" I cried.

"She's stealing stuff." Crud nodded toward her open backpack in which there was a jumble of necklaces, a silver box, and even a small framed painting. And I couldn't be positive, but tucked into the fold of a silk shawl, I thought I spotted a small glass vial with a cork stopper that contained something tiny and iridescent blue.

"Yeah, well, a girl has got to earn a living," Vanessa said, smiling. "Did you like the flying postcards? Fun, right?"

"You did that?" I asked.

"Well, I didn't think any of you guys were able to perform an Amscray Ward. Although that was some serious Dazzleshooter." She nodded at Annika. "How are those paws feeling?"

"Not great," Annika said, looking down at her palms.

I winced at the sight of her blistered hands, so red they were verging on purple.

"Wait, why are you here anyway?" I asked Vanessa.

"Luther sent me," Vanessa said. When we looked at her blankly, she added, "Mr. Boot."

"Boot? How did he know we were here?" Crud asked.

"Ooooh, Mr. Boot knows all!" Vanessa said spookily, opening her eyes widely. "He got wind of something odd happening in Central Park in the Nigh, and when none of you were in school, he made the leap. Thankfully, you guys are total slobs and left a trail of candy wrappers for me to follow. I Hanseled and Greteled it."

Crud and I both turned to Tom, who shifted his eyes away.

"So here's the deal," Vanessa said. "The Amscray Ward is a big, bad spell, really hard to maintain, and frankly, I've got nothing else in my tank. So unless you kids have a plan, this building is probably going to come down around our ears soon."

As if to drive this home, there was a tremendous crash, and a portion of Mrs. Farfle's living room wall buckled and then collapsed.

"Okay, everyone, look for a cat door," I said.

"That's the plan?" Vanessa said. "A cat door?"

"It's a way out of here," I explained. "Look through all the rooms."

This was a simple task, since Mrs. Farfle's apartment was so tiny. Except for the bathroom, there was only one room that served as a kitchen, a bedroom, and a painting studio.

I'd been in Mrs. Farfle's apartment a few times, and this was pretty much how I remembered it. Massive paintings of random household items—tubes of toothpaste, cough lozenges, rolls of silvery duct tape—were leaning against the walls under shelves crammed with jars of brushes and paints. Beneath a skylight was an easel with an unfinished painting on it, blank except for a wash of pearl gray paint. Beside a blue velvet fainting couch was a leather ottoman shaped like an elephant.

"Can you remember where the cat door was?" I asked River, looking around the room.

He shook his head. "I never said."

Oh no.

"So does that mean it won't exist here?" I asked.

"I don't know." River hesitated. "I mean, that was how the Girl with the Magic Shoes first got into the elevator, but I never thought about where the cat door actually was. Still, it was in the story, so maybe . . ."

"Okay, everybody look around for the cat door," I said. Because frankly, what other option was there? "Look behind the canvases."

We got to work, peering behind the stacks of canvases, shifting shelves away from the walls to see if the cat door was hidden behind them.

Nothing.

There was a wrenching sound, and a portion of the wall close to a window ripped away and fell to the ground outside. Leland appeared in midair, levitating by some sort of magic, his legs treading the air lightly. I think I may have screamed, but I'm not sure if it was just in my head. Leaning forward, Leland grabbed the raw edges of the wall, preparing to launch himself inside the room. But the house pivoted as he grabbed it, knocking him backward in the air. The odd thing was, though we could see the house move, we couldn't feel it from the inside. There wasn't even the slightest jostle.

"Your ward is holding," Crud said to Vanessa admiringly.

"Yeah, but this place isn't going to last much longer," she said.

There was an angry explosion, as though a giant had punched its fist into the building. The wooden studs along one entire wall snapped in half and broke through the plaster, doubling over limply. A bulge began to form in the ceiling along the edge of the wall. In a moment it was all going to come down on top of us.

I may not have been given a hefty *Last Chance Club Handbook*, and my magic was not as elegant as Crud's or as skillful as Annika's, but I could manage a decent Flatzen Spurtz Spell. I searched the room for something that might buy us a little time, and once I found it, my hands formed the spell. I even remembered to yawn to give it some extra Oomphalos, then directed it at Mrs. Farfle's painting of a huge duct tape roll. The tape roll swelled out from the canvas, as big around as a car tire, until it plopped onto the floor. It rolled halfway across the room before it toppled on its side. I directed the filaments with my hands in an Animagor Airblunken Spell, and the duct tape flew in the air, the end of it peeling up and slapping itself against the wall. It unspooled itself and rolled across the walls, bracing the broken studs, holding the slabs of plaster in place. It wrapped itself around the room over and over until all the walls were completely covered in the silvery tape.

"Nice work, kid!" Vanessa said. "I think Boot is under-estimating you guys."

The walls held steady, but after several more minutes of fruitless searching, Crud said what we were probably all thinking. "Hey, Nell, maybe your cat door theory is, you know, I hate to say this . . . flawed."

I was about to agree with him when I noticed Annika standing in the middle of the room, looking at the canvas on the easel. She cocked her head, as though assessing a painting in a museum, except that there was nothing painted on the canvas—just a gray background.

"Hmm," she said.

"What?" I asked.

"Hmm."

She backed up and ran at the canvas, her legs lifting off the floor with the elegance of a long jumper. She leapt up and dove headfirst into the canvas, and the next second she had vanished.

57

GLADYS'S DOOR

River and I looked at each other and smiled.
"Gladys's secret cat door," he said.

"I can almost forgive that disgusting cat for peeing on my quilt."

I felt a poke on my shoulder and turned to see Vanessa, who was pointing at the wall. "Your duct tape is losing interest," she said.

Indeed, the duct tape was unspooling off the wall and wrapping itself around the leg of a broken stool. Without the tape holding it, one of the broken wall studs collapsed to the ground, and the one next to it was threatening to do the same. Quickly, I recast the Animagor Airblunken Spell. The tape slapped itself back to the wall, taking the stool with it.

"You." Vanessa pointed to River. "Go next."

"No, Nell goes," River said.

"She'll have to go last to keep the spell going. Come on. Chop-chop, before we all wind up like the Wicked Witch of the East."

River hesitated, glancing at me.

"Go," I said.

River backed up and, like Annika ran at the easel, sprang through it headfirst and was gone in an instant.

"Now you, gorgeous." Vanessa pointed to Tom.

He nodded, then grinned at me. "See you in a minute." And after a remarkably nimble leap, he too had vanished into the canvas.

"You're next," I said to Crud.

Crud gave me a sad smile. "Come on, Nell. We both know I can't fit through that thing. I'm too big."

I looked at the canvas. It was true. I couldn't see him being able to fit through it.

"It's okay." Crud gave my shoulder a squeeze. "You two, go. I'll be fine."

"No, you won't be fine," I said. "You definitely, definitely won't."

"I can get him through," Vanessa said, "but I'm going to have to drop the Amscray Ward to do it. Which means"—she turned to me—"the second we're through, you're going to have to haul tail and go right after. Got it?"

I nodded.

She looked at us. "Ready?"

"Ready," we both said at once.

She bent her arms and flapped her hands down, like someone imitating a bunny. Except this bunny had major voltage flaring all around her. She was gathering the ward from the air and drawing it back into her hands—I could feel the difference in the room. The atmosphere felt lighter.

The smell of popcorn had vanished too—I guessed it was a side effect of the Amscray Ward.

"Ward deactivated." Vanessa cracked her knuckles and flexed her fingers. Then she turned to Crud. "Now let's handle this little problem."

She worked a quick but complicated spell. I watched her hands carefully but couldn't detect anything that I recognized from the spells I knew. And poof—literally poof, with a puff of smoke and everything—Crud was gone.

"Where did he go?" I asked.

"In there." Vanessa nodded up to the ceiling, where an orange balloon was floating, a white ribbon tied to it. "It's a Portable Gasbag. I put all his essential stuff in there."

She grabbed the ribbon and pulled the balloon down. After slipping her arms through her backpack—without replacing the things she'd stolen, I noticed—she said a quick "Ciao!" and she and Crud's gasbag went through the canvas.

I knew that I had to act quickly, and not just because Vanessa had told me to. Outside there was the sound of excited voices—the Magicians seemed to have figured out that the ward had been lifted. They would be in the building in no time.

I'm not agile. And I am so uncoordinated that I don't even wonder where the bruises that regularly appear on my body come from. But I had to get through the canvas fast, so I backed way up to the other end of the room in order to get a good running start. Before I could even begin my sprint to the canvas, though, the skylight panes above the easel shattered. Shards of glass sprayed the room, and the skylight's metal frame fell from the ceiling, knocking down the easel and sending the canvas flying.

"No, no, no!" I cried out, and rushed over to find that the canvas had been pierced by a section of the skylight's frame. I pulled the metal frame out of it, then picked up the canvas, shaking off the glass shards. A large swath of ripped canvas flopped down.

Gladys's cat door was destroyed.

Maybe it will still work, I thought desperately.

It *had* to work. It was my only way out of there.

I picked up the easel and moved it to the other corner of the room, away from the glass, and then propped the torn canvas on it.

I stepped back and ran, ramming my head into the canvas. The only thing I managed to do was knock the canvas into the shelf behind the easel and spill a jar of turpentine.

I was trapped.

"Hello there, Nell!"

Hovering above the broken skylight, arms spread wide, was Leland.

"Where are your friends? Hiding? And they left you all alone, huh? Grrr! Some friends, right! Hey, so, Nell, Nell, Nell, here's the deal, right. The Minister? Yeah, she's going to be up here in a minute. You're a . . . what-do-you-call-it . . . You're a pawn in her plans. She'll use you to get to your brother. And it won't be a fun time for you, Nell. So here's what I'm thinking. I make this roof collapse on you. It will be fast, Nell, I promise. You'll be dead before you know it. That's—ooof—grisly, yeah, but you do not want to spend time with the Minister, trust me. Consider it a favor, because, you know, you were nice to me when I was a ferret. You stuck up for me when Boot was being a creep. I don't forget stuff like that. So just . . . Just stay right there, right where you are, and it will be over before you know it."

He rose back up in the air and disappeared from sight.

Think, Nell, think.

A memory popped into my head. It happened a long time ago, back when Kingsley was first teaching me how to play chess. My queen was in trouble, and Kingsley had taken my two rooks and a knight, and I couldn't see my way out of a loss.

Remember, you have two knights, Nell, Kingsley had said, prodding me toward a win.

Mrs. Farfle always made duplicates of her paintings. Wouldn't there be two of Gladys's cat door as well?

I started flipping through the canvases leaning against the wall—paintings of slippers and Legos and dog bowls and keys and Pringles potato chips and nesting dolls and clothespins. And there it was, right between the clothespins painting and a painting of fungicidal cream—a pearl gray canvas, with nothing else painted on it.

I grabbed it and set it on the easel. I could hear the sounds of feet coming up the stairs now and somewhere high above me Leland's voice called, "Get ready, kid!"

I glanced up at the skylight to make sure Leland couldn't see what I was doing. I backed up, adrenaline making my muscles tremble uncontrollably, and I ran like a maniac and dove straight into the canvas.

I had closed my eyes at the impact, although all I felt was a quick sensation of falling, then several hands catching me.

And also I should mention I was screaming.

When I opened my eyes, I found myself in a very crowded elevator staring at five smiling, relieved faces and being set on my feet by Crud, who apparently had been released from his gasbag.

"What took you so long?" Annika demanded.

"Well, I wasn't having cheese and crackers with the Minister," I said. "Your mouth is bleeding."

Annika swiped at her bloody lip with the back of her hand. "Well, I didn't have anyone to catch me when I got here."

I glanced up at the open hatch in the elevator's ceiling—the one that the Girl with the Magic Shoes had tumbled through, and which I now realized I must have fallen through as well.

The elevator had scarred wood paneling and a brass-plated button panel with only one green button. Above the wooden doors was the cast-iron floor indicator with the golden dial. Instead of floor numbers, though, there were raised words across the outer rim:

NOWHERE

GETTING THERE

HALFWAY THERE

NEARLY THERE

HOME

I looked at River, who had been watching me.

"This is it," I said, marveling at it all. "This is our elevator."

He nodded, smiling back at me.

"So how does this thing work?" Tom asked, looking at the button panel. "Can I just . . . ?" His finger hovered over the single green button, and he grinned at us mischievously.

"Press it!" Annika said, her eyes bright with anticipation. "Do it!"

"Go ahead," River told him.

Tom jammed his finger against the button. The elevator shuddered. There was a loud click, then the whirring of a motor above us, and the next thing we knew, the elevator began to climb in its rickety, slow-motion way.

"Almost home," I said as I watched the golden dial above the door slide past NOWHERE and begin to move toward GETTING THERE.

River smiled too as he watched the dial. The scar across his lip turned his smile lopsided, which made him look as though he were smiling mockingly. Like his voice and his Adam's apple, it was something I'd have to get used to.

"Almost home," he said softly.

"How did the story end?" Annika asked. "Elevator World."

"It didn't," River replied.

"But remember?" I said. "There was that thing you always said when you finished the story at night."

River nodded and recited the sentence that for so many years had been the last thing I heard before I went to sleep: "After everything they'd been through, River, Nell, and the Girl with the Magic Shoes got back in the elevator, and where they would go next was a mystery."

Then Annika did the strangest thing. At least, it was strange for Annika. She grabbed my hand, and then she grabbed River's hand, and the three of us stood like that, holding hands and watching the golden dial as it slowly moved closer to HOME.

"Okay, kid," Vanessa said to River as she pointed to the dial, "almost HALFWAY THERE. It's time to tell them."

58

ᴇʟᴇᴠᴀᴛᴏʀ ᴡᴏʀʟᴅ

T ell us what?" I asked.

River didn't answer. His mouth tightened as he kept staring up at the dial.

"If you don't tell them, I will," Vanessa said.

River took a deep breath. He let go of our hands and turned to face us.

"You said you know that Mary Carpenter was poached as a kid?"

I nodded.

"She was twelve when she escaped from the Magicians," River said. "She should have been a total mess by then. Most kids are. But somehow she came out of it okay. Miraculously, she found a Wicket and hurried back home. That should have been it—a happy ending to her story—but she couldn't stop thinking about the other kids who were still trapped in the Nigh. So she watched and studied and bit by bit she began to discover where the Wickets tended to pop up in the Hither—not just in New York City, but in lots of other places too. It took her years to figure it out. She was twenty when she found her way back to the Nigh.

Soon after, she rescued the first kid and brought him back to his family. After that she rescued others. She became a legend in the Nigh, risking her own skin again and again to help the kids. It was only later that Mary found out what had happened to the children she'd brought back home." River paused and looked over at Vanessa before he turned back to Annika and me. "They died. All of them. After they returned to the Hither, they just grew weaker and weaker. It's something about the casting. It changed them. They couldn't survive in the Hither. So Mary began to hide kids in the Nigh instead. It was the only thing she could do to get us away from the Magicians and still keep us alive. The kids who've been poached—we can't go back home again. None of us."

I was silent for a moment, too shocked to speak.

"So . . . that's it?" I said finally. "We found you, and now we have to let you go again? No. That can't be the way this ends. It can't be that this was all for nothing."

"It wasn't for nothing," River insisted. "It mattered. It mattered to me. I'd been gone so long, and, I mean, I know you wouldn't forget me, Nell, but life goes on. I figured you probably thought I was dead, you'd probably given up on me, and I felt . . . left behind. Like I'd always be completely alone. But then you came here to find me."

"Yeah, and when we found you, your house got destroyed," Annika said.

River shook his head. "I built that house because it was where everyone I loved had lived. But I don't need it anymore. You all came for me. You faced *Boggedy Cats* to find me!" He smiled that lopsided smile, and I could feel the ache in my chest. "And, Nell, listen to me. It wasn't your fault that I got taken. I know that's what you've been thinking. But they would have taken me eventually. They would have found a way. If it hadn't been that day, it would have been another. So stop it. Stop blaming yourself. Promise?"

I nodded, but my eyes were filling up with tears, and I could barely choke out a word.

The elevator shuddered to a halt. I looked up at the dial. NEARLY THERE.

"Are we stuck?" Crud asked. "We're not HOME."

"The elevator takes you where you're supposed to go," River said.

The door slid open, and outside I could see piles of stones carefully stacked on top of one another, and behind them was a river. The Hudson Barrows. We were back where we had started.

I knew what had to happen. I knew it and I hated it and I could feel the pain rising, so I threw my arms around River quickly, and before I started outright bawling, I said, "I'm going to figure this out."

"Okay."

"I'm going to bring you home," I insisted. "Safely."

I felt his body tense up, and I was pretty sure he was going to tell me that it was impossible. But instead he said, "I believe you." He let go of me. "Let Dad know . . ." He paused. "Just let Dad know that everything will be okay."

I nodded. "I will."

"We'd better get going," Vanessa said, stepping out of the elevator and holding the door open for the rest of us. "We're attracting attention." She nodded toward a woman at an open window across the street who was gesturing wildly at someone else inside the apartment.

Annika kissed River's cheek, which made him turn bright red. And amazingly Annika turned red as well.

Crud gave River a hug too, then asked, "Where will you go now, man?"

River shrugged. "Wherever the elevator takes me."

I felt another stab of sorrow at the thought of the elevator door closing and River being alone again. Left behind.

River turned to Tom and stuck out his hand. "Thanks. I'm sorry I didn't trust you."

Tom shook his hand, then looked up at the elevator dial. "So . . . you don't know where this thing will take you next, right?"

River nodded.

"Okay, I'm in," Tom said.

"In what?" River asked.

"I'm going with you. I love a mystery. Tell him, Nell." He grinned at me. "Don't I love a mystery?"

"He loves a mystery." I smiled back.

River wouldn't be alone. He'd have Tom. And plenty of candy.

I hugged Tom, and in his ear I whispered, "Thank you." In response he kissed me on the cheek. It was a quick, shy kiss. The first time I'd ever been kissed by a boy, to be honest. Definitely the first time I'd been kissed by an Imp. I had a feeling it might have been the first time Tom had kissed anybody too, because afterward he went over to the button panel while avoiding my eyes.

As we filed out of the elevator, Tom let his finger hover over the green button.

"Whenever you're ready," he said to River.

River looked at us, and after a moment of hesitation, he smiled. "I'm ready."

59

ᎯOME

Out on the street Vanessa whistled, and the old-fashioned ANYWHERE TAXI careened around the block and pulled up in front of us. We piled in the back, quite a squeeze since there were four of us now. The driver—the same one as before—demanded our token. Thankfully Vanessa had one.

The ride was as quick as it was the first time. A moment after Vanessa handed the driver her token, he hopped out of the car and opened the back door on the driver's side. We stepped out of the taxi to find ourselves in front of the bodega on Bleecker Street.

Standing on the sidewalk, holding his briefcase and nibbling on a stick of beef jerky, was Mr. Boot. I spied a look of relief wash over his face when he saw us emerge from the taxi, quickly replaced with a scowl.

"I see all the miscreants are accounted for, with limbs and digits still intact. Well done, Ms. Habscomb." He glared at us all in a way that the Minister probably would have approved of. "You've broken nearly every conceivable club rule, including some I hadn't conceived of. We'll discuss punishment tomorrow." He handed Crud and me our backpacks, which he must have retrieved from Marisol in the bodega.

"Go easy on them, Luther," Vanessa said. "They've been through the wringer. And by the way, these kids have some serious skills."

Mr. Boot raised his eyebrows. "Have they? They've certainly done an excellent job hiding them from me." Mr. Boot turned to us. "For now, you all are to go directly home to your families. They won't have known you've been anywhere you shouldn't have been. Off you go!"

No one moved.

"Has this little escapade affected your hearing?" Mr. Boot looked from one of us to the other. "I said *off you go!*"

"You knew River was in the Nigh," I accused. "You lied."

"You asked if I knew where your brother was, Ms. Batista, and I said that I didn't. That was, quite literally, the truth."

"But you knew he was in the Nigh, *somewhere.* You could have told me!"

"Why? So that you would find a way back there, only to be poached, like him? Or to be used as collateral to draw him out of hiding?"

"Well, we weren't poached, were we?" I said defiantly. "And by the way, we found him."

Mr. Boot looked at Vanessa, and she nodded.

For a moment Mr. Boot seemed too surprised to say anything.

"Is he safe?" Mr. Boot asked Vanessa in a quiet voice.

"For now," Vanessa answered.

"Listen, Boot." Crud folded his arms across his chest. "There are other kids in the Nigh. Human kids."

"I'm aware."

"Then why don't you use your magic to help them," I cried, "instead of wasting your time teaching us how to find our lost phones or make toy animals come alive? What kind of lousy magician are you?"

I saw the anger flash across his face, but with some effort he controlled it. "The kind of magician who has more faith in a bloody pack of hooligans than I probably should. I expect to see you all tomorrow in Room 101 at three thirty sharp. Now go home before I turn each one of you into a knockoff handbag and let the tourists have at you."

There was nothing to do, really, except to head home, but when we turned to leave, Mr. Boot stopped me.

"Ms. Batista." He crooked a finger at me. "A word?"

Crud hesitated, reluctant to leave me, but Mr. Boot shot him a menacing look. "Alone, please."

I nodded at Crud, and he and Annika headed down the street, turning back once or twice, I suppose to check that I hadn't been turned into a handbag.

"I thought you'd like to know that the police are no longer looking for Mary Carpenter," Mr. Boot said. "It seems that the eyewitness in Spain was a bit confused about the day he was in the park. Mary is no longer a suspect."

I nodded slowly. He had no doubt used a spell to confuse the witness.

"Thank you." I was genuinely grateful.

He looked at me with a softness in his eyes. "Life rarely turns out the way we expect, does it?"

I shook my head, then bit my lower lip as I felt the sorrow begin to swell up again.

"But sometimes," Mr. Boot continued, "if we don't botch things up, it can turn out quite a bit better than we'd imagined." He smiled. "All is not lost, Nell."

I nodded.

He glanced at the beef jerky in his hand and frowned. "Awful stuff, bodega food."

"They have sandwiches in the back," I told him.

"Ah." He slipped the beef jerky into the inside pocket of his jacket and headed back into the bodega.

Back home I went directly to the bathroom—one, because I really did have to go to the bathroom, and also because I looked like a total disaster, with plaster dust and mud all over me. I showered, scrubbing off the filth and plucking minute bits of plaster out of my hair. I had a blossoming bruise on the side of my temple, but there was nothing I could do about that. By the time I had cleaned up and changed my clothes, my dad was already putting dinner on the table.

"Good day?" he asked.

I wanted to tell him everything. I wanted to tell him

that I'd seen River. I wanted to tell him that River was alive and well and that somehow I would find a way to bring him home again. I wanted to tell Dad all of it, but I knew that I couldn't. The story was so unbelievable that he would simply worry about my sanity. Besides which, it was all so wrapped up with Boot's club that something would probably fall on my head before I could get out two sentences. I glanced up nervously at the dandelion puffball chandelier above us and wondered how much it would hurt if that monstrosity crashed down on my skull.

"Yup, good day," I replied simply.

He placed a paper bag on the table, and from it he pulled out two plastic containers. He pulled off the lids, releasing steam smelling of garlic and ginger and onions.

"Hunan chicken and shrimp lo mein."

"Smells good," I said. It really did, and I was starving. I spooned some lo mein onto my plate, then reached into the paper bag and pulled out a pair of chopsticks.

"Since when do you use chopsticks?" Dad asked.

I rubbed them together just for fun. They perked right up. "I've been practicing."

Positioning the chopsticks in my hand, which felt as natural as holding a pencil now, I deftly plucked up some noodles between them and shoveled the noodles into my mouth.

"Apparently." He looked impressed.

After I swallowed the first mouthful, I said, "You know, lately, I've been thinking. . . ." I fumbled for the right words to tell him what River had wanted me to tell him. That everything would be okay. "I've been thinking about how . . . how the world is such a weird place. Weirder than I'd ever imagined."

Dad nodded uncertainly, clearly wondering what I was trying to say.

"I just . . . I just think we shouldn't give up hope on River. Not yet. I mean, things can happen that you would never expect. Things that seem impossible."

Dad smiled lightly, but I could see the worry in his eyes. I knew he thought I was still deluding myself about River, ignoring the painful truth.

An idea came to me then. I changed the grip on my chopsticks—moving the tips of my thumb and index finger to the top of the sticks, my pinkie touching the base of my palm. I tried a few quick swipes, pretending to shove a shrimp off a noodle. Now I could actually *feel* the Oomphalos. It was subtle, but I could sense the buzz of energy in the air. I shifted my chair to the right and tried again. The Oomphalos was stronger here. Really, I thought, this isn't that different from finding a cell phone signal.

"Hey, did they give us any extra soy sauce?" I asked.

As Dad looked in the bag, I lifted my chopsticks, and with as much speed as I could muster, I worked an Oifen Shoifen Spell.

The dandelion puffball–shaped chandelier above our heads shivered, making a tinkling sound. We both looked up at it, and a moment later a flutter of soft dandelion